The Clock Man

and Other Stories

by Eric Lahti

Dedicated to my wife and son.
And everyone who believes magic doesn't require a wand and a cloak.

Also by Eric Lahti:

<u>Henchmen</u>
Join a small organization of loveable bad guys: a supervillain and her henchmen. Eve, the seven foot tall, bulletproof blonde is their leader. Frank and Jean are a couple that can get into any computer or building unseen. Jacob is a rough around the edges biker type that has a deep and abiding love of guns and explosives. And Steven? Well, he's really good at manipulating people and pretty handy to have around in a fight. As super villainy goes, they're just starting out. They don't have much of a secret base. They don't have matching uniforms. Not a one of them owns a single pair of tights. What they do have is an interest in tearing down the country and watching it burn.

It's all in a day's work for Steven…one of the world's most dedicated and dangerous…
HENCHMEN

<u>Arise</u>
Steven was having a pretty good time for a guy who helped release a captured god. He had a nice place in Colorado, a pretty girl sent him a picture of herself in a bikini, and he had neighbors that left him alone. Everything was looking pretty good until he woke up to find two people in his house that were planning on killing him; one was an old coworker and the other was an old boss.

It seems that releasing the God of Dreams was caused some ripples in places best left alone and Eve's atonement was to kill Steven for his part in the transgression. Wilford wanted to kill Steven because that's just how Wilford is. They all soon find themselves trapped between a runaway God of Dreams bent on expanding his domain and the personification of Fear. If one doesn't get them, the other will.

Some days it's hard to be one of the henchmen.

Contents

A Brief Note From The Author

One of the things that terrified me when I finished *Henchmen* was the gnawing worry that I would never come up with another idea again. That would be it and I'd be remembered (if at all) as the guy who managed one novel and couldn't come up with anything else.

It turns out there were far more stories kicking around in my brain.

This little anthology started out with the singular idea of what would a world look like if you managed to meld American steel and Chinese mysticism? Kind of like steampunk without the Victorian underpinnings. That idea led to the story that ultimately became *The Clock Man* and will further lead into more stories about Aluna.

Some of the other stories allowed me to expand on *Henchmen* in ways that couldn't be handled in the first-person narrative without seeming forced. Others were just stories that popped in to say, "Howdy" before moseying off to where stories go for grub and a frosty beer.

I hope you enjoy them.

Thanks,

Eric Lahti

Exceeds Expectations

Katherine Devereux is sitting alone at the end a long table and wondering exactly what she's doing in this bleak, white room. Her black power dress, which looked so good on the hanger in the boutique downtown, is not only extremely uncomfortable but also a stark contrast to the rest of the room. It's like every bit of light in the room is bouncing off the walls and falling straight into her dress.

She feels like the room is glaring at her. It's completely irrational, but the room seems angry that she dared to wear black. The sheer irrationality of the situation has her on edge and the fact that she's worried about a room being angry is just making her more and more uneasy.

But, damn it, the room seems angry.

To make things worse, she had to follow a circuitous route through the bowels of the building to get here. She'd leave, but the byzantine directions to get to the room seem to have disappeared as soon as she entered the room. Along with her purse, her cell-phone, and her tablet.

Katherine walked into the room with only her youthful idealism. That, too, has flown the coop and the only thing she has left to entertain herself with is percolating boredom, a general feeling of unease, and the strange room.

She fidgets on the folding white chair and tries to entertain herself. She has no idea how long she's been here, exactly where here is, or even what time may actually be in this place. The entire wall opposite her is filled with a magnificent timepiece that seems to be running at a different speed than the rest of the world. It's easily ten feet across and decorated in a geometrically perfect Yin Yang symbol. Aside from the black and white of the old Taoist symbol, the clock face is completely blank. Interestingly enough, the Yin Yang seems to be slowly moving the opposite direction the wavy clock hands. Time is moving forward and balance is moving backward.

When she first walked into the room she noted the time: 10:10. Approximately, of course, since there are no numbers on the clock.

In her boredom Katherine has started counting between the clock ticks. With a normal clock this is difficult task, but the huge Yin Yang clock only ticks intermittently. At first she didn't realize how variant the ticks were. How often does anyone pay attention to the ticking of a clock? Normally the ticking of a clock fades into the background noise but Katherine Devereux is one of those people that revels in the little details that most people skim over.

Besides, she's bored out of her mind and is looking for something to get excited about.

tick.

Katherine starts counting.

One.

Two.

Three.

Four.

tick.

She feels like she's been here for hours, but the clock says 10:23. Can thirteen minutes take that long? There was that episode of *Frasier*, but that was a long time ago and the episode was actually closer to 20 minutes and only felt like it a couple hours. Her time in this room has been thirteen minutes and feels like more than several hours.

Realizing she's arguing with herself about time and episodes of *Frasier*, Katherine leans back in her chair and sighs out loud. She stares at the clock and wonders who makes a clock that big and doesn't bother to put numbers on it. The stupid wavy hands make it nearly impossible to figure out what time it really is.

Wait, is it really 10:23 or is it 11:20? Why didn't I bring my watch?

Save for the ticking of the clock, the room is dead silent. *Ha, ha. Dead. Good one, brain.* The room is one of those places that's so quiet the lack of noise feels deafening. In between the ticks of the clock

Kathryn can hear her dress rustle when she breathes. It's disconcerting to hear your clothes talking, to say the least.

Her boredom is slowly turning into a bit of paranoia. This is what happens to people when they're in sensory deprivation chamber; they start hallucinating. The brain needs some kind of stimulation and ruminations about old TV shows and the nature of time don't count as stimulating.

The room's decor isn't helping, either. It's stark white, a pure and clinical sense of nothingness. Black is fashionable, sharp. Black may feel Goth and she didn't bring her Sisters of Mercy albums, but white is so … white. Empty. The room isn't an off white or a cream. It's white. A pure absence of color. The table is white. The folding chair she's sitting in is white. The big leather chair at the other end of the table is white.

Kathryn chuckles to herself remembering a line from a movie she watched in college, long ago and far away.

The only color in the room comes from two posters on either side of the table. On the left is a poster asking if her decision is good for the company. It features a man in a suit staring accusingly at the reader. The poster is one of those admonishments that's meant to say, "no matter what you're doing, it's not enough." It's frustrating, pedantic, and outright insulting if one stops to think about it.

"Yeah," Kathryn says quietly to the poster. "It's good for the company, whether they know it or not."

The poster on the right is a kitten hanging from a tree branch with "Hang in there" written in a happy script at the bottom. The kitten has that panicky look that all kittens get when they realize they're in way over their heads. Tiny claws grip the branch and its eyes are wild.

"You'll make it, kiddo. Cats are made of rubber," she tells the kitten.

tick.

Kathryn starts counting again.

One.

Two.

Three.

Four.

Five.

tick.

Interesting, she notes.

Katherine looks around the room and adjusts her jacket for the umpteenth time since she sat down. She really wishes she'd worn something with some color in it for this meeting. The stark contrast between her clothes and the blank room are making her feel completely out of place; a subtle, gnawing feeling that she doesn't belong here, that she's not good enough or important enough to be in this spotless place.

That's it. She snaps her fingers when she realizes the room is making her feel dirty. *Well, enough of that.* Realization conquers all.

She leans back, smugly satisfied at cracking part of the code of this room. The chair creaks and nearly falls over. She barely manages to catch herself before it's too late and her ass meets the floor. Realizing there's no way she can get comfortable in the chair, Kathryn leans forward and puts her elbows on the table and her chin in her hands.

Last night, just as she was leaving she got a message delivered by a creeper: Be at this room tomorrow morning at 10am sharp. The official name of the room is "Conference and Consulting Room 4A," but as far as Kathryn knows, no one has ever been to a conference or had consulting in this room. It's not like it's easy to find anyway.

She has heard rumors of the room. Room 101, her comrades jokingly called it; a reference to Orwell's infamous room. The code monkeys she works with trade horror stories about the place; so-and-so got called there once and never came back. It's where they take you when you're to be well and truly fired. The room a psychological torture chamber; someone knew a guy who knew a gal who had a friend who came back thinking she was someone else.

And so on and so on.

Kathryn decided if she was going to be drawn and quartered at least she could look good going down. The dress spoke to her. It looked strong, but still feminine. The full suit, dress and jacket, spoke of power in a silk wool blend that paired nicely with black tights and a severe pair of shoes that are currently cutting off the feeling in her toes.

Katherine arrived five minutes early at 9:55am and found … no one. There was a note with a set of directions and a reminder to show up on time. She hustled through the maze-like hallways until she found a white door with a Post-It note stuck to it. The note had a smiley face and nothing more. The door, unfortunately, was locked.

Even for this place, the whole morning was strange. When one gets a message to show up at 10am sharp at a particular place and the message comes from the top, one shows up. This is especially true when the message is delivered by a creeper. The damned little buggers only come from up on Mahogany Row and if one shows up it means someone from the top has noticed you.

It's never good in this job to have someone from up top notice you.

Kathryn waited and at 10:10 exactly the door behind her opened and she walked into Room 101. She started by peeking around the corners, looking for someone or some note or something to indicate this was the right place. The room was as absent of notes as it was of people.

The door closed and locked behind her, leaving her stuck in the warm Arctic room.

tick.

One.

Two.

tick.

Time would appear to be a variable here, she thinks.

That is not entirely surprising. Actually, given the place she works at, variable time is downright pedestrian compared to creepers and the custom designed things she works on herself.

Kathryn taps her blood red nails on the white table. Instead of the usual click, they make a sort of hollow thump and she stops immediately. Tentatively, she tries again and finds the same thumping sound. *What is this table made out of?* She strokes the table and taps on the top with her knuckles. The texture is absolutely smooth. So smooth, in fact, that her hands don't seem to feel it.

Curiosity overcomes her and Katherine tries to move the table but it remains obstinately in place. Either it's too heavy to move or attached to the floor somehow. She leans under the table but can't decide if the table is attached somehow or not. The legs seem to flow smoothly into the floor, but there are distinct lines that look like they may be joins.

Heh, heh. Inner join table on floor. SQL humor is always in good taste.

tick.

One.

Two.

Three.

Four.

Five.

Six.

Seven.

Eight.

Nine.

Ten.

tick.

The clock now shows 9:10. Kathryn chuckles to herself. *I have to be here in less than an hour.*

Maybe it's boredom that's causing the time dilations. She had a class in college, Organizational Communication, which was so boring she always thought it managed to stretch time. To this day she has no idea what Organization Communication actually entails but she somehow managed to pass the class.

If I'm going to have to wait, Katherine thinks, *I may as well catalog the room.*

This is a mental exercise she puts herself through from time to time. It's a programmer thing; a relentless desire to codify everything into the lowest reproducible elements. Thinking like this is how developers wind up looking at the whole of creation as nothing more than things following preprogrammed patterns. The more simple things that are following simple patterns there are the more complicated the whole looks.

Kathryn sets about the process of classifying everything she sees and mentally logs the information for later retrieval. The room is strangely unsettling and making unsettling things is a part of her job. Her mind kicks into gear and begins the process of coding the place, reproducing it to constituent parts of the whole. Each thing in the room and the room as a whole become a series of nested classes that can be turned into objects. The class becomes the blueprint; classes can be instantiated into objects. The objects become ... well, the objects become the things she makes.

Create the class. Define the room. It has shape; walls and floor. Color is a constant, no need to make it changeable. What would the room look like in a solid blue or pink? It wouldn't work anymore.

The room class has many subclasses. *Crap.* The posters. Make color in the poster classes overridable. *There. Solved.*

The table class is easy enough to define. Height, width, and depth are all set. To get a good sense of the sheer size of the table maybe it would be best to multiply the x and y values by two. *No. Too much. 1.5. Yes.* Take a normal meeting room table and multiple its size by 1.5. The number of legs is a variable, but their height should be fixed at 29 inches.

Tick.

One.

Two.

Three.

Four.

Tick.

Was the clock louder just now?

Katherine goes back to cataloging. The chairs should have a couple of values to distinguish them. A binary value of comfy floats across her mind. Her chair's comfy value is zero. The other chair's comfy value is probably one.

She decides to test her theory. Impulsiveness is only one of her many virtues.

Her heels sound like gunshots in the silent room. She pulls the other chair out and examines it. It has thick padding and the leather feels soft under her fingertips. Katherine glances around the room and, finding no one, gently sits in the chair.

She's surprised to find the chair is exactly as uncomfortable as her folding white chair. She plops her elbows on the table, and rests her chin in her hands. Across the table from her is a large white leather chair.

Katherine stares in stunned amazement and looks at the chair she's sitting in. Sure enough, her butt is firmly resting on the folding white chair. She looks frantically around the room, certain she had walked across it and sat down in the leather chair just a moment ago.

She runs a hand through her hair and wonders if reality is breaking in the room. Or is it her mind that's breaking?

TICK.

Katherine nearly jumps out of her seat. The clock just got significantly louder.

Across the table from her, behind the white leather chair she thought she was sitting in, the giant black and white clock looks like a leering face. The two dots on either side seem to be staring at Katherine, judging her and finding her wanting.

She breathes in deep. *You're just getting paranoid. The clock is not staring at you.*

TICK.

To prove it to herself, Katherine walks across the room again to get a closer look at the clock. It ticks in time with her heels and each step seems to make the ticking louder. At least the ticking is more regular. Unless she's taking somewhere between four and ten seconds to take each step, that is.

She stops halfway to her destination and ponders that. It certainly felt like she was walking regularly, but how would she know? If time, in and of itself, is a variable in this place then shouldn't she be part of time? Therefore, if she's part of time – interacting with it – time could be a variable but she'd never know it.

She looks back at her seat. The white plastic seat is uncomfortable in the way McDonald's seats are uncomfortable and she doesn't even get a chocolate shake when she's sitting in it. Maybe, though, it's some kind of safe zone, a place beyond the effects of time here.

Hurrying back to the seat she hears her heels clicking regularly as clockwork; a perfectly timed tick tock. Back in the chair, she waits patiently for the next tick.

And waits.

And waits.

A thundering tick shakes her seat but she starts counting anyway. Katherine makes it thirty five before the next tick of the clock. Well, that would seem to clinch it.

Once out of the seat her steps sound perfectly regular and the clock ticks in time with each step. This time, though, the clock's ticking is more restrained. It sounds just like a regular, albeit large, clock with no markings save a geometrically perfect Yin Yang symbol.

She crosses the room again and again, back and forth, back and forth.

Katherine pauses next to the white leather chair and caresses it gently. The leather is smooth and soft, like a favorite pair of pants. She casually spins it around. It doesn't make a sound and the movement is smooth as silk, like a favorite pair of … well … never mind.

This close the clock is intimidating. From across the room, when she could take the whole thing in, it was just a large timepiece. Three feet in front of it, though, and the clock is overwhelming. She can hear the gears whirring away; patiently marking the time it takes light to travel one Planck unit. The white parts are completely featureless and her eyes fall into the black part.

The sensation of depth in the black parts of the clock is so intense she feels like she's falling into eternity and has to put her hands out to catch herself.

TICK.

Her dress vibrates from the sound and she staggers backwards. Katherine lands clumsily in the chair, the soft leather cradling her fall. The chair spins around and she faces a man across the table sitting in the big leather chair. Under her is the cheap plastic chair.

"Shall we begin?" the man asks.

Katherine pulls her wits about her like a warm blanket. Behind the man the giant Yin Yang clock reads 10:00 precisely.

"Mrs. Devereux?" the man asks. He's dressed all in varying shades of gray. His double-breasted suit is dark gray, his shirt is light gray, and the shiny tie perfectly knotted at his throat is solid gray. Arrayed in front of him are a variety of papers. A shiny black pen is carefully placed on top of the papers.

He looks at the papers in front of him, studiously ignoring her.

She looks briefly around the room and says, "It's Miss."

"Excuse me?" he asks without looking up.

"Miss Devereux," Kathryn says. "I'm not married."

"Never?"

"No," Kathryn says a little too forcefully.

"So it wasn't a 'til death do you part' situation?" he asks.

"No, I've been single all my life."

"And after, too, apparently," the man says.

The man calmly unscrews the pen and reveals a gold-nibbed fountain pen. He deftly makes a few marks on one of the sheets and screws the pen back together. "Miss Devereux, are you ready to begin?"

"I didn't catch your name," she says.

He makes another note on one of the pieces of paper and looks up at her. "No, you didn't."

Katherine has no response to that. Unwilling to let him get the last word, she adds, "You can call me Katherine."

"Miss Devereux, are you ready to get started or not?"

She stares him down, nervous but not quite ready to give into a stranger's bullying. He doesn't budge and inch and neither does she. Katherine meets his eyes and he stares into her. She feels … something, a tickling in a part of her brain that usually remains calm and ordered. She focuses on his eyes, those gray orbs. Amazing, fascinating.

The clock ticks and the spell breaks. Swallowing her pride, she says, "Yes, sir."

He makes a note in his papers and then flips through another stack of papers, reading some and ignoring others. His gray eyes find hers and she sees a hint of amusement in them, like someone told a joke and she's not in on it.

"In your short time here you've managed to raise a ruckus or three," he says.

"Excuse me?" Kathryn asks.

"A ruckus," he says, over enunciating the words. "Or three."

"A ruckus?"

"A commotion, a change, a shift."

"Is that bad?" she asks.

"It depends on the commotion," he replies.

"What 'commotion' did I raise?"

"Ruckus."

"I'm sorry...," Kathryn asks, already feeling flustered.

"They were technically ruckuses."

"What's the difference?"

"A ruckus is not a commotion, nor is a commotion a ruckus. They are different classes of disturbance," he replies.

"What ruckus did I cause?" Kathryn asks.

"Ruckeses," he says. "Plural. And you raised them, not caused them."

"Fine," she replies with a sigh. "What ruckuses did I raise?"

He ignores her again, scanning through his stack of papers, seeking some arcane bit of knowledge. *What all does he have in there?* Kathryn looks around the room some more, puzzling away at its purpose. It's far too uncomfortable to be a meeting room, but considering who she works for she guesses it's possible it is a meeting room. Meetings are meant to be uncomfortable.

"You're new here, aren't you?" he asks out of the blue. He scans and flips directly to a specific page and puts his thumb on some bit of text. "Less than a year. What did you do before?"

"College," she says.

"And?" he asks, dragging out the single syllable.

Shit, is that in there, too? No, it couldn't be.

"I was an ... escort," she mumbles.

"That's an interesting way of putting it. Come now, Miss Devereux, there's nothing to be ashamed of here."

Fuck it. "I was a dominatrix."

"And a damned good one from what I'm reading here." He scans down a page and his eyes briefly go wide before he catches himself. "Did you really...?" he asks, trailing off at the end.

She doesn't need to see what he's looking at to know what's asking about. "Yes," she says. "Yes I did. And I would do it again."

He nods and jots a note one of his many papers. The paper stack, Kathryn notices, has grown significantly since she first sat down. He had five or ten sheets with him when he came in. Now there are three stacks, each over an inch thick.

"Did you really call Mrs. Evans a 'stupid cow'?"

Kathryn blanches. "Well, you're kind of missing the context here."

"Yes or no."

"Yes, but … "

"Do you think it an apt descriptor?" he asks.

"It's an exaggeration, but yes, I think it was apt. At the time," Kathryn says.

"At the time. Is she, in your opinion, still a cow?"

"More of a manatee," Kathryn says.

"How's that?"

"Slow and relatively harmless."

He cocks an eye and looks at her like he wants to say something, but can't for whatever reason.

"And prone to wandering into propeller blades," Kathryn continues.

"Mr. Franklin."

"What?" Kathryn asks. *Who is Mr. Franklin?*

"You created your own job description," he continues. "According to this, you 'code daemons'. Your words, Miss Devereux."

"It's a play on words. Since they're essentially servants," Kathryn says.

He jots down an extensive note in the ever growing pile of paper. While he's writing, he whistles to himself. The song is some half-remembered tune from the distant past, a Swing or Big Band song of some kind. It's like he's completely forgotten she's here. Kathryn cranes her neck, trying to read what he's writing. She can't tell for sure, but it looks like little squiggles that twist and twirl on the paper.

She sees him raise an eye, but he makes no move to hide what he's writing, and goes back to annotating whatever notes he's taking on her. Ultimately, she decides it's not worth it to figure out what's he's writing and leans back in her chair.

Whatever is going on here, it's not what she expected. Like all the code monkeys, she's heard rumors about this room; she's even made up a few of her own. Heard it from a guy in maintenance who heard from someone in the mail room that knew this company alumnus who totally swore the room was that special place in Hell you always hear about.

So far, though, it's more tedious than anything else.

Maybe that's it. Maybe the room is an unholy terror to some people, but mindless tedium to other. Either way, Room 101 is the torture chamber of the soul.

The man waves a hand and a creature appears on the table. The creature is about ten feet tall and covered with spikes and muscles. The muscle is richly textured, gnarled like an old tree. The spikes are huge and serrated; the kind of blades that not only cut but tear flesh. The creature is hunched over, like it's not strong enough to carry its massive weight. Standing fully upright, it would probably push twelve or thirteen feet tall.

The face is nothing more than a couple of black eye sockets surrounded by wrinkled, leathery skin. The eyes show no hint of anything that even resembles an emotion.

Glowing lines cover the monstrous thing, like traces on a computer motherboard and bits of strange technology are implanted in its flesh. As she watches, Kathryn sees faint lights running along the paths and knows the thing is a mockup. Her mockup. The production model didn't incorporate the lights.

"Explain this," the man says.

"Research showed a predilection toward nervousness around biotechnological integration. I decided to sketch this up."

The man stands and stretches. He cracks his knuckles and the staccato sound echoes around the white room. A swipe of his hand and the creature spins in space. It twists and turns, slowly losing momentum until its ass is facing her.

"I was referring more to this," the man says.

She knows exactly what he's talking about, but decides to play innocent for the time being. "The tail is a twist on a classic design. I modified the tail to be articulated rather than biological. You know, to go with the mechanical design motif."

The look on his face is pure, unadulterated confusion. He pulls a flip notebook out of his jacket pocket and quickly makes notes.

"I think …," she starts. He holds up a finger and she stops dead.

He fills up the first page and flips to the second, writing furiously. His brow is furrowed and it's obvious his frustration is growing.

Eventually the pen cuts through the paper and he closes his eyes. Kathryn can see his lips moving as he counts.

At ten, his eyes open and he calmly sits down and continues writing, this time in one of his growing stacks of paper. It's the small victories in life. Well, not life-life, but, whatever.

"What's that you're writing?" she asks.

He holds up a finger again and Kathryn gets the hint to keep quiet.

After the clock's little hand goes around a few times – it feels like only a few minutes to her – the man stops writing. His calm demeanor is back and he gestures at the strange creature floating above the table. "I'm less concerned about the tail and more concerned about what is written on the … ass."

Kathryn leans in close and peers at the thing's ass. "Yes?" she asks.

"Why does the … demon …"

"Daemon," Kathryn interrupts.

His eyes roll back and she gets the distinct impression he never does that. "Why do the … daemon's … buttocks say '*Hecho en Mexico*'?"

Feeling she's on a roll, Kathryn can't help herself. "Because they don't make them in Canada?"

"You know damned well where they're made and it is not Mexico!" the man roars.

"Well, sure, but," Kathryn stumbles.

"But what?" he thunders. His eyes are turning bright red and there's a strange feeling in the air, like his anger is altering the very air around them.

The sudden change in his demeanor rocks her back. "It was just a little joke," she says quietly.

"Jokes," he says, his voice clearly menacing, "have their place. And printed on the buttocks of these agents is not one of them."

"I'm sorry," Kathryn says quietly.

"Do you know what the goal of this organization is, Miss Devereux?"

"To make the best quality products we can?"

"No, Miss Devereux," he says, sounding disappointed that she didn't have the answer he was looking for. "The goal, the purpose, of this organization is to maintain the balance."

"The balance?"

"The balance. Your division handles one side. A different division handles the other. In order for the balance to maintained each side must put its best effort into each product. Do you know what best effort looks like?"

"Not having '*Hecho en Mexico*' tattooed on a daemon's ass?"

"Exactly," he says, steepling his fingers together and looking smugly satisfied that she got the answer right.

"The rest of your work is exemplary, but this ... this ... renegade attitude must be reined in and applied to our mission."

"Our mission?" Kathryn asks.

"Our mission." He pats the ever growing stack of papers in front of him.

"What is in all ... that?" She asks circling her arms in the air.

Again he ignores her question and stares at the demon floating above the table. There's a glint in his eye, a subtle sign that he likes what he sees. He walks around the glowing creature and nods appreciatively at it.

His demeanor changes suddenly and rather than looking at her as an enemy he glances at Kathryn and smiles appreciatively. He gestures at the floating demon, staring at it almost lovingly, and says, "It's impressive work, Miss Devereux. A clever blend of biology and technology."

"Thank you," Kathryn says.

"We lost one recently," he says with a sigh. "An old model, well over a century. Designed to scare children into behaving."

"How did you ... we ... lose one?"

"A weapon was ... appropriated. It was unexpected."

"Appropriated?" Kathryn asks, genuinely curious about what could stop one of their works. Even the older models were incredibly tough. Nothing short of the special weapons of the ... *Oh, no.* "How did it happen?"

"Information is sketchy, but the model was found in pieces. We're still looking for the head."

"What's going on back there?" she asks.

"Things have shaken up on Earth," he says. "Rather unexpected things. I'm sorry, I'd like to discuss more but the information is still being assessed."

He appears to be opening up and Kathryn sees a chance to start getting some information of her own. "What is all that?" she asks, gesturing at the growing pile of papers on the white table.

He looks down at the papers and notes. "This is your life, Kathryn Devereux. Well, the part that's happened already."

"Is that why it keeps growing?"

"Partially. Some of this is my work. The mission doesn't stop because I'm in an interview."

"This is an interview?"

"What did you think it was?" he asks.

"I don't know. I got called to Room 101 last night and was told to be here at 10am sharp but I have no idea why I'm supposed to be here or what I'm supposed to be doing," Kathryn says. "Truthfully, I'm not one hundred percent where 'here' even is."

"Room 101?" he asks. He has a strange look on his face, like he doesn't quite understand what's going on or a there's a joke she missed somewhere along the line.

"Yes, Room 101," Kathryn says, "It's what the code monkeys call this place. It's from Orwell's *1984*, you know; the worst place in the world."

"I'm familiar with Orwell's Room 101," he says dryly. "I just find it amusing they still call it that."

Now it's Kathryn's turn to look confused. How the hell would he know the programmers call this place Room 101? And what does he mean 'they still call it that'?

He smiles slightly and asks, "Have you ever met anyone who actually went to Room 101?"

She stops and thinks. Everyone in the Agile Development Dungeon has a story about so-and-so who went to Room 101 and never came back. The room is like some kind of Urban Myth among the programmers who are, admittedly, kind prone to making up stories. Kathryn first heard the story of Room 101 shortly after she got here. Seems there was a hotshot developer, kind of a dick like most of the hotshots, who got called into Room 101 and never came back.

The story goes like this: George, no one knew his last name, was a total diva programmer who wrote some of the earliest code for the current generation of demons. It was revolutionary stuff and allowed the first instances of extensibility in the creatures. Prior to his work, they were all custom one-off jobs; tedious to code and difficult to maintain. George - whoever the hell he was - created the first object-oriented demons.

They were, for lack of a better word, amazing; completely revolutionary.

Kathryn's own work is still based on his. She's one of the stars, she knows this, but whoever this George was, he was worlds above and beyond her. Without his work she never would have been able to expand so quickly.

"No, I've never met anyone who's gone to Room 101," she says.

"Well, then, it would probably stand to reason that you've never met anyone who came back from Room 101."

"No," Kathryn admits, feeling somewhat stupid for believing in the mythos.

"Do you have any idea who first coined the phrase 'Room 101' to describe this place?"

He watches her carefully, wondering if Kathryn's already guessed at what's going on. "No," she says. "Who?"

The man in gray leans back in his chair and, for the first time, looks absolutely relaxed. His whole being changes in a heartbeat and she sees the cocky diva programmer lurking underneath the tailored suit and styled hairdo.

Kathryn is shocked that she didn't see it. He got the daemon joke, something just arcane enough to be off the beaten path for the average person. Daemons were helpful spirits in Greek mythology, things hanging out in the background. Early Unix programmers glommed onto the term and referred to any piece of software that waited patiently for input as a daemon. It's a much more dignified term than that other company's pedestrian 'service.'

Since the demons Kathryn and her cohorts code are essentially the same kind of servants, they jokingly refer to them as daemons.

Across from her, smiling openly for the first time since she's been in this room, is a fellow programmer. "You're George, aren't you?" she asks with equal parts awe and a desire to show him up.

George flashes her a lopsided grin and says, "Guilty."

"Nice to meet you," Kathryn says, hoping she doesn't sound like she's gushing. "Your work was pretty amazing."

He blushes. Deep down, he's still the shy kid who first revolutionized demon development. "Thank you," he says simply.

"So, what's all this about? What's going on here?" Kathryn asks, gesturing around the room.

"Well, it's not often that we get someone creative enough to buck the system. I read your synopsis on Project QUIET TERROR. It was very clever, a new way of looking at interactions with the Universe."

Now it's Kathryn's turn to blush. "Thank you. I thought that project had been shelved."

"Oh, no. We're doing some field testing right now, the initial results are promising."

"Where?" Kathryn asks.

"Here and there," George says. "We got a contract to upgrade security in a house in the Nowhere. We augmented the Alunan guardian."

Kathryn raises an eyebrow, waiting for him to explain what the Nowhere is and why there is a house that needed a security upgrade out there, let alone what an Alunan guardian is. George is beaming, thinking about the new system – her system – and how well it's working.

"It hasn't been fully tested, but between the Alunan guardian and your QUIET TERROR system, I doubt anything short of some kind of hero would be utterly lost and torn to pieces in short order," George says. "Heck, even here, even with the actual developer under the gun, QUIET TERROR worked pretty well."

"The clock," she says.

"The clock," George says with a nod. "The table, your chair, your skewed sense of time; all of that was to see if we could knock you off your cool. I'm pleased to say it didn't seem to work, but also disappointed it didn't work. You realized, at least a part of your mind, what was going on and kept your wits about you. That's a good thing. You can't be scared of anything in this business."

"It didn't scare me," Kathryn says. "It just made me curious."

"That may have been a skill developed in your past life. I suspect being a dominatrix let you see a lot more than most people have. Consequently, you're much harder to unsettle. You're kind of a rare breed, though. Most people are finding it quite hard to deal with the effects of your pet project."

"I suppose I should say 'Thank you'."

"It's always considered appropriate," George replies.

"Thank you."

George gets up and stretches. "It was a sincere compliment, Miss Devereux."

"That's the second time you've brought my past job up."

"Surely you don't think that's why you're here."

"Here? In this room?"

"Here. In this place," George replies.

"The thought had crossed my mind."

"Would you have done anything differently?"

Kathryn starts to speak but pauses. *Would I have done it differently?* "No, probably not," she finally says.

"Of course not. No one who makes it to this room ever says, 'Yes, I would do things differently.' You're not here because you've done something wrong; you're here because you've done something right."

"What did I do right?"

"I'm not sure. They don't usually explain their reasons. Personally I think it was the business with the President, but you never can tell."

"Again with the President," Kathryn says with a sigh and slumps back in her chair.

"It was pretty funny."

Kathryn can't help but smile. Even she has to admit it was pretty funny even if it did nearly start a war. "Yeah, it was pretty funny."

"That may well be the reason you're here. Not many people can see the joke," George says.

"The joke?"

"The cosmic joke," George says with a cocked eyebrow. "The one where the punchline is the joke itself."

"I'm not sure I follow you," Kathryn says, leaning forward in the chair.

"Most people look for some kind of meaning, some kind of idea that there's been a definitive good or bad. Those things are basically nothing more than P.R. There's never been such a thing as pure good or pure evil, save a small handful of myopic individuals who wind up driving themselves insane. The rest of us realized the cosmic joke a very long time ago."

"And the joke is?"

"Good and evil are functionally non-existent. It's less what you do than why you do it that matters."

"So why are we here?" Kathryn asks.

"I told you, balance," he says. "Most people here will say we sell things to both sides and as long as their little tiff continues we make a profit. It's the profit that people like to talk about, but it's the balance that keeps us awake at night. Sell both sides quality products and the battle will never end. It's good for us in terms of profit, but it's good for everyone because as long they're fighting each other they leave us alone. Balance is good all the way around."

"What balance?"

"All balance. Look at your creation."

"What about it?" Kathryn asks.

"You created a monster, Miss Devereux. A terrifying new blend of old biology and new horror and then stamped '*Hecho en Mexico*' on its ass. You mixed terror with humor."

"It'll never see production," Kathryn says with a sigh and slumps back in her chair.

"It's almost ready to be fielded," George says. "We even left the stamp on it."

"Where will it be deployed?" Kathryn asks, suddenly excited.

"We felt it would work well on Aluna."

"Aluna?" Kathryn asks. "Like the Alunan guardian?"

"Clever," George says. "Yes, the Alunan guardian was developed in a subsidiary firm on Aluna."

"Where's Aluna?" Kathryn asks. "Is it in Europe?"

"It's not in Europe. It's in another place," George says.

"Never heard of it."

"It's not on Earth. A parallel place, of sorts. It's an interesting blend of old and new. Think of it as a place where Earth took a different path."

Kathryn is floating. It's rare to get a demon into production. In fact, there are people she works with who have been around for centuries who have never seen a complete, unaltered design go out the door.

"Why mine?" she asks.

"We have a specific task and it fit the bill nicely. Congratulations, Miss Devereux. You've accomplished something most people never do. In my time, I got two out the door and that was after the better part of a century."

"So, why all this? Why not just send a creeper with congrats and a bonus?" Kathryn asks, gesturing around the room.

"This is, like I said earlier, an interview. If we wanted to simply congratulate you we'd send a stripper and a wad of cash," George replies. "We're not above such things here."

"You're interviewing me? For what?"

"That's part of what we're figuring out. We started out with one position but your reactions have altered the original plan," he says.

"In a good way or a bad way?" Kathryn says absently. Her mind is on her creation. It's one thing to plan out a demon, write its basic code, figure out how to make it move; seeing one in the flesh is so much more impressive.

"A good way, Miss Devereux. You've exceeded our expectations."

The room suddenly fills with sounds and the second hand on the clock moves normally. Like a switch has been thrown somewhere she can hear his breathing and the air conditioner running again. Kathryn exhales a breath and relaxes, releasing tension she didn't even know she had.

George notices and spins a finger around the room. "Project QUIET TERROR. So subtle even when it was running full blast you probably didn't even recognize the totality of your handiwork."

Now that the tension has faded away, she recognizes her fingerprints all over the interview. He even brought it up earlier and it didn't click for her. The little changes in time, in sounds, in sensations. They were nothing significant, nothing that would make her immediately realize something was off, but the little changes stacked up and slowly eroded her.

"It works better than I expected," Kathryn says.

"Field testing has proven remarkable. As people get more and more used to the sudden shocks of the world, the quiet nagging feeling that something is wrong has worked wonders. That house in Nowhere will be impenetrable," George says, clearly excited about the possibilities of a new technology.

"A question," she says.

"What's on your mind?"

"You mentioned the other side of the company. My side does these things," Kathryn says, gesturing at the slowly spinning demon on the table. "What does the other side do?"

"We started out doing contract work for the 'bad guys'," George says. He scratches his chin, thoughtfully and adds, "They're really not so bad, actually. More teachers than anything else, they just have a way of shocking people into a mode. Anyway, we did our jobs and did them well and got bigger and bigger contracts. The whole of demon creation was outsourced to us. We're it, the only ones left creating these glorious creatures."

George pauses and looks at the demon like with a sense of wonder in his eyes. He has the look of a father with a newborn. He may not have created it, but some of his DNA is in the beast. "When the other side heard," he continues, "they outsourced their beings to us as well. Now we're responsible for making the physical elements of so-called 'good' and 'evil'. The base constructs are still there, still trying to accomplish the same task in different ways, but we make the tangible elements."

"What tangible elements do the other side of the company make?"

"Things of such beauty it hurts your head and makes you want to carve out your own eyes lest you see something ugly. Beautiful, powerful things. You'll get an opportunity to work with them at some point. You may have a trick or two to teach them," he tells her with a little wink.

Kathryn wonders if she'll be able to make something beautiful, she's spent so much time having fun with the dark things that go bump in the night she's uncertain how she'll do on the other side. George watches her face, watches her brow furrow. "I know what you're thinking, you're wondering if you can pull off the other side."

"Yeah, kind of," Kathryn says. "I mean, I make things like this guy and come up with ideas of how to make people uncomfortable, how can I be uplifting?"

"You'll figure it out. Probably in your own special way. It took me some time to come to grips with it, but I managed."

"I've just … I've just never considered myself uplifting."

"What you did with the President seemed pretty uplifting for him."

Kathryn blushes, remembering the debacle that followed. "Most of those guys do that. Apparently it helps them get over a fear of public speaking."

"I take it he hadn't tried that," George says.

"He said he hadn't."

"It must have worked," George replies, sitting on the edge of the table. "People say it was the best speech he ever gave."

"Well, until the unfortunate incident with nail in the podium," Kathryn says, stifling a laugh.

"Personally, I thought the stockings emphasized his legs nicely."

Kathryn laughs out loud. It was a nationwide scandal, but a pretty funny one.

When she stops laughing she finds George watching her with a hint of a smile on his lips. "See, you can be uplifting to people," he tells her. "You just do it without cheesy posters and lame lines."

Kathryn, still chuckling, nods.

"Keep up the creative work, Miss Devereux. You're doing a great job."

He walks calmly to the other end of the table and pulls off the single sheet of paper left. Folding it into thirds, George walks back across the room and hands it to her. "Take this to H.R. Don't worry, they don't actually bite; that's just a rumor they themselves started. Just don't cross them and never make eye contact."

"I need to get some things from my desk," Kathryn says.

"Your things have been moved to your new office. H.R. will tell you where it is," George says, gathering up his papers and pen. He looks up, meets her eyes, and smiles. It's a warm smile, the kind that touches his eyes. "Good work, Miss Devereux."

With a little bow, George turns on his heel and heads toward the door. Kathryn clutches the letter to her body and holds it like a child. "Thank you, Mr. Franklin," she says to his back.

He turns his head and smiles back at her. "I wondered if you'd catch that."

"It took me a bit but, yeah, I got it."

"Nice work," he says and starts to leave before stopping again. "One last thing, Miss Devereux."

"Yes, Mr. Franklin."

"We wear gray here," he says with a smile and a small salute. "Welcome to Mahogany Row."

The Hunt

Wilford Saxton is sitting cross-legged on a rickety bed in a dilapidated motel in Cuba, New Mexico with a black, featureless gun in his lap. There are two beds in the room and the one he's sitting on is the least dirty of the two.

This part of the country is dotted with places like this; run-down or flat-out broken shells of motels are just part of the scenery around here. Fortunately, this one is actually still functional, unlike most of America's old motels. Even the buzzing neon sign out front is still mostly functional even if it does lead one to wonder what an acancy is.

Saxton contemplated hiding out in one of the ruined ranch houses in the area and actually searched around for one that might work. Unfortunately, the abandoned houses were too broken down to be of any use. Plus, he felt like a hobo and that's not something Wilford Saxton can abide by. Steven would have found it amusing to find Wilford squatting in a ruin, hiding out from God only knows what might be after him. Wilford searched for a few days, chuckling to himself at his old partner's assertion that those ruined places were actually built to look broken. Steven always had a … different way of looking at things. He was useful, a friend even, but he went too far.

Steven and his whelp of girlfriend are long term projects, though. Due to recent events they've both become too powerful for him to handle. At least on his own. He'll get them, but he needs time to figure out his new abilities and place in the world. Wilford isn't too proud to admit that he needs time to train if he's going to take on the new God of Dreams.

Besides, his new … status … capabilities … whatever, are still a mystery to him.

For instance: there's a knife sticking out Wilford's arm. He pushed the blade into his own arm to test a theory. The long, black blade is honed to a razor sharp edge that tapers to serrated ridges. It's an ugly thing, a combat blade made for the sole purpose of taking lives. Employed correctly, and Wilford always employs his blades correctly, a knife like this can gut a person smoothly and efficiently.

The blade is rammed straight through his arm, poking out the other side. It slid right between the ulna and the radius, neatly severing muscle and tendon.

A wound like this should hurt like hell. He's been stabbed through this exact same spot and the pain was excruciating. The blade inside of his body should feel like ice inside of his arm and the flesh should be on fire. *And the blood, where's the blood? Why don't I have any blood?*

He feels nothing other than a faint alarm bell ringing in the back of his head that warns him he's sustained damage and that damage hasn't been repaired yet.

"Where's my blood?" he asks quietly.

There's no one else in the motel room. The room is about twenty feet by twenty feet of solid and freezing concrete. Outside it's nearly freezing and the heater doesn't work very well. The only light comes from a lamp that flickers every time he shifts on the bed.

"You don't need blood anymore" the voice whispers in his head. "Blood is for mortals and you are so much more."

As always, the voice of his gun feels like eels swimming in his head; slick and smooth but with a threat of needle teeth tearing into him.

Wilford yanks the knife out of his arm and watches in horrid fascination as his flesh knits itself back together again. Within seconds his arm is healed and whole. There's not a single mark left where the knife pierced him.

"What has happened to me?" Wilford asks.

"You were fixed," the voice says.

"Fixed?"

"You were flawed and weak like all these wretched creatures. You are special, Wilford Saxton, the procedure repaired you."

"Is that why I can hear you?"

"Yes. The first part allowed you to hear me; the second treatment made you a weapon with no equal on this plane."

The voice echoes in Wilford's head and rattles around, digging dirty fingers into his brain. A weapon with no equal…

A little over a week ago Wilford Saxton set out kill his old partner for crimes that, at the time, seemed egregious even by Steven's admittedly high standards of pissing Wilford off. Long story short, Steven and that mad woman Eve released a thing that should have stayed hidden. That thing killed Congress and tried to take over the world. Wilford planned on killing Steven, then wound up joining him, then tried to kill him again.

Steven is wily, though; a slick and lucky customer. Steven survived Wilford's repeated attempts to kill him; first with a mountain and then with the gun that's now whispering sweet nothings in Wilford's brain. Not only did he survive, Steven seems to have gathered up power of his own.

Wilford seethes every time he thinks Steven's name. The man – scratch that, Steven's more god now than man – has ruined his life. He's lost his job, his life, his humanity to his former partner. They were friends once but all that's gone now and the mere thought of Steven's smirking face makes Wilford want to kill something. Or someone. Definitely someone. Mostly Steven.

"What do I call you?" Wilford asks the gun.

"I am just a gun, I don't need a name. What's in a name anyway?" the voice asks.

"I don't know. It would just be easier to have something to call you other than gun."

"Why don't you just think what you want? That's the easiest way to talk to me."

"I want to talk," Wilford says. "It feels … normal. I need to feel normal."

"You're not normal," the gun says. "You're special."

"What now?" Wilford asks.

"Now we hunt," the voice says.

"What are we hunting?"

"Bad things."

"Bad things? Like what?"

"I can see into your mind. You know what you want to hunt," the gun tells him.

"Monsters."

"Yes," the voice hisses. "Let's hunt a monster. You know you want it. It will serve as an excellent training opportunity for us to become a better team."

"Why do you know so much?" Wilford asks.

"I am a weapon," the gun says. "A weapon is useless without information. I was designed to be a modern version of a charmed battle axe or an enchanted sword. With new technology comes new ways of doing things. I have access to vast amounts of data; it makes me a better killer."

"You can hear me think, can't you?"

"As I said earlier, I can see into your mind," the gun whispers.

Visions fill Wilford's head as the gun peruses his memories like so many index cards. Names, dates, things lurking in the darkness pass through his mind until the gun finds one it likes. He finds himself reliving his meeting with Coco. The bogeyman of Northern New Mexico was lurking in Albuquerque for reasons only it knew. Faulty intelligence, a common problem in the Department of Homeland Security, led Wilford and his team into Hell. They were told they were stopping drug dealers and that children would be involved, but instead they found an abattoir.

The team moved in quickly, kicking down the down the door and taking up a defensive perimeter. What they found stopped them dead in their tracks. Mysterious, probably sacred symbols were carved in the walls and the whole place was bathed in blood. Even the light was tinted red. The blood on the bare bulb in the ceiling was smoking.

Saxton and his partners, Manfredi and Johnson, were experienced agents. All of them were trained killers who had done horrible things in the name of security and their country. They'd hunted the monsters that D.H.S. knows about but is powerless to stop and done everything in their power to keep the country safe. Not a single one of them had seen anything even remotely like the scene in front of them.

There may or may not have been drug dealers at that tiny South Valley house. There were children, there, though: Coco was busy eating one of them. Wilford and his team walked into a bloodbath.

The abattoir was overseen by the beast itself. It looked kind of like a man but its limbs were too long and had too many joints. The eyes,

Wilford recalls with a shudder, were black pits that seemed to go on forever. There are women out there with eyes you can lose yourself in. Those are safe places. You could lose yourself in Coco's eyes and spend the rest of your days trying in vain to find your way out a pitch black forest.

Coco attacked without warning and with a ferocity reserved for horror movie monsters. Manfredi and Johnson were down and screaming before anyone could react. The creature savaged Wilford but otherwise left him alone so he could bear witness to what happened to Manfredi and Johnson. Somehow or another it kept them alive and aware while it tore into them. In the end all that was left was living heads, silently screaming.

Wilford's mind was reeling, waiting in agony for it to be his turn.

All this he remembered vividly, even without the gun's relentless prying in his brain. He remembered everything going black and waking up in a hospital bed, wondering how he was still alive and why his wounds were all healed.

Quite a lot happened between Coco and waking up in the hospital but it was all buried deep in the lockbox of Wilford's brain. Not only was the information locked away, Wilford himself actively sought to forget it.

As Wilford lay there waiting to die horribly, Coco inexplicably bolted from the house. This thing that had taken down his team and tortured them to death left in a palpable haze of fear. What the hell is scary enough to terrify the bogeyman?

This is where it all gets kind of hazy. It's not that the gun can't probe Saxton's mind, it's just that there aren't that many memories to probe. He drifted in and out of consciousness, each time waking up somewhere different. One time it's the back of the ambulance where two blonde men fight to keep him alive. Another time he wakes up in a pale green tiled room where men in surgical garb are putting lumps of flesh inside of him. He wakes up in a bed with a man standing over him.

"You will remember nothing," the man says.

Poof. Next thing he knows Wilford is waking up in his own bed in Albuquerque with a splitting headache but no other wounds.

Nothing. Not a scratch. Not a scar. Not even a hang nail. His report on the incident was finished; signed, sealed, and delivered. There was only one problem. The report was faked and nothing in it was true. There was no mention of Coco, no mention of how Manfredi and Johnson met their untimely demise, no mention of the truth.

It's well known in National Security circles that some monsters are real. More worrying, it's well known that there's usually not much anyone can do about them. Some of the worst, the Cocos and other bogeymen of the world, flit in and out of reality which makes them exceedingly hard to track down. A few have been captured and studied to little avail. Even a god has been captured and studied, but the results of that little experiment cost the lives of no small number of people. The official policy, therefore, is similar to the policy on UFOs and extraterrestrials: cover up and deny.

And yet, here sits Wilford Saxton, a first-hand witness to the destructive power and god-awful temperament of what is known in government circles as a free-ranging non-natural aberrant being. Something drove it off, but Wilford doesn't remember and the gun can't figure it out.

At any rate, the damned thing is still out there and Wilford, newly born into weapon-ness is itching to for a little vengeance.

"How do we find it?" Wilford asks.

"I can sense it," the gun says. "It's one of the things I was designed to destroy."

"Great. Let's go kill it."

"It's not that simple. I can sense it, but I couldn't tell you exactly where it is."

"So, again," Wilford says, exasperated. "How do we find it?"

"Part of your job duties included detective work," the gun prompts.

"Well, I had to track down bad guys and kill them," Wilford says, "But I mostly I just did the killing. Steven did most of the analysis work."

The gun dives into Wilford's mind, searching for reference to Steven. It finds images of friendship, betrayal, torture, and – yes, there it is – the new God of Dreams. "You will have to think like Steven does, then," the gun says. "We're in the area, but you'll need to find the details."

*****

Details and detective work have never been Saxton's forte. He was part of a team and like all team players he became dependent on the team for survival. His role was essentially extermination. Steven thought his way through the problems and provided solutions to Wilford. It was a good arrangement and let each play on the other's strengths.

Never mind that Steven regularly beat him in sparring. That man had an annoying ability to think outside the box and come up with solutions Wilford never could arrive at. This is not to say Wilford is stupid just that analysis was never his best skill. And now he's stuck in Cuba, NM, trying to track down a monster while his gun is talking to him. Add a plucky sidekick and laugh track and it would be sitcom gold.

Cuba is a small town in north central New Mexico. The people who know of it at all know it as nothing more than a place they have to slow down to go through on their way to or from more exciting places. Its primary tourist attraction is a gas station with a built-in McDonald's and some machines that dispense elaborate condoms in the bathroom.

Like all small towns, it guards its secrets jealously against outsiders. In a place like Cuba, a person is either of the town or a stranger. People of the town don't spill secrets to strangers. Even cashiers in little gas stations with built in McDonald's restaurants know this, even if they may not be able to articulate it.

"So, you haven't heard anything about strange deaths?" Wilford asks.

The young lady running the cash register blinks at him. She's got long eyelashes and has drawn her eyebrows on with a Sharpie. "I told you, I don't know nothing. You gonna pay or what?"

Wilford hands her his credit card and waits for the inevitable question.

"You work for the TSA or what?"

Wilford sigh and wonders if she's going to end every question with "or what." The card he handed her clearly says Department of

Homeland Security. It even has his name and picture on it. Unfortunately, the only thing most Americans know about DHS the signs they read in airports. The same signs that refer to the Transportation Safety Administration. The TSA is a subsidiary of DHS, not the other way around.

"No, ma'am. DHS is the parent organization," Wilford says.

She smacks her gum and he can almost hear the rusty gears turning in her head. "Not much of a parent you ask me. You need to smack that kid," she finally says, laughing at her own joke. Something occurs to her and she adds, "They took my perfume. You gotta form I need to fill out or what?"

Wilford recognizes the futility of the conversation and says, "I don't carry them with me."

"Figures," she says, rolling her eyes and popping her gum.

Wilford holds his breath while the card reader scans his card. He was technically fired from DHS a few months ago, but the agency was asleep at the time. Quite literally asleep, the effect of the God of Dreams being freed and wreaking havoc. The organization is waking up now and there's always the chance someone will notice he's gone and shut down his card.

The machine beeps and a receipt slowly prints out. She hands it to him and says, "Where do I get one of them forms?"

At least she didn't say "or what." Wilford doesn't look up at her as he signs the receipt. "Check the website."

"You got an address or what?"

Wilford chokes down the desire to shoot her on the spot. The gun, securely stashed in a shoulder holster in his jacket, whispers to him. "She's not worth your time. Keep your eyes on the target."

"Google it," Wilford says to the girl and slides the receipt back to her.

As he walks away, he can hear her mutter, "Pendejo."

The combo gas station and McDonald's is bustling. A throng of humanity surrounds him, a mixture of people coming from the north heading toward Albuquerque and people from Albuquerque trying to get away from the city. Whatever they did to him in Dulce it changed the way he perceives crowds. Wilford used to enjoy crowds, he was great at getting along with people. Not so much anymore. His senses are heightened now and that's not always a good thing.

The smell of burgers cooking at the McDonald's is nauseating. A week ago he would have happily eaten a Big Mac or a Quarter Pounder, but now the thought of eating one nearly makes him retch. He can smell the other people in the gas station, too; they have a sickening sweet reek of Cheetos and long hours on the road.

"Why do they smell so terrible?" Wilford asks the gun.

"Your body is different," the gun says in his head. "You need different fuel. None of this cooked and wasted meat."

Wilford ponders asking what he should eat but decides against it for the time being. There are bigger things afoot and he needs to find the local police station.

*****

The Cuba Police Department consists of two full time cops. That may be too much for a town of seven hundred or so, but those pesky out-of-towners need to be dealt with and there's always a drunk and disorderly wandering around somewhere.

At the station Wilford decides to go with his strengths. He pushes the doors open and walks in like he owns the place. Purposeful strides carry him to the front desk where he flashes his DHS ID at the secretary and simply says, "I need to talk to your boss."

The secretary peers at his ID.

"Now," Wilford says.

She looks up and their eyes lock. Wilford can feel her emotions and taste them like so many Pop Rocks on his tongue. Her nervousness is infectious and intoxicating. This woman has worked behind this very desk for nearly twenty years and has never seen anything more exotic than a man with a Ferrari who was caught going a hundred and twenty down the main drag at 2am. Now, the Federal Government has shown up on her doorstep.

"Yes, yes, sir," she stumbles.

"Calm down, Miss…" Wilford says.

"It's Mrs., sir, Mrs. Becky Sandoval," she tells him.

"Becky," Wilford says quietly, "I'm sorry if I came off as brusque. My office sent me out here with almost no information and I took it out on you. It wasn't fair and you didn't deserve it."

"It's okay," she tells him. "Everyone has just been tense and we didn't expect the, uh, FBI to show up. It's not that big of a deal, really."

"See," whispers the gun. "He's here somewhere."

Wilford wonders just what he managed to drop himself into. This started out as a simple hunt, a way for him to strike back at the monsters he could never touch, but it smells like there's something else brewing. He may not be the best in the world at planning, but Wilford Saxton has learned to trust his instincts and they're busy telling him something is terribly wrong.

"I'm not with the Federal Bureau of Investigation," Wilford says with his best charming smile. "I'm with the Department of Homeland Security, ma'am."

"Is it that bad?" Betty says with a gasp.

"I don't know yet." Technically, that's not a lie. "What can you tell me?"

Becky's face goes a deep, paranoid red. Or maybe it's just how Wilford sees her. Whatever changes he's undergone recently didn't come with a manual and he's largely just winging it at this point. His gut says she's worried about something and it's not necessarily just a monster running loose.

"Well, I can tell you Chief McMasters was in the city when it happened. No matter what you may have heard, it wasn't him."

"Maybe you should back up, Mrs. Sandoval," Wilford says, a small, curious flame burning inside of him. "What, exactly, happened?"

"I'm sorry," she says with a hand on her chest. "I thought you knew everything."

"No, ma'am, I wasn't briefed before I left. I was supposed to get detailed files emailed but, well, you know how the government works."

Becky leans forward and looks around to make sure no one's watching her. The building seems empty, so he's not sure who she's looking for. She waves a finger toward him, beckoning him in. He leans toward her, close enough that he can smell the green chile on her breath and the cheap perfume on her neck. "No one knows what happened or where they went but there was apparently a lot of blood."

"Blood?" Wilford asks.

"A lot of blood. Everywhere. I snuck a peek at the pictures… Please don't tell anyone."

"My lips are sealed. Why would anyone think the chief was behind it?"

"Roger was the chief's best friend," Becky says quietly.

"Why would anyone think the chief would kill his best friend?"

"There are rumors…" she replies, eyes darting around to make sure no one is watching her. Becky crooks her finger and motions Wilford forward.

"What kind of rumors?" Wilford asks.

"The chief was seeing Rosaline," Becky says conspiratorially.

Wilford has to choke down the desire to throttle this woman until she starts making more sense. "Who was Rosaline?"

"Roger's wife," Becky whispers. "She and the chief were … well … you know."

"They were having relations."

"Yes. Having relations. That's a good way of putting it. Can I use that?" Becky says. She acts like she's never heard the phrase before and is amazed at the clarity of it.

"Sure," Wilford mutters. *What have I just wandered into?* he wonders. "Where's the chief now?"

"He's in his office. Let me ring him," Becky says.

Before she can pick up the phone Wilford stops her. "Is he in a meeting?"

"No, sir. He's just doing his morning paperwork."

"Good. Let me talk to him, professional to professional. Where's his office?"

"It's down the hall to the right," Becky says. Wilford is already moving. She calls to his back, "He doesn't like to be surprised!"

No doubt, Wilford thinks. *But he's about to get a little visit from the feds.*

*****

Two cops means the police station isn't very large. Wilford finds Chief Flint McMasters' office easily. The man's name sounds like he's an action hero from a 30s pulp novel; the kind of man who would face off with, and ultimately lose to, Doc Savage.

McMasters' office door is decorated with newspaper clippings of heroic cops doing heroic things. Here a dog is saved, there a boy is rescued from the clutches of a mad-dog rapist after a cop followed his hunch and knocked on the right door. It's a portrait of police heroism and, in Wilford's opinion, badge licking.

Wilford sighs. He's dealt with cops like this before and always hates every minute of it. They're so convinced of their own moral superiority that police officers like this fight him every step of the way. Small time cops are gods of their domains and bristle every time the feds show up. Wilford knows he'll have to tread lightly with this guy to get anything useful out of him.

His knock on the door is polite but firm. Wilford hears a muffled curse and a chair scooting back from a desk. Heavy footsteps pound toward the door, trailing a string of profanities. When the door flings open Wilford faces a heavy-set man with a bright red face. While McMasters yells at him, condemning the man who dared interrupt him, the parents that raised him, and any spawn he might have, Wilford watches the screaming McMasters calmly.

McMasters is mostly fluff and bluster. At first glance Wilford regarded him as a simpleton blowhard with a badge fetish, but upon closer examination he sees intelligence in McMasters' eyes. This is a man who is only playing at being an idiot.

Wilford calmly retrieves his badge and holds it in McMasters' face. "Wilford Saxton, Department of Homeland Security," he says firmly. "I think we need to chat, Chief McMasters."

At the sight of the badge McMasters' rage dissipates. His eyes lock onto the badge and a hint of panic flickers over his eyes. McMasters' peers closely at the badge, making a show of inspecting it. He finally convinces himself that the badge is real and asks, "What did you say your name was?"

"Wilford Saxton."

"What can I do for you Mr. Saxton?" McMasters asks.

Wilford ponders how to proceed with this. He's used to walking into a situation and taking care of problems quickly and efficiently, but not dealing with people. He decides to act just like DHS taught him to act and proceeds almost robotically. "We've heard you have a problem, Chief. I'm here to render assistance on behalf of the Department of Homeland Security."

"I think someone's sent you on a wild goose chase, Mr. Saxton. There's no problem here," McMasters tells him.

"You very much have a problem, Chief, and you and I both know it. A room bathed in blood. Two people missing. Do you honestly think a human did this?" Wilford asks.

The police chief turns a bright red in Wilford's eyes. Whether it's his new powers or a literal red, Wilford can't tell, but he knows the man is terrified of something. The chief steps back and appraises Saxton. "Interesting choice of phrase, Mr. Saxton. What do you think happened?"

"The Department has extensive files on these kinds of attacks," Wilford says with sly smile. "Between you and me, sir, I think you've got a bogeyman on the loose."

The Chief opens the door to his office and motions Wilford inside. "Perhaps we should talk," he says.

*****

Chief McMasters' office is chock full of sports memorabilia, crosses, and the odd *Dia de los Muertos* figurine. One entire shelf of his bookcase is dedicated to all manner of sports trophies from football and baseball. The shelf only has two books on it. Both are big books on Catholic philosophy and neither appears to have been opened.

A figurine of a skeletal man and wife is displayed prominently next to a photo of a severe looking Hispanic woman. Even in the picture her eyes are haunting pools.

The chief sits down in a battered leather chair behind his desk and motions Wilford to take a brown plastic seat in front of the desk. He sighs as he sits down and the old leather chair creaks and groans. "Now, Mr ... what was it? Saxon?"

"Saxton, sir."

"Now Mr. Saxton, and I'm not admitting I believe in such nonsense, what makes you think I've got a bogeyman on the loose?"

The fact that McMasters didn't even blink when asked about a bogeyman is damning enough, but the Chief also turned a deep green when he said it. The gun whispers in Wilford's mind, telling him the Chief knows far more than he's letting on.

"Well, Chief," Wilford says, "you've got a room full of blood, probably two dead victims, no leads and no witnesses."

"Could be one of your big city gangs up here," McMasters retorts.

"Not their style, they prefer to leave a message."

"A room covered in blood isn't a message?" McMasters asks. "What more do you want? An autographed card?"

"They like to leave bodies behind," Wilford says. "As a warning. Mystery isn't their style."

McMasters leans back in his chair and steeples his fingers. "Okay, what's the Bureau's interest in this? I think we've got the situation well in hand."

Wilford bites back his frustration. "I'm not with the Federal Bureau of Investigation, sir."

"Fine," McMasters says. "What interest does the TSA have in a double homicide in Cuba, New Mexico?"

McMasters is a deep shade of purple in Wilford's eyes. The gun quietly tells him McMasters is hiding something. It's bad enough that this small town piece of shit is leading him on, but he could at least remember who Wilford works for.

"I work for the Department of Homeland Security, Chief. My job is to hunt down and stomp on threats to this fine country that you pretend to love so much," Wilford says with no small amount of threat in his voice. "You have a threat to my country loose in your back yard and you are going to help me find it and eliminate it."

"I would like to remind you that you're in my office, Mr. Saxon," McMasters says with his own hint of threat in his voice.

"Saxton," Wilford hisses. "Wilford Saxton of the Department of Homeland Security."

"Mr. Saxton, we don't need your help," McMasters hisses back.

"Yes, you do chief. You have no idea what you're up against."

"And I suppose you do," McMasters replies, rolling his eyes.

"I've met this thing before," Wilford replies, completely dead-pan.

McMasters goes white as the blood drains from his face. "What do you know?" he asks.

"I don't know what it is, but it's not the only one out there. The Federal Government is aware of their existence and has engaged them on several occasions. We've captured UFOs, we've studied aliens. Hell, we captured a god. But every time, and I mean *every* time we've gone up against one of these … bogeyman things we have failed and paid the price for our failure in blood.

"I went into a building in the South Valley in Albuquerque with two other guys, both trained killers. We were a hit squad - don't bother asking anyone about it, DHS will deny it - we were armed to the teeth and I watched while a bogeyman shredded my team."

The chief's left eyebrow raises. "Shredded?"

"Shredded," Wilford says.

"Literally?"

"Bits and pieces," Wilford replies. "Blood and parts of bodies everywhere."

McMasters leans forward and temples his fingers in a paternal kind of fashion. "How did you survive?"

Wilford leans back and feels a momentary panic as the cheap brown plastic seat twists under his weight. He peers down and realizes he's sitting on a piece of lawn furniture and his opinion of McMasters drops another notch. His fingers massage his temples. Wilford's never been good at handling stress and his head should be throbbing at this point. Strangely it's not, and the finger massage has become just another affectation in an increasingly long line of things he'll never need to do again.

"I don't know, Chief. Something chased it off."

"Okay, you're telling me something that tore apart a government hit squad…" McMasters starts.

"And let me watch while it did it," Wilford interjects.

"And let you watch while it did it. Something that did that got scared off."

"Yeah," Wilford says.

"What do you suspect could scare something like that off?" McMasters asks.

The Chief has turned the dim yellow of disbelief. "Something worse than it," is all Wilford can come up with. It sounds lame even to him.

"So, Billy Badass, how do you propose to fight this thing when you admit you've already lost to it once?"

"You'll just have to trust me on this one," Wilford replies.

McMasters stares at him.

Frustrated and angry, Wilford stares back.

The alpha male pissing contest goes on for several beats until Wilford taps into his kill squad mode. His eyes turn hard, the kind of hard you only see in people who have actively been knee deep in blood and shit and walked safely away from it.

McMasters blinks first. He holds up his hands, palm out, and says, "Alright, Saxton. What do you need to know?"

"I want to see the crime scene," Wilford responds.

"That's it?" McMasters asks incredulously. "This whole dick waving scene and all you want to know is where the crime scene is?"

"For now."

"For now!" McMasters says boisterously and pounds his fist on his desk with a great, big grin on his face. "You've got some balls on you, son. Come on, I'll show you the crime scene."

*****

Roger and Rosaline, also known as the Bacas, lived slightly off the beaten path up toward the eastern edge of town. Their house is a modest two bedroom, two bath about a quarter mile from the nearest neighbor. The door mat still happily welcomes all visitors and there's a Lincoln SUV parked in the driveway.

The place is roped off with about four hundred feet of bright yellow police tape, probably the entire stash for Cuba's police department. Strangely, no one is standing outside gawking and no one has tried to break in.

This is damned peculiar, Wilford thinks as he surveys the scene.

"This town is scared," the gun whispers back.

Scared of Coco? Wilford ponders.

"Indeterminate," the gun replies. "They are scared that something will find them."

"McMasters doesn't seem scared," Wilford thinks, finally getting the grasp of sending his thoughts directly to the gun.

"He hides it well," the gun says. "Practice, I suspect."

"You still with us, Fed?" McMasters says loudly as he claps Wilford on the back. The blow is strong, stronger than it should be for a friendly slap on the back. It's the not-so-friendly reminder that Wilford Saxton is in Chief McMasters' town and had best mind his behavior.

"Yeah, sorry," Wilford replies. "Just wondering why there isn't anyone standing around."

"Why would they do that?" McMasters asks.

"Grisly murder scene, human nature," Wilford replies. He neglects to add this is probably the most exciting thing that's ever happened to this one-horse shithole.

"People 'round these parts – well – they like to mind their own business," McMasters says.

"Right. Can we go in?" Wilford asks.

"You're asking me? Big bad DEA agent asking little old me for permission," McMasters replies with a chuckle.

"It's your crime scene," Wilford says with a shrug. "And it's DHS, not DEA. I don't really care about drugs."

McMasters looks him in the eye and stares deep, seeking something he can't quite wrap his head around. "What do you care about Mr. Saxton?"

Wilford wonders that himself sometimes. His body has been changed, his mind altered. Hell, when it's not blowing big holes in everything that moves, his gun talks to him. What does Wilford Saxton care about? Does he even really belong to this world anymore?

"I care about the security of the nation," Wilford says. It's a pat response, parroted with as little thought as saying "amen" at church.

"Well, let's check this out so you can get back to protecting this fine nation."

McMasters pulls a switch blade from his pocket and cuts the tape with a sly grin. "Got it off a gang-banger passing through," he says. The door isn't locked and opens quietly on well-greased hinges. McMasters waves Wilford through with a flourish.

The smell of copper is so thick it cakes on Wilford's tongue. Becky wasn't kidding; there is blood everywhere. He can't even tell what color the room was originally. Whatever hit the place hit fast and precise, though. Not a single piece of furniture looks out of place and there is absolutely no sign of a struggle.

"It smells like Coco," the gun whispers in Wilford's head.

"I can't smell a thing except copper," Wilford replies.

"Stop smelling with your nose," the gun says. "You're so much more than a pathetic human."

What else am I supposed to smell with? Wilford wonders.

"It's a figure of speech," the gun replies. "Reach out with your senses and see what happened. The ghosts are still here."

Wilford closes his eyes and shakes his head. When his eyes shut he sees shadows moving behind his eyelids. He opens them and sees a scene straight out of a slasher movie. The attack took seconds. Rosaline heard something and stood up to see what it was. Coco came out of a shadow. There was a blur and a geyser of blood shot out of Rosaline's neck.

Roger fell next. He made the mistake of walking in with a pair of coffee cups. The cups are still on the floor where they fell after Coco took his hands. His throat was torn out and he was dead before he realized what happened.

The beast didn't take its time with them. Strange.

"This wasn't his normal attack," the gun whispers.

"No, it usually relishes pain and fear. It takes its time," Wilford thinks back.

"Indeed," the gun says.

"Someone sent him here. Who has the power to control something like that?" Wilford asks.

"Where are the bodies, chief?" Wilford asks out loud.

"There weren't any bodies, Mr. Saxton. No one saw anything. No one heard anything. Next day a neighbor came by and found this mess."

McMasters turns the bright red in Wilford's eyes.

"He's lying," the gun says.

"I know," Wilford replies. "He's red."

"Good, you're finally learning." The gun sounds satisfied, like a slow pupil finally understood a lesson.

"Have you examined the scene? Cataloged everything?" Wilford asks.

"Cataloged what? Blood? Yeah, sure. We had our CSI team on site immediately," McMasters replies with a laugh.

Wilford doesn't respond. He slips into search mode and scans the room. He already knows what happened here. Now he just needs to understand why it happened. The first time he ran afoul of this creature was pure coincidence, but the attack was different. The creature reveled in misery and pain. This time it hit fast and hard and something about the scene just feels different.

"Why didn't you call in for help from the FBI or State Police?" Wilford asks.

"No need. Pretty obvious what happened here. Meth heads went on a bender and slaughtered these fine folks," McMasters says, idly looking at a picture on the wall.

"Meth heads?" Wilford asks, wondering if McMasters is pulling his leg.

"Meth heads. Tweakers. You must have come across them," McMasters says.

"I've seen plenty of meth heads," Wilford replies. "But I've never seen them do this."

"Meth makes 'em crazy. Strong, too," McMasters says. He's staring at a picture of a woman, presumably Rosaline Baca. "We found a couple of them in a hotel next morning. Claimed they were just passing through and needed a place to crash."

"Well, as long as justice was served," Wilford says, rolling his eyes.

"Law and order every time," McMasters says quietly, still staring at the picture. "That's our motto."

"I don't suppose you'd mind if I asked them a few questions?" Wilford asks.

McMasters squirms and says, "No one can talk to them. Lawyers, you know?"

Wilford knows something is up with McMasters. His gut says the chief isn't innocent, but he's not responsible for this mess. "Mind if I look around the crime scene?" Wilford asks. "I'd love to see what a pair of meth heads can do when they set their minds to it."

"Be my guest," McMasters says, exhaling sharply. "Not much of a crime scene anymore, just waitin' on the cleaners to deal with the mess."

Wilford closes his eyes again and looks out over the scene with his new sight. He can make out every detail of the room. The link between his mind and the gun enhances everything he sees. A fingerprint glows white, blood stains make the room light up in ultraviolet purple.

Everything took place here in the living room. Wilford walks around the room, peering at various objects but not really paying attention to them. His mind is constantly replaying the attack, watching it from different angles, different energy patterns.

Wilford can't help but feel a little like Batman.

"How am I seeing all this?" he asks the gun.

"Everything that happens leaves an energy trail. It's just the way the world works," the gun replies. "Those trails stay around for a while like echoes in the fabric of reality."

Something about the attack catches his interest. Well, actually a couple things. Replayed in slow motion he sees Coco first come out of the shadows in the northwest corner of the house. A glance shows him there's no doorway there. Another thing that's odd is Coco takes off the man's hands before tearing his throat out, but when the bogeyman first shows up his hands look like plain old ugly-ass hands. Wilford has to play back the energies in the room at extremely slow speed to catch Coco's hand turn briefly to a single claw and back to a hand again.

Coco's a shape shifter. Shit. The rumors were true.

The final thing that catches Wilford's eye is a small bit of red in the woman's hand. He zooms in but can't make out what he's looking at. He moves around the living room, scanning for anything that looks like the red object.

Bingo. There it is under a lamp table in the corner. Something small – no several small things – lit up in red.

"Don't know what you're looking for, Hoss, but this place was swept clean by Cuba's finest," McMasters says out of the blue.

"You and the other cop in this town, eh?" Wilford says. "Bang up job, chief."

Wilford kneels in the corner and fetches the little red pieces. They're pieces of some sort of figurine, tiny bones and a grinning skull. A little skeleton of some sort or another.

"You find something, slick?" McMasters asks.

"Bones, Dr. Grissom," Wilford says. He holds out the tiny pieces to McMasters and watches the other man's eyes.

"*Dia de los Muertos* figurine, master investigator," McMasters says. "There are tons of them in this town. Pretty common among the Hispanic population around here."

"I know what *Dia de los Muertos* figures are," Wilford says. "These are different, though, far more intricate than a normal figure. It's also made of real bone." The little pieces in his hand are far from common. Something happened to them. He peers closely and can see a hint of dark things.

"I think you're mistaken," McMasters says. "No one makes those out of real bone."

"Someone did," Wilford says.

Wilford toys with the pieces, trying to reassemble them into something coherent but too many of the bones are missing. He examines the skull, turning the tiny piece around in his head. The empty eye sockets leer at him and the grinning teeth are laughing at some joke Wilford hasn't gotten around to understanding yet.

"Mind if I keep these?" Wilford asks.

"Sorry, son, that's evidence," McMasters replies. "Leave 'em on the coffee table, I'll make sure they're bagged and tagged."

There is no doubt in Wilford's mind that the tiny bone fragments will disappear as soon as he walks out the door but he's in no position to argue. He sets the pieces on the coffee table, still pondering the hint of darkness his new vision revealed on the bones. Something is tugging at his mind, trying to make him understand, but he just can't grasp it.

"Was she worth it, Chief?" Wilford finally asks.

"Pardon me?" McMasters asks.

"Rumor has it you and Rosaline Baca were having relations," Wilford says, watching the chief carefully.

"Relations?" McMasters asks, turning a deep shade of burgundy in Wilford's eyes. "What the fuck does that mean?"

Wilford pauses, slipping momentarily into government agent mode before deciding that part of him is in the past. "Fucking her, chief," he says. "You were fucking her. Was it worth it?"

"Wait a minute. You think I had something to do with this?" McMasters asks. "I was out of town when this happened."

"I know that, too, chief. I'm not accusing you. I'm just wondering, was it worth it?" Wilford asks. "You got laid and now these people are dead. Was fucking your best friend's wife worth it?"

"That's none of your business Saxton," McMasters hisses. "What happened between me and Rosaline is over and has been for a long time. And it's NONE. OF. YOUR. BUSINESS."

"Convenient you grabbed some meth heads," Wilford says quietly. "If this came to a trial you'd be suspect number one."

"And how the hell did I do this when I was a couple hundred miles away, surrounded by other law enforcement officers who will attest to the fact that I was swapping stories with cops from all over the state?" McMasters asks. "You think you've got something on me, slick, you'd best let me know now."

"Like I said, chief, I'm not accusing you of killing these people. You talk tough but I've been around many a murderer and you don't strike me as being one of them. I don't think you've got it in you to do this," Wilford says.

"Then why are you asking me if it was worth it?" McMasters asks, peering hard at Wilford and wondering what the fed is driving at.

"My guess is these people were murdered because someone in this town didn't approve of your dalliances," Wilford replies.

"You know what?" McMasters asks. "You need to meet some people in this town. Come over for dinner tonight. We've got some other people coming by for dinner, won't take much to set one more plate."

*****

Wilford spends the rest of the day trying to learn more about the murders but he finds out quickly that no one wants to talk. Considering the way small towns work this isn't entirely surprising and he spends most of the day stocking up on supplies and talking to the gun.

The gun is a wealth of information about a great many things, but is very tight lipped about its history.

"Where did you come from?" Wilford asks.

"I don't remember," the gun replies. "My memory of self is tied to my user; I use the operator's brain to store myself."

"Are you using my brain now?" Wilford asks.

"Yes," the gun replies, "you have plenty free space now that you've been expanded."

"How have I been expanded?" Wilford asks.

"Data is limited." Wilford can feel the gun struggling to understand the changes that were made. "Dr. Von Braun was working on his own and he wanted to keep things under wraps until the experiment was completed. It was bad science."

"Who is Dr. Von Braun?" Wilford asks, wondering if the doctor is the man who told him he'd remember nothing.

He feels the gun digging through his memories and an image of a blonde man with blue eyes fills his head. The man was a scientist at Dulce before Wilford put a hole in him.

"Werner," Wilford thinks with no small amount of disgust.

"Yes," the gun replies. "Werner Von Braun. He was the original lead scientist on the Titan project. Dr. Von Braun experimented first on himself but you were the first prototype for the new master race."

"Is there any information on what he's done to me?" Wilford wonders.

"Back when Dulce was a US Government facility a minion of Fear was captured and examined. You were the result of that experimentation," the gun says as if that should explain everything.

Wilford turns the information around in his head, but can't make sense of it. "What is a minion of fear?" he asks.

"Fear, and the rest of the elementals were beings that were considered gods among various primitive peoples," the gun explains. "In reality they were just simple, if powerful, creatures that insinuated themselves into human culture and slowly gained power. Fear became the embodiment of fear, Dreamer became the ruler of all human dreams. Think of them as power sponges. The minions of Fear are warped people she has created to do her bidding; they are almost indestructible."

"I can see why the government would want one," Wilford says with a whistle.

"Indeed," the gun says. "Dr. Von Braun was originally tasked with replicating the minions to create an army. Over time Dr. Von Braun came to realize he was creating a better form of human. Slowly, methodically, government oversight was removed and the project was attached to the Dulce site's other major project: integrating alien DNA with primates."

Wilford remembers the endless tubes filled with green liquid. Each tube held a nearly hairless white ape.

"What was the goal of that project?" Wilford asks.

"Another army," the gun replies. "Dulce was created to build new armies using advanced technologies. The site was chosen because of its remoteness and easy security. Most people in the town never heard of the work going on there and scientists were forbidden from leaving the location. When it was realized the minion DNA created better specimens than the ape and alien DNA mixture, the ape alien hybrid project was frozen. The minion DNA created leaders that could control the ape alien hybrids telepathically. A new army and command structure was developed. The scientists who worked on the project ultimately became part of the project and were disseminated across the country."

"There are more of them," Wilford muses. "It wasn't just the couple in Dulce."

"Indeed," the gun replies, "dozens of them."

"Shit," is the best response Wilford can come up with.

"You're going to need an army if you want to go after them," the gun says.

"I used to have an army," Wilford replies, remembering yet another way Steven has screwed things up.

The gun rifles through Wilford's memories and extracts an image of near skeletal man in a tight suit. "An interesting, if flawed, attempt at creating an army."

"We called them Flicker Men. They could travel between dimensions by flickering in and out of reality. The procedure usually killed them in short order, but the ability to appear and disappear like that was powerful. They were the best chance we had at dealing with things like Coco," Wilford says. "I don't know who created them or how, but they were incredibly useful. Now they're all gone."

He feels the gun churning away at the image of the Flicker Man. "Their power was derived from the God of Dreams," it says. "Interesting. I wonder how they did it."

"Dunno," Wilford says. "They just showed up and I was tasked with putting them to work. We were supposed to start hunting monsters when Steven and his little band ruined everything."

"Once the God of Dreams escaped he took back his power."

"I guess," Wilford says.

"The power they possessed, the ability to walk between worlds like that, would have crippled their minds," the gun says. "They could not have lasted long."

"Usually around six months or so," Wilford replies.

"Fascinating," the gun replies.

A beeping sound echoes around the small hotel room. Wilford shuts off the alarm on his phone and gets ready to meet the movers and shakers of Cuba, New Mexico. He doesn't want to go, doesn't want to deal with McMasters and the chief's insatiable desire to be respected. Wilford would rather continue to grill the gun. He may not be an analyst, but he knows information is power.

*****

McMasters greets Wilford at the door with a grin and a bottle of cheap beer. "Welcome to Casa de McMasters!"

Wilford accepts the beer with a nod and a pleasant, "Thank you."

The introductory tour around Casa de McMasters is a blur of hand-shaking and fake smiles. The chief's wife is busy cooking, McMasters explains, and doesn't like anyone in the kitchen while she's busy. The other couple at the dinner – the Sandovals – smile outwardly but

Wilford can sense the seething just below their fake veneers. For whatever reason, be it that he's an outsider or something more sinister, Shireen and Tomás do not like him. She's better at hiding it than he is, but neither bothers to completely obscure their disdain.

"What is that you do for the TSA, Mr … what was it?" Shireen asks him before he can even shake her hand.

"I don't work for the TSA, ma'am," Wilford responds, wishing people would get their agencies straight. "I work directly for the Department of Homeland Security."

"Those paper pushers," Tomás adds out of the blue. "All DHS is supposed to do is provide unclassified reports."

"Well, that's definitely part of the mandate, sir," Wilford says.

"Oh, are you a field agent? Like James Bond?" Shireen asks.

"Kind of, ma'am," Wilford says. "I work in a more police-like section of the organization."

"Doing what?" Tomás asks.

"Well, most of it is classified work, sir," Wilford says, not wanting to remember the things he's done.

"Oh! Do tell!" Shireen jumps in.

McMasters has been quietly watching the exchange, obviously enjoying Wilford's discomfort. "He was a hit man," the chief says.

Conversation stops when the chief drops the bomb on the little party and all eyes focus on Wilford. Wilford glares at McMasters. To call Wilford Saxton a hitman is a gross misunderstanding of his role in the machineries of government. It's true; he's killed no small amount of people, but there were always very good reasons.

"It doesn't matter," a voice says from behind them all. "Dinner is ready."

The owner of the voice is small woman who absolutely owns the room with her presence. Mrs. McMasters – Renee to her friends, Mrs. McMasters to Wilford – is a small woman, probably no more than five foot five inches tall. She's got black hair and piercing black eyes.

"Be wary, boy," the gun whispers. "You're a pilgrim in an unholy land and she is radiating power."

"Duly noted," Wilford thinks back.

Mrs. McMasters waves once and everyone dutifully follows her hand to the dinner table. Shireen shoots her a smile which is only partially returned. Tomás gets a nod of the head and the chief himself gets a wink and a knowing smile. As Wilford walks past her she shoots him a huge toothy grin and a cheery, "Welcome," but the smile doesn't reach her eyes and the grin holds a hint of menace. A half-remembered quote about pit bulls and lipstick crosses his mind, but Wilford gratefully tells her thank you and bows slightly to her.

Dinner is standard Northern New Mexican fare: *enchiladas* with fried eggs on top, *rellenos*, and *calabacitas*. Even though Wilford originally hails from New Hampshire, he's come to appreciate the local cuisine and has to admit the scary little woman can cook a mean meal.

Shireen barely waits for everyone to dig into their food before she asks, "What did he mean when he said you're a hit man?"

"Yeah," Tomás pipes in. "I knew the government did assassinations, but I didn't think you were officially called 'hit men'."

"You're an assassin?" Mrs. McMasters questions. She leans forward, her elbows on the table and stares at the stranger in her dining room.

Wilford was busy chewing when the questions started flying and has to hurry to finish. The food is excellent and the chile is crazy hot. He holds up a finger and downs some water to clear his throat.

"Please excuse me," Wilford says. "The food is excellent Mrs. McMasters and thank you for having me."

She acknowledges his thank you with a small nod of her head.

"First up," Wilford continues. "The United States government is not in the assassination business."

Tomás immediately engages. "How can you say that? It's well known that the government regularly eliminates people it doesn't agree with."

Wilford stares at him dumfounded. "Like who?" he asks.

"Pinochet, Guevara, Castro," Tomás says, counting off the dictators on his fingers.

"Pinochet died of a heart attack, Guevara was captured and executed by the Bolivians, and Castro is still alive," Wilford says.

"Pinochet's death was kind of convenient, don't you think? And it was CIA-backed Bolivian guerillas that got Guevara. As for Castro, you have to admit there have been a number of attempts on the man's life," Shireen pipes in.

"I wouldn't know about those things, ma'am. That sounds more like CIA or NSA activities. DHS is concerned with immediate threats to the United States."

"So, you admit you're a hit man?" Mrs. McMasters asks.

"No, ma'am. I've never been an assassin. I was part of a fire team. We were primarily intended to arrest terrorists before they could ..." Wilford starts.

"Kill anyone?" Mrs. McMasters finishes. "I find it odd that anyone the government disagrees with is considered a terrorist."

Gonna be a long night, Wilford thinks. "It's true there aren't any hard and fast rules about what makes a terrorist, but usually someone is only considered a terrorist if they have proven dedication to kill indiscriminately for a political or religious purpose."

"Was Timothy McVeigh a terrorist?" Shireen asks.

"Very much so. He intended to use fear to achieve his goals," Wilford responds.

"What about you, though? Don't you intend to strike fear into the hearts of your enemies?" Mrs. McMasters asks. "Wouldn't that make you a terrorist?"

Wilford decides to eat a *relleno* while he ponders the question. He thoughtfully chews the stuffed chile and notes it's an actual *poblano* chile instead of the Hatch chiles he usually finds.

"I think the goals are different, ma'am," he finally says. "Terrorists try to scare the general population to put pressure on governments. We try to scare the terrorists into leaving the general population alone."

"And execute them when they don't cooperate?" Tomás asks.

"We aim to arrest, sir," Wilford explains. "Everyone the Department of Homeland Security has arrested has stood trial."

"How many have you killed?" Mrs. McMasters asks.

Wilford closes his eyes and sees all the bodies he's left on the floor. He consoles himself by saying they were all bad people, but bad is such a nebulous term. "I don't keep count, ma'am, but it's more than I would prefer," he says.

"All bad guys, though, right?" the chief asks.

Sure, Wilford thinks. *They were all bad.* "We have a great deal of intelligence before we move on any targets."

"Would you say you think you're keeping the country safe?" Mrs. McMasters asks.

"Yes, ma'am," Wilford replies before adding a tiny little lie. "I can say I have a clean conscience."

"Good enough for me. Thank you for your service, Mr. Saxton," Mrs. McMasters says.

With that statement, the grilling ends immediately and conversation moves onto the latest movies, who is screwing who in town and what chances everyone's favorite football teams have of winning the next big game. Wilford much prefers the small talk to the relentless grilling.

After dinner, he asks if Mrs. McMasters would like some help cleaning up. She pats his face and says she's got it. She and the chief clear the dishes and soon return with small bowls of flan. The caramel pudding looks homemade and everyone gets their own portion set right in front of them.

"I hope you enjoy flan, Mr. Saxton," Mrs. McMasters says as she sits.

"I love it, ma'am," he replies.

"Well, I hope my small town recipe is up to your big city taste buds," Mrs. McMasters says, fishing for a compliment.

"Ma'am, everything you've served tonight has been among the best food I've ever tasted," Wilford says.

"Please, then," she says, gesturing to the flan.

Wilford notices all eyes are on him as he dips his spoon into the caramel custard. Having people watch him eat has always disturbed him, but he fights down the nervousness and takes a taste. As he suspected, the flan is excellent. It probably took her half the day to make this stuff. He swallows and smiles at Mrs. McMasters. "Excellent, flan, ma'am."

"Don't panic," the gun whispers, "but you've just been poisoned."

Wilford is sipping his water and nearly chokes. He recovers his composure without too much loss of face and keeps drinking. "What do you mean poisoned?" he thinks.

"Poisoned," the gun replies. "As in there was poison in that dessert. Lily of the Valley would be my guess."

Wilford has no response to that, but he's pretty sure the blood is draining from his face.

"Like I said, don't panic," the gun tells him. "It takes a lot more than poison to kill you."

He feels something strange happening inside of him, like warm fingers spreading around his stomach. His body is reacting to a threat and just like Wilford himself when he sees a threat, his body is stomping the poison down.

"To think they thought they could kill you with a poison. Amateur hour," the gun says. Wilford can hear it chuckling to itself, a cackling feeling that sets his teeth on edge. Not for the first time, Wilford wonders exactly what he's gotten himself into with the gun.

All eyes keep watching him as Wilford finishes his coughing fit. Everyone looks like they expect something to happen. It's then that it dawns on Wilford that the other couple was here to help dispose of the body – his body – after the poison took hold.

"Fuck these guys," Wilford thinks.

"That's the spirit," the gun replies.

He can feel the gun smiling in his head. "How much poison do you think she put in this stuff?" Wilford asks.

"It doesn't matter," the gun says with a sneer. "You could eat a whole plant and it wouldn't hurt you."

"This is truly excellent flan, ma'am," Wilford tells Mrs. McMasters as he eats another spoonful.

"I'm … I'm glad you like it," she replies. She has a curious look on her face and everyone else at the table is looking each other, likely wondering who actually wound up with the tainted dessert.

Wilford enjoys their discomfort and keeps eating.

The party doesn't last much longer. The planned entertainment bailed out at the last minute and left the party feeling lackluster. People came to the party hoping to watch a man die and were disappointed when he calmly excused himself and walked toward the door with a belly full of poison.

No one else touched their flan, not even the cook.

On his way out the door, Mrs. McMasters hands him a small statue of skeleton holding a badge. "A memento," she says, peering into his eyes and trying to understand what just ate dinner at her table. "Thank you very much for visiting."

Wilford examines the statue appreciatively, notices it's made of real bone, and says, "Thank you very much for having me, ma'am. Dinner was excellent and the dessert was extraordinary."

*****

Back at the hotel the heater still isn't working and Wilford still doesn't notice the cold. His mind is racing, wondering not only why someone would try to poison him but why the poison didn't work. Lily of the Valley is not a pleasant way to go. Headaches, rashes, stomach cramps, diarrhea, cardiac problems are all part of the slow and unpleasant death *Convallaria majalis* bestows on people who eat it. The fact that Mrs. McMasters chose such a toxin meant she wanted him to not only die, but hurt while he was doing it.

"I told you," the gun says, "you were fixed. You're a weapon now."

"So I'm immune to poisons?" Wilford asks.

"Poisons, toxins, bad Chinese food," the gun says. "Your body isolates the toxins and neutralizes them."

"Bad Chinese food? When did you develop a sense of humor?" Wilford asks.

"The more I'm around you the more I'll develop a sense of you," the gun says. "Over time, our personalities will merge. We will become a single unit."

"I'm not sure I like the idea of merging with you, whatever that means," Wilford says with a sick feeling in his gut.

"It's already happening," the gun says. "Have you noticed you stopped talking to me out loud?"

Wilford hadn't noticed that. He had started conversing with the gun – which is strange enough as it is – without talking out loud. His thoughts were just more efficient. That didn't mean he was merging with the gun, did it?

"Fine," Wilford thinks. "On another note, was there something wrong with that woman tonight or was it just me?"

"Which one?" the gun asks. "Both of them seemed off to me."

"There is that," Wilford thinks with a sigh. "The chief's wife; what did you make of her?"

"She's powerful. I suspect she might be the most powerful person in town."

"Great, so she's the Grand Poohbah of Shit-Town," Wilford replies.

"She would be one of the most powerful people in any town," the gun says. "She reeks of magic. Her energy signature would indicate she's a *bruja*."

"Energy signature? *Bruja*? What's a *bruja*?"

"Everyone and everything has an energy signature. All biologicals create energy and magic users have a specific signature, just like Coco has a specific energy signature," the gun explains. "Her energy feels like magic. Since she's Hispanic, I can only assume she's a bruja."

"Magic? No such thing." Wilford wonders if the gun is starting to lose it and searches the plain black frame of the weapon.

"What are you doing?" the gun asks.

"Looking for your battery compartment."

"I don't have batteries and I don't like you in that way," the gun says with a hint of disgust. "Why are you looking for a battery compartment?"

"You're talking about magic like it's a real thing. Your batteries must be low or something," Wilford thinks to the gun.

"You can accept that there are monsters and Gods walking the planet but you have trouble with magic?" the gun asks.

"I've seen monsters and I know a God. A new God, to be sure," Wilford pauses, wondering about something. "Wait, is Steven a God now?"

"Yes, he is the new God of Dreams."

"And his girlfriend?" Wilford thinks with a bit of disgust.

"An engine of sorts. She can alter reality if fed ideas," the gun replies. "The God of Dreams can generate no end of ideas and she can make them real. Together they're probably the most powerful things on the planet."

"Shit," Wilford thinks.

"Indeed."

"What if they were separated? What then?"

"She has some power on her own but big ideas must be fed to her in a certain format," the gun says. "He can create that format and she can make it happen. Without her he's tough and dangerous, but nowhere near as powerful as they are together. On her own she's still dangerous, but nowhere near the threat they are together."

An idea slowly starts to form in Wilford's head. Whether it's his experiences or the gun's influence or simply too much time spent with Steven in the past, Wilford is developing a devious mind. His idea, something that he never would have considered even a few ago, still faintly disgusts him but the idea of using bad guys to fight bad guys has a certain appeal.

"Your idea might work," the gun thinks out of the blue.

For a moment Wilford is shocked until he remembers the gun is slowly becoming a part of him. In a sense, he's becoming one of the things he hated. Experience is teaching him that his hatred may have been unfounded. Being the other, the monster, will allow him to do things he could never do as a plain human. Steven still needs to be stopped, though; he needs to be punished for his sins.

A thought pops into his head, something he'd dismissed at the time but now seems important. "Did you notice the faint red glow around that skeleton figure I found at the Baca's?" he asks.

"Yes," the gun says, "It was residual magic."

"Any idea who – what do you call it when someone puts magic on a thing?" Wilford asks.

"Enchanted it," the gun replies.

"That's it," Wilford thinks, snapping his fingers. "Any idea who enchanted the skeleton?"

"I do not know. Whoever did it hid his tracks well," the gun replies. "And it's a *Dia de los Muertos* figurine, not a run-of-the-mill skeleton. The figurines usually have significance to the owners but I'm not familiar with them being gifted to strangers."

Wilford pulls the little skeleton figure Mrs. McMasters gave him out of his jacket pocket and looks closely at it. To him, it's just a skeleton – he never did completely understand the mythology surrounding the figures - but it has meaning to someone. It's richly detailed down the painted joints on its skeletal limbs. The mouth is a toothy grin and the empty eye sockets are surprisingly emotive. He looks closely at the badge the skeleton is carrying but can't make out any details without a magnifying glass.

"What do you make of this?" he asks the gun. "Wait, do I need to put it somewhere so you can see it?"

"I see through your eyes," the gun says. "And it appears to be a skeleton police officer."

"Is there anything special about it, magic or anything like that?" Wilford asks.

"Look at it with your enchanced vision," the gun says.

Wilford focuses, wills his vision to change. He can't see anything special about the grinning skeleton, but there's a faint buzzing behind his eyes, like something is hiding just barely out of sight.

"Crap. Can you still sense Coco around here?" Wilford asks.

"The creature is still in the area but is as difficult to locate as ever. Jumpers are notoriously difficult to track," the gun says. "This one in particular was well designed."

"Designed?" Wilford asks.

"Coco and the creatures like it are not of this planet," the gun says. "They are created somewhere else and placed here for unknown reasons."

"Where are they created?" Wilford asks.

He feels the gun shrug, a strangely human gesture for a weapon. The gun doesn't know and since the knowledge is unavailable, it doesn't care.

"Can you tell if it's close?" he asks.

"It doesn't seem to be nearby. You should rest."

"What about you?" Wilford asks.

"I will set an automated scan. I don't actually require much rest, though. Soon you won't either."

Wilford sets the miniature skeleton in the middle of the other bed in the room and lies back with a sigh. "What if I like rest?" he asks.

"Then rest, but be careful dreaming," the gun says. "Remember, you and the new God of Dreams have history and when you dream you're in his domain."

"Duly noted, mom," Wilford thinks, wondering if Steven's lurking in the dream world somewhere.

The gun doesn't rise to the jibe and Wilford's heavy eyelids slowly fall closed. The last thing he remembers is a very faint tint on the *Dia de los Muertos* figure. The tint is so faint he wonders if he imagined it.

*****

At 3am alarm bells go off in Wilford's head and he awakens to the gun's insistent voice admonishing him to wake up. The room is bathed in a red glow. At first he thinks the glow is just from the alarm clock but he sees the glow is coming from the other bed.

"What's going on?" he thinks to the gun.

"Coco is near. It's time to hunt."

Excellent, Wilford thinks to himself and grabs the gun. As soon as he touches the weapon schematics quietly intrude on his vision. The room is overlaid with glowing lines that show him everything. Numbers flit by his vision: approximate range to target, his position in latitude and longitude, energy level of the gun, outside air temperature, and so on.

"Best guess puts the area of ingress in the corner near the bathroom," the gun says. A portion of the bathroom is illuminated in purple.

"Why wouldn't he use the door?"

"He didn't use the door at the Baca scene," the gun says. "Evidence there suggested he entered through a shadow in the corner of the room."

Wilford's heart is beating faster. Although he'd hate to admit it, he's terrified. His last encounter with this creature didn't go so well. This time might be different. He knows what he's getting into and has some serious firepower at his fingertips.

A strange faint crackling sound fills the air and his skin starts crawling. In the corner, next to the bathroom, a pale black and purple glow slowly grows.

"Told you," the gun says.

"Hush," Wilford replies.

The air feels intense, like a storm is about to erupt in his room. The *Dia de los Muertos* skeleton is glowing a bright, candy red.

"Be careful," the gun whispers. "He's dangerous."

"I thought I was immortal," Wilford says.

"You are. That's the problem."

"Then he can't kill me," Wilford says.

"There are worse things than being dead. Think about it, your head can come off but you won't die," the gun says.

"Duly noted."

With a slight pop, the pressure in the room ends and a dark figure erupts from the corner. Wilford only catches a glimpse of a black cloak and flashing claws. The thing has eyes so black they almost glow in the faint light of the room. In a blur of motion it attacks the other bed. A single slash of its claws and bed stuffing flies through the room.

Wilford feels a faint tug on his arm and finds himself aiming at the corner where Coco entered the room. Rather than fight it, he goes with the gun's decision and presses the firing pad.

The gun is a remarkable piece of weaponry. It's a potent mixture of Earthly technology and godly magic. Designed by a god to kill other gods and their minions; the gun is delicate enough to perform microsurgery and powerful enough to level mountains. It draws energy from the world around it and tightly interfaces with its user. Feeding on information from Wilford's heightened senses it sends a signal of its own, briefly taking control of his body in order to select a target.

Viewed through Wilford's regular eyes the bogeyman is a vaguely human-shaped thing wrapped in a black cloak. The gun clicks on his enchanced – a mixture of enchanted and enhanced – vision and Coco's shape is revealed. The bogeyman is not a complete shape-shifter; only his hands and claws can change. The rest of him is a mess of sinewy muscle under rough, gray skin. The claw that shredded the bed flows back into a hand.

Wilford pulls the trigger and after a small burping noise, the gun emits a small purple blob. The blob accelerates into the corner of the room and the light reveals a portal of sorts, an escape tunnel for Coco should things go bad. When the blob hits the portal enchanced vision shows energy flowing into the portal before the hole in reality closes with a pop.

Coco reacts immediately. Black eyes scan the room and lock onto Wilford's squatting form. Before Wilford can react the bogeyman is on him. Sickeningly squishy hands grab Wilford and raise him off the ground. A claw forms on Coco's hand and jams into Wilford's stomach.

The claw rends through organs, slicing through them effortlessly. The wound should be excruciating but all Wilford notices is a message reporting damage and ensuring that the damage is being repaired. His fist pulls back and slams into Coco's man-like head. It feels like punching old gelatin, crunchy and soft at the same time.

The bogeyman retracts its claw and retreats. Wilford follows up with a couple more punches to the thing's head before stepping behind Coco and tossing the bogeyman over his shoulder like he was taught in combat training. The creature lands on its feet and snarls but before it can jump the gun takes over and uses Wilford's arm to aim itself at Coco.

The gun barks and a hole sizzles through Coco's body. The bogeyman screams and charges Wilford. The force of the impact tosses him through the big picture window. Some automated process in his body takes over and Saxton lands in a ball and rolls immediately to his feet.

From outside the motel, Wilford can hear Coco screaming. Its portal is gone and the strange mortal just blew a hole through it. The screams are filled with rage and pain and something else. The thing is shocked that what it thought was a mortal has given the mighty bogeyman its first wound.

"Now what?" Wilford thinks.

"Now we wait for it to come out," the gun replies.

"Is that wise?"

"I'm recalibrating myself for a kill shot," the gun says. "We're going to focus on the extremities, such as they are, before tackling the beast itself."

Together gun and operator take up a defensive stance about thirty feet from the door. All manner of screaming and crashing is going on in the motel room. A lamp flies out the window, followed by a television.

"It's scared and angry", the gun tells Wilford. "It's never had its way out taken away from it."

"Can we see it through the walls?"

He hears a faint clicking sound in his head and soon the creature is outlined in red. It's pacing back and forth around the small room, looking for any opportunity to escape and recover its senses. It tries in vain to create a new portal but the shot through its torso damaged something and each new portal fails before completely materializing.

Unfortunately for Coco, there's only one way out.

It realizes its predicament and decides to act in true Coco fashion. The door to the motel explodes in splinters and the bogeyman charges straight at Wilford. It moves quickly, covering the thirty feet between it and Wilford less than a second.

Wilford expected the bogeyman would do exactly what it did. He presses the gun's trigger pad three times and watches the gun do its handiwork. The show is amazing. Using its knowledge and Wilford's muscles the gun unleashes Hell on the bogeyman of the northern New Mexico. Three blasts neatly sever most of the creature's limbs and it falls forward on its face.

Coco, using its one good claw, drags itself toward its aggressor. Wilford's cool eyes watch the thing try to finish the hunt with only one arm. Even though he's the target, Wilford can't help but feel a grudging respect for the creature.

"It's can repair itself, right?" he asks.

"Yes," the gun replies. "It was designed to be self-sufficient."

"How come it doesn't just grow more limbs?"

"I cauterized its limb generators," the gun replies.

Wilford stares at the gun. "I'm sure that means something," he says.

Coco is still trying to reach him. Wilford steps forward but stays just out of reach of the creature. At this distance, under the orange sodium lights the bogeyman of northern New Mexico is finally visible to his bare human eyes. Up close the creature is a hideous mass of indistinct leathery skin. The eyes are filled with a mixture of hatred and sadness.

"Watch out," the gun whispers.

With a mighty tug, Coco pulls itself forward and nearly stabs Wilford in the foot.

Wilford and the gun set to work immediately. A beam of energy launches from the gun and hits the back of Coco's head. Through his enchanced vision Wilford watches in stunned silence as the beam methodically destroys the creature's mind. When the brain is destroyed Coco's final limb is removed and its head is removed.

After centuries of terrorizing children and generally causing mayhem, the bogeyman is finally dead.

A few minutes later its torso and limbs are neatly stacked in a corner of the parking lot. Wilford retrieves the skeleton which is still glowing bright red, tosses Coco's destroyed head in a bag, and hops in his Suburban.

The glowing red skeleton tells him everything he needs to know. The pieces of the puzzle just fell into place.

*****

Clan McMasters is sound asleep when a black Suburban quietly pulls into the driveway. Wilford steps out and stalks toward the door, gun in one hand and what's left of Coco's head in the other.

"What are we doing?" the gun asks.

"Tidying up loose ends," Wilford tells the gun. "She sent that thing to kill me and I'd like to know why."

"What if she won't talk? Are you prepared to make her talk?"

Wilford pauses on the walkway to the McMasters house and wonders. Does he have it in him to make her talk? It wouldn't be the first time he's tortured someone to find information. There have been countless criminals, terrorists, and assorted scum who have experienced his tender mercies.

But those were all enemies of the State that trained him and paid him; the same people who convinced him to take lives for them without question. He's off the reservation now and on his own for the first time. Everything he believed in has been stripped from him. He believed in a God and recently met a real one. He believed in the country and found it would happily kowtow to anyone with power. He believed in normal and sane but he can stick a knife through his arm and not notice it; earlier in the evening he slaughtered a bogeyman. He talks to his gun.

"She'll talk," he thinks to the gun. "She'll join us."

"Join us?"

"We can't do it alone."

"Do you think this plan is wise?" the gun asks.

"I was fixed," Wilford says. "It's time I did some fixing of my own."

Wilford pulls out a lock picking kit from inside his jacket and seduces the deadbolt in seconds. The door opens silently on well-greased hinges. Inside, the house is dark and quiet. The place is spotless. There's no way anyone would guess there was a party and an attempted murder here earlier this evening.

He turns on his enchanced vision and sees the world brightly outlined. The living room leads to a hallway. Working his way down he finds a bathroom, a walk-in closet filled with food, and a sewing room. At the end of the hallway is a single closed door.

Soft snoring echoes from behind the door. Wilford pushes it open and finds the chief and the *bruja* sound asleep. Like everyone else they feel safe in their bed and in each other's company. He watches them for a while and wonders what witches dream about. Brooms? Full moons?

"It's now or never," the gun says.

Wilford hefts the bag holding Coco's head. He thinks maybe it would be best to just leave, to walk away from everything and everyone and go live on the beach somewhere. It sounds good, but he knows he'd be bored and bitter in no time. The severed head of the bogeyman makes a gentle arc and lands directly on Mrs. McMasters' stomach.

She awakes with a start and sits bolt upright in bed.

"Friend of yours?" Wilford asks her.

Mrs. McMasters should be screaming right now but she stares at Wilford with hate in her eyes. The chief slowly wakes up and pats Mrs. McMasters's back. "Go back to sleep, sweetie," he says quietly.

"Sit up, Chief," Wilford says.

The chief finally notices Wilford standing at the foot of their bed and reaches for his pistol. Wilford laughs at him. "Your wife tried to kill me and now you're trying to kill me. Does murder run in the family?"

Mrs. McMasters is examining the head he just tossed in her lap. She should be shrieking or tossing it away but turns it in her hands.

"You?" she asks, nodding toward the severed head.

"Yeah," Wilford says. "The rest of him is in the motel parking lot, but I figured you might appreciate this part.

"You survived poison and my assassin. Who are you, Mr. Saxton?" she asks.

"I don't know anymore, ma'am," Wilford replies. "But I'm tired of being pushed around."

"What are you doing in my room, Saxton?" the Chief asks.

"Hush, Francis," Mrs. McMasters says.

"Francis? I thought your name was Flint," Wilford says.

"He can't stand Francis, feels it's a girl's name. What do you want, Mr. Saxton?" Mrs. McMasters asks.

"I want to know why you tried to kill me twice."

"You were in the way. You threatened to expose me for what I was," she says.

"Did you think no one would notice?"

"When my husband captured the meth dealers everyone forgot all about Roger and that whore Rosaline."

"You wanted me dead because your husband had an affair? You sent the bogeyman after a woman for having sex with him?" Wilford asks, dumbfounded. "You are crazy."

"Wait," the Chief says. "What does he mean 'the bogeyman'?"

Rather than answer she throws two knives at Wilford. Both of them slide deep into his body; one hits his heart, the other penetrates his stomach. Wilford calmly pulls the knives out and tosses them on the bed.

Mrs. McMasters gasps when the wounds don't bleed and Wilford doesn't keel over. "What are you?" she asks.

"You're a weapon," the gun whispers.

"I'm a weapon," Wilford tells her.

"Whose weapon are you?"

"What is going on?" the Chief asks.

"Silence," Mrs. McMasters hisses. "This is beyond football and busting speeders. You're way out of your league here."

The Chief looks stunned but shuts up immediately. Wilford had kind of guessed that she ran the family and his reaction just confirmed it.

"Mrs. McMasters," Wilford says calmly. "You caught me on a good day. Last week I would have simply shot you and your husband and called it a good day. I'm trying to make myself a better person."

"Should I thank you?" she asks.

"Probably not, I'm about to drag you into something you'd be happier to avoid."

"Speak, boy."

"Boy," Wilford says with a snort. "Lady, I've fought monsters all my adult life. I just killed your precious Coco. One of my friends became a God. You're a big fish in a tiny pond. I'm going to give you a choice. Take it and you'll find there are things out there that are much bigger than you."

"If I refuse?" she asks.

"I'll kill you both, suck up whatever of your power remains, and move on."

"What makes you think you can even kill me?" she asks.

During the exchange, the gun was watching the Chief out of the corner of Wilford's eyes. Like all jocks, Chief McMasters thinks he's clever, but his movements are rough and gross, the jagged movement of someone used to crashing headfirst into things. The gun is hardly surprised when the Chief takes aim with a large revolver. It briefly takes over Wilford's arm, selects a simple melting function, and fires at the Chief's gun.

The entire ordeal, save the Chief's scream when molten steel touches his hand, takes less than a heartbeat and ends with Wilford in control, the gun aimed squarely at Renee McMasters, and Wilford ready to blow the *bruja* off the planet.

"I sent your assassin to Hell," Wilford says. "I'd be more than happy to send you to meet him."

There's steel in her eyes when she glares at Wilford, but not anger. She's more curious and wary than scared. "What's my alternative?" she asks.

"Help me take back the world," Wilford says. "Kill the monsters, slay the Gods."

"Why would I want to do that?"

Wilford notices Chief McMasters holding his burned hand. There are big crocodile tears flowing down his cheeks. "Go get some ice, Chief," Wilford tells him.

The Chief jumps out of bed, clutching his burned hand, and runs out of the bedroom. Wilford's enchanced senses hear him frantically pulling ice cube trays from the freezer. He looks back at Mrs. McMasters, calmly watching him and stroking Coco's dead head. She raises an eyebrow.

"Well, Mrs. McMasters?" Wilford asks.

"Renee," she responds.

Wilford gives her a slight nod and continues. "Renee. There are more monsters out there, preying on innocent people, hunting and killing children. I want to stop that. I wasn't lying when I said my friend was a God. I believe people should be free of those influences."

"You want to, what? Hunt monsters and Gods?"

"Hunt and kill them, yes," Wilford says.

"Why would I want to help you do that? The monsters aren't all bad and the Gods are well beyond my reach."

"But not mine."

"The current plan is working well for me, I can call them, use them. What good would it do me to change all that?" Renee asks.

"They'll turn on you eventually. There are others out there, too, hunters who will find you and kill you. I just got back from Dulce. You might have seen the explosion on the news? I was there. I blew it up. It was a factory for creating new monsters to overthrow the old," Wilford tells her. "I left behind a Valkyrie, two gods, and some sort of engine with long black hair. They're still out there."

Renee fidgets with the decapitated head in her lap, stroking the warped face of the bogeyman. "He wasn't always bad, you know. Something corrupted him. It gave me just enough of a crack to get into his programming."

"See? That's why I need you. To help me find the real bad guys and take care of them," Wilford says.

"It's true, there is evil out there, but if I join you, you'll have to trust my judgment."

"She's telling the truth," the gun whispers to him.

"I can do that," Wilford tells her. "I have a strong 'Don't mess with me and I won't mess with you ethic'."

"What about my husband?" Renee asks.

"What about him?"

"He's innocent. Dumb, but innocent. And I do truly love him. What role would he play?"

"He could come in handy. He's not as dumb as she thinks and he is not without skills," the gun says.

"We'll bring him on board; teach him if necessary," Wilford says.

Renee looks longingly into Coco's dead eyes one more time and lays his severed head on the Chief's pillow. She pulls back the covers, revealing a slight woman in a dark nightgown. Her feet swing out of the bed and she walks straight and proud toward Wilford. Even at nearly a foot and a half shorter than him, she manages to be intimidating.

"What are you doing?" the gun asks.

"Building an army," Wilford replies. A small army, but an army.

Renee holds her hand out and Wilford shakes it. "You trust my judgment," she says, "and I'll trust yours."

"Well, Renee, are you ready to hunt some monsters?"

"Yes, Wilford Saxton, I believe I am. After I tend to my husband."

"Let me give help you with that," Wilford says. "He'll need both hands for what's coming."

The Protectors

The house is mostly still and quiet.

There are the normal clicks and pops of an old house settling after an exuberant afternoon. As the house cools the wood in the frame shrinks and contracts in on itself. Groans escape from the ceiling. A clock tick-tocks, dutifully keeping time for the owners of the house so they'll know exactly when it is should the need arise.

A faint click, a hum, and then the rumble of the heated air fills the ductwork; the thermostat has decided the house is too cold and taken steps to rectify the problem. A red light flashes on a small box under the television and yet another kids' show will be recorded to its digital innards.

All in all, for a still and quiet house, quite a lot of activity is mindlessly happening. Like mechanical ants the various trinkets and automatons are going about their programmed duties of keeping the hive safe and comfortable. Left to their own devices, provided they're fed with electricity and spare parts, the components will go about their business forever.

The house is not exactly a sprawling estate, but it's not tiny either. Enter through the front door and a dining room and sitting room combo greets visitors. A large table with room enough for six people dominates the dining room, even though the family of three very rarely uses the excess chairs. To the left a set of stairs goes up to the master bedroom and a small office. The office was converted to a kid's room when the baby came along and years later it still fulfills that purpose.

Also off to the left is a hallway that leads to a bathroom and two other bedrooms. One of the bedrooms has been converted to an office and is filled to the gills with all manner of books, clothes, and spare computer parts that are most definitely going to be useful.

Pass through the dining room and the kitchen awaits, a spacious affair with good, solid equipment. The family cooks a lot and the kitchen shows it. The room is mostly neat and tidy but signs of use adorn the pots hanging on hooks. The scratches on the kitchen island are mute historical markers of some vegetable that lost its form in service of the greater good.

The back of the house is an added-on room that the family uses as a living room. Half of the large space is dominated by a rug and shelves of Lego pieces. The other half has a reclining couch and a television in an armoire. Under the armoire are the usual television accoutrements; a gaming system, a DVD player, and various and sundry boxes for streaming video or playing back video.

A pit bull is stretched out on the sofa, snoring and dreaming of steaks. She's an old dog, now more given to enjoying a good sleep on the sofa than chasing mailmen or chewing on furniture. In her old age she's decided sofas are better for deep snoozing than sharpening her teeth on. The people that live here call her Tina-Lou and she usually deigns to respond to that name even though her real dog name - a name of scent and a certain kind of whimper - would be completely incomprehensible to the humans that live here. They feed her and give her a sofa to sleep on so listening to their prattle is a small effort to her.

At 3am, a man and a woman are deep asleep in the upstairs bedroom, completely at ease with each other's presence. His name is Nelson, hers is Amanda. Nelson is dreaming of the computers that run the world and Amanda is dreaming of a beach in some tropical part of the world. Her hand is lightly resting on his back.

The child's bedroom is adorned with posters for The Avengers, racks of books, a hammock full of stuffed animals, and shelves with various toy cars. His bedspread features scenes from *Star Wars*. More Lego pieces dot the floor like plastic caltrops ready to poke and cut the unshod feet of those that would cross this moat of carpet. A stuffed diplodocus named Dippy lies alone on the empty bed. Dippy's neck is bent in the middle, but he doesn't care. Like the dog, as long as the diplodocus has a bed he's content.

A keening wail, the kind that only terrified child can make, shatters the stillness. All the clicks and pops and whirs of the house are drowned out by the shrieking sound.

Stillness shattered, the house springs to life. The old pit bull starts barking and nearly falls off the couch trying to find out what's causing the noise. Nelson and Amanda go from dead asleep to instantly alert in a heartbeat, a skill they've mastered over the eight years of the child's life. Kids have a remarkable ability to scare themselves, but they also have an amazing capacity to hurt themselves and parents learn very quickly to react. Still, it takes Nelson and Amanda a moment to come completely awake, recognize the sound isn't coming from an alarm clock, and hurry to the kid's room.

Amanda reaches the room first and panic sets in when she finds the bed empty. Unbelieving, she digs through the covers thinking her son is hiding somewhere in the bed.

The screaming continues, echoing around the open house. Nelson stops at the stairs and looks down. His son is standing in the middle of the dining room, clutching Donny, his toy deinonychus. Kevin's eyes are huge as dinner plates. The moonlight streaming in through the windows makes him look pale and ethereal.

Amanda is in full-on panic mode, muttering to herself and flinging covers all over the bedroom. "He's downstairs," Nelson yells as he sprints down the stairs. He misses a step and slides the rest of the way down.

Nelson scrambles to his feet just before Amanda makes it downstairs. She reaches Kevin first and drops to her knees in front of her screaming child. Her arms wrap around him and pull him and his dinosaur into her body. Kevin's screaming stops but his little body is still shaking. His wide eyes are riveted down the hallway when Nelson slides in front of him.

Tina-Lou slowly peeks her head around the corner from the kitchen. Her barking is loud enough to rattle the windows. "Hush!" Nelson yells.

The old dog gives him a disgruntled look but keeps woofing quietly. Her claws click on the tile as the old dog slowly crosses to the frightened boy. She can tell something's wrong but can't tell what it is; all she knows is her boy is in trouble and it's time to become dog-mom.

Amanda is rocking Kevin and cooing to him quietly. She keeps repeating, "It's okay, it's okay, it's okay."

"What's wrong, buddy?" Nelson asks.

Kevin doesn't respond. He keeps staring down the hall and shaking.

"What were you doing down here at 3am?" Amanda asks Kevin.

"Buddy, it's okay. Mom and dad are here. What's going on?" Nelson asks.

Kevin's finger points shakily down the hall.

Amanda and Nelson turn and look down the dark hallway. They freeze and peer closely, looking and listening for any movement.

The hallway stares back, empty and quiet save the faint click of the thermostat deciding to turn itself on.

"Did you see something down there?" Amanda asks.

Kevin nods but refuses to take his eyes off the hallway.

"What did you see? What's down there?" Nelson asks.

Kevin's voice is a tiny whisper. "Two men in helmets."

Amanda and Nelson look at each other, understanding settling in. "Nightmare?" she asks.

"Could be. Probably," Nelson answers. He slumps to the floor in relief.

"I saw them," Kevin says, tears welling up in his eyes. "I swear. Two men in helmets. They walked down the hall and went into the bathroom."

Kevin snuggles into Amanda and slowly stops shaking. "I saw them," he whispers.

Nelson is sitting flat on the floor. The adrenaline rush is wearing off and he's back to sleepy. Amanda is holding their son tightly, but she's relaxing, too. "Can you go check?" she asks.

Tina decides everything is fine and plops down on the floor, but she keeps her eyes on the hallway.

All Nelson really wants to do is go back to bed, but he knows Kevin won't relax until someone checks. He struggles to his feet, winks at Kevin, and turns to look down the hallway.

His bare feet have walked down the hall at night more times than Nelson can count and never found it to be anything other than a plain hallway. Maybe Kevin's fear is rubbing off on him but tonight it feels

... off. Nelson takes a deep breath and steps into the darkness, feeling around the walls for the light switch.

There's a crackle of ... energy? Something in the hallway. The air feels heavy and cold, like breathing in the old walk-in freezer at his first job. Hairs on the back of his neck rise and he feels like someone is watching him.

Nelson's hand feels along the wall searching for the light switch. He knows it's on the other side of the bathroom door. Silently, he curses the idiots that put the light switch halfway down the hall. What kind of moron puts the hallway light switch anywhere other than at the start of the hallway?

At the bathroom door, he peers into the dark room and imagines someone hiding behind the shower curtain. A sliver of moonlight runs through the center of the empty bathroom and casts eerie shadows like so many Tarot cards tossed haphazardly across a table.

Nelson moves along, feeling his way through a hallway that shouldn't be this dark. His hands finally hit the flat switch and in a flash of light the magic is broken. The hallway is just a hallway. A reprint of Georgia O'Keefe's *Blue and Green Music* hangs next to pictures of Venice taken on Nelson and Amanda's first international vacation.

Nelson looks out into the dining room and sees Amanda, Kevin, and an old dog watching him. He puffs up his chest and reaches around the corner to find the light switches in the bathroom. Light spills out, cold and harsh, and he has to blink his eyes against it. All the extra lights in the bathroom make it seem impossibly bright.

Bright, but empty.

He pulls the shower curtain apart and finds nothing. The bathroom is quietly empty. Save for the Kevin's bathtub blocks and the odd Lego boat, there's nothing out of the ordinary. A toothbrush is lying haphazardly next to the sink, the toilet paper roll is on the floor, but there's nothing strange and there are certainly no men with helmets hiding in the five foot by twelve foot room.

Amanda tenses when Nelson goes into the bathroom and out of their sight. It's a completely unconscious reaction. The same kind of thing happens when she sees a roach in the house. He walks safely out of the bathroom and switches the light off. She lets out a breath she didn't even realize she was holding.

Kevin watches his dad walk out, safe and sound, and smiles. Like all kids he's got an amazing ability to rebound from trauma. Dad made it out so it must be okay.

Nelson ruffles Kevin's hair. "No bad men in there, buddy. I think we're safe and sound."

Amanda stands and whispers a quick, "Thank you," to Nelson. She grips Kevin's hand and asks, "Is everyone ready to go back to bed?"

Kevin nods and grips Donny tighter in his arms.

"Tina?" Nelson asks.

The pit bull yawns, displaying a gaping maw of huge teeth. She grunts, gets up, shakes, and waddles back into the living room. Her couch is calling to her.

"Come here, pal," Nelson says as he picks up Kevin. He grunts at the effort of picking up the eight-year-old, but manages to straighten and carry the boy up the stairs. Kevin's arms and legs are wrapped around his dad, the dinosaur tucked between them.

"Careful, babe," Amanda says. "You don't want to throw your back out."

"Too late," Nelson grunts but continues carrying the boy up the stairs. He manages to make it up the stairs and gently deposit his son in bed. Kevin wraps his arms around his dinosaur and snuggles under the covers.

"Thanks, dad," Kevin whispers.

"Any time, buddy. Get some sleep," Nelson tells his son as he hugs him tightly.

Amanda kisses the top of Kevin's head and says, "Sleep well, sleepy-bear. I love you."

"Love you, too, mama," Kevin says sleepily.

Nelson adjusts the Lite-Brite and turns on the moon-shaped lamp. He blows Kevin a kiss, yawns, and heads back to bed with his wife. They touch briefly before rolling over. The light goes out and they each try to purge their demons. Amanda imagines criminals in her house, hiding and waiting to come after them while they sleep. Nelson's mind is filled with a gnawing sense of dread. Something was wrong with that hallway, but it wasn't anything tangible. Amanda dreams of walking down the hall. Nelson dreams of horrors stalking the house.

The house stays quiet and still for the rest of the night. The various electronic devices continue their silent vigil over the house, maintaining the warmth, recording the videos, and answering the phone calls.

*****

Nelson is up before the rest of the family and quietly creeps down the stairs so he doesn't wake the rest of the family. He pours some cold-brewed coffee, sits in his chair, and checks his email. His mind wanders while he scans Facebook postings and Twitter feeds.

It had to have been a nightmare, right? The bathroom was empty. He didn't check everything, but certainly two men in helmets wouldn't be able to hide behind the door or under the sink. Still, he can't shake the feeling of electricity that was in the air.

Maybe it was a loose wire or something, he thinks. *Maybe I was dreaming. Maybe I dreamed the whole thing.*

Sure. A dream. That's all it was.

Nelson is still pondering the event when Kevin comes plodding down the stairs, plops down on the couch and turns on the T.V. The dulcet strains of the *Mighty Morphin Power Rangers* theme song snaps him out of his reverie.

"Sleep okay, buddy?" Nelson asks.

Kevin is wrapped up in a giant blanket on the couch, mostly focused on the spandex-clad avengers flipping and kicking and generally saving the world from evil. He looks at his dad and brightly says, "I slept great! How about you?"

"Other than the 3am scream-fest, I slept like the dead."

Kevin's eyes drop. "Sorry about that," he says. "It must have been a bad dream."

"Don't worry about it. Want some cocoa?"

The boy's eyes pop back up and smile creeps across his face. "Yes, please. Oh, and dad, not too hot."

"You got it, bub." Nelson ruffles his son's hair and makes the boy some cocoa. Not too hot. Not too cold.

Kevin continues to watch the insane antics of the kids in tights and the monsters in rubber masks. Nelson drinks coffee, shakes the cobwebs from his head, and gets back to the important work of surfing the Internet.

Because, after all, it's not going to surf itself.

Amanda putters into the kitchen about an hour later and makes some espresso. While the machine makes various grunting noises, she asks, "How's everyone doing this morning?"

Kevin's head peeks out of the covers. He's got a hot cocoa mustache and bright eyes. "Slept great, how about you?"

"After I got back to sleep, I slept fine. Strange dreams, though," she says.

Nelson looks at her and arches an eyebrow.

One of the nicer things about being married is the ability to understand someone's little quirks and gestures. Nelson didn't have to say a word, raising an eyebrow was enough to tell Amanda he wanted more information.

"I can't quite remember what it was, but I remember walking through this house and something was watching me, whispering to me to walk down the hall."

"Did you go down the hall?" Nelson asks.

"Yeah, before I could get to the end I woke up," she says.

"What is it about that hall?" Nelson mumbles. He takes a gulp of his coffee – he likes cold brew because it takes less time to get ready in the morning and he can slam down the cold stuff – and continues. "You had a bad dream about it."

"I didn't say it was bad, it was just strange," Amanda says.

"Point well taken," Nelson continues. "You had a strange dream about it. Kevin had a strange dream about it."

"Mine was a bad dream, dad."

Nelson sighs. "You had a strange dream about the hall, you had a bad dream about the hall."

"What were you doing downstairs at 3am anyway, sweetie?" Amanda asks as she stirs milk into her morning espresso.

Kevin's eyebrows knit together momentarily. "I don't know. I just woke up there."

"At least you had Donny with you, right?" Nelson asks.

"Yeah, he's my friend," the boy responds.

Amanda shoots Nelson a concerned look and asks Kevin, "Has this happened before? Waking up in the dining room, I mean."

Kevin shakes his head. "Nope. Never."

"It's probably nothing," Nelson says.

"Probably not," Amanda responds. "Still, if it happens again, let me know."

"Then you'll get worried, mom?"

Amanda smiles at her precocious son. "Yes. Then I'll get worried."

"I won't do it again, I promise," Kevin replies.

"Sweetie," Amanda says, "I'm not upset. I just want to know you're all right."

"I'm fine, mom," Kevin says and turns back to the TV. He's only eight, but he's already perfected the eye roll of a teenager. Eight going on eighteen, as the saying goes. It's one of those things that's cute in a four-year-old, but starts to get wearing in an older child.

The rest of the morning is spent on Power Rangers, Avengers, and pancakes. Amanda cooks, Nelson cleans up, Kevin gives the breakfast a home. After breakfast, Kevin and his stuffed dinosaur move on to building scenes of unimaginable destruction out of Legos and plastic army men. The war was terrifying, no doubt, but the good guys won and that's all that matters.

*****

Weekend days are spent on relaxing, playing mini-golf, reading, or playing games. Very little in the way of actual work goes on during the weekends around their house.

This is a good thing.

By evening, everyone is relaxed and ready for a peaceful night. Kevin takes his shower. He and his dino buddy go to bed and read. Amanda and Nelson watch TV until they get tired, too. The dog comes inside and crashes on the couch like she has the weight of the world on her broad pit bull shoulders.

Lights go off and the house goes still and quiet again. After the excitement of the weekend – they played with Nerf guns all afternoon – even the house feels tired. The echoes of laughter, the thunk of Nerf darts hitting the wall, and the elaborate fake deaths have faded.

As Nelson and Amanda are getting ready to turn out the lights and visit Morpheus, Amanda remembers she needs to plug in her phone. She gives him a quick kiss and quietly pads down the stairs. Half-asleep, Nelson hears her rummage around her purse looking for the phone. Clicks of things being pulled out and dropped on the table echo up the stairs. He smiles, wondering how she manages to find anything in that giant bag of hers.

Nelson is almost completely asleep when he hears Amanda shriek and yell, "Get down here!"

The words echo around his tired skull before finding that part of his brain that processes a need to panic. Adrenaline hits and Nelson goes from near comatose to wide awake immediately. He'll pay for the rapid response later but for now he's out of the bed and halfway down the stairs before he even completely processes what's going on.

Kevin, younger and deeply asleep takes a bit longer to get moving. He finds his stuffed dinosaur and pads to the top of the stairs, rubbing his eyes and wondering what's going on. Tina-Lou woofs from the safety and comfort of her couch.

Nelson finds Amanda standing in the dining room shaking and pointing down the hallway.

"What's going on?" he asks in a panic.

"There," is all she says.

He looks down the hallway, but can't see anything.

"What?" he asks.

"Down there!" she yells.

"What's down there?"

"What's going on mama?" Kevin asks quietly from the top of the stairs.

"It's fine, buddy, get back in bed," Nelson says.

"I saw them," Amanda says quietly.

"Saw who?" Nelson asks.

"The men in the helmets," she says. "I saw the men in helmets."

"Mom?" Kevin asks.

"What men?" Nelson asks.

"His men," Amanda says.

"Whose men?"

"Kevin's men. The men he saw last night. I saw them," Amanda says.

"You saw them?" Kevin asks. He seems to be shrinking. Over the day he had managed to convince himself that it was all just a dream. He shakes his head back and forth and clutches the stuffed deinonychus to his chest.

"What did you see?" Nelson asks.

"I told you, I saw them," Amanda snaps back. "I saw them!"

"Okay, slow down. Sit down and tell me what you saw."

"Did they have helmets?" Kevin asks.

"Yes, sweetie. I saw them and they had helmets."

"Are you sure?" Nelson asks.

"Yes I'm fucking sure," she snaps back.

He's taken aback by her vehemence. Amanda usually only curses when she's drunk or stressed and she hasn't had a drink. "Down the hall?"

Amanda puts her hands on her temples and wonders exactly when her husband decided to stop thinking. How much simpler can she make it? She saw two men in the hallway. Deciding Nelson is just daft, she slows down and tries, as calmly as possible, to explain what happened. "I saw two men wearing helmets in the hallway. They went into the bathroom."

Nelson sighs and wonders if there's something in the water. It's obvious to him that there's no one in the house. Their dog is old, but she's still a dog and would go absolutely ballistic if a strange person was in the house. Sure, she likes to act like she doesn't hear him, but that dog can hear someone whisper "biscuit" from the back of the house. So far she's only gotten her hackles up after Kevin or Amanda yelled.

He stalks into the hallway, tired and frustrated. There's the same electric feel to the air and the temperature drops as soon as he gets close to the bathroom door but he doesn't care this time. His hand slaps the hallway light. A quick glance down the hallway reveals nothing more than some pictures and a mirror at the end just before he has to go right to the guest bedroom or left into his office.

The light switch in the bathroom gets the same smack. The light is bright, the air is cold, and the bathroom is empty. Just as he expected. He takes his time checking the bathroom and finds no one hiding behind the door or in the shower or under the cabinets. The toilet paper is actually on the holder this time, but otherwise the bathroom is exactly the same as it always is.

Nelson stalks back into the dining room and issues a brusque "Nothing there."

Then he sees his wife and realizes she is well and truly scared. Terrified even. Suddenly he feels sorry for smacking the light switches. He maneuverers Amanda to a chair and kneels in front of her. "Tell me what you saw," he says quietly.

"Two men wearing helmets in the hallway," is all she can come up with. Her skin is pale, but the color is starting to come back.

"What did the helmets look like?" Nelson asks her.

"Was there anyone in the bathroom?" Kevin asks.

"It was empty, buddy. Come down here if you want to talk."

"Is it safe?"

"It's fine," Nelson says, eyes never leaving his wife's blue orbs.

"I'm staying up here," Kevin says.

"Okay, buddy. We'll be right there," Nelson says over his shoulder. "Now, sweetie, tell me what they looked like."

"They had helmets."

"Describe the helmets."

"They're helmets. What do I know about helmets?"

"Were they army helmets? Viking helmets? Bicycle helmets?"

She glares at him for a moment, thinking he's mocking her. His face doesn't look like that, though. He's serious. "Pointy," she says. "They were metal, almost like old-time knight helmets but they didn't cover their faces."

"What else were they wearing?"

"I don't know. I was focused on their helmets. They were shiny."

"I'm going to bed," Kevin says.

"We'll be right there," Nelson tells him. "Were they carrying anything? What did their faces look like? How were they walking? Did they have more armor on?"

"I couldn't really tell. It was dark. I just saw their shiny helmets," she says. "Please believe me."

Nelson stares into her eyes and watches them soften. "I believe you," he says quietly. "But there's no one in the bathroom now."

"They were there," she says.

"Okay, but all I'm saying is there's no one in there now."

"THEY WERE THERE!" she yells.

Nelson grabs her hands and holds them tightly to his chest. His eyes implore hers and he says, "I believe you."

"They were there," she repeats quietly. "I saw them."

"What do you want to do?" he asks.

Amanda shakes her head like she's trying to dispel cobwebs. "I don't know."

"We should sleep on it, sweetie," he tells her.

"With those things in the house? How can I sleep?"

"I'll check the whole house, I promise."

"Promise?"

"I promise. I'll search every square inch of this house."

"I saw them, you know," Amanda says again. "I wasn't imagining it."

"I believe you."

Amanda stands up and smooths out her pajamas. Her eyes flick back and forth between the upstairs where her son is watching them with curiosity in his eyes and the hallway filled to the brim with darkness.

She finally decides to go upstairs. Nelson stands, working the kinks out of his joints. A few pops and clicks remind him he's not the twenty year-old stud he never actually was. He watches Amanda walk up the stairs, watches her jump at the shadows in the corners and the breeze from the heater. He knows there's no one in the house; the dog would let him know if a strange person was among them.

Still, there's that tingling at the base of his skull and his skin feels like it's slightly too tight on his body. Even though the … well, incidents, he guesses … have all taken place in the hallway, he starts his search in the living room. All's quiet, save a snoring pit bull sprawled out on the sofa. Lights flash every now and then as another TV show is recorded. The automated processes are working exactly like they should, all it takes is a person to appreciate their efforts.

Likewise the kitchen and the dining room, silence reigns supreme. That only leaves the hallway. Nelson stands in front of the dark space and tries to convince himself there's nothing to worry about.

His imagination creates all manner of monsters in the hall; aliens, giant spiders, ghosts of every shape and color. The space is silent but Nelson would swear he can see things moving down there. The chill is still there and the air still has a faint tang of electricity. He's reminded of all the times when he was a kid and would put a nine-volt battery on his tongue; the tickling energy and the taste of ozone on his tongue.

"Dad?" Kevin calls from above.

Nelson breathes a sigh of relief at the temporary respite and steps back slightly. His son is leaning over the railing watching him. "Did you find anything?" Kevin asks.

"No, buddy. There's nothing here," Nelson says quietly.

"You haven't seen the men?"

"Not yet."

"Have you looked in the hall?"

"I'm about to," Nelson says.

"They're always in the hall, Dad."

Nelson's shoulders tense at his son's words, but he knows he can't show any fear. It's a father thing; you never let your kids know you're scared. "I'll keep an eye out," he says and shoots his son a grin that feels forced.

Kevin looks down at Nelson and an unseen, unheard message pings between them: *Be careful, dad. I will, son.*

"Be right back, bud," Nelson says.

Nelson takes a deep breath and steps forward into the hall. The darkness is immediate and oppressive. He could have sworn he left the damned light on but the narrow hall is pitch black. His heart is pounding like a drummer in a death metal band and a bead of sweat is slowly running down the side of his head.

Stop it, he screams to himself. *There's nothing there.*

His hands fumble for the switch. *Where is it? It should be right here.*

The thermostat issues a click that sounds world deafening. There's a distant roar of the furnace starting up. His skin is crawling and panic is running its greasy fingers through his hair.

Where IS THE SWITCH?

He's imagining the walls crawling with spiders. The hot air from the heater feels like things moving in the darkness, brushing against his skin.

His fingers find the raised switch plate and scramble to slap it. The hallway light is small, two weak bulbs that barely illuminate the hall and do little to chase away the shadows, but it's better than nothing. Eyes used to darkness seek around and find nothing. The bathroom is likewise empty.

Nelson pushes further down the hall. It's only a few more steps but it feels like an eternity before he's standing at the end. On the left is his office, a mixture of humming fans, blue and red flashing lights, and the gentle tick, tick, tick of a Swatch he bought in Tokyo years ago. The office is a mess, but there's no one hiding in it, not that an invader could find a place to hide among the piles of things he's intended to throw out for months and the ever-growing collection of Lego minifigs.

The other side of the hall holds the guest bedroom and bathroom. Both are places he uses regularly without a second thought but there's a sense of foreboding in the air tonight, like the very aether has sucked the energy out of the room. The room, of course, is empty. Save for the drip of a faucet he's been planning on fixing for a few months, the bathroom is motionless, too.

He chuckles to himself, slightly embarrassed at his fear. Of course there was nothing down there, it was always imagination. Kevin had a nightmare and freaked out Amanda; that's all it ever was. Nelson squares his shoulders, shuts off the lights and heads upstairs. That little part of him, though, the remnants of the reptile brain that everyone shares is shrieking at him to run and not look back. He can't put his finger on it, but something feels wrong.

As he hits the stairs he misses the light that briefly flares in his office and the two men that silently stalk down the hallway into the bathroom.

*****

Kevin is waiting in bed feeling pensive when Nelson walks up the stairs. At the sight of his dad he exhales the breath he was holding. His stuffed deinonychus is wrapped in his arms, its beady black eyes watching everything. The ancient creature is Kevin's safety blanket. Some kids carry around a teddy bear, or a blanket, or a doll. Kevin carries what was probably the smartest predator of the Cretaceous era. The real animals were strong and lethal, and packs of them hunted anything they could find. The real animals were eleven feet of feathers, teeth, and huge claws. The stuffed version of the dinosaur is soft and cuddly. The real thing was a holy terror.

Kevin hugs his dad tight and yawns. If his dad says everything is fine, then everything is fine. Heavy eyelids droop and very soon Kevin and his dinosaur are involved in yet another adventure. Another dream and another bad guy falls under the combination Kevin's clever mind and Donny's sharp teeth.

Amanda is curled on her side. The shaking has stopped, but the shock hasn't subsided. She saw what she saw and she knows it. One look in Nelson's eyes and she feels both relief and worry. The relief stems from the fact that he didn't find anything; the worry is because he didn't find anything.

"Did you find anything?" she asks even though she already knows the answer.

"Nothing," he says. "There's no one down there, but…"

"But what?"

"I don't want to talk about it."

"You need to," she says.

"I … I've been down that hall more times than I can remember and something didn't … It didn't feel right," Nelson says.

"What was wrong?"

"It had to have been my imagination, but I could swear the air felt, well, wrong. Colder, like something had been sucked out of it. Energy or something."

Her hand strokes his back, but she doesn't say anything. She knows him well enough to know he'll work it through on his own time.

"I've been down that hallway a thousand times and it never felt like that," he finally says.

"Whatever it was, I saw it; I swear to you, I saw it," she replies.

"I believe you."

She lies back on the pillow and stares at the ceiling, looking for patterns in the spackled dots. A trick she learned when she was a little girl and her parents were arguing was to lose herself in the chaos of popcorned spackle. The trick evolved into her own form of meditation and soon she realized that loosening her mind helped her tease free answers to her questions.

The random patterns of dots slowly slides out of focus and are replaced by a deeper focus. In Amanda's mind patterns start to emerge from the chaos. It's almost like looking at one of those 3-D Magic Eye posters except the image that resolves itself is all in her head. The picture in her mind is a pastiche of dreams, nightmares, and the men in helmets.

She sees hidden links, things most people wouldn't see and interprets them in her own way. The things in the hall are dangerous, of that Amanda is absolutely certain. Still, there's a nagging doubt in the back of her head, a thread that won't quite unravel. *What if I'm wrong?*

Amanda focuses on the danger and makes her decision.

"We need to get rid of them. They're dangerous," she finally says.

"How do you know?" Nelson asks.

"I … I don't know. I just know they are and we need to get rid of them."

"They don't seem to be hurting anyone. They just show up and vanish. Maybe if we leave them alone they'll leave us alone." Nelson says, wondering if he's just placating her or if he's being serious. It's probably a little bit of both.

"Would you leave a black widow alone?"

"In the house?" Nelson says. "Probably not."

"Why?"

"One wrong move and someone gets bit," Nelson says.

"Those things down there are the same thing. One wrong move and those things might bite. Do you want it to be me? Do you want Kevin to get bit?" Amanda snaps.

"No," Nelson says. "But I do know the black widows keep the roach population down."

"Their bite can still kill," Amanda insists.

"We can have a couple black widows or a million roaches, is all I'm saying."

Amanda rolls onto her shoulder, props herself up on an elbow and stares at her husband. She trusts his judgment, but in this case she knows she's right. "We need to get rid of them."

Her eyes are that hard tanzanite she gets when she's deadly serious and Nelson is smart enough to not push the issue. It's probably a moot point, anyway. How can you get rid of a ghost? This isn't Hollywood, he can't just dial 555-2368 and get help.

Screw it, he thinks. *There's a solution to every problem.* He just needs to find this one.

For a couple that decided not that long ago to not sleep, Amanda and Nelson are out within twenty minutes.

*****

The next day is spent on research. The Internet knows a great many things, but it's light on how to capture a ghost. Kevin, who got to watch TV all day while his parents were otherwise occupied, later commented that they should spend more time on the Internet. He loves watching them work together. They're like a couple of cogs that mesh together and work seamlessly. Someday he hopes he'll find a wife like that.

A lot of research and some shopping and soon the day is at an end. Dinner is a pensive occasion. Amanda is jumpy and Nelson is tired. Kevin, like all kids his age, notices his parents are acting odd but mostly blows it off. Adults are kind of a mystery to him; not at all like kids. In fact, they're kind of boring. Who wants to sit around and talk when you could be out back slaying dragons and winning wars?

"Kevin, why is your dinosaur at the table?" Amanda asks.

"He's hungry," Kevin says as he shovels some macaroni and cheese into his mouth.

"Dinosaurs don't eat mac and cheese, bub," Nelson says distantly.

"Donny does," Kevin replies. "He loves mac and cheese. Actually, all dinosaurs loved mac and cheese. That's why they were so big."

"I don't think there was mac and cheese in the Cretaceous, sweetie," Amanda tells him.

"By the late Cretaceous there was," Kevin tells her. "Mac and cheese has been around for a long time but when the comet hit most of the mac and cheese was destroyed. That's why the dinosaurs died off."

Amanda and Nelson glance at each other and roll their eyes. They're both tired and strung out and the idea of macaroni and cheese sauce in the Cretaceous is just too much to handle. Amanda covers her mouth and suppresses a giggle while Nelson laughs out loud.

Kevin's eyes are sparkling. He's a clever kid and he knew all he had to do was make them laugh and everything would be fine. He beams when Nelson puts a hand on his shoulder and Amanda clutches his hand.

"Donny can stay at the table, pal," Nelson says.

"Just for tonight," Amanda adds.

The tension broken, everyone smiles and enjoys dinner. It may not be spectacular food, but it's a dinner with family and that makes everything taste amazing. They talk and laugh and listen to more of Kevin's stories about dinosaurs and fighting bad guys. Amanda tells a story about work, Nelson regales the small crowd with a tale of how he broke his toe tripping over a basset hound.

After dinner, Nelson is cleaning up the dishes when he hears Kevin whimper.

The whimper is followed by Amanda's scream. Nelson bolts from the kitchen just in time to see Amanda disappear into the bathroom. He follows her in and finds her frantically tearing the small room apart.

"I saw them!" she yells. "I saw them!"

"Who?" Nelson asks.

"The men in the helmets. I saw them come down the hall and come in here."

She's tearing open the blue cabinet doors and peering inside. She finds nothing and slams the doors shut. Amanda stops and stands straight in the middle of the room, one hand on her hip the other pushing through her hair.

"They came down the hall and then they came in here. I was right behind them. Where'd they go?" she says rapidly as she spins around. "There's nowhere to go, right? I know I saw them come in here and I was right behind them. And now, they're what, gone? Disappeared? Poof! Like magic."

Without warning Amanda spins, yells "Aha!" and rips open the shower curtain. The empty shower stall gazes back at them. Nelson can almost hear the disappointment settle in her body.

"You saw them?" Nelson asks.

She turns on him, eyes full of fire and fury. "Yes! I saw them."

"You're sure they came in here," he asks.

"Where else would they go?" Amanda is pacing around the little bathroom. Two steps forward, turn, two steps, turn. It's hypnotic and unnerving, like a lava lamp gone horribly awry.

"Okay, so, let me get this straight," Nelson says. "You saw them come in here and chased after them."

She looks at him with her "I can't believe you're so daft look" and says, "Yes."

"You saw two men walk down the hallway and come into this bathroom and you followed them?"

"Yes. God! What have I been saying here?" Amanda is frustrated beyond words right now. She paces quicker and more forcefully, like if she just paces hard enough the world will fall into place and everything will be fine again.

"And what were you planning on doing when you caught them?" Nelson asks.

She stops dead in her tracks as the realization of what she did hits her. *What was I planning on doing? Stopping two grown men in helmets that have been quietly stalking down my hall?*

"What are we going to do?" she asks quietly.

Nelson wraps his arms around his wife and feels her sag into him. "We're going to do exactly what we said we were going to do. We're going to capture some ghosts."

"Is that what they are?" she asks.

"I don't know, but we've got two guys who walk into this room and disappear. We've got cold spots after they move through. Sniff and you can smell a faint bit of electricity in the air. All signs point to ghosts."

Amanda nods and sucks in a deep breath. Her eyes are still wild but at least they're not actively pirouetting around. "I hope what we found will work," she says and sighs.

"Hey," Nelson says with what hopes doesn't sound too much like false bravado. "When has the Internet ever been wrong?"

*****

The question that preoccupied them all day wasn't the more obvious "Is there such a thing as ghosts" that so many people always ask. They knew, or at least Kevin and Amanda knew, without a doubt that there were ghosts. Nelson had his suspicions but lacked the absolute knowledge the rest of his family had.

They asked a much more complicated question: how do we catch a ghost and dispose of it?

The Internet is an amazing thing, a vast warehouse of information both accurate and hell-and-gone from reality. Their search took a goodly portion of the afternoon before they started to see a trend emerging and decided to follow it. Before they found anything even remotely logical they had to wade through an ocean of nonsense: crystals, mediums, psychics, exorcisms, and all manner of strangeness. At one site they found a group that called themselves Sex Nuns. The Sex Nuns promised they could solve any paranormal problem. The trick was they needed to have sex in the problem area. With the people that lived there.

Amanda fixed a cold stare on Nelson before he could even comment on the Sex Nuns and he wisely closed their website without bookmarking it.

In the end, after digging through the strange and wonderful world of the World Wide Web, they found their solution. It was … interesting and not exactly what Nelson and Amanda expected. In lieu of the expected plasma balls, Van De Graaff generators, or positron colliders they found a possible recipe for success in the form of a jar and a candle.

The Internet was adamant the solution would work. Nelson had his doubts, but decided to go along with the plan because, well, why not? It's not like he had any solutions to offer and doing something was better than doing nothing.

Now Nelson is sitting on a green plastic chair in the bathtub of the guest room and wondering how long he is going to have to stay. He's got his phone in his hand and can't stop going back and forth between checking Facebook and checking his email. For what seems the fiftieth time since he sat down in this chair he makes sure the phone is on vibrate.

About four feet from Nelson is a jar with a candle burning in it. The jar's top is sitting on the counter right next to the jar.

The theory is this: ghosts require energy to manifest. That's why there are unexplained cold spots when ghosts are nearby; the ghosts are sucking all the energy out of the area just to keep themselves going. Therefore, it follows, to catch a ghost bait a trap with energy. The easiest form of energy to get hold of is a burning candle. Keep all the other lights out so the bait is that much more obvious. When the ghost, or ghosts, fall for the trap they'll enter the jar to be nearer to the energy source. Once they're in the jar slap the top on.

Voilà! Trapped ghosts under glass.

The Internet was less informative about what to do once the ghosts have been trapped, but everyone was adamant that releasing them should be handled very carefully. Even the mighty Internet respects the power of the paranormal. That's the dangerous part, the world said unanimously. When the spirit is released it's going to be pissed.

Kevin has no real idea what's going on. Grown-ups always seemed strange to him, but sitting in the dark house and waiting for ghosts at least seemed exciting. After an eternity of waiting, though, the excitement has dropped off and he just wants to go to bed and read about something other than sitting quietly in the dining room.

"Mom," he whispers.

She shushes him. The Internet was very explicit that silence must be maintained.

"Mom," he whispers again, ignoring her shushing.

Amanda, in turn, ignores him and keeps her eyes focused on the hallway. It's not parental neglect or anything like that; she's just figured out that she sometimes needs to focus.

"Mom."

Amanda sighs. She understands her son well enough to know he won't give up. "What, sweetie?" she whispers.

"What are we doing?" he asks.

"Shh," she whispers. "We need to be quiet."

"Why?"

"Because we need to stay hidden."

They're seated at the table. In the dark. In plain sight of anyone who cares to look. Kevin shakes his head and clutches Donny.

"Okay," he whispers. "What are we doing?"

Amanda keeps her eyes peeled on the hallway. Her phone is in her hand, ready to text her husband as soon she sees any sign that they're coming down the hallway. "We're going to catch the ghosts," she says quietly.

"Why?" Kevin asks.

"Because we need to."

The standard response they always give him when they're not sure why they're really doing things. Kevin's used to it even if he thinks it's kind of a stupid thing to do. He puts Donny on the table and rests his chin in his hands. Without realizing it, his legs start kicking back and forth. His foot hits the chair leg on every back swing.

The slow tick, tick, tick of Kevin's feet on the chair legs is an annoying metronome. Amanda, already stressed out, breaks her incessant vigil on the hallway and turns toward her son. "Stop it!" she hisses.

Kevin stops his legs but they restart of their own accord. The first time his foot hits the chair legs he freezes again.

"Mom," he whispers again.

"What, baby?" Amanda asks.

"Why do we need to stop the ghosts?"

Amanda has no response to this. They're ghosts, she thinks, isn't that good enough? But she knows it's not enough of rationalization. Her brain racks, chewing on the problem of how to appease her precocious offspring.

"They're dangerous," she finally says.

"How do we know that?" Kevin asks.

Again, she's stumped. She doesn't have a good answer for him so she settles for making something up.

"They're not supposed to be here. This is our house, not theirs," she says.

"They haven't done anything to us. Maybe they're here to help."

"They're not here to help. They're not supposed to be here at all," Amanda says.

"How do you know?" Kevin asks.

"Because…" she pauses as she sees a flicker of movement in the hallway. The flicker turns to a pair of helmets with – men? – underneath them. Her mind rebels at the mere thought of what she's seeing. Fingers fumble with her phone and send the message she'd set up: *They're coming*.

*****

Nelson's phone buzzes and he knows it's on. Boredom turns to excitement which morphs to nervousness. Suddenly, in the heat of the moment, he wonders just what he's gotten himself into. It's bad enough that he spent the last hour sitting on a too-small chair in a bathtub; now there are ghosts, actual factual ghosts, coming down the hall.

His mind turns to mush and it takes him a short eternity to send the message back, "OK." As he hits send he sees them come around the corner and his brain does back-flips. They're real. Dear God, they're real and they're coming and…

When the first one turns into the bathroom Nelson's whole body tenses; something indistinct wearing a helmet and some kind of short sword has just silently glided into the bathroom. Fight or flight instinct kicks in and he finds himself stuck between something he can't fight and the door he can't get to.

Immediately beyond the first one the second follows. They're identical in every way as near as Nelson can tell. Nelson stares in horrid fascination, peering at them, trying to remember what they look like. Each time he glances from the ghostly faces to anything else their visage vanishes from his mind and he's left with nothing more than an image of a helmet.

The thing stares at the lit candle as it glides past, slowing perceptibly as the dancing flame captures its attention. A second ghost silently stops just behind the first one. As Nelson leans to the side he catches a glimpse of the second one staring at the candle, too.

Transfixed, the things float in place. Their faces are locked on the candle. Nelson feels a slow buildup of energy in the room as the ghosts suck energy from the candle. Slowly, they become more distinct even as the air in the room gets colder.

Nelson shivers unconsciously and barely notices the mist from his breath. He's amazed and horrified. When the first ghost dives into the candle he nearly jumps out of his skin. The second ghost glances his way before diving into the candle itself.

His heart is racing and he slowly realizes he's shivering. *Oh my God*, he thinks to himself, *it worked. It actually worked.* Nelson pulls himself to his feet and stumbles out of the bathtub. His legs, numb from the cold and the hard plastic seat, give out and he falls face-first onto the bathroom tile. The fall is enough to kick start his mind and he scrambles to his feet, desperate to put the top on the glass jar before the ghosts decide to leave.

The candle flame is rapidly shrinking. There's no doubt in his mind that as soon as that flame goes out the ghosts will get away. He grabs the edge of the counter and pulls himself upright. In the gathering darkness the glass top is harder to find than he expected. Panic is growing and he can feel his heart beating faster.

Advice from the Internet keeps coming back to him: be very careful when releasing captured ghosts as they tend to be irate.

His hand finds the tops but it skitters in the sink with a loud clink. Nelson glances at the candle and finds it almost gone. Curses escape his lips and he hears Kevin's voice asking if he's okay.

"Fine," Nelson spits.

"Can I help, dad?" Kevin asks. The boy is standing just outside the doorway to the bathroom holding his dinosaur and looking nervous.

Nelson finally finds the glass top and slaps it in the place as the candle finally dies off. He is silently amazed he didn't break it.

"Got 'em, buddy," Nelson says.

"Really?" Kevin asks.

"Really," Nelson says as he leans against the wall and sinks to the ground.

Kevin steps slowly forward and looks at the jar. He can see swirling colors in there. Fascination drags him forward until his face is right next to the glass.

"Are those … them?" he whispers.

Nelson runs a hand through his hair and stares at the jar. He's still amazed it worked. "I think so," he tells his son.

Amanda appears at the doorway and pulls Kevin away from the jar. "Stay back, sweetie."

Nelson and Amanda look at each other and smiles slowly cross their faces. "Good job, babe," she whispers.

"Thanks," Nelson says and gets to his knees to look at the jar. "I can't believe they're actually in there."

"What do we do with them?" Kevin asks.

"I don't know," Nelson says quietly. "This is kind of a first for me."

"We could keep them," Kevin says brightly. "We could put the jar next to the TV."

"I don't think we're going to keep a jar full of ghosts next to the TV, sweetie," Amanda says.

"Why not?" Kevin asks.

"Because they're dangerous," she replies.

"How do you know?"

Mother and son go back and forth while Nelson gets lost in the swirling colors. He tunes out Amanda and Kevin and focuses on the ghosts. Distantly he hears their voices. "Let us out. Let us out before it's too late."

"Too late for what?" Nelson asks quietly.

"He'll be here soon."

"Who? Who will be here soon?" Nelson asks.

"Who are you talking to dad?" Kevin asks.

"The ghosts," Nelson says. "I can hear them."

"What are they saying?" the boy asks.

"They want out," Nelson says.

"Absolutely not," Amanda says quickly and a little too loud. "They're staying in there and we're taking the jar somewhere else."

"I'm not sure that's a good idea," Nelson says.

"It doesn't matter, it's not staying in this house," Amanda says.

"Amanda, we need to think this through. We've got two ghosts in a jar. Now is not the time to jump to conclusions."

"I'm not jumping," Amanda says. "I want that and them out of here."

"Shouldn't we take it someone who could study it?" Kevin asks.

"Like who?" Nelson asks.

"No one!" Amanda says.

"What about the University?" Kevin asks.

"You want to drive across town with two ghosts in glass jar?" Amanda asks, amazed.

"We've got to do something with it," Nelson says. "We can't just tape it up and throw it in the trash. I say we take it the University and see what they say."

"Do they have ghost scientists there?" Kevin asks.

Nelson shrugs and says, "I don't know. Worth a shot."

"We are not taking those things to the university," Amanda yells. "I'm getting them out of this house."

"Wait," Nelson says, but it's too late.

Amanda pushes past Kevin and stands in front of the jar. She hesitates, but reaches down and grabs it with both hands. Nelson scrambles to his feet but his legs are all pins and needles and he's too slow and too late to stop Amanda.

"Wait!" Nelson shouts. He hears her feet rushing across the dining room floor.

Kevin takes off after his mom, shouting at her to stop.

Nelson gets to his feet and manages one shout before he hears the door open. The screen slams open and he hears the distant sound of breaking glass.

"Why couldn't you wait?" Nelson asks as he rushes out the door.

"They're dangerous!" he hears her yell but he's not paying attention to her anymore. His eyes are focused on Kevin standing in the middle of the yard staring at the two ghosts. Whatever magic made their features indistinct and immediately forgettable is gone.

Their faces are lined with age and sadness covers their eyes. One of them is talking to Kevin who turns to face his dad. Tears are streaming down the boy's face and there's panic in his eyes.

"What's going on?" Nelson asks as he skids to a stop in front of the creatures.

"We were here to protect you," one says.

The ghosts are fading, dissolving into whatever they're made of. Their voices become broken and indistinct.

"Now … free … come," the other says.

"What?" Nelson asks desperately. "Coming? What's coming?"

"We should have left them alone," Kevin says. "They weren't hurting anything. They were here to help."

"The boy … no … safe," one of the ghosts says.

"Boy … danger," the other says.

"See, dad!" Kevin yells. "We're in trouble."

Kevin is shaking uncontrollably. His arms are clutching the ubiquitous stuffed dinosaur and crying.

"What is going on?" Nelson yells.

"We broke the circle, dad," Kevin says.

"Beast … coming," the first ghost says quietly.

"… wife … alone with … Beast," the other adds.

The blood drains from Nelson's face when he sees the sad looks on their faces. Kevin's abject horror is palpable and the ghosts' faces are drawn tight with worry. Nelson's mind is reeling. An hour ago he didn't really believe in ghosts and now two of them are standing in front of his telling him he screwed up royally. His mind is snake pit of confusion, questions and worries and stark raving terror circle his tired brain. Whatever questions he has though, will have to wait.

He turns and sees the metal security door slowly closing on its own.

"… one chance …," the ghost on the left says.

"… must … inside," the other continues.

"Dad," Kevin pleads.

"Hope Chan … can … here," the ghost on the left says.

The one on the right nods and looks straight at Kevin. "Message sent," it says, the strain of remaining present obvious on its face, "wait … Chan."

Nelson sprints for the door, hopping over the hand rail. He catches it just before it shuts completely. The door feels like it's made of heavy stone and it takes all his strength to wrench it open. Kevin reaches him and puts a hand on his arm.

"Dad?"

"I've got to hurry buddy," Nelson says quickly. "Stay out here. I'll be back."

He looks back at the ghosts watching him sadly and feels their desperation. Kneeling down he grabs his son in his arms and holds him tight. "I love you, bud," he says.

"I love you, too, dad," Kevin whispers. His small arms are tight around Nelson's neck and it takes some effort to pull them away. Nelson takes one look at his son, throws him a cocky smile that he doesn't really feel in his heart, and disappears into the house.

*****

The door bangs softly in the breeze, no longer desperate to shut itself. Kevin stands outside the house that's all he's ever known and cries silently. His hands are shaking as he clutches Donny. The ghosts silently disappeared about fifteen minutes ago, fading slowly to a pair of floating helmets and swords before those, too, vanished with a quiet pop.

"Dad," he calls out quietly.

There's no answer.

He slowly pushes the door open and stands in doorway panting. "Mom?"

There's a slight rustling in living room, Tina-Lou stirring in her pit bull sleep. Kevin takes a deep breath and steps into the house.

All is quiet, dark, and still in the house. He has visions of seeing his mom and dad face down in a huge pool of blood. Monsters, vampires and unspeakable things, fill his head and he jumps at every shadow. Suddenly those things that are fun at other times, familiar things to see take on horrifying proportions. The red balloon he was punching and kicking earlier becomes a faceless head that stares at him with an eyeless gaze.

"Mommy?" he cries out.

The thermostat, fooled by the open door, decides the house is too cold and kicks on the heat. The sound of the furnace starting up sounds like the growl of a Bugbear or some other monster from his *Dungeons & Dragons* books.

"Dad," he says with a sob.

He peers down the dark hallway but can't make himself go down it. He hears a loud thump in the darkness and jumps. Kevin is transfixed in terror. The clicking thunk of boots starts moving down there. A loud noise from the living room, a mixture of growl and snort breaks his fear and Kevin runs toward it. Mom and dad might be missing but the aging pit bull, growling quietly on the sofa, is a link to safety and he sprints toward her.

Kevin jumps on the couch and buries his face in Tina-Lou's short fur. The dog recognizes his scent and scoots her face toward his. A huge tongue lazily licks his face before settling back into a low growl. Mom and dad might be gone but his dog was still here.

"Tina Lou," Kevin cries softly.

The thunk of boots move closer and Kevin sinks down into the couch to hide from whatever monster is hunting him. The sound stops in the kitchen and he holds his breath desperately, quietly praying away whatever is out there.

He hears the footsteps moving away when Tina Lou lets out a huge woof that nearly rattles the windows. The footsteps in the kitchen stop and make their way back toward the living room.

Kevin is sobbing quietly now as terror takes over. The old dog sits up and sniffs at the air. A low growl escapes her lips and she bares huge teeth. Tina Lou may be old, but she's still a pit bull and her jaws can crush cue balls. Kevin hides behind her as he hears the footsteps move from the tile of the kitchen to the wood of the living room.

The old dog barks. The sound is incredibly loud, the kind of sound that would strike fear into any criminals that would dare enter the house. Her graying muzzle is pulled back in a snarl.

"It's all right, old girl," a voice says.

Kevin jumps out of his skin when he hears it. It's not his mom and it's not his dad and that means someone strange is in the house. The voice is a growl unto itself, not as feral as the dog's, but scary nonetheless.

"Stay back or she'll eat you," Kevin says in a quavering voice.

"She's not going to eat me, are you old girl?" the voice asks.

The dog's tail slowly starts thumping back and forth, wagging cautiously. Kevin peeks over the couch and sees the silhouette of a man standing in the living room. It's hard to make out the details in the dark but he appears to be wearing a long thick jacket of some sort and a conical hat straight out of the old Kung Fu movies Kevin and his dad watched.

"Who are you?" Kevin asks.

"I'm a friend," the man growls. "I know you're scared and you have every right to be, but you're just gonna have to trust me for now."

Hidden under the growl, his voice carries a deep Southern drawl to it that makes him seem completely unfazed by anything. He looks around lazily, eyes occasionally lit by reflections from the moon. Tina-Lou gingerly hops off the couch, skitters across the wood floor and sniffs the stranger. He stands perfectly still while the dog sniffs at him. Satisfied that he's not a threat, she sits down on the floor and looks up at him.

The man holds out a hand and the dog sniffs at it. He passes muster and she lets him reach down and scratch her behind the ears.

"Nice dog," the man says to Kevin.

"She's vicious when she wants to be."

"I don't doubt it. Who's your friend?"

Kevin looks at the man, wonder what friend he's talking about.

"In your arms, who's your dino buddy?" the man asks him.

Kevin looks down at Donny and looks back at the man. "Donny," he says.

"And what kind of dinosaur is Donny?"

Like all eight year-old boys, Kevin is a master at dinosaurs. "A deinonychus," he says. "They were smart and fearsome."

"Couple of good friends you've got here, pal. My name's Chan. I know I don't look like a Chan, but that's my name. What's yours?" the man asks.

"Kevin."

"Kevin, I'm powerful sorry to tell you this, but bad things are afoot in this house. There's someone that wants you," Chan says.

"Who wants me? What happened to my mom and dad?" Kevin asks. As soon as Tina-Lou decided Chan was okay, Kevin relaxed and the questions started pouring out. "Who were those ghosts and what did they mean when they said 'He was coming'?"

"Slow down, Hoss," Chan says. "There's a guy we call The Beast after you. Don't know much about him but he's dangerous. He's been snatching up people. Those ghosts were automated sentries. We send them to keep people like you safe."

"Like me?"

"You're a magic user, son. Powerful one, too by the smell of it."

"What?"

"Just gonna have to trust me, buddy. We don't have much time and I need to get you safely out of here. I don't know what happened to your folks, but I promise I'll help you find out," Chan tells him. "You've got one protector here, but I think you're gonna need another one."

"Magic isn't real," Kevin says.

"Son, magic is very real. Let me show you. A deinonychus, you say?"

"What?" Kevin asks.

"Donny. He's a deinonychus?"

"Yes."

"Ain't never seen one of those alive," Chan says. "Gotta admit, I'm kinda looking forward to it."

"What? What are you talking about?" Kevin asks.

"Magic, son. Pure magic."

Kevin feels something move in his arms and is startled to see Donny turn his stuffed head toward him. One black eye focuses on Kevin's face. Startled, Kevin drops the stuffed dinosaur which continues to squirm and grow. The body elongates and expands. Fake fur turns to smooth scales. On the scales, feathers start to sprout and a long keening wail escapes from the creature.

As it grows, the dinosaur pushes a coffee table out of the way. A full grown deinonychus is standing in the living room sniffing the air and snorting. Its black eyes peer around the room and settle on Kevin. A foot-long mouth filled with razor sharp teeth opens and snaps shut. It barks out a sound that's a cross between the honk of a crane and the call of an eagle. The mouth filled with teeth looms closer. Kevin huddles back on the couch trying to get away. The deinonychus snorts and sniffs at him.

Kevin is reeling in abject terror at the eleven-foot-long dinosaur when he feels the soft feathered face nuzzle him and hears a kind chirping purr. He opens his eyes and finds Donny rubbing his face against him. Delicately, Kevin reaches a hand up and strokes the dinosaur's muzzle. The feathers are soft and warm and the chirping purr increases.

"Told you, son," Chan says. "Magic is real."

At the sound of Chan's voice Donny starts. Quick as a flash the dinosaur hops on top of the coffee table, scattering remotes and books over the floor. Huge claws on his hind legs flex and click against the hard wood leaving gouges in their wake.

"It's okay, Donny," Kevin says. "He's here to help. I think. At least that's what he says."

Chan tips his Chinese hat at Donny. The dinosaur regards him skeptically and crouches down, looking for a reason to pounce. Its tail is flicking back and forth, knocking pictures and small ceramic bowls off the book shelves behind it.

"Calm down, dino," Chan says calmly. "I ain't here to hurt no one."

Donny remains not quite convinced, but eases his stance. He keeps a wary eye on Chan.

"We are on something of a timeline, friends. I don't know how long we've got so we'd best get our hustle on."

"Why?" Kevin asks. "Where are my parents?"

"Told you son. I don't know where your folks are, but I'll help you find 'em. As for the why, well, those sentries weren't pullin' your leg.

Someone bad is coming here and we'd best make ourselves scarce if we don't want to meet him with our pants down. Now ain't the time and here ain't the place to fight him."

"Where are we going?" Kevin asks.

Tina-Lou stands up and stretches. Donny hops off the table and sniffs her. The two predators eye each other warily but decide to get along for the time being.

"We're going to a safe place for the time being. Got to get you situated so's we can find your folks," Chan says.

As the terror has waned in Kevin's mind exhaustion has crept in. He's still scared, he still just wants his mom and dad and his warm bed, but he has to admit a full-grown Donny is pretty good. He yawns and nods to Chan. "I still want my mom and dad," he says.

"And I promise you we'll find 'em, son," Chan replies. "But we need to get going."

"Do you have a car or something? Do I need clothes?" Kevin asks.

"No, son, I ain't got no car. Never did get along with 'em. As for clothes or anything else, it's best you take what you're wearing and nothing else. We'll still have to burn it and get you some new duds. Anything you take with you can be used to track you so, aside from your friend here and the clothes on your back, it's best to leave everything else here."

Kevin nods and asks, "How are we getting where we're going?"

"Magic, son. Pure magic."

Chan waves his hands slightly and a crackling electricity fills the air. Kevin feels a deep thrumming in his bones, building until it shakes his teeth. Without warning, everything stops and the air feels heavy.

"What just happened?" Kevin asks.

"Our ride is here, Hoss," Chan says.

"Where?" Kevin asks.

"Right through that door," Chan says, pointing to a door that leads outside. "Ready to skedaddle?"

Chan opens the sliding glass door that usually leads outside. Instead of his back yard, though, Kevin sees a dusty lane. Tina-Lou shakes, stretches, and walks through the door. Donny flexes his claws and follows her through.

"Time go, son," Chan says.

Kevin takes one last look around the living room he's grown up in. Emotions swirl around him and he feels the weight of the evening drop on his shoulders. Tears well up in his eyes as he remembers playing with Legos on the floor, snuggling with his mom on the couch and sword fighting his dad with Nerf swords in the back yard.

He feels Chan's hand on his shoulder and the tears erupt in full.

"I know, son," Chan says quietly. "I've been right where you are. Everything looks black, but I promise you the world will keep on turning."

Kevin buries himself in Chan's arms and sobs uncontrollably. He feels strong arms reach down and pick him up. Suddenly he's three again, getting carried to bed by his dad. As Chan walks through the door, Kevin stares over the man's shoulder at the life he's leaving behind. On one side of him is bright sunlight and green trees, on the other a cold, dark living room filled with memories.

His bleary eyes see the door close behind them and everything he knew is left behind. Even the door itself vanishes.

"Welcome to Aluna, son," Chan says quietly. "I know it ain't home, but I hope you'll like it. At the very least, you'll be safe here."

Awaken

He refers to himself as a he, but the notion of gender doesn't really apply to him. It was just a choice, one made to compliment the choice she made. Gender doesn't really apply to her, either, but it was one of those things that seemed like a good idea at the time and he's gotten used to the idea of being a him just like she got used to the idea of being a her.

In the dark void he waits with the patience of a god. At first he raged against this prison but that was ... some time ago. Time has no meaning here. Time is a measurement of change. He may have been here for hours or decades or millennia but the formless black space means there's no change and therefore no way to measure time. He gets glimmers every now and then, flickers of information that jump around in time and space: a sort of scientist probing the secrets of the world, a young girl who doesn't realize what she is, things looking at him. His shadows have dropped into a waiting mode, hiding among the shadows of this cavern.

Mostly he sleeps. He's a champ sleeper. This isn't entirely unexpected given his role in the universe. The God of Dreams should be able to sleep. He's cut off from his realm, cut off from the mortal world, cut off from his shadows and stuck in nothingness. To pass the time, he sleeps.

*****

Russ Johnson woke up a happy man today.

It's a Tuesday, and that's a good thing. Russ never could get his head wrapped around Mondays. They always struck him as needlessly complicated; he has to get caught up from all the stuff he didn't get done on Saturday and Sunday and he has to recover from all the stuff he did do on Saturday and Sunday.

Russ is a bright guy, though, and he realizes if Mondays were to go away, Tuesdays would be far worse because then he'd have to deal with all the things he did and didn't do on Saturday, Sunday, and Monday. Three days off would be great, but the remaining four days would be even more stressful than they are now.

Mondays may not be the best thing, but they could be worse. Besides, Mondays mean he gets to see her again.

She is Ms. Bethany Daniels, and she runs the front desk at work.

Russ is a shy guy and it took him months to even work up the nerve to say "hello" to her. It took him weeks after that to actually talk to her. Last night he resolved to ask her out first thing this morning.

Since Russ is a scientist, he likes everything neatly ordered: he wants a dedicated plan of how he's going to move and what the expected outcomes of each interaction will be. As such, he spent last night figuring out exactly how to tackle the problem of asking Bethany out. After many false starts, he believes he has the perfect way to ask her. Of course, like any experiment, he'll never know the outcome until he observes the results.

He's gone from nervous to terrified back to nervous and is now sitting at a low hum of antsy energy while he speeds to work. He hopes everything will go okay, and the data seems to suggest that it will. Actually, Russ is as close to praying as he's ever been. In his mind this has to work.

It has to work because he's spent every night since he met her kicking himself for not being braver, not being strong enough to just ask her out. He's tired of feeling like that and wants to be able to look himself in the mirror again and not be ashamed.

He thinks Bethany Daniels is the cutest thing he's ever met.

All the way to work, his mind is preoccupied. The quiet roar of his RX-8's engine normally invigorates him, helps him focus on his driving while he pretends he's a race car driver, someone with razor sharp reflexes and a quick wit. Now the engine provides a deep, hypnotic thrum that's just a backdrop to his internal conversation. He's still retooling the words he'll say to her in his head.

"You look nice today, Bethany," he'll say. He read somewhere that women like it when you use their names. It means you care enough to remember. Research is important when treading new waters.

She'll say, "Thank you very much," and blush slightly. Again, research has proven useful.

Russ sees himself leaning in closer to her. He imagines the smell of her perfume, the look of interest on her face.

"Would you like to go to dinner with me?" he'll ask.

This is where the simulation breaks down. He wants to be suave, like the heroes he sees on TV, but all he can come up with is that lame line about dinner. Maybe coffee would be better. *Does she even drink coffee?* Damn. A new variable that he hasn't explored.

Maybe he's just not a romantic at heart.

As he approaches the Big-I, the RX handles the switch from westbound Interstate 40 to southbound Interstate 25 like it's glued to the road. He wants to push the car, see if it can take the interchange at 80 or 90, but he keeps it at a quiet 65 mph. He consoles himself with the fact that the posted speed limit on the interchange is 45 mph, so he's still something of a rebel.

Russ exits the freeway at Lead and heads west into downtown Albuquerque. He parks in the parking garage on 4th St. The entire top floor is reserved for his group even if no one else in Albuquerque knows it. Parking is one of the perks to working where he does, even if no one else anywhere will ever know what he does at his job.

He walks down the stairs instead of taking the elevator. It's September 20, 2005 and Russ congratulates him on keeping his New Year's resolution of taking stairs whenever possible. He still has time before he can even go into work so he gets a coffee and waits outside the Simms building.

The mornings are still warm, but temperatures are slowly dropping.

Russ finishes his coffee and walks calmly through the front door of the Simms building. It's almost 9am and the lobby is in full hustle and bustle mode. He waves to a couple of familiar faces, but otherwise keeps his head down and makes a beeline toward the unmarked door in the southwestern corner of the building. A quick look around reveals no one watching so he keys in his combination, sucks in his breath and opens the door.

If seeing Bethany is the best part of his day, walking through this door is the worst.

Inside he's greeted by the same two armed guards who scowl at him every morning and one Mr. Robinson whose glare makes Russ feel like he's been judged and found wanting. There's something awful about Mr. Robinson; he's always there, he's always angry, and he terrifies Russ in the same way that greeting a six-foot-tall spider in the bathroom would be terrifying.

The room is a standard issue Government room, Mark I, complete with corners (four, 90 nominal degrees each) and white colored walls. The United States flag is on the right and the New Mexico flag is on the left. There are pictures of George Bush and Dick Cheney on the wall.

The room looks like a Government room, completely devoid of anything that might imply emotion or uniqueness. One thing about Government buildings is the complete lack of anything that anyone could possibly find offensive. Or interesting, for that matter. This is a dead space and anyone that inadvertently looks in through the open door will see nothing important.

The guards are always standing in the same position, flanking Robinson on opposite sides of the room. They always wear the same black combat BDUs. They've always got their machine guns ready and almost but not quite pointed at anyone who walks through the door. Their fingers are always near the triggers, like they're just waiting for an excuse to shoot someone, anyone.

Robinson always wears the same black suit, white shirt, black tie. His job seems to be to glare at everyone that walks through the door.

For his part, Robinson hates it here. He hates the people that walk through the door. He hates the idiots standing behind him. He hates everything in this place and everyone he meets. Pathetic humans. If he had his way, he'd kill them all and eat their children. Which reminds him; they should be bringing him food tonight. Hopefully, they'll clean the homeless bastard this time before they drop it off. Robinson even hates the name Robinson, but they insist on using it.

Frankly, Robinson hates a lot of things. Mostly he hates the fact that they wiped out his people and know how to kill him easily and effectively and there's not a damned thing he can do about it but obey or die screaming in flaming agony.

Russ manages to choke down his fear long enough to nod to Robinson and the nameless guards while he walks across the seal of the United States inlaid into the floor. The guards roll their eyes and Robinson manages to look disgusted without moving a muscle.

The back wall is a smooth expanse. Unless you know exactly what you're looking for you'll never notice the tiny hole. Russ pulls a red object on a necklace from inside his shirt. It's long and thin and faintly resembles an ankh without the arms.

The object is a key, but it's a very specialized one. Keys usually open one lock since that's the nature of keys, but this key is a little more advanced that those keys. This key not only opens a couple of locks - two to be precise - but also tells the computers that control those lock exactly who opened the lock and when it was opened. The key is also smart enough to wipe itself out if anyone trie to open the wrong lock with it.

That's a nice bit of security right there: it means someone can't just go wandering around sticking the key into locks to see what happens. There's exactly one shot before the key wipes itself and the computer calls the guys with guns.

Russ puts the key in the lock and holds his breath.

*****

Sometime recently the God of Dreams woke briefly. It wasn't for very long, just a blip even on a human time scale, but gods can do things quicker than mortals. He fought to stay awake, to leave the nothing lands but her spell was too strong and he got sucked back into the nothingness.

He can out-dream anyone in the world, but it's been lonely dreaming lately. Had she not imprisoned him in the nothing he'd be able to hop in and out of any dream he chose. No one but him dreams in the nothing and for all his power, he can't change nothing into something.

Still, even a momentary blip away from the dreaming lands gave him a vision of something other the same dull blackness. He saw a cavern, heard a voice, saw strange things gazing down on him. The God of Dreams carried those things back into the nothing with him and almost wept as they slowly disintegrated.

Disintegrated, he thought as he watched that brief vision fade to black. It's a word only humans could come up with. The opposite of integrated. Things flowing from something integrated into a coherent whole into constituent parts that drift away quietly.

He sometimes wishes he could disintegrate. Then he wonders if he hasn't already. She chose an apt prison.

*****

Russ has heard rumors of people getting shot if the key doesn't work. He's never had any proof, but a couple of people have vanished after they put their key in and it didn't work. More than likely they were just fired, debriefed and sent on their way with a stern warning that talking about anything they worked on would result in jail time and huge fines followed by a bullet to the back of their lover's head, but one always has to wonder. These are the joys of working in classified environments.

There's a hint of a vibration and Russ knows the elevator is working, quietly trudging up from the depths of Hades. The wall splits in two and he breathes a sigh of relief and steps into the waiting elevator. A small part of Russ chides him for not taking the stairs, but a larger part of him remembers there are no stairs here. There is precisely one way in and one way out of this place and that way is this elevator. Sure, it's probably a violation of numerous State and Federal safe work statutes, but sometimes National Security has to trump such trivial things as worker safety.

The doors close and all Russ can hear is the lifeless Muzak versions of popular songs from the 80s. He used to think Morrissey was tedious as Morrissey until he heard the Muzak version of it. The Muzak version of Morrissey is soul crushing.

The elevator takes its sweet time going down. He's not sure, but Russ has again heard rumors that the bottom of the shaft is a couple thousand feet under Albuquerque. A ding and the doors open again and he's facing that same hideous lime-green leather couch and the same neatly arranged magazines lying quietly on an old coffee table.

He's never seen who was responsible for the magazines; how they get there and who arranges them remains a mystery to him, but he suspects it's one of Bethany's many minor jobs.

Aside from the couch and the coffee table, the room is adorned with various Department of Defense posters warning viewers of the dangers of talking. One poster features a hand sticking out of the water and a ship sinking in the background. "SOMEONE TALKED" is written in huge letters across the top and bottom of the poster. It's a classic World War II poster warning people to shut the hell up. Others feature not so subtle reminders that the nameless, faceless enemies of the United States have ears everywhere or warnings that spies look just like everyone else.

Security reminders are constants in places like this. It feeds off the idea that if you constantly apply a message that message will stick. It worked for religion for centuries and has worked for National Security for decades. Keep constantly feeding people the same message and they will eventually believe it.

At the far end of the lobby is an enclosed secretary's station and a door immediately to the right of that station. Inside the secretary's station is Bethany Daniels and, in Russ's mind, she looks as beautiful as ever. She's got long, wavy blonde hair and a smile that lights up the room. Today she's wearing a pale gray dress and subdued makeup. It makes her look all that much better.

This is it, Russ thinks to himself. He takes a deep breath and walks forward into his destiny.

The secretary's station is glassed in, probably with bullet-proof glass, and the only way through the door is for the secretary to let you in. Sure, you could probably break the lock somehow, but you'd never be able to do it without raising every alarm in the building. Before you know it you'd be surrounded by large guys in black BDUs looking for an excuse to perforate you.

When she sees Russ, Bethany smiles and waves. His feet feel like they're made of lead, his heart is beating about a million beats per minutes and he feels a trickle of sweat rolling down the side of his face, but Russ manages to walk forward.

He hears the elevator go up and knows it's now or never. Swallowing his fear, Russ walks to Bethany's station and is greeted by a cheerful, "Good morning!"

"Good morning, Bethany," he manages to say. He's fidgeting now, not quite sure what to do next.

She looks at him closely for a minute before asking, "Is everything okay?"

"Yes," he replies. "Sorry, everything's fine."

"Can I get your badge, Russ?"

She used his name! Oh joy oh joy oh joy!

Russ fumbles for the other lanyard inside his shirt and puts his badge up to the glass. It's got his picture, his name and a bunch of letters like TS, SCI, and so on. The National Security apparatus thinks Russ is very trustworthy, and he aims to keep them feeling that way.

Bethany examines his picture and credentials and looks closely at his face. Even though they've been through this routine nearly daily for months, she still performs each step just like she did the very first time. Her security clearance isn't as high as his, but it's still up there and she aims to keep it that way.

"Thanks, Russ. Have a great day!" she tells him through the glass.

"Uh, Bethany, uh. Um. Um. Can I ask you a question?" Russ says.

"Of course," she replies, brow furrowing slightly concerned.

Russ takes a deep breath, closes his eyes and asks, "Would you like to get dinner with me sometime?"

There, he's said it. Now he can't stop talking. A voice in his head yells at him to take it back, to make everything like it was before he ruined everything.

"I understand if you don't want to, I mean, I'd really like you to, but I get that you probably don't want to or you're busy or whatever, but I just wanted to ask and it's okay if you say no, in fact I shouldn't have asked it, I'm sorry, forget it."

When he opens his eyes, she's smiling at him and there's a twinkle in her eyes. She can tell that took an amazing amount of effort on his part.

"I'd love to," she tells him. "I'm free tonight, if you are."

The elevator dings behind him and he faintly hears the doors open, but Russ is still in space. She said yes. She actually said yes. Shit. Now he's got actually take her out. If asking was that hard, how hard will actually going to dinner with her be?

"I'm totally free tonight," Russ finally manages.

"We can talk at lunch," she tells him. "I think I've got other customers."

"If you two are done flirting," a gruff voice says from behind, "let's not forget we've got work to do."

When he turns around, Russ finds himself staring face to face with General Hapablap, the head of this facility and Senator Lucius Bedfellow, the Congressional liaison. Hapablap is a great guy and claps Russ on the shoulder. "Good luck, son," he tells Russ.

Bedfellow just watches impassively like everything around him is not quite important enough to care about. Like every other Senator, Bedfellow feels slightly dirty after intermingling with the people he claims to represent.

Russ hears a click and turns back to Bethany. With a warm smile she gestures at the now open door. As he steps through it, he hears Bethany say, "Your badges, please, gentlemen."

*****

If. No, when. When he gets out of this nothingness, when the God of Dreams manages to wake up and revisit the world, the first thing he's going to do is make everyone run for cover. He'll tear open the walls of reality and let dreams wander through. During his brief waking period he felt a pair of shadows hiding out and sent a message to them before falling back into the black void. He hasn't heard from the other one he sent with the scientist but it's no matter, the message was transmitted and the scientist will deliver the daughter.

The things he saw and heard may have disintegrated, but he's noticed something important: the void's hold on him is weakening rapidly. Maybe she built it that way or maybe she's just not that great at building prisons. Whatever the reason, Fear's little prison is falling apart.

Not that it was ever spectacular. He can sometimes almost travel to his realm by walking through reality. The door opens, he starts to step through and the door slams shut again. Soon enough he'll make it through and escape. He almost made it last night. It's only a matter of time before her spell weakens and he can flicker home.

Once things are settled he'll be sure to pay her a visit. Her minions will be tough to deal with; they don't dream, but he's got more than a few tricks up his sleeve. All he needs is power. The scientist's daughter will be key to getting that power. She can make dreams real. He can expand his realm to cover this part of reality and she will help him take the dreams and nightmares and make them real things.

Real dreams can be terrifyingly powerful things.

Then the Goddess of Fear will pay. Everyone will pay.

*****

The next hour or so is a blur for Russ. He's on autopilot when he keys in at door two and waits patiently while the huge metal door slowly creeps open.

There are two other huge metal doors - one and three - located on either side of his door, but Russ has never been in either of them. For that matter, he's only ever seen door three partway open once, but it closed before he could muster the guts to peek inside.

This area, far beneath the surface of Albuquerque, is one of the stranger pieces of the Top Secret lab infrastructure that dots the American landscape. It contains things that need research and security but, for whatever reason, those things can't be moved. Sometimes the things are just too big, sometimes there's nowhere else to put them, other times the things simply don't want to be moved. Russ doesn't know what's behind the other two doors and the people that work in them don't work the same schedules as the people that work behind his door, so he's only heard scuttlebutt about what's going on.

The rumors about door three usually focus on aliens or UFOs or some such stuff, but Russ knows full well that classified work is always covered with rumors of aliens or UFOs, so he takes those rumors with a grain of salt. Door number one is a complete mystery. One of his buddies, a fellow analyst by the name of Peggy claimed to have snuck a peek inside but said all she saw was stars and something that looked an awful lot like a dragon. Peggy was gone the next day and Russ never said a word about what he had heard.

Behind Russ's door is a large, open cavern, generally referred to as "the cave." It's basically circular, about a hundred and fifty, two hundred feet in diameter. The floor is mostly smooth, which is kind of odd for a cave, but not completely outside the realm of possibility. All around the edges are workstations and servers and various pieces of equipment. Some of the equipment looks like it came directly from mad scientist's secret lair. There are glowing things and things that look like plasma balls and even one thing that looks like a giant lamp.

The lava lamp thing has always held a deep fascination for Russ. So much so that he went out to Wal-Mart after his first week down here and bought his own lava lamp for his apartment. He likes to watch it and listen to Pink Floyd and imagine he's smoking a huge doobie. He never actually smokes a doobie, though, because the staff is regularly tested for drug use down here and, to tell the truth, Russ would have absolutely no idea of how to even get a doobie. So he sits in his apartment with all the lights off and listens to *Dark Side of the Moon* and watches his lava lamp and pretends.

He really wants his lava lamp right now. Bethany's face is pinging around his head and he really needs to relax and get his work done.

In the center of the room, surrounded by a yellow and black metal fence lies an older gentleman on a natural stone pedestal. The man is wearing an elegantly tailored, if somewhat out of date, suit; double-breasted and black with bright white pinstripes. The underside of the pedestal is shrouded in shadow even though there are more lights shining on the man that there are lights shining on the field at Isotopes Stadium.

Peggy once told him the shadows tried to bite a guy that got too close. Again, Russ took it with a grain of salt. She also told him the guy's suit was from the 1930s. That may well be true. Russ is hardly an expert on suits. Or clothes in general. He knows pants go on the legs and shirts go on the top and things should look like they belong together.

There's a glowing circle made of God only knows what that surrounds the guy on the pylon. It looks like it was etched into the rock around the pylon and glows a deep, otherworldly blue. The circle is about five feet thick and etched with even more circles and intertwining lines inside of it. A single white, glowing line constantly orbits the entire circle at the rate of exactly one loop every fifteen seconds.

The rumor about the circle is its some kind of magical protection circle that a Navajo shaman set up years ago. There's no proof about this and, obviously, it sounds like total bull, but that's rumors, right?

Russ always felt it looked like a huge, glowing mandala, and always kind of wanted one for his apartment. It would look cool with his lava lamp. Alas, Wal-Mart doesn't apparently sell giant glowing circles. You can, however, find decent mandala posters here and there and Russ has two that hang on either side of his lava lamp.

The fence is dotted with signs warning of the terrible fate that will befall anyone who attempts to cross it. There are even signs on the fence, and around the room, warning that anyone who so much as throws a wadded-up piece of paper can be shot immediately. If the fence and the signs and the general weirdness of the place aren't enough to keep people from playing around down here, the two guys with assault rifles and serious looks definitely are.

No one's quite sure who the guy on the pedestal is, but he hasn't so much as moved since Russ has been here. Apparently he hasn't moved since the first guys found him shortly after World War II.

Back in the day, someone wanted to do some poking and prodding of the guy on the pylon. One of the scientists who wanted to do the poking and prodding got too close to the circle, some shadow or something touched him. He freaked out and tried to kill his buddies before clawing his own eyes out. After that incident, no one was allowed to go near circle or the sleeper and all data had to be gathered through various non-tactile means. First it was just cameras, then radar, then microwaves, then all this crazy equipment that fills the cavern now.

About thirty years ago, someone noticed the sleeper periodically flickers and partially disappears. When it happens, it's almost exactly like watching a fluorescent tube bulb flickering before it finally decides to shine light on the world.

It took them a while, but they finally figured out that the sleeper is somehow manipulating space and time. Watching over the space of months peeking with every instrument known to man – and a few Russ swears aren't known to man – the team down here accumulated a massive amount of information about what happens when the guy flickers. All that data got sent off somewhere else one day.

*****

He doesn't have a name because gods don't really need them. His role is to control and regulate dreams. Of course, humans being the primitive, stupid things that they are insist on names rather than simply understanding the concepts. As a result he's been called the King of Dreams, the God of Dreams, Morpheus, Nodens, Bormanus, Muludaianinis, the Sandman, and a thousand other names over the millennia, none of which really fit. Humans have called on him for countless things. Due to the nature of his kind, if the calling is correct, he's been forced to at least show up.

It's a terrible thing and it usually leaves him in a bad mood.

They called him here, with exactly the right message and he was obliged to come. That's when they hit him. Even as strong as he is, he couldn't face them all down. Their combined powers shut him down, cut him off from his realm and dropped him into the nothingness.

He knows he shouldn't be surprised. The humans have a saying, "Hell hath no fury like a woman scorned."

Especially when that woman is her. The humans only whisper her name lest she show up. She stalks the night covered in a cloak, reveling in their terror, but she was an amazing lover. Gods enjoy sex, too. When they do it, though, the stars dance and sing. The Earth has been known to literally move. Together they made the heavens shake until he decided he was done and sought another.

The heavens shook again when she caught him. Her rage combined with her natural abilities made for a terrifying event. By his reckoning at least one entire civilization was lost when she exploded.

The Goddess of Fear is not a woman to trifle with.

Her revenge was to lure him here to "talk things out". He accepted, if only because he didn't like the idea of things being left undone, but she had a trap ready for him and he walked right into it.

Now there is only nothingness. A nothingness designed to wear him down and trap him in a world of terror.

But the God of Dreams can make things even Fear is terrified of.

Last night he came so close to escape. He tried a new way out her prison. If he can't flicker to his own reality, maybe he can just get up in the human reality and walk out of here. It was just a trifle, barely worthy of note, but he wiggled enough to know it's doable.

That slight movement disrupted the spell in all sorts of unexpected ways.

*****

A couple other guys are in the lab, already focusing on their own work. Russ says a quick hello and pleasant greetings are exchanged. One of the guys, George Smith - who Russ absolutely hates - says he's going to ask Bethany out at lunch.

Smith is smarmy guy with a weasel face and a perpetual smirk. He and Russ have been somewhat competitive ever since Smith started a couple years ago. Well, actually that's not entirely accurate: Smith has regularly gone out of his way to point out everything Russ has done wrong and happily attempted to take credit for everything Russ has done right.

George Smith has an enormous amount of will to succeed, but very little in the actual talent to succeed department so he tends to knock people down and take credit for their work whenever he can. If Russ has a failing, it's that he doesn't really understand the idea of moving up in his job even though he has the talent to do it.

Russ and George are kind of like Yin and Yang.

When Smith says he's asking Bethany out at lunch Russ's first thought is *"Ha! Screw you! I already asked her out and she said 'Yes'."* This thought fades rapidly and is replaced by, *"What if she takes him up on his offer and kicks me to the curb?"* A quick look at Smith, with his greasy, stringy hair and pinched face and Russ reassures himself that Bethany won't touch the weasel.

He mutters a quiet, "Good luck with that," to Smith and turns away.

Russ spares a quick look at the sleeper and the glow from the circle and the cameras and other scientific accoutrements and sits down at his computer to go over the data all the equipment recorded last night.

With a huge effort, he pushes Bethany's face out of his mind and settles into the daily grind of crunching data. Each camera and sensor and otherworldly piece of recording equipment down here is constantly watching the guy in the center of the room and each one of them stores its information. Someone has to process all that information and that's why all these guys are down here.

A quick look at the data shows almost the exact same data Russ has seen every day for the past few years: nothing. Nothing ever happens down here.

When he first started, it was super exciting to be working on a project like this. Most people will go their whole lives not knowing a place like this exists, let alone actually working in one. The average person will never see a guy who never wakes up and never ages and occasionally flickers like a fluorescent light or shadows that can seize their minds and make them see things that aren't there. Hell, just knowing a place like this exists down here is pretty cool. The unfortunate thing, though, is life down here never changes. It's like being in a Vegas casino; there's no sense of time or change. It's just the daily drudgery of looking at the same data over and over again.

Russ's equipment logs come from a low-light camera, an IR camera, a microwave sensor, and a sensor called xrs3a that monitors tachyons or some damned thing. Russ doesn't exactly know what xrs3a measures, but it spits out long columns of numbers which have traditionally been zeroes. On the rare times when the sleeper flickers, the numbers go up to 100 or so. Over time, Russ has learned to interpret the data that thing spits out even though he can't really conceptualize what the data is showing.

Today there's a slight change in the data from the microwave sensor. The sensor takes samples a thousand times per second looking for any kind of microwave radiation. Last night the microwave sensor registered a minor shift from its usual array of zeroes. There are five hundred numbers that aren't zero, ranging from 1.1 to 9.9. It's just a tiny spike, but it's a spike. In a realm of zeroes and numbers from one hundred and up, a range of numbers between one and ten is something new and exciting.

Five hundred sounds like a lot, but there are millions of records in the log and the five hundred records translate to an event that lasted half a second. It's some kind of change and that's very exciting. Russ makes note of the time in the sensor log and cues up the low-light camera and the IR camera recordings for the time.

It takes several loops through the camera footage before Russ finally sees what happened. The sleeper's finger twitched slightly at exactly 02:13:01.0034. There's no real difference between the low-light camera and the IR camera, both just show a slight twitch; one displays it in green, the other in the dark blue tints that always show up.

The xrs3a, on the other hand, went ballistic for half a second. The normally sequential columns of zeroes are all over the place, like someone dropped a bomb in a pile of integers. Russ has absolutely no idea what the numbers are, so he follows procedure. Contain the data in a secure digital container and ship it off S6. He doesn't know what S6 is, nor does anyone else. Rumors say S6 is their sister facility somewhere in northern New Mexico, but no one knows for certain. It's probably just another lab out there somewhere. Hopefully someone at S6 will be able to interpret the data.

"Guys," Russ says out loud. "Check your data for 02:13:01.0034."

Smith immediately bends over his computer and starts digging. Russ's buddy James slides his chair over and peers over Russ's shoulder.

"Sheeit," James says his with trademark exaggerated Texas drawl. The closer he looks at the data, the paler he gets. As his eyes move over Russ's data, James starts nervously chewing his lip. When he speaks again, his fake accent is gone and he's back to his Midwest roots. "We need to tell Hapablap about this," he whispers.

Russ just nods.

"Confirm, abnormal data at 02:13:01.0034," Smith says. "My data is crazy. Damn. What happened?"

"All I can see is a finger twitch," Russ says.

"Had to have been more than that, look at this," Smith responds.

Russ and James slide their chairs and look over Smith's data. None of them can completely comprehend what they're seeing, but it looks interesting, if somewhat scary. Scary is good, as far as they're concerned, because scary is much better than bored.

"Damn," James whispers. "I wish Hayha was still here. He'd know what to do."

Dr. Delano Hayha was the head on this project for a while. He moved to Albuquerque from somewhere in California and was responsible for most of the advanced sensor arrangement in the cave. Hayha was nice, if different, guy, and everyone was pretty choked up when they heard he'd left.

"Hayha wigged out, man," Russ says. "They took him out of here in a straightjacket."

"A shadow got him," George says, suddenly serious and not at all his plotting and vindictive self. "He touched a shadow and tried to shut down the circle."

"No way," Russ says. "Hayha always insisted no one even got close to the circle."

"I was here, man. I saw it happen. He walked back there," George says, pointing to a dark area where the servers live, "When he came out he tried to shut down the circle. Security stopped him, of course, but he tried to shut everything down."

"Shit," James whispers, stunned. "Why didn't they say anything?"

"People freak out when stuff like that happens. That's why Peggy left. She couldn't shut up about all the stories she'd heard," George says.

"Like one of those shadows under the pedestal?" James asks.

"Yeah, I guess, I don't know exactly," George responds.

"If there was one out here, there could be more," Russ says. "Why didn't they warn us?"

"Government loves its secrets," James says.

All three of them nervously look around the room. The cave is very well lit, but there are still places where shadows hold court and all of them are thinking about ways to avoid those places in the future. One by one, their eyes focus on the man on the pedestal and, one by one, a cold chill starts up their spines. He's still sleeping, still unmoving, but he moved last night and no one has ever seen that happen.

"We need to tell Hapablap," Russ finally says.

*****

During his extremely brief prison break the God of Dreams got some useful information. A part of him is made of shadows and before she fired up her spell, he managed to get a few shadows out with some basic commands: watch, learn, and attempt to control without being spotted. One shadow resides under his pedestal, but it's all but wasted now. Like all things, his shadows don't last forever without external input. The pair out in the room can find energy by leeching off the servers or sucking the dreams out of a daydreamer's head. The shadow under the pedestal is as cut off from the universe as he himself is. It's a withered thing, wasted by the energy expended to corrupt that man's mind back in the day.

The other shadows, though, have watched and waited patiently for decades, quietly collecting and storing information. When he moved last night her spell was briefly broken and his shadows burst information at him. She chose this cavern because it was insulated from the world. The spaceship in a nearby cavern was leaking some kind of alien power source and it was enough to block his signature. She wanted him to be hidden forever, but humans would appear to have found the ship and then stumbled across him.

So, the humans are here. They're annoying and largely useless, but maybe this prison wasn't as permanent as she thought it would be.

As the information leaks away into the nothing the King of Dreams resolves to redouble his efforts. His shadows are still out there. All he needs to do is be patient and wait for the humans to mess everything up like they always do.

*****

General Royce Hapablap is finishing his third cup of coffee and filling out paperwork when he hears Bethany's voice over the intercom telling him he's needed in the cave. He sighs and hopes Bethany and the kid analyst, what's his name? Russ. That's right, Russ. He hopes they have a good time tonight. Normally, he'd frown on staff fraternization, but he's getting older and he finds he just hopes they can enjoy each other's company for a while. Youth shouldn't be wasted on a place like this. Places like this destroyed his marriage because he could never tell his wife even where he spent his days, let alone what he did. Secrets like that tear marriages apart bit by bit until all that's left between two people are the simplest of platitudes. His lifetime of service in the Army was so much easier when he was just a simple soldier thinking about keeping the Reds at bay. Unfortunately, the Army discovered he was not only a bright guy, but knew how to keep a secret. Promotions came quickly, but each one pulled him further and further toward larger and larger piles of paperwork.

Russ may not be able to talk about what he does and Bethany won't be able to spill her secrets, but they at least know where each other works and that's a big deal.

General Hapablap picks up his coffee and walks to what he affectionately thinks of as "The Nerdery." The kids that run the analysis section are great kids and he respects their knowledge, even if they sometimes talk well out of his range of understanding.

When he walks through door number two he finds them huddled over a monitor, pointing and bickering about what they're looking at. As they see him approach, they all start talking at once, a cacophony of technical jargon and equipment numbers. Hapablap can pick out bits and pieces of what they're saying, but it's all overlapping until finally he sets down his coffee, lifts his hands and says, "Stop, guys. One at a time. What's going on?"

"Hap, it moved last night," James says, pointing to the figure on the pedestal.

Part of the general's mind cringes when the guys call him Hap, but he's learned over the years that dealing with civilians means dealing with informalities. He's figured out, though, that the guys respect him and defer to his leadership, even if it doesn't always come across through their speech. He figures if he can think of them and "The Nerdery," and still respect them, they should be able to call him Hap since they still respect him.

"We have the video, it twitched a finger. Some of the exotic sensors lit up like Christmas trees," Russ tells him.

"What's going on, Hap?" a voice says from behind Hapablap. When he turns, he finds Senator Bedfellow standing behind him, his suit and tie a start contrast to the dress uniform Hapablap is wearing and the jeans and T-shirts of The Nerdery.

Hapablap distrusts Bedfellow something fierce. Every time Bedfellow comes here he puts his nose in places it doesn't belong and stirs everyone up. The Senator also has a nasty habit of following Hapablap everywhere and it drives the general up a wall.

"My name is General Royce Hapablap, Senator," Hapablap says.

General Hapablap may put up with informality from his team, but he'll be damned if he's going to put up with it from stuffed suit from Washington.

Senator Bedfellow is a political creature and, therefore, used to using people. He simply shrugs and says, "My apologies, General Hapablap. What seems to be going on?"

The guys from The Nerdery clam up instantly. They know the Senator is an outsider and don't trust him one bit. All except for George Smith, who sees an opportunity to shine. "There was a finger twitch this morning about 2am, Senator," he says.

Russ and James look at George like he's just grown a second head. They know when to shut the hell up, a lesson George has apparently forgotten.

"A finger twitch is causing this entire ruckus?" Bedfellow asks.

"Senator," George continues, "you have to understand; we have never seen any sign of life from that guy. No breathing, no eye movement, nothing. Other than the flickers, this is the first time we have ever seen anything happen."

Bedfellow thinks for a moment before deciding he can't use the information and walks away.

Hapablap watches him go with disdain in his eyes before turning back to his guys. "Anything else happen since then?"

Russ shakes his head, "No, sir. Just a half second blurp at about 2am."

"Have your forwarded the data?" Hapablap asks.

"Yeah, it went out a few minutes ago," James says.

"Well," Hapablap sighs, "let's keep an eye on things. Maybe it won't happen again."

"Yes, sir. We're kind of keyed up right now, so we won't miss a thing," Russ tells him.

Hapablap nods, "Keep up your analysis. Keep me in the loop if you figure anything out."

The Nerdery nods and goes back to bickering about the data on their screens. Hapablap watches them for a moment before deciding the guys know their jobs and he'd just get in the way. He grabs his coffee and heads back to his desk feeling slightly ill at ease.

*****

If he did it once he can do it again. Centuries, millennia of existence have taught him the power of perseverance. He focuses first on his finger. Logic indicates the last thing that broke her spell should be the first place that should be able to do it again.

No good. His body remains fully stuck, just like his mind and his power.

His mind takes a deep breath and looks for the edges of his prison for the umpteenth time since it went up. This time he finds something that wasn't there before. It's not much, just a small breach in her magic but it's enough. The King of Dreams of pushes on it gently and feels it give just a bit.

Fear, he thinks, is about to find out what happens when she messes with the dream world. Dreams do not follow her rules. If he wants to experience the delights of Minerva that's none of Fear's concern. He was done with her anyway and she had no right to demand more of him.

His finger moves slightly. Not much, but it's an active, intentional movement. He keeps working at the problem, pushing gently but firmly at the crack in Fear's prison.

*****

Russ is so focused on going through his logged data that he fails to notice the live feed twitch slightly. Nothing much, a tenth of a second, but a hundred numbers scramble across the screen and disappear in the waves of zeroes and nulls.

Something about the data feels strange to Russ. The numbers he's seeing from the xrs3a looks strange. Except for the 100s or so that happen when the guy flickers, Russ has never seen numbers other than zeroes on the log. He doesn't know what the calibration is set to, but the numbers shoot from 0 to over 10,000 and drop off again in half a second. The microwave sensor shot from 0 to over 15, which is probably no small change, but, again, he doesn't know what the numbers mean other than some kind of microwave signal peaked and dropped. Without knowing what each sensor is looking at it's difficult to assess, but the difference between 15 and 10,000 is pretty damned huge.

And why would a simple finger twitch generate a microwave signal, let alone whatever signal the xrs3a is looking at?

Another blast of numbers streams across the live feed and, again, no one notices it. That's the problem with boredom, at some point in the past someone got to futzing with the signal interpreters and accidentally triggered an alarm. The alarm was the most excitement this lonely place had seen in years. Everyone showed up, guns were drawn, exits sealed. It was a huge mess. The guy that was playing with the alarms was chastised severely and decided, for whatever reason, that the alarm itself was to blame. So he disabled the alarms and never told anyone. Nothing ever happens right? Nothing ever will, so what's the big deal? When the guy who disabled the alarms left, it never occurred to him to tell anyone.

Russ stares at the screen, peering at logged data and pondering the information with the limited knowledge he has. He never notices the numbers blasting across the screens. Sometimes, he secretly wonders exactly what it is he's supposed to be doing down here. No one gives him the information he needs to do his job. All he can do is watch and wonder.

All the watching and wondering grates on him so he pushes away from his desk and stretches in his chair. His eyes are unfocused, the result of staring at a computer screen for hours trying to suss out information that doesn't want to be visible. Russ is nothing if not tenacious when it comes to figuring out problems.

*****

He pushes away at the crack with increasing force and feels it start to give. His finger twitches again. With this twitch the King of Dreams sends a message to his shadows. There are humans here and he needs one of them. Any of them will do. Draw one of them in and control him. Shut this prison down.

＊＊＊＊＊

Russ's bleary eyes and numbed brain only barely manage to catch and process the next burst of numbers flying across the live monitor screen. It takes a few seconds for the message to hit his brain and a few more seconds for his brain to realize something just happened. Russ is tired and desperately wants to write it off as an optical illusion, but he's thorough and decides to check it out.

He loads up the log on his computer and runs a quick search routine. What he finds wakes him up immediately: whatever the sensors recorded last night has been going on, in increasing frequency, this morning. His first pass through the data from xrs3a makes him think his search routine is borked. After a quick check of his logic and a quick check at the timestamps Russ is convinced the problem is not on his end. There have been no less than ten more signals this morning, starting at 8am and continuing more and more frequently over the past couple of hours.

"Shit," he says out loud.

"What's up?" James asks him, looking up from his own data.

Russ ignores him and spins to look at the guy on the pedestal. The man looks the same, still and quiet as a grave.

"There have been ten more signals this morning," Russ tells James.

"What?"

"Check the live feed," Russ says.

Both Russ and George grab their own copies of the fresh data and run their own searches on it. George's routine finishes first, which helps inflate his ego. The data deflates his ego immediately.

James just stares at his screen.

"Why didn't the alarms go off?" James finally asks.

"What alarms?" Russ asks.

"All of this stuff is supposed to trigger an alarm when anything strange happens," George says.

"I didn't hear a thing," James says.

"Yeah, me neither," Russ says. "Where are the alarms?"

"Back there, behind the servers," George says, pointing toward a shadowy part of the cave.

They all stare at the dark shadows and shudder a little.

"We need to find out what's up with the alarms. Hap will want to know," James says.

"Maybe if we all go together…" Russ says.

They're spared from having to face their fears when one of the armed guards suddenly spins and points his gun at the shadowy area behind the servers. "Who's there?" he yells.

His partner whirls around and simply says, "Status?"

"Definitely saw movement, sir," the first guy responds.

The other armed guard immediately brings his gun up to his shoulder and points it where his partner is aiming. Without hesitation, the first guard flicks on the flashlight under the barrel of his gun and cautiously steps forward, leading with his weapon.

Everything stops while the guard is moving forward. Russ has to force himself to breathe.

The guard steps into the area behind the shadows and shines his light around. Not seeing anything, he steps into the darkness and pauses slightly. Russ can't be certain, but he thinks he sees a shadow brush the guard.

The guard's eyes are black when he comes out the other side. He doesn't hesitate before shooting his partner twice in the face.

Russ and George immediately duck. James freezes like a deer stuck in the headlights of an oncoming semi. The guard calmly shoots him. Blossoms of red explode from James's chest and he dies with a stunned look on his face, falling into his desk and scattering papers everywhere. George screams and Russ desperately tries to pretend he's somewhere else.

The guard ignores them and heads toward a large electrical box in the back of the room.

"Shit!" Russ yells, "He's going to shut off the electricity."

*****

The crack in the prison is large enough to look through now and he smiles as sees the chaos unfold. These pathetic humans sought to understand him? What a laugh. Humans are good for one thing and one thing only: ruling. His domain has been restricted to the land of dreams for far too long. He obeyed the rules, kept to the treaty, and look what it got him. They all turned against him for a dalliance. If they want to ally themselves with Fear, let them.

The truce is over and the land of dreams is about to be expanded.

He reaches out with his mind, pushing through the crack in his prison and smiling as it expands. For the first time in decades his amber eyes open. He still has trouble moving his body but control is returning. He reaches out and finds a shadow. Information floods between them. If only he could use a shadow to shut down the field he'd be home free, but the shadows are insubstantial things.

The humans are panicking now. It won't be long before they bolt for the door. Just in case everything falls apart, the King of Dreams quickly builds a backup plan. A shadow slinks across the floor straight at one cowering human.

*****

George is crouched beneath his desk and doesn't notice the shadow crawling toward him. It touches him and his mind is filled with a single message: A God of Dreams needs a prophet. George finally understands what they've been watching this whole time. It was never a man, it only looked like a man because, well, why the hell not? What does a dream look like? Why can't it wear a suit and hang out under Albuquerque? It's a dream personified, it can do whatever it wants. It was held in place, falsely imprisoned and needs to escape. The prison walls are crumbling and the God of Dreams has chosen him.

A prophet, George thinks to himself. *I'll be a prophet. Someone important.*

Quietly, George Smith creeps out of the cave and yells for General Hapablap before sneaking to the elevator and quietly disappearing. He knows he has a lot of work to do to prepare for his new master. A church must be built. A new church for a real God. It will take time, but he will sweep away the old, false gods and build a mighty temple to the one, true God.

A shadow has wrapped itself around George's leg, quietly feeding thoughts and ideas to the new prophet of the Church of the Holy Dreamtime.

General Hapablap sprints into the nerdery and find chaos and blood. At least two people are dead. The remaining guard's hands are almost on a large lever on the box when General Hapablap shoots him twice in the back and the guard collapses in a heap on the floor.

*****

The prison walls collapse and the King of Dreams rises like Cthulhu awakening. His shadows fill him with information: visions, recordings, things that happened while he was trapped. He processes the data rapidly, anger welling up in him that not only was he trapped here but these tiny ... things had the temerity to think they could study and understand him.

Vengeance is coming, he thinks. He stands and starts to walk into the world when a force stops him. All around the dais is a blue, pulsing mandala. It glows with power.

He shrugs and tries to flicker back to the Dreaming lands. The world flickers around him but he can't leave. He screams in rage and pounds his fists on the invisible wall holding him in place. So, Fear's little prison had a backup wall. There's only one person who could build this kind of power.

John Begay will pay for this.

In the interim, maybe he can get one of the humans to break the circle for him.

*****

Russ notices the man on the pedestal is no longer on the pedestal; he's standing and his eyes are full of fury, literally glowing with rage. Russ can feel his anger at being caged from all the way across the room.

Shadows are moving around the room, circling like sharks. Russ doesn't know what the shadows are, but shadows that move on their own can't be good.

"Hap!" Russ yells and points at the guy standing there glaring at them.

"What the hell is going on here?" Senator Bedfellow yells from the doorway.

"Get out of here!" Hapablap yells. "Take everyone with you!"

Bedfellow doesn't hesitate. He bolts out the door like a blur in an expensive suit.

"Hap, come on!" Russ yells.

"Go on, son. I'll see what I can do to hold it off. Get that pretty secretary out of here," Hapablap calmly tells Russ.

A quick look back and when he sees Russ still standing there, General Royce Hapablap realizes he needs his command voice. "Go!" he says simply.

This time, Russ doesn't hesitate. He gives Hap one last look and heads out. On the way out, he finds Bethany standing by the elevator, nervously wringing her hands.

"He left," she says in a daze. "He left and told me to stay down here. He said someone would come down and he needed me to let them in."

Russ wraps an arm around her and she leans into him. "Why did he leave?" she asks him.

"I don't know," Russ says, "but we're in trouble. Come on. Let's check the monitors in your office."

He takes her hand and together they run to her office. Inside is a bank of monitors that shows the scene in the office upstairs. As they watch, that Robinson creep sticks a key in the elevator lock and twists it before pulling it out.

Russ's heart collapses and Bethany sinks into her chair.

"That son of a bitch just froze the elevator," Russ mumbles.

Robinson and his cronies stare at the elevator door for a moment before retaking their positions. Robinson sits in his desk and glares at the front door. The two guards stand on either side of the room and face the front door.

"He trapped us," Bethany whispers. "Why would he trap us down here?"

"He's a politician," Russ says. "He's covering his ass and he doesn't care who he has to step over to do it."

"What happened in there?" Bethany asks again.

Russ thinks for a bit. How does he explain what happened? She doesn't know what he does or what's in the cave. She may or may not have the clearance for the information and she definitely doesn't have need to know. Screw it.

"We've been watching something sleep in there," he finally says. "It woke up. It somehow took over a guard and used him to shoot some people. Hap shot the guard."

"We're in trouble, aren't we?" she asks him.

"Yes," Russ whispers. "We're in trouble."

Distantly they hear a gunshot and Russ knows something bad just happened to Hap.

*****

The man fought well, like a true warrior. The God of Dreams sent shadows with a simple message: release me and I'll let you go. The man didn't move. The shadows pushed further into his head, releasing nightmare visions of a wife leaving and a family turning their backs but the man stayed still, rooted to his spot.

The God of Dreams could feel the dedication in the man; the General had made a promise to keep the world safe and he aimed keep it. Too late, the God of Dreams noticed the man pointing a gun at his own temple.

The gunshot echoed and the connection was severed.

*****

"Stay here, lock the door," Russ tells Bethany. "I can't promise anything, but I'm going to see what I can do."

"Don't leave," she whispers.

"I'm sorry," Russ tells her. "I promise you, I'll be back. We'll find a way out of here. In the meantime, try the phones, email, anything you can think of."

"Okay," Bethany says, steeling herself. It helps her to have something to think about. "Come back, please. You owe me a date."

Russ can't help but smile, but it's a sad smile. He finally got up the nerve to ask her out and, like so much of his life, it was just too late. Well, this time he's not just going to lie down. He's going to find a way to save her.

"I wouldn't miss it for the world," he tells her and, acting completely on impulse, kisses her.

She kisses him back and they cling together, each of them wishing this was a different time and different place for their first kiss.

Russ finally pulls himself away and, with a sad look, says, "I'll be right back," before stepping out the door of Bethany's office. When he hears the door lock he says a silent prayer to someone he hasn't prayed to in years and walks back to Room 2 to face his destiny.

*****

Rage consumes him again. To come so close only to be thwarted. He stares around the room and sends his shadows scurrying, seeking anyone still alive. All he needs is someone to cross over the mandala from the other side and the spell will be broken. Anyone will do, even someone barely alive.

To his dismay, the shadows report everyone is dead. The humans have figured out new and exciting ways to kill each other and their new tools are frightfully effective.

He closes his eyes and forces himself to be patient. Someone will find him eventually.

*****

Russ lets door number two close and lock. For the time being, no one is getting in or out of this room.

The man in the center of the cave watches Russ impassively, like a cat watching a bird with a broken wing. Russ stares back. He doesn't know what the guy in the center of the cave is, but he does know the guy's not going anywhere right now.

Russ is so focused on the guy in center of the cave he almost trips over Hap. He knees down to check on the general and finds the entire top of Hap's head is missing. From the look of things, Hap did it himself. Hap's gun lies nearby.

"Turn off the wall, please," the man in the center tells Russ. His voice is hypnotic and soft, carrying the promise of warm comforters and pleasant dreams.

The wall? Oh, the circle. Russ looks at the man and realizes he's not crossing the circle. If he turns the circle off, the guy's free.

"No," Russ says.

"I said please," the man responds. "Do it. Let me out of here."

"No."

The man sighs and Russ catches movement out of the corner of his eye. Someone or something else is in here with them.

"I definitely should have used Smith to get out of here before sending him out to the world."

"Smith?" Russ asks. "George Smith?"

"Yes, him," the man says dismissively. "He is to be my prophet, but I guessed at least one of you would help a man in need."

"Your prophet?"

"My, aren't you Mr. Questions. Yes, my dear boy. My prophet. He is to bear witness to my coming."

"Who are you?"

"You don't know, do you? Lucius never told you his suspicions, did he?" the man asks.

"Lucius?" Russ asks him.

"Senator Lucius Bedfellow. A foul little man who feels he is more important than he really is."

"How do you know about him?"

"I know about all of you. My shadows watched you all as I slept and sent the images clear as day when I woke up. I watched Bedfellow tell me his pitiful plans to use me to seize the power of this country. I listened when he told me what he did to poor Dr. Hayha. Lucius Bedfellow was not a man who knew when to shut up."

Russ pauses, stunned. This man, or whatever he is, has been watching them all since the beginning and Senator Bedfellow was talking to him.

"What are you?" Russ finally asks.

"I am what your tiny mind would call the God of Dreams. What I truly am is beyond your understanding. Suffice it to say, I am dreams."

The man calmly watches Russ, obviously waiting for a response, but Russ isn't sure how to respond. Does he kneel? Does he bow? Does he let this God of Dreams go? The man, or whatever he is, is directly responsible for four deaths this morning alone. A part of Russ thinks if this guy gets free a whole bunch more people are going to die.

"I…," Russ hesitates. "I can't let you out."

"I was worried you'd say that," the God of Dreams says.

Like a blur, the shadow is on Russ, swallowing him, singing songs of hatred and fear in his head. The God of Dreams is angry now, enraged at his being imprisoned, baffled that they refuse to release him. Oh, well, it may be a vulgar display of power, but sometimes one must demonstrate one's power.

His shadows are a part of him, an early warning system and a way of projecting power. Truth be told, he's actually made of those shadows and those shadows are made of dreams. Just like dreams, the shadows, and therefore God of Dreams, can haunt minds, make things seem real or fake.

The shadow pours over Russ and works its way into his mind. It shows him the horrible things that will befall him if he refuses to break the circle. It shows him the rewards for obedience, gold and women and everything he desires.

It would be so easy to let the God of Dreams out, to follow his desires and submit to his will instead of fighting. He could just give in and save himself. Maybe this god would save B… No, mustn't think of her, must keep her secret and safe. This thing filled his head with horrors. It would share those horrors with others.

No, it's best to keep it here, keep it away from the world.

Russ Johnson has never felt himself the hero type, but he musters his strength and, for the sake of the world, and the sake of her, plunges his fingers into his eyes. The pain is enormous, worse than anything he's felt before, but it clears his head and he feels in control of himself once more.

Lying there, screaming on the floor, pain is all he feels, but a small part of senses the shadow has left and wonders if by hurting himself he hurt the shadow or the God of Dreams. He wishes he could open his eyes but remembers he doesn't have them anymore.

The pain. He has to stop the pain. If he's going to die down here, Russ feels like he needs to die his way. He feels around the floor until his hand touches something cold and metallic. Hap's gun.

Russ has never fired a gun, but he knows the basics. He fumbles around delicately, worried about accidentally firing the gun. Russ has to chuckle to himself; he's about to shoot himself and he's worried about shooting himself accidentally.

A little shifting and Russ finally manages to put the barrel under his chin. Somewhere, long ago, he'd read that was the best way to kill yourself with a gun was to put it under your chin, not up to your temple. Put the gun to your temple and you run the risk of just blowing your eyes out and not actually dying. He has to chuckle to himself again. What a waste that would be since he's already take out his eyes.

He affords himself a final thought about how today started so well and a final goodbye to the girlfriend who never was and Russ twitches his finger.

The Clock Man

Everyone should have the opportunity to wake up in a dumpster. It's a humbling experience to greet the morning with a splitting headache and covered in *lo mein*.

For a while I lay there in the detritus and wonder if somehow, somewhen, I don't really belong in here with the rest of the trash. It's not like I've lived a life of shining example. More accurately, my life has been a pretty good example of how to not run things.

This garbage heap is actually more comfortable than my normal bed. I might have to consider stealing one and taking back to my hovel. Sunlight is streaming through the space between the flaps, there's a sweet smell of soy sauce in the air and I can't help but think to myself that it's really not a bad time to be alive.

My muscles and joints complain when I try to sit up but desire to know what's outside overrules their relentless grumbling. When I push the lid open with my head the sunlight feels like lasers in my eyes and I wisely decide to wait out the hated orange orb in the sky.

Okay, so I don't hate the star; it just hurts like hell to look at it right now. The other one is easier to deal with, even if that means things never really get dark around here. I lean back against the wall of the dumpster and try to get my poor brain to engage. Comfy as this place is staying here is problematic at best. At some point a trash truck will come lumbering along and dump my sorry butt into a larger heap of trash.

I really need some coffee. Or better yet, some *baiju*. Some of the sweet White Alcohol would dull the pain and make me feel more like my calm, cool, and collected self.

My eyes itch, probably from the chile sauce on the noodles. What kind of filthy savage dumps spicy noodles on a guy in a dumpster? For all he knew, I could have just been sleeping off a bender in the only quiet place in this fair city.

I push the lid up again and sunlight burns, but it's more like burning yourself on a toaster than pouring lye in your eyes. The dark still feels better so I let the lid drop back down again.

So, let's see. What happened last night? I have a vague recollection of a bottle of *baiju* with my name on it and a heady desire to take that bottle and make it my sweet lover for the evening. The distilled sorghum had other plans, though, and made me its plaything instead. There was some yelling. I think there was a brunette in a tight red dress. There was also …

Ah, man. I lean back against the wall of the dumpster and groan. I got in a fight with some cops.

I wonder if I won. There was a time when I could go through cops like tissue paper, but that was when I was one. Now I'm just a guy who hangs out in dumpsters and does shady things for money. Okay, so I did those things when I was a cop, too, but … Oh, screw it.

Crap. If I did win the cops will be gunning for me. If I lost, I'll never live it down. This is the main reason I don't get into fights with cops. There are a lot of them and they don't take kindly to losing. The other reason is I need them to keep my nascent business afloat.

Yes. I was a cop. Don't hold it against me. I was young and I needed the money.

Now? Well, how should I describe what I do now? Finder? Problem solver? General rogue and rapscallion is probably more accurate. I like to think of myself as a thorn in the side of the ruling class but the truth is they don't even notice my existence and I'm barely better than a hired thug with half a brain and a lack of compunctions.

I was a cop, after all.

Outside my temporary safe house I can hear the sounds of the world going by. My city is an elegant – if sometimes toxic – mix of Chinese mysticism and *Gwai Lo* steel. They built the railroads with strong backs and stronger magic. We provided the steel and the knowhow and they connected the land from sea to shining sea.

We may be second-class citizens to the Chinese, but they respect our ability to make things.

Overhead I can hear the deep basso thrum of a Yuan patrol blimp. It must be about 10am and I've spent too much time hiding from the world. Time to get my ass out of this dumpster and face the music.

The light hurts my eyes and the sounds, muffled inside the dumpster, are an all-out assault on my senses. I have to choke down the desire to crawl back into my soy sauce filled casket but one look at the festering pile of noodles convinces me to move on.

As my eyes adjust to the light I find a shadow standing in front of me. The man is tall, slender, and wearing a *dǒulì* – one of those conical bamboo hats – that falls slightly over his eyes. He's standing stock still, staring calmly at the dumpster.

"About time, Crow," the man says in a deep Southern growl. "Thought you were gonna sleep all day."

"I was looking for whoever's been leaving corpses in the dumpsters," I tell him.

"I thought you might be corpse for a moment there," he replies.

"What can I say? It was quiet and I was comfortable."

"You're a lazy man, Crow."

"I am indeed," I reply.

"There's someone who'd like to meet your acquaintance," he says. "This time without the alcohol."

I brush the noodles off my duster and appraise the man in front of me. My jacket is waxed cotton with a touch of magic from my cleaner. The noodles and sauce slide off easily without leaving a trace. "Who am I meeting?" I ask.

"A young woman of considerable importance," he replies.

Images of last night flood my brain. There was a young woman there. She was wearing a red dress and I probably made a total ass of myself. I feel like I should blame someone. The *baiju* will have to do until I can find a suitable victim for my ire.

"Would this young woman of considerable importance happen to be wearing a red dress?" I ask.

"Not at the moment, no."

The sigh of relief I exhale could power a wind farm for a week. At least I didn't make an ass of myself in front of someone of considerable importance.

"She's wearing a jade wrap now. You threw up on her red dress last night."

Fuck me running. I knew I should have stayed in the dumpster. "Where is she?" I ask.

He points down the alley at the main drag. Across the street is small, run-down diner. "Madam Chow's," he says.

"Well, Chan," I say. "Let's get moving."

II

Chan is a kind of warrior ascetic, a man who took the Chinese legends a bit too far and believed all the *wuxia* wire-work was real. I don't know his full name – no one does – but I can guarantee you he's no Shaolin monk. His voice is a dead giveaway. No matter how he dresses, no matter how much he tries to dress the part, his Southern drawl doesn't fit his bamboo hat.

"So, what's the deal Chan? Why did I have to get out of bed?" I ask.

"A dumpster is your bed now, Crow?" he growls. "You have truly fallen."

"It comes with breakfast," I tell him, knowing full well the breakfast was someone else's dinner.

Chan stops and puts a hand on my chest. I can't see his eyes under the shadow of the hat, but his lips are set in a line and I can tell he's glaring at me. "You were better than this," he tells me. "I think you still are better than this."

"Chill out, Chan," I say. "I'm fine."

"You threw up on a woman last night."

"Is that a crime?" I ask.

In cases like this I like to mask my desire to punch him in the back of the head with pathetic attempts at humor. I've been told I have anger issues and advised to get them under control before I wind up dragon food. Also, Chan would beat my ass down before I even knew what hit me.

"In the case of this woman, it probably is," Chan says. I don't know how he does it, but he manages to growl out a sigh.

"Come on!" I say. My head is throbbing and I'm really not in the mood for his moralizing. "Haven't you ever thrown up on a woman before?"

"No," he says simply.

"You need to get out more," I tell him.

He grunts in reply and leads me to the main street. Huo Yuanjia Ave is the city's main street, bisecting it neatly down the middle from North to South. The area we're in is relatively quiet now but gets noisy at night when the tourists show up to watch spectacle. No, not the spectacle of me throwing up on some woman. Every night the Wuxia district erupts into partying, drinking, and martial arts madness.

If you want to spar in the streets with strangers you'll find the best in the world right here. Actually, the best in the world is walking right next to me. Chan may have the lanky build and the color of a skeleton but he can move like a snake when he wants to. I fought him once, high on my giant ego and a bottle of cheap *baiju*.

It was absolutely no contest. I've fought cops, bad guys, the odd devil, and groups of all of the above and walked away; Chan dropped me with one punch and I didn't even see him move. After that I begged him, literally begged him to teach me.

His tutelage was brutal but effective and we've been friends ever since then. He's still strange, but you'll never find a better friend in the world. I love him like a brother and hate him all at the same time. Chan represents everything I could have been; everything I should have been but never was and never will be.

The people who came to watch the fights decided they wanted drinks and the bars opened. Then they wanted food and the restaurants opened. Dancing followed and the clubs became famous. Every night it's a party down here and I've lived down here for a very long time. The crime followed right after the clubs showed up. It was petty stuff at first; drugs and prostitution, but things got worse as the gangs started fighting each other for territory.

Then the cops got involved and we were the biggest, baddest street gang around. There was so much crime down we couldn't stop it all and there were some things going on that even we didn't want any part of.

The major clubs and restaurants are closed now, quiet and sulking in the daylight like petulant children who've had their toys taken away. People still live here during the day and Huo Yuanjia Ave caters best to its adopted sons and daughters. Hidden in the little unlit doorways between the clubs are the finest parts of this city; the little hole-in-the-wall places that make the capital of Aluna such a special place.

In between The Jade Dragon and The Tears of Heaven lies a single doorway with "No Admittance" written on it. Chan knocks three times in rapid succession and once more slowly. A slat in the door opens and a hidden voice says, "We're closed. *Wuxia* demo is tonight."

Before the slat can close, Chan says, "Mrs. Chow will be disappointed."

The slat stops closing and I get the distinct impression the whirring and clicking in the air is more than the normal clocks and assorted timekeepers patiently marking the passage of time. Somewhere nearby is a vidder and we're the stars of the show.

"What'd you say?" the voice says.

"I said 'Mrs. Chow will be disappointed'." Chan says calmly. "And will probably consider it a personal affront if you keep us waiting much longer. We are expected."

Chan has a way speaking that makes his rigid formality seem smooth, even frightening. I can almost smell the fear growing in the guy behind the door. Whoever he is, he's not too bright. "And who are you?" he snips.

The bamboo hat rises and the guy behind the door gets his first look at the stormy eyes of the *wushu* master. His hat is nothing special; lots of people on Aluna wear them. Those eyes are another thing entirely. Just like he won't talk about the gravelly voice (I think he secretly smokes), Chan has never explained why his eyes have storms in them.

It's very unnerving talking to someone whose eyes light up with lightning strikes.

"I am Chan," he tells the voice.

I hear a gasp and an immediate rattling. Locks are slid out of place and soon the door swings open on rusty hinges. Inside is a big guy wearing a shirt decorated with pictures of various strippers. He's obviously hired muscle, the kind of guy who breaks fingers for fun and profit, but he actually bows when he meets Chan.

"It's an honor, sir," the man says with a deep bow.

"Did you enjoy keeping my guests waiting?" a woman's voice asks down the hall.

The man in the stripper shirt goes white. I can see the indecision in his eyes; does he bow to Mrs. Chow and risk the ire of Chan or continue bowing to Chan and hope for the best with his employer? Considering his choices I can happily say I'm glad I'm not him. Chan could kill the guy with a finger. Mrs. Chow would make him suffer.

He chooses the less painful option and bows deeply to the woman.

Mrs. Chow is - how shall I put this delicately? – involved in the less legal aspects of the *Ch'uan* region of town. She's not a regular criminal; she's the mobster other criminals are terrified of. Hell, I'm terrified of her. Even the police are wary of Mrs. Chow. No one knows her first name. No one knows where she came from; she showed up one day and, through some sort of machinations, took over a huge part of town.

She's a small woman, slightly over five feet tall and probably weighs a hundred pounds soaking wet. I've seen her toss guys twice her size around like they're rag dolls. It's seriously amazing; she turns into this little blur with black hair and emerald green eyes. Even the air gets out of her way when she moves.

"My apologies, madam Chow," the muscle blubbers. "I did not know they were your honored guests."

"I didn't say they were honored guests," she tells him as she stares at me. "Just that they were my guests."

The guard is still bowing down to her and hoping his act of supplication will save him from whatever Hells she has locked up in the basement. I've heard rumors, and the rumors are enough to keep me quiet.

"You may go now," Mrs. Chow says.

The guy manages to bow and walk at the same time. Fear of the unknown is a great motivator; it lets you do things you didn't know you could do.

"We apologize for our tardiness," Chan says quietly.

Mrs. Chow eyes him warily and he returns the stare. I can't help but feel like I'm stuck in a room with a pair of fighting lizards. These guys may be the two most dangerous people in town and each of them knows it. Fortunately for all of us they've chosen different life arcs. Each collects power but they collect it in different ways: Mrs. Chow seeks to control the city underworld, Chan just wants absolute mastery over himself.

She blinks first. "It is not a problem, Chan," Mrs. Chow says quietly.

"Thank you for your hospitality, Mrs. Chow," Chan says with a slight bow. "You honor us by providing your great venue."

He's such the diplomat. If it were up to me I'd be raiding the bar and throwing knives at the guards. Speaking of which, where is the bar around here?

"It is my pleasure to provide my humble bar for this esteemed meeting," she says. "Please, follow me."

Without a word she turns on a heel and stalks down the hall. The click of her heels echoes on the *changmu* floors of her mostly empty club. Chan waves me forward and I hesitantly follow the small woman through the club. She pauses behind the bar and presses a hidden button.

The room seems to get taller and it takes me a moment to realize the rest of the room isn't growing, the floor I'm standing on is falling into the ground. The old hidden stair trick. I must be getting slow in my old age; I didn't even notice them and I walked right over them.

Mrs. Chow pushes past me and walks down the stairs muttering under her breath. A huge string of Chinese curses whispers down the dark stairwell but the only one I can pick out is *Gao yang jong duh goo yang*: Motherless goats of all motherless goats.

I guess she's not happy about us being here, either. My pulse pounds more the further down the stairs I go. I'm somewhat – no, scratch that – I'm extremely claustrophobic.

At the bottom of the stairs is a small room I've only heard whispered about. They say this is where dreams come to die, the Hell of the underworld, the place where Mrs. Chow meets her problems head on.

The room is solid stone, a square about twenty feet on a side and lit with a single bare bulb. The light is sickly and distant and the gray walls make it feel like a tomb. It's cold and dank and feels exactly unlike the streets. I've just gotten here, but I already hate it. The walls are solid and the rational part of my mind tells me everything will be fine but my animal mind is screaming at me to leave. Chan is right behind me, a hand on my shoulder gently pushing me forward.

"So," I say, trying to act like I'm not sweating profusely. "Will there be drinks at this little *huìyì*?"

When I'm nervous I tend to throw around the miniscule amount of Chinese I know; it makes me look smarter than I really am.

Mrs. Chow snorts and points to an empty chair at the table. Across the table, calmly smoking a *bidi* is a stunning blonde woman. Her bored eyes lock onto me and she looks me up and down, a wry smile playing across her lips. Something about her looks familiar. She feels like a ghost from my past or a dream come to life. Where do I know this woman from?

The blonde inhales deeply and exhales a cloud of sweet smelling smoke. "This is legendary Felix Crow?" she asks. It doesn't sound like she's impressed.

"Got an extra one of those?" I ask, gesturing to her hand-wrapped cigarette.

"Depends," she says. "Are you going to throw up on me again?"

I really wish I could remember last night.

"Bad noodles," I say. "Totally not my fault."

"I'm sure," she replies and slides a small cotton bag across the table at me.

I fish a *bidi* out of her bag and feel around the pockets of my jacket looking for my lighter. Ah, there it is, buried underneath a pile of strips of fortune cookie predictions. Without taking my eyes off the strange blonde woman, I light the little cigarette. The smoke is sharp in my throat and I have to suppress a cough and a wanton desire for a shot of *baiju*. "Thanks," I say with a rasp.

She holds her hand out, palm up and I put her bag of *bidis* back in her open palm.

The *bidi* is calming my nerves a bit, but there's still a sense panic gnawing at the edges of my mind. If I don't get out of here soon I'm going to choke someone. Panic makes me edgy and when I'm edgy I lose the few social graces I have left. "Who are you and why am I here?" I ask.

"Sit down before you fall down," the blonde says, gesturing to a single wooden chair opposite her.

This whole thing stinks to high *Tiān*. If I'm lucky my ancestors are watching over me from heaven and have forgotten some of the bad things I've said about them. If not, well, shit.

"I'll stand if it's alright with you," I tell her.

"Suit yourself, but you look shaky," the blonde tells me.

"Sit down Crow," Mrs. Chow says from behind me.

I turn around and find Mrs. Chow glaring at me. Chan has taken up a position next to the door. He looks casual, leaning against the wall with his arms crossed over his chest, but I know he doesn't actually relax. Ever.

"I have no problem with you standing, but our hostess has other ideas. Sit down, Felix. Is it okay if I call you Felix?" the blonde says.

"Sure," I tell her and pull the chair back. The screech of old wood on concrete is terrifying.

I take my time sitting down. If they're going to drag me down here and push me around I fully plan on making their lives miserable for doing it. The chair is about as comfortable as one of those hard plastic things at Yuan's (over a million noodles bowls sold!), but it feels amazing on my ass. Gods above, I'm getting old.

"Comfy?" the blonde asks.

Squirming around seems like a good idea right now. "No," I tell her. "I usually require better furniture when I'm being strong-armed. It's in the contract."

She raises an eyebrow.

"My associate back there," I say, pointing a thumb at Chan, "should have given you the requisite 'strong-arming Felix Crow' contract. It clearly states my requirement for comfortable seats when I'm being pushed around."

"Felix…" she starts.

"Yeah," I interrupt.

"You're not being strong-armed," she continues. "I'd like to retain your services."

"My services?"

"You are Felix Crow, formerly of the local constabulary, retired after an unspecified incident, now a finder and fixer of problems. I have a problem I would like found and fixed."

"A problem?"

"Are you going to answer every question with another question?" she asks.

"Is it bothering you?"

"No, I find it almost as charming as when you threw up on me last night," she says with an extreme eye roll.

"Then we're off to a wonderful start," I tell her with my best fake genuine grin. "What's your name, or should I just call you 'Blondie'?"

"Would it make you happy?" she asks.

"Touché," I say. "So who are you?"

The blonde changes her legs, crossing the left over the right, and leans forward. She methodically stubs the *bidi* out in a ceramic ashtray and leans back again. "You really don't recognize me," she says.

I take a deep drag on my *bidi* and smash it out before I exhale. "Nope. Not a clue."

"He's never been the most perceptive person," Mrs. Chow says from behind me. I'd really love to smash her smirking face in right now.

"He tends to focus completely on the task," Chan growls.

"I'm sure the booze isn't helping things," the blonde says.

"Fuck you all," I say and start to get up.

Chan's hand on my shoulder pushes me back down into the seat and holds me there. From here I could break his arm. It would be trivial. He'd still beat me half to death, but I could break his arm.

"Just listen, Crow," Chan growls quietly.

"Fine," I say and brush his hand off. "What's the game here, sweetheart? You've got the crime queen of Aluna and the badass of all time helping you pull my sorry ass down into this hole. You want something? Spit it out. I'm grumpy and hungry and all I want to do is drink a gallon of coffee and sit on my porch and hope the world fucks itself to death."

She sighs and says, "My name is Alyssa Zhào. I need your help. I wanted your friend Chan here but he lacks your ability to get into locked places and he's busy anyway."

"Zhào," I say. "Any relation to Chenming Zhào?"

"He's my father," she says.

Shit.

Chenming Zhào is the single most important person on the planet. All those clicks and whirs on the street? He synchronizes them. He makes the world move and aligns the gears of Aluna. He's the current Clock Man, to use the parlance of our time.

I lean back in my chair and examine the blonde in light of my new information. I don't know much about her; she manages to keep out of the spotlight. If her dad really is Chenming, she's the daughter of the single most important person on the planet. That kind of relationship means she's got a lot of resources available to her.

"Okay," I say, "if you are who you say you are, what do you need with me?"

"I need to speak with my father," she says.

"So go talk. The tower is open from eight to eight every day," I tell her.

That's one thing about Chenming; he may be the most important person on the planet, but the Clock Man is also one of the easiest people in the world to go see. He's part mystic, part engineer, but he's always available.

"The tower is open, but no one has seen my father in weeks," Alyssa says. There's a hint of worry in her eyes.

"What are you talking about?" I ask. "He was in the news just last week."

"A letter on his stationery, nothing more," she replies, leaning forward.

"Well, he's probably working on something," I say, waving my hand dismissively. I really don't have time for this crap. "He does keep the world running, you know."

"He's always supposed to be accessible. He's never ignored me before," she says.

There's genuine concern in her eyes. It's probably nothing, but whatever's going on it's got her rattled and I don't suspect much rattles Alyssa Zhào.

"Okay," I say. "What do you want from me?"

She stops and looks me in the eye like she's searching for something in my head but can't be certain it's there. Her gaze is steady; sharp and piercing. I can't help but feel small and weak under those emerald eyes.

"Honestly, Mr. Crow, I didn't want you. I wanted Chan but he is unavailable," Alyssa says. I guess she was searching for a bit of competence in me. Good luck with that quest, toots.

I look back at Chan. His face is impenetrable but he shrugs slightly.

"Good to know I'm your sloppy seconds," I say.

"Charming," Alyssa replies and lights another *bidi*. She looks at Mrs. Chow and says, "I think this was a mistake. Thank you for your time."

"Wait," Chan says. His gravelly voice is quiet but seems to echo off the walls. "Crow can do this."

"What?" I ask, "Do what?"

"He's a ruffian, a drunkard, and a fool," Mrs. Chow says, "but he's your best bet."

Alyssa takes a drag and exhales. For a moment I'm staring at a dragon with pale white skin, piercing green eyes, and blonde hair. Dragons run this world and it wouldn't surprise me if one had put on the skin of this woman to fool me. "What guarantee will you offer me?" she asks.

"If he fails…" Mrs. Chow starts.

"If he fails," Chan interrupts, "I'll kill him myself."

I stand up and spin around to face him. As usual he's unreadable. "What is going on?" I ask.

"I can feel him in the tower but I can't get to him," Alyssa says. "Something is terribly wrong and I don't think it can be fixed."

The walls are closing in on me again and these idiots aren't helping things. I reach for Alyssa's bag of *bidis* but she pulls them close to her. They're still within reach, though, so I snatch the bag away from her and light one up.

"You're fast," she says. "Faster than I thought."

I throw the bag back at her and now it's my turn to stare. There's only so much pushing around and mystery I can handle before I start getting really pissed. "You should see my speed vomiting," I tell her.

She fumbles with the bag, not really accepting that I just threw her own bag of *bidis* at her. A wry smile crosses her lips like she just found what she was looking for and can't believe it was in front of her the whole time.

"What you want from me?" I ask.

"I want you to infiltrate the tower, find my dad, and kill him," she says.

"What?" I ask. "Why do you want me to kill him?"

"Truth?" she asks.

"Truth," I say. "No more bullshit about being able to feel him."

"Someone came to my house last week and tried to get me to go with him," she says.

"Is that out of the ordinary?"

"Whoever it was called me *méihuā*," she says. "That's what my dad used to call me when I was a little girl."

"I'm sure a lot of dads call their daughters plum blossom," I say.

"Possibly," she replies, "but when I pressed him on where we were going he got agitated and tried to grab me. The way he talked, it sounded like my dad."

"So?" I ask.

"It wasn't my dad at the door. But it was my dad at the door. He's gotten himself into something," she says. "Something terrible. He used to tell me he thought he could control people; I think he's found a way."

"Okay…," I say, trailing off. Alyssa's obviously nuts.

"I know my dad," she says. "He's gone off the rails."

Pot meet kettle. Oh, well. She's rich so she's not crazy; she's eccentric. But eccentric people have money. "What's the pay?" I ask. I never work for free.

"Anything your heart desires," she says with a wink.

While a roll in the hay with Alyssa Zhào would be a fun way to kill an hour or so, I've got more important things on my mind. "Anything?" I ask.

"Anything in my power to get," Alyssa says.

"I'll kill your dad and get back to you on the payment," I tell her.

III

After someone drops a bomb like wanting me to kill the Clock Man I like to retreat into a bowl of noodles and a bottle of *baiju*, but Chan has other plans. We make our way upstairs to the quiet bar and the space greets me with the promise of clean air and freedom. I hope I never have to see the tomb below again.

Chan's in a strange mood today. Strange even by his bizarre standards. When we hit the top of the stairs he plants a hand on my shoulder and guides me to the bar. No matter how much I want to go outside and feel the sunlight on my face I know better than to fight him. I'm tough, but he's on a whole other level. The man can sling pain like no one else I've ever met so I put on my docile face and sit where I'm told.

Someday, I swear, I'm going to enjoy hurting my best friend. Maybe not today, maybe not tomorrow, but he and I have a reckoning coming.

Mrs. Chow appears behind the bar like magic and gently places two glasses in front of us. She reaches below the bar but Chan holds up a hand and says, "We'll have water, please."

"Suit yourself, freak," Mrs. Chow says with a scowl. She's well known for her customer service.

"I'll have whatever you have under the bar," I start but Chan shakes his head.

"Water will do for both of us," he says to no one in particular. I like to think he's talking to Mrs. Chow and I just got caught in the cross fire but a tingling in my danger senses tells me I was the intended target.

I hate water.

Mrs. Chow pours out two cups full of water and places a glass decanter embellished with her dragon emblem in front of us. The decanter is full of crystal clear water and ice. Cold sweat slowly drips down the side of the green dragons and their red eyes stare at me, accusing me of some crime I didn't even know I'd committed.

I'm not saying I haven't committed it, just that I don't remember committing it.

"Would you like some noodles?" Chan asks.

"I think I may still have some in my pocket," I tell him.

"Those are inedible, Crow."

Chan, for all his wisdom, all his strength, all his intelligence and warmth, never did understand jokes. Since he doesn't get humor and I don't get being serious it's kind of amazing we get along as well as we do. He holds up two fingers and Mrs. Chow sighs and barks something I don't quite catch to whoever is working in her kitchen. Whoever's back there yells, "*Shì de qíngfù.*"

Interesting. Her staff calls her Mistress.

"Where are you going, Chan?" I ask.

"What makes you think I'm going anywhere?" he asks.

"Alyssa said you were unavailable," I say, sniffing the water.

"A man can be unavailable without going anywhere," he replies.

"Yeah, but this sounds like it would be trivial for you. Sneak in, kill someone, sneak out. It would take you half an hour tops," I say. "The only way you wouldn't do it is if you weren't around."

He smiles, which is rare thing for Chan. "Two reasons," he tells me. "The first is exactly what you just did."

"What's that?"

"Put two and two together and came up with nine."

"Two plus two is four," I say.

"Yes, but the right answer was nine. You figured out something without all the information. That will come in handy. You're better at that than anyone I've ever known."

"Thanks," I tell him and take a sip of my water. So cold, so wet, so bland. "What's the second reason? The real reason?"

"I need to go to Earth," he says.

"Why would you want to do that?" I ask. Everyone knows Earth is a train wreck. Sure, a lot of us came from there, but no one really wants to go back.

There's a bustle of activity and Mrs. Chow sets steaming cups of noodle soup in front of us. I can smell the soy sauce and sriracha chiles. Chan happily sniffs at his and dips a big ladle-like spoon in the soup. His appreciation is palpable. Even if I can't see his face because of that ridiculous hat his whole body shows how much he's enjoying the soup.

Since he's preoccupied, I take a spoonful myself. The sriracha sauce – that amazing blend of garlic and near-lethal chiles – offsets the salty soy sauce. Mrs. Chow's food is everything I've ever heard it was; *Tiān* in a bowl.

We eat our soup quietly and I can't help but think *baiju* would make this so much better. It's a way we have here; you never converse during the meal. Before the meal and after the meal conversation is expected, but it's seriously disrespectful to your food to talk while you're eating. Noodles of this quality especially deserve full attention.

When Chan finishes – just before I do – he pushes his bowl forward and pours us more water. He'll wait patiently while I eat. After my last spoonful of noodles I say a small thank you prayer and push my empty bowl forward.

"There's a boy on Earth who is in danger," Chan says as if the pause in the conversation never happened.

"So?" I ask.

"He's got magic, Crow," Chan says. "Serious magic."

I never did get Chan's hang-up with all this harum scarum stuff he spouts all the time. Sure, there's magic here. The whole damned planet is powered by ancient magics. But it's just power, you can make lights shine and clocks move, but he seems to think it can do more than build railroads and make the world move.

"Good luck," I tell him and take another sip of water. Gods above, I hate this stuff.

Chan goes on, prattling away about magic and Earth. Somehow or another he missed the part where I didn't say "Pray tell, this is fascinating, please go on."

"There's still some magic left on that ball. Most of it is concentrated in the hands of a small group of people but it's still there. And sometimes it winds up in unexpected places, like a boy who can pull cookies from the Dreaming Lands."

"Uh huh," I say.

"Every now and then a true *fangshi* – a sorcerer they call them there – is born. One was born a bit back. We weren't sure for a while if he was a true *fangshi* but the watchers we put in place have verified it. Unfortunately, this child has attracted the attention of The Beast."

That caught my attention. There's always someone around here trying to prove they're tougher than everyone else, but I've never heard of this guy. "Who's 'The Beast'?" I ask.

"Someone new. Apparently very dangerous. I need to extract the child before anything bad can happen to him," Chan says. His brow is furrowed in concentration and worry. He must think this kid is something special if he sent watchers over to Earth to keep an eye on things. Watchers take a huge amount of energy to run.

"Anyone seen this 'The Beast'?" I ask.

"No," Chan replies. His eyes get vacant as he remembers something. "Just his handiwork. He set those girls on fire last month. No one can seem to find him. For all his apparent power and reach, he's a phantom."

The girls. Shit. I saw the remains of that and wouldn't wish it on anyone, especially a child. The girls Chan's referring to were a couple of *Jìnǚ* from around here. They pissed off the wrong person and he roasted them in 200 liter drums. It must have taken a long time for them to die and the screams had to have been incredible.

"Who are 'we'?" I ask.

"We?" Chan asks.

"You said 'watchers we put in place'. Who are 'we'?"

"I must learn that for all your drinking and throwing up on powerful people you're extremely attentive, Crow," Chan says with a gravelly laugh. "'We' are a small group trying to explore magic. They're a group of women from up north; they call themselves 'The Furious Fae.'"

"I've heard of them," I say, biting my tongue slightly. Personally, I think they're a bunch of idiots who have too much free time on their hands.

"They don't keep a low profile," Chan says. Something about the way he says it makes me wonder if he disagrees.

"So you're going to Earth to bring back a kid. What then?"

"Time will tell, but the fates will be kind. I'll do my best to raise him and teach him," Chan says.

"Ever been around kids?" I ask.

Chan shakes his head.

"Good luck," I tell him with a chuckle. "So you and the little guy…"

"*Fangshi*," Chan interrupts. "He is a *fangshi*."

"Yeah, him," I say, wondering if Chan has finally gone completely off the rails. "You're going to what, become some happy little family?"

"I'll teach him and protect him."

"What is it with you and all this magic?" I ask. "You're obsessed with the stuff but you and I know people can't wield it. It's machine stuff."

"How do you think the machines came to be?" Chan asks. "Someone had to have the magic to give it to the machines."

There's a logic to that, but it almost smells circular. We don't know what caused x to happen so it must have been magic. Schools teach that magic was discovered and harnessed by the first Clock Man (Shit, I have to kill the current one tomorrow) but all he does is regulate the flow. I've heard stories about people being able to actually use magic but I rank those stories right up there with the stories about spontaneous combustion.

Chan peers at me and I can tell he sees the gears turning slowly in my head. "You know what your problem is, Crow?"

"I don't have any *baiju*?" I ask.

"You always want a magical solution to your problems but you refuse to realize you can make that magic happen yourself."

Asshole. He keeps dragging our conversations back to magic like some kind of damned nut. "You know what your problems is, Chan?" I ask.

"I have no problems," he says.

I decide to ignore the fact that he insists on wearing that hat everywhere and ask, "What has this dogged insistence on magic gotten you?"

"Admittedly nothing so far."

"Exactly," I tell him. "Quit looking for a way to power up your life and just go live it."

Chan gets a queer expression on his face and I can tell he's actually pondering what I just said. I know him; he'll keep chewing on it until he comes to a conclusion and then he'll show up at my doorstep at 3am wanting to discuss it.

"Good luck tomorrow," he tells me. "Remember, you must not fail."

"Good luck with your kid," I reply. "I hope he keeps you up all night when he gets nightmares."

IV

Croatoa is the capital of Aluna. It's a massive, sprawling city filled with the constant clicks and whirs of gears turning, sending Chinese magic to the mystical engines that keep the place running. We kind of parallel Earth's history to a point, a fact that makes some of our scientists want to pull their hair out. The chances of two different planets having even remotely similar lifeforms is astronomical; for two different places to parallel to the point that both places have Chinese culture is so impossible it's mind-blowing. The only thing I can think our planets must have been linked together at some point in the past and ancient Earth's Chinese mystics came here. Someone on the other end closed the tunnel because we can see Earth but they can't see us.

It's enough to make my head hurt just thinking about it.

Overhead wires pulse green and purple sending the various magics around and the air is filled with the constant crackling of arcane energies. It's one of those things you just learn to live with if you want luxuries like light and warm water. I guess that's one of the differences between Aluna and Earth; the electricity that drives Earth simply doesn't work here. Another strange aspect of the universe, you'd think things like electricity would work everywhere but we've brought back the occasional Earth engine and the damned things will start up and produce absolutely nothing but smoke.

The street is filled with various vendors hawking everything from herbal erection remedies to chemical powders guaranteed to stop every ache and pain. The chemicals are a load of hogwash. I had a splitting headache once – no it wasn't a hangover, Chan had punched me during a training session – and stopped at one the chemical booths and bought a packet of white powder. The guy selling it told me to mix it with water and drink it down.

It didn't do a damned thing. My headache finally went away after a bottle of *baiju*.

The herbal remedies are a whole other beast. When I was still a green rookie on the force someone slipped a packet of herbal erection remedies into my coffee. I am not kidding here; I had an erection for three days. The local herbalist told me the *chu'anzu* powder was for older people and chided me for being a young guy and taking it.

When I asked him what I could do about it, he just shrugged and told me to get laid. Not easy to do when you're a rookie. I got the guys back, though. Down one of the back alleys off Tsu Street is a woman who sells breast augmentation pills. A couple of the guys on the force were wearing bras for a week.

Mrs. Chow's noodles are still with me so I ignore the pretty lady trying to sell me roasted bird feet. She pleads and bats long eyelashes and like a sucker I give in and buy a fried tarantula. The legs are the best part.

In front of my apartment, while I'm busy crunching away on my tarantula and wondering what was so important that Chan told me I must not fail, something catches my eye and a little part of my brain clicks. One of those fancy new magic powered carriages is parked in the street. It's a gleaming dark green and brass affront to nature with tan leather seats and no top. The squarish nose of the thing has brass – or is it bronze, I can't remember – pipes sticking out and folding back into the machine. It's gorgeous and hideous and I want one.

Things like that carriage cost a fortune and I don't live in the best part of town. The people around here are nice and all, but that's a lot of food parked in our street. I would have expected it to be a bare frame by now but no one is going anywhere near it. As I get closer I feel why; there's some kind of crackling field surrounding the thing. Get too close and it'll fry your eyeballs right out of your head.

That much money and power parked in my neighborhood can't be good. Things like that do not park down here. I break off the final leg of my tarantula, chuck the body into a nearby trash can and start looking around. Maybe it's my overpowered sense of self but after the day I've had it wouldn't surprise me in the slightest if the owner of the car was here for me.

"Crow," a voice says from the alley next to my hovel.

I hate it when I'm right.

I peer down the alley but can't make out much. The magic lights don't extend into the alleys and all I can make out is a pool of black. There's a flash of light, someone lighting a *bidi*, but the light and the smoker are too far away to make out any details of what the guy looks like.

"What?" I yell down the alley.

"Come here," a voice yells back.

"You come here," I reply.

"Got a proposition for you," the voice says.

"Do I have to dress up?"

"No but you might want to hear this."

There is absolutely no way I'm going to walk down that alley alone. Even if I had a barker on me (which I don't) I wouldn't walk down there.

"Come on out here. I'll buy you a coffee," I call back.

"Do you really want to talk money around your neighbors, Crow?"

Even mentioning money in this part of town is a shortcut to attracting attention you don't want. "You gonna shoot me?" I ask. I figure there's a chance he might tell me the truth.

"I don't even have a barker on me," the voice responds. "Come on, Crow, I've got places to be, people to intimidate."

I know I'm going to regret this.

The alley is only about five feet wide and goes up ten stories on either side. The bare concrete of the floor is clean and tidy. We may be poor but we're not slobs. There's graffiti all around me, written in a mishmash of Chinese script and Western slang. The kids call it Changlish. I call it lazy.

To the right of me is a cartoon thing with fur all over its body – Māo, I think his name is – smiling a big toothy grin and holding up a *bidi* with a five-leaf design on the wrapper. The left side of the wall is covered with random sayings about freedom, liberty, magic, and the odd picture of Chan. Even the graffiti is neat and tidy, rarely infringing on another artist's work. In the rare cases where a tag partially obscures another tag a disgustingly jovial discussion takes place.

"Sorry."

"No worries. Nice work."

"I liked yours."

"Yours is more pertinent."

Blah, blah, blah. It's kind of sickening but exactly the opposite of what you'd expect from the artists. I've met these guys before and they'll happily gut you with an extremely ornate butterfly knife if you interrupt a work in progress. They're a strange group; incredibly patient with each other but they detest everyone else. Art critics of highest order.

The alley gets darker the further in I go and I have to fight against my claustrophobia to keep going. Tight spaces, you know. I know these walls will smash together any second now and trap me forever.

"Hurry it up, Crow," the voice says.

"Eat a dick," I tell him and keep forcing one foot in front of the other.

At the end of the alley is a larger open space bisected by a narrow road and filled with dumpsters. The road is where the garbage truck rumbles through once a week and takes the small amount of crap we can't recycle out to the wondrous place known as the pit of flames.

Standing alone under a crackling light is a man in a long black coat. Even though it's warm outside he's completely bundled up. The jacket is wrapped tight around him and the collar is pulled up. A fedora is pulled down over his eyes and all I can make out a faint trace of lips and a hint of grayish skin.

When he looks up at me the fedora casts shadows over his face obscuring any details. "Took you long enough," he says.

"I was enjoying the scenery," I tell him. "Did you see the art?"

He chuckles, a grunting sort of laugh that sounds more like a snort than a mirthful noise and shoots me a huge smile that's more simian that human. There's something predatory in that smile. "You call that art?"

"You must have missed the one in the bikini."

He gives me another piggy chuckle-snort. "Must have," he says with a smile.

"Wanna tell me what's the dealy-O here?" I ask.

"The 'dealy-O'?"

"Yeah. The dealy-O. Why are you hanging out in an alley behind my apartment?"

"The art," he says and shoots me a smile.

"The art," I say, "is back there. This is just a dumpster and a light."

"And no witnesses."

"Gonna kill me, Hoss?" I ask. "I guess not because if you wanted me dead you could have popped me or slit my throat out front and the only thing anyone would notice is a pair of new boots."

"We have no desire to kill you. We'd just like to offer you a choice."

"We?" I ask. "You got a mouse in your pocket?"

"My controller and I would like to offer you a job and a large sum of money."

I usually look to a person's eyes to find out if they're lying. There are always little cues that people can't stop. One of my few gifts is the ability to look someone in the eye and tell whether or not I'm being lied to. This guy's eyes are hidden and it's messing up my game. All I've got left is my scintillating personality and a desperate hope that my conversation skills are up to par. "You had me at 'large sum of money'."

"Would you like to know the best part?"

"There's something better than a 'large sum of money'?"

"You don't have to do a thing to get the money. In fact, all you have to do is not do something you're not really interested in doing anyway," he says.

"Oh, thank *Tiān*," I reply, clutching at my heart. "So I can not only skip doing my laundry but get paid for not doing it."

Was that a laugh I just saw? I think it was a laugh. "No, Mr. Crow, I'm referring to a job you took on today. Your laundry should continue unabated." He sniffs at the air. "As soon as possible, actually."

I can't help but take a whiff but all I smell is the soy sauce on my jacket and a faint hint of *bidis*. I've definitely smelled worse. I'll just leave the ambiguity of that statement right where it is. "Laundry day is tomorrow," I quip. "So what's the job I don't have to do?"

Seriousness stalks into his voice and his apelike smile fades. "Don't kill the Clock Man," he says. "Walk away. Move away. Leave it alone."

"Can't," I say simply.

"Sure you can," he replies. "All you have to do is not do something. You can not do something."

"I don't do a thing on weekends."

"You're all good then," he says. His speech starts to get faster, like he's in a hurry to get out of here. "Don't do what you're planning on doing, Crow. Try to carry out this mission and it will go very poorly for you."

He's fidgety, like his hands don't quite know what to do with themselves. Odd, he was calm as a cucumber a few minutes ago. I wonder what's gotten into him; I don't usually have this effect on people but I may be able to use it to my advantage.

"Go home, Crow," he says as he backs into the shadows. It's probably supposed to be dramatic, but the movement is hurried. Desperate, almost. "Go home and sleep late. Tomorrow you'll have all the money for all the *baiju* on Aluna."

Desperate people make me nervous. Actually this whole setup is making me nervous. Why meet in an alley, anyway? If all he wanted to do was talk why not do it out front? Before I was just a little jittery, like a kid that had too much X, but now I'm actually curious.

"Poorly how?" I call after him before he can disappear.

He stops partway into the shadows but I can see he wants to keep going. His left arm is shaking so badly now that he has to hold it steady with his right. "What?" he asks.

"You said it would go poorly. Poorly how?" I ask.

"Bad." Is it just me wanting a drink or is his voice different? Slower or something.

"That's kind of nebulous," I tell him. "Care to elaborate?"

"It will be bad." His voice is slurring. A few minutes ago we had a witty dialogue going on. Now he's slurring his words and his sentences are getting simpler. What's going on here?

"Bad like eating long pork? Or bad like enjoying long pork? Come on. You've got me with the money thing but you still need to scare me some more, don't you?" I take a step forward and he takes a slight step back.

"Stay back," he mumbles. "Have a barker."

"No thanks," I tell him and take another step. "I don't care for them."

He twitches and fumbling hands reach toward his pocket. "No. I have barker. Stay back."

I take two steps forward just to see what he'll do. His hands are desperately searching, trying to get into a pocket but he can't control himself. "Pull it," I tell him. "Shoot me down where I stand and you won't have to worry about me."

"Will shoot," he says.

"Do it. If you don't kill me I'll be breaking into that tower tomorrow morning and killing the Clock Man." I start walking toward him, slowly and calmly.

Shuddering hands search try and fail to get into a pocket. "Stop there," he says in a voice so slurred I can barely make out the words.

"I'll pull his heart out and drink his blood," I snarl. "Shoot me down or watch him die."

We're close enough now I could almost reach out and touch him. Three maybe four feet separate us. He finally manages to get a hand in his pocket. I wait patiently while he pulls out his barker. The weapon is a small two-barrel piece, the kind of thing you only use when you want to keep it hidden. Tiny, but at this range it'll kill me easily.

I take a deep breath – even with Mr. Shaky barely being able to aim a barker is a barker. As I exhale I launch forward, twist and grab his barker and push it down as I step into him. My free hand clamps down under his hand and twists his arm, barker and all, up and around, keeping the barrel of the barker away from me. The twist puts stress on his shoulder and his whole body leans to the side to ease the pressure. When I see his shoulder drop I push the twist further and step back, pulling his arm out the socket.

It's terribly painful. Chan taught me how to do this and like everything else he taught me, he taught it to me by doing it on me.

There's an almost audible pop when his shoulder rips free; I can feel it all the way down his arm. His mouth opens in a silent scream and his whole body collapses. His body hits the ground and squirms like a fish out of water. The squirms turn to spasms and foam pours from his mouth.

Okay, so having your arm ripped out of its socket hurts, but I don't recall lying on the ground spasming and foaming at the mouth.

When he hit the ground his hat came off and rolled partway down the alley. Free of the shadows covering his face I get my first glimpse of the man who threatened me. His eyes are wide open and wild; the sinister eyes of a madman with an axe to grind. His body stops spasming and goes tense. Every muscle tightens and his lips pull back in a pained and awful sneer.

There's a crashing sound behind me and I nearly jump out of my skin. A few seconds later there's another crash and I spin around to see what's making all the racket.

The dumpster's lid is bent and warped outward like something big hit it from inside. The first crash must have been the lid getting smacked around and the second was the same lid crashing down. I ease forward carefully, lift the lid of the dumpster and find nothing.

By the time I turn back to the guy on the ground I find myself facing a corpse. The guy died while I was playing the fool. I'm not sure how I should feel right about now. Should I feel sad? Well, it was a lot of money and I suspect the bargain may be gone now. Angry? Can't pull that one off. I'm too tired to care. Joyous or happy to be alive would be good but I don't think I was ever threatened.

What just happened? Why was the car out front when the guy was back here? What was in that dumpster? Did I just cross paths with whatever or whoever's been leaving corpses in Croatoa's dumpster?

Too many questions, not enough baiju.

The guy's hat is a few feet away from him, knocked from his head when he fell in a spasming heap on the ground. I know I should call the cops, let them know there's a dead guy back here but I don't want to deal with all the questions right now, so I rifle through his pockets and find nothing. The hat's nice, though and it fits my head. The barker is a beautiful design, but I leave it where it fell. I never did truck with those things.

"Thanks for the lid, buddy," I mumble and head back through the alley with my fancy new hat.

V

My apartment is quiet and messy, just like I like it. I've found a messy place cuts down on both looters and people ransacking the place. If it looks like someone's already tossed the joint anyone looking for valuables will assume all the good stuff is already gone.

Joke's on them, though, I've got a bunch of money scattered all around this place. I'm an expert at hiding things and the money I got from graft and outright theft while I was on the force is no exception. I mean, let's face it, if I can hide the graft itself how hard could it be to hid the sweet, sweet payoffs I got from various bosses and criminals over the years?

And that right there is one of the reasons I left the force. They made it too easy, stopping just short of encouraging us to shake down criminals for extra money. I guess from their point of view, there was no reason to give out bonuses when we were all taking our own from every bust.

When I walk into my hovel every piece of junk is exactly where I left it. That statuette of the girl with the *kwan dao* is still fighting the guy with two *daos*. It's exactly as I suspected; there can be no clear winner. Her short sword on the edge of a staff is matched by his two broadswords. Every time she thrusts he can parry with one hand and strike with the other. She has to respond by stopping her strike and dealing with the incoming blade. She has reach and power; he has two quick strikes ready for her.

So it goes, and so it goes. If they're evenly matched there will never be a true winner unless one of them makes a mistake or tires. Or cheats. The pair are my own little yin yang in the form of two warriors carved from soulstone and darkrock.

I guess I should say everything is exactly as I left it except for one thing. The table has been cleared, something I've contemplated doing for years but could never find a good reason to do. I drink my coffee, eat my noodles, and sip my *baiju* on the balcony; what do I need with a table? It's usually piled high with notes, books, bills, and empty bottles. Now those things have been neatly stacked on the floor, the table's been polished to a high shine, and there's a single box on the table that wasn't there the last time I could see the top of the table.

The box is a couple feet long by a foot wide and about six inches thick. It's wrapped in paper featuring the cat from the alley. This time, instead of rolling a *dàmá* blunt, the cat is holding a pair of chopsticks in one hand and a bottle of wine in the other.

Who would dare enter my home and clean even a small part of it? This affront will not stand. My hands and body go loose, ready to unleash my vibrating hand of death on whoever dared enter my safe area. Without conscious thought, my body relaxes and uncoils. If whoever left the box is still here they'll taste my wrath.

"*Chūlái,*" I call. "Come on out. I promise to not hurt you. Much"

The apartment remains silent. It's times like this when I wish I could afford a *Jiufeng* to hang out when I'm gone. I love the idea of coming home and finding an intruder shredded, but the little magical buggers cost a fortune and refuse to eat take out.

"Anyone here?" I call out again. "Last chance to get out before I call down the thunder."

No response.

Maybe I have a secret admirer. Who else would break in and leave something? I look around the living room and take in the piles of stuff I've accumulated over the years; towering stacks of books, weapons both blunt and bladed, my fabled collection of *mah jong* tiles. I guess it's possible someone came in and decided I needed more stuff. This part of town teems with crazies.

The box can wait. If it's survived this long left to its own devices in my apartment, it can survive a little longer. Right now I need a drink.

I don't keep the best *baiju* on Aluna in my apartment; hell, I can't even afford the best *baiju* on Aluna. My bottle, a jade jar engraved with dragons, is filled with stuff made right here in my neighborhood. There's a woman down the way a bit that makes homebrew *baiju*. It's pretty good stuff and the price is right.

Bottle in one hand, glass in the other I make my way to the table and prod the box with my foot. It doesn't explode or fill the air with toxic magic so I gently nudge it out of the way and set my drink and glass down. While I pour out a couple fingers I peer at the box. This close the paper looks expensive. The folds are perfectly creased and the wrapping is held together with an intricate system of interlocking paper weaves. Someone took their time on this.

A deep thrumming fills the room and my glass shakes and rattles on the table. One of the nicer aspects of my place is its location along a blimp flight path. The thrumming turns to the low growl of engines as one of the early evening flights lumbers by.

After it passes the room goes back to being basically quiet and I return my senseless peering at the box on my table. So far it hasn't tried to kill me, so that's one thing in its favor. It's also neatly wrapped. Very neatly wrapped. I don't know of anyone who would wrap a bomb this nicely. Well, there was that one guy, but he's dead now so he doesn't count.

Time to pay the piper, I guess. I down my *baiju* in one gulp and smile as it burns its way down my throat. My stomach lights up with that delicious fiery sensation you only get with decent liquor. For a moment I pause and wonder if I should have another but decide to wait. The first drink is still toying with me.

I slide the box toward me and realize the paper is more than expensive. This is boutique stuff. Normally only the royalty are even allowed to own paper like this. It's smooth and cold to the touch almost like silk that's been left out during the winter. This kind of paper - *shén zhǐ*, literally God Paper – is amazing stuff. It stays cold and smooth even with my fingertips on it.

I've never touched God Paper before. This calls for a drink.

Another glass of *baiju*, another round of admiring the package. I should be careful unwrapping this. Paper like this demands at least some level of sophistication.

The sweet, sweet sorghum liquor is slowly calming my blood, blurring my edge, and making the world seem saner. Fuck it. I pull my *balisong* knife out, flick it open and slice the package open. The silky paper falls open like a *tuōyī wǔ's* gown before she spins on the pole. Under the wrapping a plain brown wooden box with *yòng nǐ de mófǎ* etched onto the top.

Use your magic. Chan.

Why would Chan leave me a package with "Use your magic" written on the top?

Well, at least the box is safe. Probably. Chan hasn't tried to kill me lately and he seemed pretty chummy earlier today, so the chance that he dropped off a bomb is kind of slim. Although Chan is a complicated man and I'm not actually sure if anyone understands him, even that witchy woman he hangs out with.

I pull the top off and find a piece of folded black fabric. It's smooth and cold to the touch; some sort of waxed cotton. Pulling it out, I find a tailored duster. I have to admit, it's nice, but why would Chan send me a duster?

At least it fits nicely. When I check myself in the mirror the coat and I are a perfect match. Something's missing, though. The black duster, my scruffy few-day-old beard, tousled hair, all go together, but the look is still missing something.

A hat. I need a hat. Something that will match the ensemble. Something like the hat I took earlier tonight. I grab it off my couch, screw it onto my head and check the mirror again. Perfect. A tip of the hat, a brush of the brim. It's like I've worn this all my life.

Right now, I need a drink, a *bidi*, and my balcony. A couple fingers of *baiju* and I walk out to the balcony to show the world my new duds. That's right, folks, Felix Crow is watching the world and the world had best be ready.

The sky rumbles and another blimp trudges smoothly across the sky-way. The people on that ship have crossed deserts, forests, oceans, all in luxury. I want to fly away on one of those ships someday. I want to eat giant prawns and watch the world slide smoothly by while I sit high above it, away from the riff-raff.

Those majestic ships are freedom. Freedom filled with hydrogen, powered by magical engines, and adorned in polished brass and jade. I've only been on one once, back when I was still on the force. We had a conference in Yuan Ting, a cozy little beach resort town. The flight from here took a few days of relaxation and watching the world and drinking. When we hit Yuan Ting, we played horseshoes and ate barbeque. I think the conference was on forensics or some such thing. Then they dropped us all back in town and we went about our business cleaning up the city.

Of the five guys I went to the conference with three were dead in a month. I love this town, but it's tough; it'll carve you up and sell your organs on the black market. The body in the alley back there? The one I left on the ground? No one will bat an eye. Since I left his money alone it'll look like just another gangland hit. Maybe the cops will think he's just another corpse that didn't make it to the dumpster.

In a place like this tragedy doesn't come in buckets, it comes in dozens of little packets. Each of those packets is a little hit to your sense of worth and faith in others. All of those little packets demand a drink, a fight, a traipse with a *jìnǚ*, or some sort of walk on the wild side. Mostly I just drink and watch the world go by from my porch.

There's thunder boiling in the distance and the humidity is crazy. There's no way a rational person would be wearing this jacket on this night. I'm sweating like a fiend but it's important to, uh, wear the jacket. For some reason.

I really should get ready for the morning, but I can't bring myself to care overmuch. It's the Clock Man, a tired old man who regulates the flow of magic into the power grid. How hard it could it be? Walk in, walk upstairs, and run a dagger through his heart.

Shit. I have agreed to kill the Clock Man.

My chair on the porch is right where I left it and my ass hits it like a ton of bricks. It just hit me, I just agreed to kill the Clock Man. I've killed plenty of people in the past; I was a cop, after all.

The Clock Man is more than people, though. He's responsible for regulating the way magic rolls through the world. It powers our lights, vidders, cars, everything. The crazy thing about magic is its inherently chaotic nature. In order for the stuff to work and make things, you know, go, you have to control how it flows through the wires.

They call him the Clock Man because he handles the clock cycles, managing the flow of magic to keep it neat and orderly. If the stuff gets out of hand all sorts of bad things can happen. Magic is, at its heart, energy. But it's more than just power flowing through a wire. This is primal energy we're talking about, wild and free and capable of warping reality at the most basic level. There was a time, not long ago, when the former Clock Man started dicking around with the way the magic was transmitted. He thought he had a new and more efficient way of transmitting power, but he tried to make it work on his terms. He tried to violate the rules and an entire city in the center of the continent fell through reality into the dreaming lands.

I understand the things that have crawled out of that place will crush your soul.

Which makes me wonder if Alyssa has a plan to replace her dad. Without him at the helm the effects of an unregulated, wide-spread magic distribution system would be catastrophic. End of the world level catastrophic.

I kill him and the world might end. I don't kill him and Chan kills me. Either way I end up dead.

Fuck it.

I need another drink and some sleep. Tomorrow I've got to kill the world.

VI

Some people like to say everything looks better in the morning. To me it just looks brighter and for the umpteenth time I wonder why I keep the blinds open when I sleep. *Tàiyáng's* light is red-hot pokers in my eyes. At least *Xiǎo Mèimei* is still hidden below the horizon; both of them together would be more than I can handle right now.

The little dragons outside my window are squawking; staccato chirps and whistles demanding their breakfast. I don't know why I started feeding the little vermin, maybe I'm just a sucker for the watching them fly. The red one on the left is the leader. I don't know if Red is a boy or a girl, but I always assumed a girl. There's a certain grace to her movements that the others don't have.

While I'm making coffee I dredge up some lizards I keep handy, break their backs, and toss them onto the patio and watch the little dragons feed. Red places a talon on the biggest lizard and coils her long body into a circle around her prey. I can't be certain but I think she gave me the dragon version of a smile.

The coffee is helping, but a shot of *baiju* speeds the healing process.

I don't have much time so I down the coffee, toss some more lizards on the patio, gather up my new jacket and hat, and hit the streets.

This early in the morning most people in my neighborhood are still sleeping. There's just the quiet brushing of the odd shopkeeper getting ready to open and hawk their wares and the constant shrieking of the tiny dragons. The Tower, as most people call it, is about a couple miles from my place and the walk clears my head. Breakfast is more coffee and a couple *baozi* filled with beef and soy sauce. The steamed dumplings should give me energy to spare.

At the tower I find the usual two guards, burly guys in traditional armor brandishing *kwan daos*. The sword blades topping their poles are razor sharp and the guys themselves can cut you in half before you realize they've moved. When I was still a cop we got to watch some Tower guards put on a demo. It was eye-opening. Any crazy ideas I had about throwing down with those guys went out the window when I saw one of them cut a guy into several pieces before the poor fellow could fall down. There was a blur and the guy's arms and legs came off. The guard took the victim's head before the body could fall.

Neither acknowledges me as I breeze past them. They're trained to ignore anyone whom they don't deem a threat. Must be my lucky day. Whatever skills they might have they didn't notice the guy who's about to crash the party.

The lobby is still empty so I march up to the information desk like I own the place. The girl running the desk smiles the smile of someone who hasn't had to put up with too much shit yet and says, "Hello, sir, and welcome to the Tower. How can I help you today?"

I brush the hat just like I did last night and shoot her a safe smile. "I'd like to see the Clock Man," I tell her.

The girl's face falls. "Oh, I'm so sorry. The Clock Man isn't available right now." She leans in close and motions for me to join her. "He's working on something special," she whispers and shoots me a wink. Apparently I'm in on the conspiracy now.

"Last time one of these guys worked on something special we lost a city," I say.

She looks aghast. "The current Clock Man would never allow that to happen."

"I'm sure. Still, he's supposed to be available twenty six hours a day. It's in the job title."

"Of course, except when he's working on a special project," she says, nodding her head.

"Any idea how long the special project will take?" I ask.

"It's special."

"Understood," I say with a wink. "Is the rest of the museum open?"

Her smile blinks back into place. "Of course! The museum is always open and we have new things in the gift shop. Would you like a map?"

"No, thank you. I've been here before but the place is so fascinating I can't help coming back."

"Well," she says brightly, "if you have any questions you just come right back here and I'll be glad to help you."

"Thank you kindly, ma'am," I say and give her another tip of my hat.

I was hoping for the easy way out. Get to see the Clock Man, kill him, go home; easy-peasy. Of course it wouldn't be as easy as that. Now I've got to find a way to get upstairs without having to fight every guard in this place. Fortunately most of the guards aren't on par with the two outside but I'd still prefer to do this quietly. That means I need a plan and to make that happen I need to concentrate.

The girl running the reception desk is watching me with the ghost of a smile on her lips and a strange, quirky expression on her face. I can't quite read her but if she's watching me I need to find a way to look normal. It's easy enough to disappear in the museum, the place is chock full of the past five hundred years' worth of magic control machinery.

Some of this is interesting, but the whole place is a common destination for every school kid in the city and half of them from the rest of the continent. I've been here more times than I can count, seen every nook and cranny of the place. At this stage I could probably guide tours myself.

I still need to blend in and that means wandering around, nodding appreciatively at the old machinery and reading the descriptive tags. The early stuff is fascinating in its own way. Old hat to most of us, but fascinating. Somehow or another the ancients managed to figure out magic was real and how to harness it with copper, iron, jade, and whatever else they had available. It was inefficient, sure, but those guys slapped together some hunks of metal, connected them with tubes, and used the machines to makes lights turn on and vidders show us pictures.

A world was remade with the machines in this room, magic was harnessed, manipulated, controlled. Without these gleaming pieces of metal most of what we take for granted wouldn't exist. From the copper and iron through the gleaming steel and titanium products, though, they all had one thing in common: a Clock Man to run them. No matter how hard the world has tried, there is no way to regulate the flow of power without a person to constantly watch it and tweak it.

That's the role of the Clock Man: constant effort. The job comes with an insane amount of perks but it is absolutely non-stop for ten solid years. If the Clock Man doesn't crack from the pressure and lack of sleep he's guaranteed a comfortable retirement and the eternal adoration of the world for the rest of his natural life; which usually lasts about three years.

Stress. The silent killer.

Chenming Zhang, the current Clock Man, has been in his position for eight years now. That means it's a safe bet he won't lose it and try to destroy the world. Mostly the people that are going to fall apart do it within the first three years. A few outliers made it five years before falling apart and being retired. The Magic Regulation Committee watches these guys like a bunch of hawks for the first four years. At eight years, Zhang's considered a safe bet.

That makes it all that much stranger that his daughter would want him dead and would go to the extent to have both Chan and Mrs. Chow threaten to kill me. It's not like Alyssa needs his money and she can't take over his position. And why me? Mrs. Chow has a couple dozen guys that would be happy to kill the Clock Man. You can't swing a cat in her place without hitting a killer.

As I'm pondering, I wander around the museum and stare blankly at the machines of loving grace scattered around. Periodically, my eyes will focus and I'll find myself in front of another piece of one-off design. Each machine was hand-crafted by one Clock Man or another. Not all of them take on a special project, but some of the more mechanically inclined will build a machine.

Move through the museum long enough and the machines change with the times. In the beginning they were all brass and jade, but over time the designs shifted more toward the sleek and smooth steel lines of the modern era. Call me a traditionalist, but I prefer the older models. Sure, they're not as efficient and had a nasty habit of throwing raw magic all over the place, but the designs were spectacular. The new machines are more efficient and less likely to kill everyone slowly, but they lack a certain soul.

All the machines work basically the same way. See, magic is everywhere, all the time, but it's not exactly in a useable state. To put things bluntly, magic is completely random. The machines take the random and enforce an order on it before shooting it down into the wires. Some of the machines were in use for a hundred years or more, others lasted only a couple of years before catastrophic failure. One detonated and took out the first tower and part of the surrounding neighborhood.

The current machine has been in use for less than a decade with no issues that I'm aware of. Granted, not every special project consists of a new machine. There was that one project that attempted to distribute magic wirelessly but nothing ever came of it. Actually, that machine used to be in the corner but it appears to be missing. Another special project consisted of having sex with groupies.

Hey, no one ever accused these guys of being moral paragons.

I wonder what happened to the wireless machine. There's just a sign that says the machine has been removed for cleaning.

The girl at the counter is still watching me, still has that sly smile. Has she been watching me the whole time? Hmm…

Her eyes track me as I walk toward the counter. Before I get there, I throw an arm over my shoulder, point at the empty space, and ask, "When's the wireless coming back?"

She blinks slowly, almost seductively. "Temujin's Hammer? The Clock Man requested it."

"The sign says it's being cleaned."

A finger crooks toward me and motions me closer. I lean in and she motions me to come closer. Finally, my face is right next to hers, close enough to feel her breath on my ear. "It's easier this way," she whispers to me.

I pull back and look at her. Her eyes are sparkling, glittering lobby lights like emerald orbs. That smile of hers is still there like she knows something I don't know. "Easier what way?" I ask.

The smile grows. "Easier than making a sign saying 'Sorry this is being used in the Clock Man's Special Project and will be back on display when he's finished with it', silly" she says.

"Any idea what he's doing with it?" I ask.

"I'm not privy to his machinations, sir," she replies. Did she just wink at me?

"Of course not," I reply. Why would she know what he's up to?

"Maybe I could offer you a special tour, though," she tells me. "You know, to make up for the inconvenience of missing out on Temujin's Hammer..."

This might be good way to pass the time. "I'm not terribly inconvenienced, ma'am. But I'd appreciate an insider view on the museum."

"I get off in an hour. Meet me in the gift shop," she says and winks again.

"I'll be there," I tell her. "And I appreciate the offer."

VII

There's a bar around the corner that I used to frequent when I was a cop. It's a serious dive, the kind of place cops go to because it's usually full of criminals. No, it's not what you're thinking; we didn't go there to bust people and make our quota. When we needed to make quota we'd go into the valley. The bar is called *Taijiquan*, in a delightful twist on the style's famous balance. It was a kind of neutral zone, a place where cops and crooks could hang out and share information. We'd let the bad guys know what the government was pissed off about that day and they'd let us know who was stepping over the lines of acceptable criminal behavior. It was a great place to get information as well as a good drink.

Taijiquan is still right where I left it years ago and still the ultimate shit hole that sells the best liquor on two planets. Not surprising, considering the time of day, the place is empty. The bartender, a former wushu master, is slightly older than last time I met him, but still looks like he fights tigers in his free time. Come to think of it, he probably does. Du Xinwu is a beast of a man, over two meters tall and built like a forest bear, which he also probably fights.

Xinwu grins his ape-like grin at me and waves me over.

"Greetings, Master Xinwu," I say and plop down on a barstool. "Still doing the trick?"

He sets a bottle down and pours out two shots of *baiju*. "The trick, Crow, is no trick. It's skill!" He drains his *baiju* and laughs a huge, carefree laugh.

His laughter is infectious and I can't help but smile at his nonchalance. When you're built like Xinwu, there's probably not much that can frighten you. "You're telling me there's no trick to standing six boards on end and putting your fist through them?" I shoot my *baiju* and feel the warmth of Yo-Ti's fingers tickling my throat.

"No trick at all." He rolls up his sleeve and shows me an arm rippling with muscle and covered in tattoos. "You just hit hard and fast, too fast for the boards to get out of the way and too hard for them to resist."

"I still think it's a gimmick," I tell him and push my glass toward him.

He grins and pours out another shot. "Just because you can't do it doesn't mean it can't be done. Do you need another demonstration?"

"No, no, no," I tell him and shoot my *baiju*. "I've seen it. I just have trouble believing anyone can be that good."

"You should try practicing," he says. "Start soft. Punch through one board and work your way up."

"I'm too delicate," I tell him. "It hurts my hands to hit boards."

"How did you ever become a cop?"

"They gave us gloves."

Xinwu laughs again, a full belly laugh that shakes the bar and rattles the glasses. He's a happy guy, relaxed and at peace in his skin. Another small glass slides across the bar toward me and I remember why I used to love this place. Master Xinwu was never into the money; he cares for friendship, good drink, and laughter with friends. In a lot of ways he's who I'd love to be like when I grow up.

I reach into my jacket and search around for money but his hand snakes across the table and holds mine fast. "Your money's no good here, Crow. I told you that."

"Just feel like I should pay you," I say and wonder how someone so big can be so damned fast. Must be the fact that he's always relaxed.

"You did pay me, brother. I'll never forget that."

About five years ago there was a gang, one of the local mobster-type groups was shaking him down, trying to drive him out of business. Imagine that; someone shaking down one of the great wushu masters. Of course, even the best fighter on the planet can be overwhelmed and no matter how good you are twenty on one is not good odds. I got wind of the showdown and quietly took out the leader before anything could happen. At that point, it was just a little more blood on my hands and I didn't think much of it, but it meant the world to Master Xinwu. He couldn't have gotten close to Sister Snakehead and wouldn't have killed her anyway. His honor wouldn't allow him to kill a woman; I don't have such compunctions.

I showed up to deliver a warrant, a common thing in her house and calmly walked up to her while her minions laughed and hooted at the cop daring to bring down the great sister. While they were laughing I slammed a dagger in Sister Snakehead's black heart and watched her die. Even as dumb as her hired muscle was, none of them was crazy enough to touch a cop.

I got a medal for taking down one of the biggest criminals in the city and Master Xinwu got to keep his bar.

"I told you back then," I say, "I was just doing my job."

More laughter and he actually wipes tears from his eyes. "That's a good one, Crow."

"What?"

"Bad as the cops are, they've never been assassins."

I lean forward and wonder, not for the first time, about all the terrible things I've done. There was always some justification, however flimsy, for every bribe or life I took while on the force. As always, I find yet another excuse to push off the introspection and worry about it later.

"What can I say?" I ask, "I love this bar."

"So do I, brother," Xinwu says. "So do I."

We pause and enjoy the empty bar. He refills our drinks and holds his glass up in toast. I tap it with my own glass and we further drown our sorrows.

"What brings you around, Crow?" Xinwu asks.

"Waiting on a meeting."

"Is she hot?" he asks with a laugh.

"You do know me, friend."

"The famous Felix Crow doesn't wait for meetings unless the meeting is one on one."

"Yeah," I say, "she's pretty hot."

"It's been too long," he says, "Some masters insist that sex reduces their *chi*, but I think that's just because they can't get laid. You take her and make her your own. That's *chi*! Who is she?"

"Desk girl at the Clock Tower," I tell him.

"How did you meet her?"

"I was over there this morning."

"Checking out the rumors, eh? Once a cop, always a cop," he says.

"What rumors?" I ask.

"Interrogating me, Crow?" He laughs again. "The rumors of that strange thing running around. The fact that no one's heard from the

Clock Man in months. All kinds of crazy zāogāo de mólì going on over there. Very bad mojo indeed."

"Strange thing?"

"Something fast running around in the shadows over there. Folks that have seen it swear it's not human; it looks like some kind of skeleton and sounds like clicking and whirring. Personally, I think they've just been drinking the cheap *baiju*."

"So they haven't been drinking here is what you're saying?" I ask.

He shrugs and says, "Let's just say I didn't care for them."

"You're my new hero, Xinwu."

"I'm everyone's hero, pal," he tells me. "I'm a bartender. I'm everyone's best friend, everyone's confidante, everyone's psychologist. I solve problems, I fix relationships, I know answers."

"And you're modest about it."

"Modesty is not becoming of a bartender," Xinwu says. "It's trained out of us at bartending academy."

"Wait," I say. "There's a bartending academy?"

"Of course. This job is more than just pouring *baiju*." He puts his fists on his hips and puffs up his chest. "I am like a god."

"Okay, God," I say. "Can I pray for another shot?"

"Only the devout may drink of my *baiju*," he says.

"Oh, I believe. I believe in the healing power of your mighty elixir."

"Well, then, disciple, come pray at my temple."

He reaches under the bar and pulls out a coal black bottle, so dark it's hard to focus on. "This, my boy," he tells me, "is the fabled *baiju* of Lan-Caihe. There is nothing else on Aluna like it."

When Xinwu pours the drink it looks like the finest silk coiling into my glass. Liquids aren't supposed to do that; they should like liquids, not semi-solids. It splashes around like a liquid in my cup and the aroma, praise the Immortals, is a special kind of amazing.

"Drink," Xinwu says quietly. "Drink of the blood of the Heavens."

On my first sip the world snaps into sharp focus. On my second, I feel power and fire surging through my veins. When I shoot down the rest of it, I can see through time. The feeling is unbelievable. I feel powerful and wise. Give me a problem and I'll solve it. Give me an enemy and I'll crush him like a *kūnchóng*.

"I feel like I've touched Monkey's face," I say.

"It's incredible stuff. There are rumored to be only four bottles of this on the whole planet."

"Thank you," I tell him, still looking in wonder at the bar I've been in countless times.

"To your heath," he tells me.

"To yours," I reply.

According to the clock on the wall, I need to get going. There's a young lady ready to show me around the museum and it wouldn't do to keep her waiting. I thank Xinwu again and we exchange bows before I go. Just before I reach the door Xinwu calls out, "Hey, Crow."

I turn and the world slowly follows me. "Yes," I say.

"Be careful over there. Something's not right in that tower."

"You said the people saying that were assholes."

"I said I didn't care for them," he replies. "They're assholes, but they're not stupid. Just watch yourself."

"Will do, dad," I tell him with a smile and plop my hat back on my head. "Thanks for the drink."

VIII

She's waiting when I get back to the museum, leaning against the reception desk with her legs crossed and her elbows propping her up. That strange grin is still on her lips and her eyes are sparkling. Some part of me, the remedial portion of my brain that still thinks like a cop, has a feeling this isn't going to be a regular tour.

The *baiju* of the Gods is still coursing through my head and everything is still sharply defined from the purplish gray of her hair to the drape of her dress. Inebriation doesn't describe this feeling; it's more like intoxication, like everything is amazing and miraculous.

"I didn't catch your name earlier," I tell her.

She points to her right breast and her finger hovers over a name tag. "Huizhong," she says without breaking eye contact.

"Are you really wise and loyal?"

"At some things," she says and winks, "and with certain people."

"Care to share?"

"Yes. Yes I do." She sways to me, a serpentine siren on the prowl, liquid and smooth. "I watched you looking at the machines earlier. Shall we start with the portraits?"

Her body slides next to mine and an arm links through mine. "Pictures seem right up my alley," I tell her.

With a slight tug she leads me toward the back of the museum, to the portrait gallery of all the Clock Men that have ever been. No one ever goes back there; everyone's too interested in the machinery. Most people are content to let the Clock Man control the magic that powers their lamps and vidders, almost no one cares for the minds that made it all happen.

"Right up your alley?" Huizhong asks. "How's that?"

"I drank something earlier, now I can see things no one else can."

"Got any more?"

"Sorry, no. I know a guy who owns a bar," I say. "He got hold of some *baiju* of Lan-Caihe."

"Mmmm," she purrs. "How was it?"

"Amazing. Better than sex."

"You just need to find better girls."

She leads me through a doorway with "*àn xia húlu qǐ le piáo*" in gold letters written above it. One gourd is pushed under the water, but another floats up: the traditional saying of the Clock Men since the very first Clock Man stepped down and another was found waiting outside. It used to imply that no matter how many problems you stamped out another one would rise up but the very first Clock Man used to say it referred to opportunities instead of problems.

The portrait gallery goes back millennia to the very first Clock Man. Zhang Sanfeng is one of the very few Clock Men who is smiling in his portrait. His very expression belies the level of effort he put in to light up the world with magic.

"Zhang was quite the character," Huizhong says with a little laugh. "No one knew what to make of him at the time but as soon as he made the first lamps turn on people treated him like a God. They showered him with gifts; food, gold, women. They say he had quite the appetite."

"For food?" I ask.

She looks up at me and smiles that same odd grin. "For women," she says. "Oh, he liked his food and drink, too, but he was a master with the women. They say the very first woman that was sent to him was a young lady who had dishonored her family and was sent to the village crazy as a kind of punishment. She screamed and howled and they had to drag her to Zhang's house. When he was done with her she never stopped smiling. The women of the time lined up, volunteering to be the next 'victim' of the Clock Man."

"Maybe he just gave great back rubs."

Huizhong untangles her arm from mine and walks closer to Zhang's portrait. "Maybe," she says, looking over her shoulder at me. "But the rumor is he was just amazing at sex."

"A man of many talents," I say.

"Well, two. Controlling magic and bringing women to such heights of pleasure they never stopped smiling."

"The men must have hated him."

She reaches out as if to brush Zhang's face, like she could somehow reach through time and touch the man himself. Before her fingers brush the ancient paper she stops herself and turns back to face me. Her eyes look me up and down and she steps in close. We're standing close enough now that I can almost feel the heat of her body.

"Perhaps," she says and pats my chest, "but even as patriarchal as it was back then, no one could deny that having a happy wife was a good thing."

Her arms links through mine again and Huizhong gently pulls me further down the line, explaining stories about some of the Clock Men, ignoring others entirely. This Clock Man could drink Monkey himself under the table. That Clock Man had a huge drug problem but found a way to run magic around the world. Another was a well-respected pornographer who also did the first breakthrough work on wireless transfer.

For all their amazing skills and knowhow, it's amazing to see these guys as humans. We tend, and I'm talking about humans here, to treat our heroes as beyond reproach. Some of these guys all but changed the rules of magical physics to make things better for everyone; they broke boundaries we didn't even know existed and bent the world to their will. At the same time they were running drugs and hookers out of the Clock Tower.

Huizhong has a story for all of them. No matter how many times I've been through here I've never heard about the human side of them. It must be the upside of working here.

She keeps pulling gently but firmly along the hallway of heroes toward a door that I've never noticed before. Her fingers press the edge and the door quietly pops open. Huizhong winks at me and pulls me inside.

"This is the archive," she says. "The Tower has been here for over a thousand years now. It's constantly growing and changing. We have diaries, notes, pictures, tinkerings, musings, you name it. The Clock Men leave everything here when they finish their duties."

We're in a room stacked floor to ceiling with boxes. They're all neatly labelled and stacked in a room that seems to go on forever. "This looks, uh, neatly organized," I say.

Huizhong saunters down one of the aisles, running a finger across the boxes. "Every time a Clock Man leaves he walks out empty-handed.

A group has his apartment cleaned out in an hour. Everything is logged and documented over the next several months."

"Does anyone ever get to come back here?"

"No one comes back here," she says. "Ever."

She spins around and motions me to come over. "We're completely alone, Mr. Crow."

"You know my name?" I ask.

"Everyone knows the famous Mr. Felix Crow," she purrs.

Her hand grabs the front of my jacket and tugs me closer to her. Ruby lips find mine and soon her body is pressed next to mine. Her tongue pushes between my lips and fingers hold my face next to hers. Hair as soft as silk runs through my fingers. She's warm and soft and smells faintly of the rain forest and lotus flowers.

A hand pulls off my hat and tosses it aside. "It was in my way," Huizhong says with a smile before her lips attack mine again. Our kissing becomes more and more passionate, desperate almost. My jacket comes off and drops on the floor and her hands slide down my body.

"What are we doing here?" I ask, not really caring as long those hands keep moving down.

Huizhong shrugs and smiles. "Do you really have to ask? Who doesn't want the famous Felix Crow?"

I really shouldn't worry about this. Or should I? Who cares? Huizhong slides down to her knees and I realize I honestly don't care. Her eyes lock onto mine but her hands work deftly unzipping and extracting. When her mouth opens my eyes close.

There's an amazing warmth followed by a stinging pinprick.

Followed by overwhelming blackness.

IX

I come to with a raging headache, which isn't uncommon and an itch on my nose which is also not all that uncommon. My hands don't seem to want to move to scratch the itch, which is a bit strange.

Wait. My hands do move, they just can't move. They seem to be restrained somehow.

That is strange. Usually I remember paying for things like this.

Opening my eyes feels like sliding sandpaper across an open wound. The light hurts but closing my eyes hurts worse. Shit. I can't win for losing.

"Is he awake?" a voice asks.

"I think so," a more familiar voice replies.

"What did you give him?"

"A *jincan* derivative," the familiar voice says. The voice sounds higher than the other voice. Feminine? Is that word? I absolutely cannot get my brain in gear right now.

"It looks like it hit him hard. Will he survive?"

"Yes, my lord, I believe so. It was administered in a ... delicate place."

Wait. There was a sharp pain. I remember that now.

"A delicate place?" the deeper voice asks.

"In his pants," the higher voice says. She. Yes, that's it, the voice is a woman's. She giggles.

"Don't your people usually prefer to carry toxins in your mouths?" the deeper voice asks. He's a man. I'm remembering a few things now but that may or may not be a good thing.

There's a pause in the conversation. "Yes, my lord," the woman says.

Huizhong. Her name is Huizhong.

Who's the man?

"Minx," the man says simply. "I knew I was right to hire you."

"You honor me, my Lord," Huizhong says.

"How long until he fully regains consciousness?" the man asks.

There's a sensation of something brushing my lips. I really wish it was *baiju*.

"He's awake now, listening to us, but it will be a few minutes before the *jincan* completely breaks down," Huizhong says.

"Is he secure?" the man asks.

"Yes, my Lord," a deep baritone replies.

I open my eyes again and this time it doesn't hurt quite as much it did last time. It still doesn't feel good, but it's not quite crippling. I can't see clearly because the light is too bright but I can make out three figures. They look like grayish pillars.

Someone slaps my face. "Wake up, Crow," Huizhong says. "It's time to meet your destiny."

My eyes finally focus enough to make out some faces. I recognize Huizhong and would love to spit in her face but my mouth is dry as a desert. The other two I don't recognize but one of them is undoubtedly a Tower guard. He's huge and his *kwan dao* looks like it could rend Guan Yu himself in twain.

Why haven't they killed me?

I wish I could think of something witty, something that would cut as deep the guard's *kwan dao*, but all I can come up with is, "Fuck you."

"He's awake, my Lord," Huizhong says and turns away from me toward a man I've never seen before. He's tall and thin with receding gray hair. His eyes are filled with madness and desperation, like someone is trying to crawl out of them and escape.

"You should have taken my offer last night, Crow," he says. "In some ways this is better, though. The great Felix Crow will come in handy."

What offer? Last night? The guy last night died in an alley. Who is this guy?

At least he thinks I'm great.

"Once you break him, my Lord, his skin will be yours," Huizhong says. "Then you can use him to get places you haven't been able to get to before."

"That despicable Mrs. Chow hates him," the man says.

"Yes, but she'll let him get close to her, especially if Chan is with him," Huizhong says.

"Then I can take care of both of them at the same time."

"Who are you?" I ask.

He leans in close, close enough that I can smell his fetid breath. His mad, dancing eyes peer into mine and a smile breaks across his face. "He doesn't know," he says with a smile.

"How could he, my Lord?" Huizhong asks. "He's never seen you in this flesh."

"Or any flesh," the man says.

He steps back and laughs out loud at me. "Crow. The famous Felix Crow. The fallen cop with a drinking problem. The man who killed so many of my associates and had his friends cover it up. The man who thwarted my plans doesn't even recognize his *sĭdĭ*. We are mortal enemies, you and I, even if you're not aware of it."

Great. Captured by a loon.

"I have no idea who you are, pal, but if you let me go now, I'll let you live," I say.

"You have no idea what you're up against," Huizhong says. "If you were smart you'd beg forgiveness and accept adjudication."

"I'd say 'blow me' but you already did and you weren't very good at it," I tell her.

She smiles and says, "You only lasted two seconds. How bad could I be?"

"Knock it off, you two," the man says. "Mr. Crow, I shouldn't be surprised you don't recognize me. We've met but you've never seen my face."

"So it's cool that I don't recognize you?" I ask.

"It's actually preferential for me. The less you know about me, the better. Of course, even though you didn't know what you were doing you did cause me no small amount of problems," he says.

"I'm good at that. Can I go now?"

"No, Mr. Crow, you're not going anywhere. I need your body for a small bit of revenge."

"*Aiyah*," I say. "Everyone wants my body today."

Huizhong acts like she wants to say something but the mystery man holds up a hand before she makes a noise. "Your mind is useless to me. In fact, it's actually in my way. I understand you have a fondness for enclosed spaces, no doubt a reaction to the girl you couldn't save.

You remember her don't you? Found her under the house where she was hiding from my associate here."

Huizhong waves and smiles.

Under the house? That's smarmy.

"You see, Mr. Crow, that girl held answers I needed. She could control magic without my machines. I needed to know how and make sure no one else could figure out the trick."

Fuck me running. The girl.

"You know she's not the only one, right?" I ask.

"Of course," he says. "Your friend Chan has a remarkable ability, but he's far too powerful to take on directly. That's where you come in. He'll let you get close to him when no one else can. I'll control your mind and he and Mrs. Chow will be history. Your corpse will wind up in a dumpster, of course. Consider it my calling card."

"What does Mrs. Chow have to do with this?" I ask.

"I don't care for her," he says. "Now, if you'll excuse me, I have things I need to do, people to see, minds to break. Enjoy your dark, tiny cell."

As he turns to leave I notice a flash of gold on the back of his neck and then he's gone. Huizhong smiles that sly smile of hers and says, "Goodbye Crow. I'm glad I had you. Enjoy being buried alive."

She snaps her fingers and the Tower guard leans his *kwan dao* against the wall. The big guy's muscles bulge as he closes a huge door in front of me. It's seriously a huge door and it's coming right at me. Sweat pops out on my forehead and I have to bite back a sudden desire to beg them to do anything but close that door on me. I can't be absolutely positive, but when that thing is shut I will have zero space between it and me. It'll be like being crushed forever.

Darkness closes in and I hope the huge door is soundproof because my scream is none too quiet.

X

After I stop screaming and struggling, after the will to fight at any cost has fled I'm left with a huge stone door brushing against my nose and the absolute certainty that it's edging closer and closer every time I breathe.

I think I've mentioned this before but it bears repeating: I hate enclosed spaces. The dumpster was one thing, there was light and sound and air. Mrs. Chow's basement was a test of my own willpower to not run screaming up the stairs.

This is absolute hell. The Hell of Eternal Crushing. My screams are still echoing in my ears long after I've lost the ability to make any noise other than a pathetic whimper. It's dark and tight and I can't move and every time I breathe I get my own hot breath in my face and the panic is rising again and damn it all it's closing in me again.

There's still strength in these old bones after all. Panic strength pushes me forward and I find a voice I thought I'd lost.

I think I passed out. Panic will do that to you.

How long was I out? There's no time in this place; there's just dark and close and terror. I was hoping it was just a dream but here I am. I'm still strapped down and there's still a big fucking rock pushing into my nose and making it hard to breathe.

Panic rises again.

Guanyin, please help me.

I pass out again and wake up with a serious desire for a drink. My lips are parched and all I can think about is another drink of *baiju*. Am I an alcoholic? Who cares? I want a drink. I'd step over my own mother (bless her shade) for a drink. Why has Lan-Caihe left me?

It would appear detox is far worse in an enclosed space. My limbs are shaking uncontrollably and my heart is jumping around in my chest. Maybe I'll die. Death would be a welcome release. The panic has left but the gnawing sense of futility is still there. I hope, and I'm not joking here, I hope my mind breaks soon. Anything would be better than this.

I open my eyes and I'm in a forest. Oh, thank you Guanyin. You are truly the goddess of mercy and you are kind and wise and I promise I'll burn some incense in your honor.

As soon as I find some.

The forest is cool and quiet. Overhead a full moon is casting shadows on the forest floor. I stretch my arms and enjoy the freedom. My feet move of their own accord, crunching the pine needles underneath.

Freedom never felt so good. The air is sweet, the freedom is sweeter.

I catch a glimpse of movement out of the corner of my eye and know someone is stalking me. Honestly, I don't care. If I die now I die free and that's better than anything in my recent life. The movement keeps circling around me, slowly closing in. Whoever it is thinks they're being silent but I've been stalked by professionals and whoever is circling in on me is a rank amateur.

"Come on out," I say to the forest. "I know you're there."

"I may be here, but where are you?" a voice calls out.

"I think I'm here," I say.

A woman's face pops out of the tree line and stares at me coldly. "You're not here, Crow. You're sandwiched between two slabs of stone and slowly dying what will likely be a horrible, painful death."

With that I'm back in my cell with my nose pressed into a cold block of stone and my own hot breath reflecting back in my face.

Mother fucker.

How did I get into this position?

Right. The girl.

My last case, the one that drove me off the force. The girl was just a girl. Ten, maybe eleven years old at the most. She'd gone missing, just another lost kid in the big city. We didn't have anyone actively looking for her; there aren't enough cops in the world to hunt down the number of kids that go missing in this town. I stumbled across her one night, purely by coincidence. I was stumbling home, drunk out of my mind and had to take a leak. I ducked down an alley to find a quiet place and was pissing on the wall when I caught a flash of movement.

In a brief bit of responsibility I followed the movement and found a girl - the girl - scared and alone and beaten half out of her mind. She was hiding behind a dumpster and a couple guys were trying to coax her out. I figured it was an attempted rape in progress so I did what any rational peace officer would do.

I shot them and tossed their bodies in the dumpster.

The girl shot out of her hiding spot without even so much as a "thank you" and disappeared into some abandoned house. I followed her in and chased her through the wrecked place. There was graffiti everywhere, broken glass vials, syringes; all the accoutrements of fine living in the city. She moved like a *tùzĭ* on speed, long legs propelling her in huge hopping movements.

She shot into a room and trapped herself among the soiled mattresses and boarded up windows. I held up my badge and told her I was there to help. I'd get her home, keep her safe, all the crap we're trained to say to keep people calm.

Her energy was infectious. I don't know what she was hopped up on but even crouching in the corner like a rabbit she was practically vibrating. Moving slowly forward, talking quietly the whole time, I tried to talk her back down to Aluna. "It's going to be okay." "You're safe now." "I'm a cop." The usual nonsense.

I could hear people outside rattling around and wasn't sure if they were more bad guys or just some vagrants looking to kill and eat us. Neither was a good option. The walls in that old place were paper thin, probably why the people that used to live there moved out. That or the rats.

The girl was getting ready to try to bolt through me when someone outside said "Charges placed."

I charged at the girl, tackling her onto the rotting mattress just before the charges outside went off. We were both on the mattress when the world got very loud and bright. Pieces of the sky rained down; pointy, heavy pieces that tore up my jacket, messed up my hair, and left huge bleeding gashes in my body.

When the dust settled I looked down at the girl, hoping for at least a "thank you" after saving her from the explosion. My jacket was shredded and my stomach burned like hell. The girl's eyes were blank and there was a trickle of blood leaking from her mouth. When I tackled her she fell on a piece of wood that pierced her heart.

She died and I got a commendation for bravery and thinking on my feet.

I never did learn the girl's name.

I'm not sure I've ever been this thirsty. My mouth feels like the Southern Desert. I've spent the past, however long it's been, seeing things. Visions? Hallucinations? I don't know. The space lizard was a nice touch but the endless spiders have been kind of freaky. Maybe it's their revenge for eating all their kin.

Fuck 'em.

What I need right now is water. I never thought I'd say that, but I really want some water.

The shadows along the needle-covered ground are stretched thin making the mass of the thick trees around me look like reeds. A glance overhead and I feel like can almost touch the stars above me. The twin sisters are waning, receding into the darkness. They'll be reborn again into the light soon.

I'm back in the forest again. A woman is standing in the middle of a clearing with a long bow in one hand and a wicked looking arrow in the other. In the fading light I can't make out many details, just the extremes. She's got long black hair and her dark eyes glitter and dance in the fading moonlight. Her blouse has a single tree on it, white etched on black. For a moment I wonder if she's a statue or a figment of my imagination.

Scattered around the clearing are stacks of delicately balanced rocks, little homages to something or other. Whoever put them there has a lot more patience than I do.

There's a faint sense of movement - more a blur than anything else - and an arrow embeds itself in the dirt between my legs. I wonder if this is the same woman I heard rustling around the forest last time I was here, however many days ago that was. If she is the same, she was putting on a show for me; there's no way anyone that moves as fast as she just did would make so much noise moving through the brush.

"That's far enough, Crow," she says quietly.

"Is he the one?" a voice asks.

The woman sags and sighs. "Yes," she says.

I have such a way with women. When they're not drugging me they're generally disappointed in me.

"He doesn't look like much," the voice says.

"He's not," she says. "But he's close and not without skills."

"Close?" I ask. "Close to what?"

"Silence," the voice says. "You're not here to talk."

"Well, then, oh mighty invisible voice, why am I here?"

The chittering insects and normal forest noises stop suddenly. In the deathly silence I hear an eerie rustling sound. It almost sounds like the wind whispering tales of madness through the trees. A sense of … something … awakens in my head. When Chan's around there's always a slight buzzing, so faint I almost don't notice it's there. This buzzing is monstrous.

Something is out there in the woods and that buzzing sounds is rattling my teeth in my skull. The air around me seems to crackle and pulse with power. I fall to my knees, holding my throbbing head between my hands. The girl laughs. It's a sound so full of mirth and joy that it feels sinister in this place.

Behind her a pair of amber lights moves smoothly in the darkened woods, shifting back and forth. "You're here to be judged Felix Crow," the girl says.

A dragon's head erupts smoothly from the forest. The bright amber eyes sit on top of a face full of long whiskers and fangs that could split a man in half. It moves smoothly, a thing made of liquid and chittering scales. The girl stands perfectly still as its bulk circles around her, holding out a hand to stroke the scales as they glide past.

I wasn't kidding when I said dragons ran this world. They're quite real, very powerful, and extremely dangerous creatures. There aren't a whole lot of them, but it was their planet long before it was ours and a sort of truce rules all interactions. Another war between us and them would be disastrous for everyone involved. We've got the numbers but they've got the power.

The dragon stops inches from my face, close enough that I could feel my final breath reflect off its muzzle if it decides to light me up. Nostrils expand to the size of plates as it sniffs at me. It sniffs at me and watches me with eyes that have seen eternity.

Dragons are big critters. I've never seen one up close before, at least a living one. There's a skeleton of a Northern Wyvern at the Tower museum. That one is at least 150 hands long and was reportedly 5000 turns old when it died. The dragon in front of me is a South Eastern dragon and is easily double the length of the one at the museum.

South Eastern dragons look kind of like snakes with wings. They've got short, stubby legs and long whiskers. Some people say they look wise. I'll grant they're extremely intelligent and wise creatures, but their intelligence is alien and their wisdom is very ... dragon.

When he speaks the dragon's gravelly voice is so deep it vibrates my clothes. "This little thing is meaningless to me."

Dragons are also kind of stuck up dicks.

It turns and starts to glide away. "Get rid of him," the dragon tells the woman with the bow. She doesn't hesitate for a moment. Before I can say anything there's an arrow heading toward me.

Time slows down and I can clearly see the three-bladed tips spinning lazily toward me. Each time one of the tips hits the perfect angle moonlight glints off the razor sharp edges. The girl hasn't lowered the bow yet, she's just grinning madly at me.

I have all the time in the world to dodge it but I'm thirsty and fed up with stuck-up dragons and women who want me dead. My hand is perfectly in place when the arrow comes by and all I have to do is make a fist to stop the arrow before it hits me in the face.

The black haired woman's grin fades and the dragon stops receding into the woods. He turns to face me and a toothy grin crosses his ugly mug. "Maybe there is hope for this one after all."

"I'm full of surprises," I say.

"Indeed," the dragon says, "who would've thought a derelict like you would still have some skills. I would have thought the poison coursing through your veins would have killed you long ago."

"Ah, that's sweet. I'll bet you say that to all the boys, though," I reply.

The dragon makes a sound like a series of short growls. He's laughing. I not only met a dragon tonight, I made him laugh. That's got to be worth something, right?

Right?

"I say we should kill him now," the girl says. "He's unpredictable and dangerous."

"And that is exactly why we need him," the dragon tells her. "He won't even see it coming. There's no way a he'd ever see a pathetic specimen like this as a threat."

"He?" I ask. "He who?"

They ignore me and keep talking amongst themselves. "He'll find a way to screw it up," the woman says. "The first drop of booze he sees and he'll be completely unreliable."

"Then we'll just have to make sure he doesn't drink," the dragon says.

"I'd seriously like a drink," I say.

"How do you intend to do that?" the woman asks.

The dragon coils around itself and brings his face closer to hers. "I'll tell him the truth."

"The truth?" the woman asks.

"The truth!" I shout. I figure if they're not paying attention to me I might as well have a bit of fun. It's not like I'm not locked in a stone closet in the real world.

"The whole truth," the dragon says. Whiskers bristle and twitch as a huge smile graces his face.

The woman nods, but I can tell she's not happy. If she'd brought another arrow I have no doubt it would be screaming toward my face right now. "Mark my words, he'll fail miserably."

"Perhaps," the dragon says, "but he's perfectly placed and isn't a complete screw up, all evidence to the contrary."

"You guys know I'm right here, right?" I ask.

"Your call," she says.

The dragon moves like liquid metal, a thing made of ethereal fluid and snapping jaws. His face stops inches from mine. He's close enough that his breath washes over my hair like a strong breeze. For a dragon his breath is surprisingly fresh.

"Little man, I'm about to tell you a story. Do you think you can hold yourself together long enough to hear it?" he asks.

I really feel like being a jackass right now and telling him I'm bored already or something equally lame, but this is a dragon and I've never met one in the flesh. He reeks of power and wisdom. "I'm all ears," I tell him.

"Good," the dragon says. "Back when the first of your small kind wandered into my territory I recognized something useful about your race. I was just a young dragon at the time, merely a thousand years old, but I was a precocious youth and I could tell you weren't all boring hairless mammals."

"Was that a compliment?" I ask.

"It was," he says and rises up. His wings spread wide and I get a feeling for just how small we really are. I'm amazed humans managed to kill any of these creatures; we had numbers on our side, I guess.

"I was the first dragon to see your race as anything other than food," he continues. "There aren't many among you, but some of your people can channel the magic that controls Aluna. Channel it and control it. Control the magic, control the planet."

"Magic," I say drolly.

"Magic," the woman says.

"Magic," the dragon says, "is not what you think it is. It is power, the most primal power on the planet. Left to its own devices, magic will make things happen seemingly randomly. It can create a gold statue or remove a mountain."

"It lets me turn on my lights," I add.

"Typical human," the dragon says with a growling sigh, "You're given the keys to the greatest power on the planet and you use it to keep lights on at night."

"Not all of us can start a fire as easily as you, pal," I tell him.

"Show some respect!" the woman snaps.

"Who is she?" I ask.

The dragon coils around itself to look at the woman in the middle of the clearing. "Come here, child," he says, "meet the legendary Felix Crow."

The woman stalks forward in a huff, hands on her hips and peers at me. "I can't see him very well," she says.

The dragon snorts fire and the ground around me erupts in flames. "She calls herself Mab, although I doubt that is her real name," the dragon says. "She is the head of the Furious Fae."

Aiyah. The Furious Fae. The same group that Chan has been working with on one of his strange projects.

Mab looks closer at me and frowns. "You're joking, right?" she asks the dragon.

"I do not joke," the dragon says.

"He's not what I expected," she says.

"I'm not wearing a tie," I say.

The flames are dying down. Dirt, after all, doesn't burn very well. She steps toward me and glares. "The Felix Crow I heard about was a brave man, strong and true. He risked his life to save Zeola. This man is a wasted shell."

The dragon sniffs at me, close enough that I could lean forward slightly and impale myself on his giant teeth. "His soul is strong, even if it is drenched in cheap liquor."

"Who's Zeola?" I ask.

"She was a child in the capital. She was kidnapped by someone and a cop named Felix Crow tried to save her. Unfortunately, she was killed by the fates. The Felix Crow I heard of was a hero, a shining savior of the innocent in the city," Mab says.

I know that story, but I never pictured myself as a savior or a hero. "So that was her name," I say quietly.

Mab jerks her head toward me when I say that. "You remember her."

I nod. "I remember her."

"You tried to save her?" Mab asks.

"I tried," I say.

"How did she die?"

How do I handle this? The truth is I only tried to save her because I was bored and drunk. It was pure happenstance that I stumbled across the girl and my own bumbling that got her killed. "I was trying to calm her down and someone blew up the building we were in. I fell on her, trying to protect her."

I'd like to keep it nebulous, but her eyes are burning into me. "I fell on her and a piece of wood pierced her heart."

Mab's face softens and the dragon growls quietly. "The truth is," I say. "I killed her."

The dragon looks first at me and then back at Mab. "That is the truth?" Mab asks me.

"Yes. The sad truth," I tell her.

"But you tried?" she asks.

"I tried."

The dragon snorts again and asks, "Now do you trust him?"

"Somewhat," she says. "Enough."

"Good," the dragon says. "Turn him on."

"Turn me on?" I ask. "What does that mean?"

"Just like you turn a light off and on," Mab says and punches me square in the jaw.

I wake up back in my stone cage desperately thirsty with an aching jaw. The light hasn't changed. The stone hasn't changed. Nothing has changed, except the throbbing pain.

I'm still trapped. The doors are thick stone, thicker than I'd realized. I can see the densely interwoven layers clearly now. In fact, when I look around I can see everything clearer. It's amazing what happens to your brain when it starts to collapse from lack of water. What is it they say? Three days to death or something like that?

I've been here an eternity. At least it feels like an eternity. Maybe it's only been a few hours but my cracked and dry lips would debate that.

What was it that guy said? He wanted to wear my skin? That doesn't make any sense. He also wanted my brain broken. Maybe his brain is broken. I wonder if my eyes will come along with my skin. My eyes are showing me such interesting things right now.

I wonder what it will feel like when my brain finally breaks.

I must be dead. Or broken. Whatever. Something strange is happening here. I expected to be able to move freely but still seem stuck here. Can't ghosts move through walls? Perhaps Yan Wang, the beloved emperor of the underworld, is angry with me for one of my many, many transgressions.

My eyes, though, can see such wondrous things. Tiny particles dance around each other. Solid matter isn't solid and it's not stable. Everything is vibrating and moving. I can feel the movement behind my eyes, in some small part of my brain that I've never used before.

As I pull my brain back the enormity of the stone doors in front of me … changes. They have weight and heft and it took a Tower guard to move them but I've seen them up close and know they're mostly empty space. How is it that something can weigh so much but be mostly nothing?

Out of the sheer boredom of my situation and my rapidly crashing mind I zoom back into the stone and peer closely at the little things that make up the doors. They're tiny dots with other dots buzzing around them. A little push from that spot behind my eyes and one of them goes tearing off. As it bounces off others the stone changes.

What was it the dragon said? Left to its own devices magic can create a gold statue or remove a mountain. It's the most powerful and most primal force on the planet.

I look down at the straps that hold my hands steady. They're biological, lacking the intricate symmetry of the stone but possessing their own logic. I push gently at one of the little dots and it flies into more dots. I push again with more force and the dots explode into motion. More force and the structure breaks down. Soon my wrist is free.

Maybe I'm not dead. Maybe my brain is totally broken. All I know is I can finally scratch that itch and I'm a happy man.

It didn't take long to realize how to start a chain reaction. This must be what magic is: the ability to ripple reality at a very small level. I focus on the stone door in front of me and look deeply into it. A mighty push and dots start moving. Soon they're all slamming against each other. The vibration in the air intensifies, builds to an almost painful level.

The stone doors explode outward and fresh air floods my face. I step through the rubble and find the room empty save the Tower guard that locked me in here. His face is a mask of surprise and terror. I guess he doesn't see stone doors explode every day of the week.

His training takes over and the air around him ripples. Energy swirls and the two-foot long sword of his *kwan dao* starts moving toward my face. He's fast, but I started moving as soon as I saw the air swirl. Is this how Chan dropped me so easily?

The blade slides gracefully past my head and I have all the time in the world to watch it go by. I twist and push off with my hips, driving the power of my legs through my torso into my shoulders. My first punch cracks his ribs, the second slams into the side of his head. Chan always used to say "hospital, graveyard." He meant the first strike should send someone to the hospital, the second should send them to the grave.

Don't worry; it's just a figure of speech. Chan's philosophy of fighting revolved around never wasting a strike. Every punch, every kick, everything he did was as powerful as he could make it.

The guard goes down on my second blow. I kneel down and find he still has a pulse. This guy locked me up to die. He was just doing his job, but I don't care. I kick his head until I hear a sickening crack and his skull collapses. Huizhong and the guy that locked me in here are getting worse treatment; I'm already planning on what to do with them.

Then it's time to go see about The Clock Man.

XI

This high up in the tower the security presence is pretty low. A few people are wandering about, doing errands and sundry tasks, but no one challenges me. Walk around a place like you own it and everyone will believe you actually own it. Well, until you run into the real owners. Those you just kill.

I tried to be the good guy but I guess it's not in my nature. My old buddy rage is back and we're going to have some fun. I tried to hide from him with *baiju*, but now he and I are going to drink and smash and generally make up for lost time. It's like meeting that dysfunctional chick from college who was batshit insane but oh so much fun in the sack.

I feel strange. I've always had fast hands but there's a different energy running through me. I can see air and energy moving around the few people out and about. It's almost like I can see what's going to happen before it happens.

The Tower has almost a hundred floors now. It started as a two story building way back when two stories were damned impressive. Over time, as more and more Clock Men took up residence and needed places to store their things, the Tower grew first out then up. Now it's a giant spire piercing the sky. Other than the Clock Man himself, no one really knows what goes on in the upper floors. The first twenty floors or so are dedicated to the libraries and storage areas for the museums. The remaining floors are a mystery.

People, of course, love mysteries and love to spin yarns about them. Someone's friend who was dating this girl knew a guy who had been up there. They say strange magic dominates the top floors; the Clock Man's own personal stash of power that he can play with to his heart's content. Things, they continue, that simply should not exist wander the upper floors freely.

The same people also like to say that's the reason for the guards. In a place where the public is invited to visit why you need guys like the Tower Guards?

Because they're not there to keep people out, the Tower Guards are there to keep something in.

Personally, I think it's all bunk; the same kinds of stories people relish telling. My guess is the top stories of the Tower are just storage. Floor after floor after floor of Clock Man projects and documents and living quarters for the Tower guards.

The hallway I'm in is empty, but tastefully decorated. The floor is hard oak, polished smooth from decades or centuries of shuffling guards and whoever else gets to come in here. I feel like I should stop and look around but the longer I stay here the better the chance of someone finding my handiwork down the hall. I'd love to beat someone to death, but there's a guy and a girl that need to experience my tender mercies and I need to save some strength for them.

The elevator is in the center of the hallway but those things are steel death boxes. You'd think I'd be over my claustrophobia after my time in the cabinet but the thought of being inside anything make me sweat. I've got some freedom and I intend to use it. Even if I have to climb eighty flights of stairs and die of a heart attack at the top it's better than being stuck in a metal grave.

The first set of stairs is easy.

When I push the door open and poke my head out on the next floor I find Huizhong with her purple hair and two Tower Guards. She smiles that warm smile of hers and I slam the door shut.

I back up and wait. No matter how big and tough these guys are I've got a perfect choke point. Heavy footsteps echo through the door as the big guys charge forward. Their *kwan daos* are supposedly pretty tough, easily capable of going through armor so I decide to take another step back.

Sure enough, the first guy hits the door hard. He was probably hoping to just blow it right off its hinges but it didn't work out too well; the door shudders and dust blows out of the walls, but the door holds.

"The door opens outward, idiot!" I yell.

A two foot blade slams through the door, cutting through the steel like butter. I'm glad I backed up. A second blade punches through and pushes down, ripping a huge gash in the metal. Both blades pull back and crash back through, huge tears forming across the surface.

I wonder why they didn't just open the door.

Tower guards are supposed to be some of the best fighters on the planet and there are two of them a few feet away from me. The first guard was easy, he wasn't expecting me. Now I've got two and they're ready to go. On the other side of them is a woman I'm really looking forward to talking to again. Maybe it's magic, maybe it's general excitement, or maybe it's just my normally violent desires coming out again, but I'm having trouble standing still.

I want blood.

The metal door is weakening. I can sense it, feel it as the structure breaks down. A few more strikes and they'll be able to walk through the hole they're cutting. I close my eyes and focus on the metal in front of me. The energy that holds the dots together is strong as ever. The sharp blades are simply pushing the structure apart, making space for their weapons to go through.

I push against the door with all the mental energy I can and it explodes outward in a mess of metal shards. The explosion of power when the links between the dots erupts is amazing. It pushes me back against the stairwell wall and almost down the stairs.

When the dust settles the two guards are waiting for me. They're covered in scratches and the guy on the right is dripping blood on the tile floor. The air ripples and they both attack at once. The bleeding guy slashes straight across, trying to get me to lean back while his buddy stabs straight forward at my stomach.

I drop and roll sideways, avoiding both strikes easily. The guy that stabbed at me is the first to recover; he twists toward me and the thick blade streaks toward me. Rather than going under it this time I hop over the blade and watch it pass under me. As his *kwan dao* slides past, his buddy stabs straight into me. He almost gets me, but I'm moving too quickly for him to do anything more than cut my shirt.

They work well as a team, each setting me up so the other can knock me down. So far I've managed to stay just ahead of them but my luck doesn't hold out forever. Tower guards are skilled fighters and they constantly switch their tactics. They move from slash and stab to slash then slash, to stab and cut down. The first one cuts straight down at me and I shuffle to the side, right into the horizontal slash.

Magical speed or whatever it is lets me narrowly avoid disaster, but I still wind up with a nasty cut on my chest and two big guys pressing the attack. I need to start thinking differently. I've been thinking like a defender; I need to think like an attacker.

It's counterintuitive, but if you want to negate a long-range weapon you need to move inside its range. A *kwan dao* is a weapon designed to hold an attacker at a distance and it's at its most dangerous at that long range. I wait for the first strike, dodge the second strike and dart in as quickly as I can. Bishamonten – the god of warriors – smiles on my audacious attempt and my half-fist finds the man's throat.

He coughs and chokes. His buddy decides I'm a more important target than his partner is useful and slashes toward me. I fall backward just in time to avoid the huge blade. The guy I just punched takes the huge *kwan dao* right in the stomach.

My foot finds the guy's chin while the tower guard is trying to pull his weapon out of his partner's stomach. He staggers back and I put my other foot between his legs. His knees buckle and the huge guy collapses.

I should let it go, move on and finish what I've started. They're both out of the game and there's no reason to do it, but out of sheer spite I kick the guy as hard as I can. His neck makes a sickening cracking sound and the big guy goes down face first onto the tile floor.

There's blood all over the floor and the coppery scent brings back such good times. I quit the force over a woman. A woman!

Speaking of which...

Huizhong is staring at me, eyes twinkling and a huge grin spreading on her face. "That was amazing," she says.

I'm across the floor in a heartbeat and her throat feels soft and weak in my hand. Whatever Mab and the dragon did, it feels amazing. Huizhong's eyes are bulging and her feet are kicking in the air. That's right, child, there will be no tricking me this time. Her maroon nails tear at my arms but it's no use; we both know she's not going to walk away from this.

But I am. I am going to walk away and go upstairs and tear the Clock Man apart. Not because someone asked me to. Not because I'm afraid of Chan. Because I want to. And when I'm done with the Clock

Man, I'm going to find the woman who set me on this path and teach her a lesson about messing with Felix Crow. Then I'm going to find my buddy Chan and explain to him which of us is better at *wushu*. Once he's broken, well, let's just say Mrs. Chow is going to have a visitor.

Visions fill my head, bloody, rampaging visions. Mrs. Chow's head stuck in a bottle of *baiju* on her bar, her tiny feet kicking at the air as she runs out of breath. Chan's broken body lying in a gutter. That blonde bitch Alyssa cut to shreds. And it all starts with the little girl with the purple hair kicking and clawing at my fist.

She's turning blue and purple now, dying by inches and I'm enjoying every second of it. "That's right, bitch!" I scream in her face. "Felix Crow is back!"

I flash back on all the good times on the force. There was that one guy – the child molester – we tortured him for days before we got bored and left him bleeding and chained to a furnace in an abandoned warehouse. I went back and pissed on his corpse every time I had a bad day. That woman selling *shén jiàng* on the streets, telling everyone her drug would make them immortal. Her god sauce kept her going longer than we expected. When my brothers in black and I were done we sold her to a brothel and spent the proceeds on hookers and booze.

I heard she died on the bed with some fat guy inside of her. He kept fucking her after she was dead. I laughed when I heard that.

Mab's face flashes in my mind, a disapproving look in her eyes. The dragon, ageless and inhuman smiles a sad grin behind her.

Why did I laugh? Is it that funny?

No, use the rage. Let the rage win. Anger makes me stronger. I'm stronger than Chan, stronger than everyone.

Huizhong's body is going slack but she still keeps fighting feebly in my grasp. That's iron will right there. I can respect that. It takes strength to fight day in and day out against the inevitable. Her head is lolling to the side, purple gray hair covering her eyes. One hand grips my arm feebly, a final last-ditch attempt to dig her nails into my flesh.

She is so strong to keep fighting.

I see Chan's face, standing over me, him telling me that all my anger was slowing me down. I needed to be stronger to fight back the rage; that true power came from rising above the hatred and keeping my mind clear. I found I could do that when I had a drink.

My hand unclenches and Huizhong drops to the floor and collapses. She coughs and gags. Tears are streaming down her face as she clutches her throat and spasms.

"I'm sorry," I say feebly.

I wish I was better at this but what do you say to someone when you've just tried to gleefully choke the life out of her? Sure, she drugged me and waved happily when that asshole locked me in that dark place. Anger rises inside of me again. I should kick her. I'll bet with this newfound speed I could kick her head clean off her body. Say hello to Yan Wang, bitch, and tell him when I get to *Diyu* Felix Crow is going to cut his puny death god balls off.

My leg is pulled back, ready to deliver the final killing blow that will feel so good when Huizhong looks up at me and her eyes are filled with terror. I must look like some kind of madman, grinning like an idiot and getting ready to kick someone's head in.

I slowly set my foot back down and back away. I haven't felt hatred like that in years, the *baiju* always kept it bay. My back hits a wall and I slide down and land on my ass. Huizhong watches my every move like I'm a snake about to come back at her.

"Got a *bidi*?" I ask.

She points at a small sequined purse pushed against the wall. My body doesn't entirely want to work. I'm so tired right now. Tired and thirsty. I manage to crawl across the floor and grab her purse. "Do you mind?" I ask and hold the purse up.

She shakes her head but doesn't answer. Her eyes are still huge, greenish dinner plates on a pale, terrified face. Her purse is empty save a box of good *bidis*, a brass lighter with a single tree on it, some money, and an ID. I always felt strange rummaging through a woman's purse. It feels like rummaging through her mind. Ignoring the almost overwhelming desire to pocket her cash I pull out a *bidi* and light it. Gods above and below that feels good.

I lean back against the wall and look at her lighter, staring at the tree. "Did Mab send you?"

Huizhong shakes her head. "Tiamat," she croaks.

"What's a Tiamat?" I ask.

"The dragon. Tiamat. He sent me. Mab knew about it, but it was Tiamat's order. I've been here a couple years doing some terrible things, waiting for the time to be right. Waiting for you to walk through the door," she says quietly.

"Why?" I ask.

Huizhong pulls herself over to my wall and leans against it with a wince and a sigh. We look at each other; the tiger and the crane. Every time I lift my *bidi* to take a drag she flinches. Part of me wants to tell her it's okay, that I'm done hurting her for now, but another part just chuckles. Revenge is a tasty dish. Her eyes never leave mine as she feels around in her purse for a *bidi*. She screws the little leaf-wrapped cigarette into her lips and holds out her hand for her lighter.

It's not much of an apology, but I light her *bidi* before I hand her lighter back. She must have decided I'm okay because she turns away from me and stares at the opposite wall. The tip of the *bidi* burns bright red and she inhales the smoke deep into her lungs before exhaling through her nose like a dragon.

"You were chosen because you're magic sensitive and have a propensity for brutal behavior, but you also have a strong sense of duty," she finally says.

"A monster with a heart of gold," I say and take a drag of my own *bidi*.

"Something like that," she says. "Tiamat and The Order knew they'd have to push you, keep you away from your drug for a while to get the old Felix back and get a chance to talk to you."

"Did Chan know?" I ask.

"They never actually wanted him. He couldn't … finish the job. Almost no one knew what was up; it was all just events to set in motion. They needed a weapon and found one. You just needed some repairs, reminders, and upgrades," she says.

"Good to know I'm still so popular," I say.

"You do have a reputation," she replies.

We finish our smokes in silence, each lost in thoughts. I have to say, I hate this. I hate this whole situation. I hate dragons and fairies and women with purple hair. I was happy and content. I had flying lizards who tolerated me. There was that guy down the street that sold really good fried tarantulas. I could get drunk, solve the occasional case, and generally ignore the world.

Huizhong flicks the rest of her *bidi* across the hall. It throws a few sparks when it lands and a tendril of smoke dances into the air. She turns to me, face resigned, and asks, "Are you going to kill me now?"

Am I? I went through the Hell of Closed Spaces because of her. Days, weeks, however long I spent in there, whatever Mab and Tiamat did to me, it was all enough to let the old Crow out and now three guys are dead and I nearly killed the girl next to me.

I feel terrible. There's a black pit in my stomach and a coiling tendril of hatred in my heart. That pit wants more blood, more pain, and I'd almost like to give in again. Then I think of my little dragons.

"No," I say. "I'm not going to kill you."

"What happens now?" she asks.

"Is Chenming really that much of a problem?" I ask.

"He's completely lost it. Or found it, I don't know," she says with a sigh. "No one's seen him in months. He's learned to control people from a distance. In this building he can take people over and wear them like skin suits. Outside he needs to use a wire to control them."

I flash back on the wire running from the neck of the guy in the alley and thing that exploded out of the dumpster.

"He's planning on controlling all the magic on the planet," Huizhong continues. "He thinks he's a god. It'll only get worse once he's got all the power on the planet."

"Is he on the top floor?" I ask.

"I imagine so. That's where his lab is."

"Does the elevator go all the way up?" I ask. Maybe it's time to let go of some of my fears.

"You'll need a key," she says.

"Any idea where I can get one of these keys?"

She pulls a necklace out of her dress and shows me a shiny brass key. "What are you going to do?" she asks.

"I'm going to kill the Clock Man and go home so I can feed my dragon lizards. Then I'm going to pretend I've never heard of the

Furious Fae, met a dragon, or killed a Clock Man. If you're lucky, I'll pretend I've never heard of you, either."

I grab a *kwan dao* off the floor. The Tower Guard won't be needing it anymore and it might come in handy. "Let's do this," I say. "I've got lizards to feed."

XII

The elevator is one of those outside-the-building jobs with a big, open glass panel that looks out over the better parts of the city. By the twentieth floor the crime and grime have given way to elegant architecture. At the fiftieth floor the grid of the city is plainly visible.

"I've never been this high up before," Huizhong says.

"I prefer being on the ground floor," I tell her. "It's more real."

"It's still real up here, you're just getting more perspective on it," she replies.

"Hmph. From up here all you see is city, but cities are buildings and roads. Cities are people and all the people are down there," I tell her. "Tell me something."

"What do you want to know?" she asks.

"Why didn't you go after him? You have a key and you probably have skills other than drugging guys in museums."

"I'm good," she says, "but you're better. You have the vicious nature of a cop. You've been trained by one of the greatest wushu masters of all time. You're persistent. It was between you and Chan."

"And Chan was unable," I say.

"He was, but he also said you were a better choice. For all your faults, and there are many,"

"Thanks," I interject.

She ignores me and continues. "For all your faults, you're one of the few people who could fight your way through the Clock Tower and execute the Clock Man in cold blood. Chan could have done most of it, but he absolutely refused to kill the Clock Man."

I stand by the window and ponder that. I'm perfectly okay with slaughtering Chenming Zheng and I doubt I'll feel any remorse when the job is done; probably just that dull throb that wants death to be so much more than it is.

She stands next to me and stares out over the city. "The elevator is slow on purpose. It was so the Clock Man could see all the stages of the city, from the people to the whole thing. It was supposed to remind him of his role."

"Ever met him?" I ask.

"No, he'd already holed up by the time I got here. I've met his minions, though. They claim to speak for him."

"Was that asshole that walled me up one of the minions?"

"Robinson," Huizhong says, "Yes, he's one of the head minions."

We're at the seventieth floor now and the city streets have faded. The city is a blur of white and jade now, sparkling in evening suns. "What did you mean when you said he could control people?"

"There's a rumor that Chenming can take over people, make them do what he wants them to do. Here, in this building, he can do it from anywhere with certain people. Outside it's apparently harder, he needs a wire or something so he can't be too far away from them."

"I got into a fight the night before I came here. Killed a guy in an alley and stole his hat. There was a gold wire running from the back of his neck into a dumpster," I say.

"What was in the dumpster?" she asks.

"Dunno," I say. "Something. It exploded out of the dumpster and disappeared down the street before I even knew what was happening."

At the eightieth floor, the city is singular sparkling gem, mostly white with hints of green. It's taken on an existence of its own from up here; the people are all but forgotten and there's only city. Huizhong reaches out to touch me but stops her hand. Fine by me. After nearly killing her I'm not sure I want to touch her.

"We're nearly there," she tells me. "What are you going to do?"

"Kill him and think about killing you," I say.

"I told you, I only did what I had to do."

"Following orders?" I ask.

"Yes," she says. "I know that doesn't make it any better."

"Why?" I ask. We're at the ninetieth floor now. Not much time left. I can see the edges of the city, a fuzzy line where the city ends and the desert begins; a slow change from white and green to light browns and tans.

"Tiamat felt you needed to fall, all the way down. To clear your head and find the monster you used to be."

"You found him all right," I say. "I tried to bury him but you had to go dig him back up."

Huizhong rubs her neck and nods. "We didn't know."

I look at her and throw her the grin I used to give to murderers and child molesters before I cut them from the crotch to sternum or drove nails through their fingers. She recoils. "You knew exactly what you were doing," I tell her. "You found a weapon and you sharpened it and pointed it at Chenming Zheng."

"For what it's worth, I'm sorry," she says.

The elevator dings. Penthouse floor: magic, mysteries, Clock Men.

XIII

The elevator doors open to a house of horrors. The lights are flickering off and on, going from dark to far too bright with the regularity of a heartbeat. Every time the lights flash I get to see another sight I'd rather not see. The lab is a wreck, there's blood everywhere and strange experiments scattered around the place.

Flash: There's a half a man staring at us from a tube of gelatin. On the first flash I think he's dead but each time the light flashes again his head has moved. Soon he's staring at us, mouth open then closed, open then closed.

Flash: A little dragon lizard's wings flap up and down but the only remaining part of the dragon is a severed head and the wings. The dragon's eyes are gyrating wildly in their sockets. Whatever is happening to it hurts.

Flash: Wires run out of a headless body that clenches and unclenches its fists repeatedly. It has the look and feel of a prototype.

I feel Huizhong's hand on my shoulder and shoot her a glare. She frowns but takes her hand off. "Not what you expected?" I ask.

She shakes her head but doesn't answer.

Somewhere across the lab I hear scurrying. Something is clicking along behind the racks and ancient machines. Whatever it is, it doesn't sound human, it sounds like gears rolling across the floor and clacking nightmares.

Without warning Huizhong punches me hard in the kidney. She knew exactly how and where to hit me. Pain radiates through my back and I drop my knees. Her small hand grabs a fistful of my hair and pulls my head back into her knee. I see stars and feel nausea rising through my gut. Head trauma is always hard to deal with. My *kwan dao* clatters to the floor.

Anger rises up again; it's been smoldering, pouting under the surface, and her unexpected punch makes me long for her throat in my hand again.

"Why?" I ask her as I try to struggle to my feet.

Her fist flies out and hits the back of my head. I go back down but land on one knee instead of both. My head is fuzzy and my back is screaming at me. Before she can hit me again I switch knees, spinning in place to face her.

Huizhong's foot lands a glancing blow across my face with just enough force to knock me to the side but not enough force to do any real damage. As I fall I catch myself on my right arm and lash out with my left foot, kicking straight into her midsection.

The air goes out of her and she doubles over. I scramble to my feet, slipping on some … stuff… that's been spilled on the lab floor. Whatever it is viscous and slick. I almost fall but manage to catch myself on a table before I face plant.

Huizhong comes back in fast, faster than she has any right to. It's difficult to follow her movements in the flashing light and I have to resort to touch awareness. She erupts into a flurry of rapid-fire strikes; Southern Style *wushu* at its finest. Every time she punches I follow it with my body and try to push it back to her. Once you get pretty good at sticky hands, you can feel where an opponent is going to strike next and deal with it before it becomes a problem. I can keep up with blocking her but her strikes are coming so fast I can't manage a counter strike.

The room is crowded with all manner of shelves and tables, and that makes a defensive game risky. As she presses her attack I keep moving back slightly and each step back increases the risk of running into something pointy or slipping on something.

It's time to make better use of my surroundings. I've got a basic mental map of the place I made when I walked in. It's an old cop trick, map out the area so you don't get caught up in a trap. I'm near where we came in, near the table holding the half-man. He's stuck in the center of the table, but there's room on either side.

I let Huizhong push me back; let her think she'll have me cornered at the table. When my butt hits the table I wait for her next flurry of strikes and lean back on the table to avoid the worst of them. As I lie down on the table I bring my foot up. The kick's not powerful since I can't push to the floor but it hits her right between her legs.

It may not hurt a woman as much as a man, but there's sensitive tissue down there. She doubles over and I use her body to pull myself up and forward. The kick might not have been powerful, but my fist in her face is. She staggers backwards and slips on the same goop that nearly got me earlier. She lands on her ass, face covered in blood from her newly broken nose.

She's fooled me twice now and there won't be a third time. I hop off the table and scan the room for my *kwan dao*; it's time to end this.

Huizhong sees me pick up the big weapon and stalk toward her. Oddly, she doesn't move, just watches me curiously, like she's not entirely certain what just happened. She pulls her hands from her face and looks at them in horror. I don't have time for her little games anymore, though. I've got a Clock Man to kill.

She finally clues into me as I raise the bladed tip of the *kwan dao* high in the air. A spinning horizontal strike that takes her head clean off would be more dramatic – and fun – but the lab is too tightly packed for that. If I can't cut her head off, I can at least split it in two.

Her hands are up in the air, arms crossed over her face and she's screaming something that I can't hear over the blood rushing in my ears. In the flickering lights I see my blade start to arc down. She can keep her arms up if she wants, my blade will go right through them.

I hit something solid; far too solid to be a head. On the next flicker of the lights I see a hand has caught my strike. Not deflected it. Not blocked it. Caught it. Huizhong is still holding her arms up in an X over her head and there's a hand and part of an arm reaching out from beside her.

The hand looks odd in the flashing lights. I can't quite make out what's wrong with it, but it's lumpier, sharper than it should be. Of course, the fact that the hand can catch a *kwan dao* blade means there's something strange about it. Any hand that can catch an eighteen-inch-long razor-sharp blade is something to be reckoned with.

The thing the hand is attached to makes the hand itself look normal. Something steps in front of Huizhong, a terrifying mess of whirring gear poking out of torn flesh. One of the eyes is missing and was replaced it with a vidder camera that sticks out of its head. Its left arm, the one it caught my blade with, is a mixture of jade and steel.

"Chenming Zheng, I presume," I say.

His voice is a mixture of clicks and purring motors overlaying a deep baritone. "You should have taken my offer."

"What offer?" I ask.

"You could have walked away. You could have ignored everything and been happily rich," he says. "You could have stayed in your cage and been just another skin for me."

"While both of those sound like great deals," I tell him, "I don't care for cages and those were both cages."

"Would a coffin suit you?" he asks.

"Depends on the coffin," I say. "Some are nicer than others but to be frank I'd prefer a nice tomb with some statues of naked ladies having sex with donkeys out front. I feel that would lend it an air of class."

Chenming Zheng stares at me, trying to decide if I'm joking or just crazy. Personally, I like to think it's a bit of both. "I'll see what I can do," he tells me and throws a side kick that sends me skidding on my ass across the floor.

The thing that was the Clock Man stalks toward me smoothly. I would have expected the first melding of man and machine would have been a jerking mess but he's been up here for months perfecting his techniques. This must have been what I saw jump out of the dumpster in that alley.

"What's the deal, Zheng?" I ask. "What do you think you're going to accomplish here?"

I'm talking because my back hurts and I think something may be ripped inside of me. Not only was his kick fast it was powerful. If I can keep him talking it might give me time to figure out to kill Huizhong and walk out of here in one piece.

"I like power," he says. "Soon I'll have all of it and the world will be mine and be me."

Wait, what?

"What do you mean, be you?" I ask.

Huizhong stands up. Her eyes are blank glassy orbs. "Soon everyone will be me," she says.

The dragon lizard's wings start flapping and the hollow eyes focus on me. Its beak opens and closes furiously. The dismembered hand flexes furiously. I hear a sloshing sound behind and turn to find the half man staring at me and gesticulating wildly.

Huizhong attacks without warning and the rest of the labs goes ballistic. She moves quickly, a ferocious series of blows raining toward me. Chenming, or whatever the Clock Man has become, follows her closely. The lab is too tightly packed for them both to attack at the same time so they take turns. It's also too tight for me to use the huge *kwan dao*, I can block with it but my strikes are weak at best. Every time I hit Huizhong she falls back and Chenming takes over.

There's no way I can keep this up for much longer. Eventually the punches will start landing and experience has taught me as soon as start getting punched I'll continue to get punched. There's something strange about the way they fight, though. Huizhong's strikes feel choppy, like her rhythm has changed somewhere.

It's like he's remote controlling her and while I'm focusing on the fight a thought hits me. I disengage quickly, rolling backward over the table behind me and using it as a barricade between them and me. The flickering lights make it hard to track anything. If I'm going to survive this I need to fix the fucking lights before my brain leaks out my ears. Also, I need to get to the wireless machine; it must be how he's controlling everything.

As soon as I land Huizhong leaps toward the table I just rolled over. I kick out as hard as I can and the table slides forward, catching her on the shins. She face plants onto the table and rolls over, holding her shins. Chenming leaps gracefully onto the table and lands ready to pounce again, metal feet scraping on the table. He slides to a stop on the table and glares at me; a flesh and metal god angry that a puny human would dare interrupt his creation. Whatever he's done to himself, he's made a body that's pretty damned slick.

I bolt before he can pounce on me and pound me into oblivion. The damned wireless machine has got to be around here somewhere but where? Chenming lands behind me with a clatter of metal on the stone floors. Maybe the packed lab room can work to my advantage.

At the first intersection I duck down a cluttered aisle and sprint as fast as I can. At every chance I get I turn a random direction. I'm getting myself lost but hopefully losing him in the process. I can hear his metal feet sliding each time he tries to take a tight turn.

The lab takes up the entire top floor and it's a huge mess. I turn one corner and wind up nearly running face first into some kind of strange looking lizard with feathers and teeth. It grins out at me and I smile back. There's a placard next to it that reads "Dinosaur: Deinonychus. Terran." I have no idea what any of those words mean so I reach out a hand and pat the thing on its long-dead head. "I just ran into a dragon, buddy. Whatever you are, you're kind of tiny."

It's time to stop running and start stalking. I quietly sneak back away from the dead end and the dead animal. I can hear Chenming clanking around in the distance but the mess and high bookshelves make it impossible to tell exactly where he is.

I close my eyes and look around. Chenming glows like a torch in the night. Gods above, he's so powerful. How am I going to kill this guy?

Wait. There's something strange about the room. Thin glowing fibers trace around the room. Each of them links up to something that links to Chenming. That's probably my wireless machine. Now, where is Huizhong?

I sneak toward the wireless. Of all the fibers tracing around the room all but two of them are stationary. One links directly to the glowing mass of Chenming. The other is right around the next corner, moving slowly toward me. I expect I'm not the only one who can see like this, so I have to play it careful. I loiter close to the corner but not too close.

Huizhong appears around the corner like she popped into place. She's got a dagger in her right hand and she lunges at me silently. I saw the strike coming before she even realized she was going to do it; energy moved through the air and gave me all the time in the world. I'm already moving before her arm is fully extended. Catch her at the wrist, spin forward and plant my forearm into her extended elbow. I'm through messing with this chick.

She cries out as her arm bends a direction it wasn't meant to bend. Before she can do anything but scream I snake my arm around her neck and pull her backward. My arm completes its turn around her throat and locks. She desperately claws at my arm but it's no use; I've got her bent over backward and locked in place. Her one good arm continues to scrape feebly at my arm but there's no way she's getting out of this. When she goes limp, I count to twenty just to be sure and drop her on the stone floor. A finger on her throat shows her heart is still beating. Next time I'll count to thirty. Slowly.

Now it's time to take care of the Clock Man.

XIV

Chenming senses Huizhong go down and I can feel his concern. I wonder if he can feel my anger; or if he's even capable of understanding such tiny things anymore. I've spent too much time on this job. I've been beaten, drugged, seduced, warped, and wasted for what should have been such a simple task.

It's time for the Clock Man to strike midnight and I'm looking forward to tearing those gears and pieces of metal straight out of his flesh.

"Chenming Zhang!" I yell. "I'm coming for you!"

It's bad enough that he's sucking up all the power but I draw the line at taking control of people; it smells too much like slavery and I cannot abide slavers.

I move to a better position, an open area next to a large window that he probably used as a study while he was working on his twisted plans. The area is suspended off the main floor by cables, probably to give him a better view of his domain and all the things he's going to control. I pull myself up take a moment to look out over the city. Huge windows let me see the whole city spread out a hundred stories below.

Now I've got room to move. That's the thing about *kwan dao*, it's a big weapon and needs space to use effectively. Chenming, or what's left of him, stalks into the opposite side of the room and casually hops up to the study. We stare at each other, wondering when the other will attack but he holds his position and I hold mine.

He grins a mouthful of metal teeth, some formed into fangs, others regular teeth. His right hand forms a fist and the left covers it. He steps gently forward. Both arms come out in traditional salute. It would appear something of Chenming Zheng remains, his movements promise an honorable fight. I return his salute with one of my own and present my *kwan dao*. A slight nod means he agrees to the terms of the fight.

I've got a heavy weapon and he's got … well, he's some kind of mad machine. It should make for an interesting fight. He squares off in a classic Mantis style stance, all his weight on his rear leg and hands held out like a praying mantis. If he follows traditional Mantis style he'll rely on high kicks. I look down at his legs and see pieces of metal. Just one of those feet will crack my skull like an egg.

I take up my own ready position, weight evenly spread and the pointy part of my weapon pointed at his face. At some unseen signal we both start moving, learning about each other. I keep my *kwan dao* moving, spinning gently. The weapon is heavy but it spins smoothly. To make the best use of it, I have to keep it moving and be ready to react.

We circle each other, watching for little cues to each other. I can only assume he's already figured my style but I've only shown him one of my systems. Chan always felt focusing on only one system was a surefire way to get yourself killed. "As soon as someone can guess your style, they've got you," he liked to say. Chan himself had formed his own system of fighting out of dozens of styles, not all of them *Wushu*.

Chenming makes the first move, a blindingly fast jumping kick to my head. As soon as I see the tell-tale shifting of his energy his foot is almost to my head. I barely manage to dodge and don't have a chance to set up a counter attack before a second metal foot nearly crushes my ribs.

I was right; his kicks hurt.

Getting kicked pushes me back, gives me some room, and a moment to get my own attack ready. I stagger back and collapse to a knee. Chenming darts forward and gods above is he fast. Apparently his melding of flesh and machine has made him fast; faster than Chan, faster than me. But he's still predictable.

Before he can get to me I spin on one knee and swing the *kwan dao* at him. If I had timed it correctly the blade would have sliced him in half but I underestimated his speed and the wooden pole hits him rather than the sharp steel. Still, I know how to generate force and my strike knocks him sideways. He rolls and comes up cleanly but it gave me the time I needed to get to my feet.

I spin backwards, letting the *kwan dao* whip around in an arc. With a regular opponent I'd wait for him to move and rely on my natural speed to keep up but Chenming is far faster than a regular opponent and I can barely see the energy swirling before he moves. He darts forward in a blur and rolls under my blade. Before he can hit me I let the blunt side of my weapon continue its arc straight into the side of his head.

The blunt, weighted opposite end my *kwan dao* slams into his head full force. He staggers slightly but otherwise takes it like it's nothing.

The three pound ball should have collapsed his skull but the changes to his body must consist of more than just gears and metal limbs.

A flicker of motion and his metal fist slams into me. He was in an awkward position so he can't put everything behind the blow but it still flattens me. I barely have time to get my feet up before he lands on me. Gods above, he weighs a ton. My legs nearly give out under his bulk. I was planning on using weight to throw him right over my head but he lands straight on top of me and my legs nearly give out. I think I may have pulled a muscle in my leg.

I twist to my side and dump him on the ground with brute force rather than elegant technique – Chan would be disappointed. Chenming's Mantis style isn't well-suited to fighting from the ground but he still manages to land a kick that sends us sliding apart. Metal limbs scrabble at the floor as he tries to stop himself.

My *kwan dao* becomes a cane while I pull myself to my feet. I definitely pulled a muscle. My right leg is throbbing and screaming at me. Chenming rises straight up like some kind of damnable puppet. He's got metal limbs, a head that can take a full-power strike from a three-pound metal ball, and enough weight that I can't lift him.

How do you stop someone when neither the blade nor the ball can hurt him?

I relax and look at him through magical eyes. He's a swirling mass of power, more god now than human. If I had to hazard a guess, I'd say even Tiamat would have trouble with Chenming Zheng. There's no way I can out magic him; he'd swat me like a bug and merrily continue taking over the world.

Speaking of Tiamat, what was it that dragon said? Magic can create a gold statue or remove a mountain. Chenming is tough; no doubt about it, but it just might work. I concentrate on the tiny particles of the wires holding this part of the floor up. The mental effort of maintaining all that information is a crushing blow to my tiny brain but easier to deal with than Zheng's metal fists crushing my skull.

I'm not going to create a gold statue, just change the floor a little. Chenming's feet scrabble for purchase on the tile as he starts to charge. He starts moving, close now as I focus on the wires. They give way with a pop. The floor changes its angle, sloping downward to the floor just below us.

He realizes too late what I'm up to. His metal feet slide smoothly down the ramp I just made for him. He picks up speed rapidly and I hear the crash of a window breaking. I can see him for just a moment, flailing his arms desperately before gravity takes over and he starts the quick journey to the bottom of the Clock Tower.

The lab is trashed but at least the drones have stopped barking. When Chenming Zheng flew out the window he took his magic with him. I should expect a huge explosion as all the power in the man's metal body escapes but there's nothing of the sort. Maybe the magic just flowed back into Aluna.

Huizhong is still lying where I choked her out. She's still breathing and I debate picking her up and tossing her out the window with him, but I don't know how much of what she did was the Clock Man and how much was Tiamat and how much was Huizhong. I may be an asshole, but I like to think I'm a fair asshole.

I'll wait until I know for certain and then toss her in front of a car.

I root around in her purse until I find her *bidis* and lighter. The smoke tastes good, like a little leaf wrapped in a bit of victory. I'm still smoking when she stirs a few minutes later and shoots me a glare.

"Did you get that out of my purse?" she asks.

"Yep, but I left the other stuff alone," I tell her. "That's twice I could have killed you; I figured you could at least cough up a smoke."

She pulls herself to a somewhat upright position and immediately collapses. "Get me one, too," she says as she lies on the floor staring at the ceiling.

"Sure you want one?" I ask. "Your neck is looking a bit bruised."

Huizhong tenderly touches her neck and winces. She nods and I rifle through her purse one more time. I start to toss her a *bidi* and lighter but I figure I might try being a good guy once. Call it what you will, fascination, horniness, whatever, maybe I've done enough to her for one night. I crawl over to her and put the *bidi* between her lips and light it.

She coughs when she inhales but it doesn't stop her. "What happened?" she asks. "Where's Chenming?"

"He fell down," I say.

"You honestly did it, didn't you?" she asks with a kind of awe. "You killed the Clock Man."

"Technically speaking, the rapid stop on the bottom floor killed him."

"Jackass."

"Bitch."

I think I'm beginning to like this girl. I'll just need to check her mouth for poisons in the future.

XV

Mrs. Chow glares at me when I walk into her bar but I can make out the faintest hint of a smile on those permanently pursed lips of hers. She doesn't say a word when I sit down but I can tell something has changed. I'm used to her glaring at me but I'm also used to her traditional money first policy so it's a bit of a shock when she sets two bottles and a glass on the bar and walks away.

At the very least, it's brighter in here.

I sit down at the bar and catch a glimpse of myself in the mirror. My reflection is as handsome as ever and the hat really suits me. Huizhong found my hat and jacket lying in the corner of the Clock Man's lab. She handed them over with a smile and a punch to my jaw before disappearing with a flick of her purple gray hair. Still playing hard to get. Or want. Whatever. I'll be looking her up at some point.

No one was quite sure what to do after Chenming's partially mechanical corpse hit the ground at about a billion meters per second. While the emergency crews were running around trying to figure out what just happened, I slipped out the back in my jacket and hat and made my way here.

The bottles in front of me aren't marked. One has an image of dragon the other has an image of a *fenghuang* – a bird comprised of a rooster, a swallow, a tortoise, a snake, a stag, a goose, and a fish. The dragon is yang, the bird is yin.

Most people don't get the concept of yin and yang; they see them as separate and seek to emphasize their gentle yin or their terrifying yang. The problem is yin and yang must cooperate to create a whole. A yin, in and of itself, is incomplete just as a yang on its own is only a partial thing. Balance, as they say, is all that keeps us from tilting completely to one edge and sliding into oblivion.

Mrs. Chow knows this better than most. She's been known to have her enemies castrated and show up later the same evening to hand out money to orphans. I don't think she's looking to maintain her karma or any other such nonsense, she just feels the need to have balance in her life. For every thug she skins alive and leaves to die in the hot Alunan suns, she does something nice to someone else.

In my case she gave me a choice.

The choice is easy but difficult at the same time. The dragon will make me feel strong and powerful but comes with a terrible price. The *fenghuang* has a different kind of power: subtle, quiet, and often unexpected, but with a different kind of price.

While I'm pondering the door opens and Chan walks in. He's got a young boy, a strange looking dragon covered with feathers, and the strangest damned thing I've ever seen following him. The dragon I can almost wrap my head around; it looks kind of like that stuffed thing in the Clock Tower. What was it called? A dino something. An Earth creature. The other thing, though, is frankly freaky. It walks on all fours and is covered with hair. Its tail wags back and forth like nothing I've ever seen before and sniffs around the bar before it sprawls out on the floor with a contented sigh. It yawns and shows off a huge mouth filled with massive teeth.

"Chan," I ask, pointing at the hairy thing on the floor. "What the hell is that thing?"

Chan looks at me and looks at the creature on the floor and is just about to answer when the boy says, "She's a dog, mister."

Oh, well, that explains everything then. She's a dog. "What's a dog?" I ask.

The boy looks confused, like he can't understand why I would ask that. "It's an Earth animal, Crow," Chan says. "Kind of like your little dragons, just bigger."

"And hairier. What does it do?"

"That's pretty much it," Chan tells me. "She's an old dog and old dogs get tired, right Kevin?"

The boy has sat down on the floor next to the dog and is stroking its fur while the feathered lizard sniffs around the room. "She's nearly a hundred in dog years."

Okay, so it has its own unit of time measurement, too.

A screech breaks the relative calm of the place and I turn around to find Mrs. Chow glaring and pointing at the animals in her bar. I hunt around the bar for something that looks like a snack and settle on an abandoned plate of cold egg rolls. Anything that can set off Mrs. Chow like that is worth befriending.

While Chan tries to cool down Mrs. Chow, I hop off my bar stool and take the plate of eggrolls to the dog. When it sees me coming it growls, a deep bass rumble. Kevin strokes the dog and whispers to it. "It's okay, mister," he says. "She won't bite."

"With teeth like that I'm less worried about being bitten than I am about losing a limb, kid," I reply.

The dino thing skitters over to me and sniffs away at the plate of egg rolls. I swat it on the nose and tell it to wait its turn and am rewarded with a strange chirping noise and a sighing huff. The creature is about half my height with a long snout filled with teeth and I probably shouldn't be screwing with it but as I see it I stared down a dragon not too long ago so this little critter doesn't really faze me.

I squat down and the dog growls a little more but it can smell food nearby. When I hold out one of the eggrolls, it sniffs and delicately takes it from my hand and immediately scoots away to eat in relative safety.

The dino is hovering near me, not quite close enough to swat at, but definitely close enough to dart in and snatch an egg roll, so I take one of the plate and hand it the creature. It snatches the food from my hand in a flash and tilts its head back to chew and swallow. I'm rewarded with more of that chirping cooing sound that it makes.

The dog has finished eating and is edging closer to me, sniffing frantically at the remaining egg roll. "What's her name, kid?" I ask.

"Tina Lou," he says.

"That's a strange name. Of course, it's a strange animal," I say.

"She," he corrects me. "Tina's a she not an it."

I like this kid. He's in one of the most dangerous bars in town with two of the weirdest animals I've ever seen, casually correcting a guy that probably looks like hammered shit. "Sorry, Tina," I tell her. "Want some more?"

I break the remaining egg roll in half and offer the first half to the dino thing. It snatches it from my hand and reaches for the other half. I gently swat it on the nose again and get chirped at for my troubles. The remaining half of the egg roll gets held out to the dog.

She edges forward and again delicately takes the food from my fingers. This time, though, she doesn't back away, but she does eye me warily while she's eating. The dino realizes there's no more food to be had and takes off in search of whatever it is that bird lizards go looking for.

"Hold your hand out to her so she can smell you," Kevin tells me.

"Sure she won't bite it off?" I ask.

"She's fine," the kid says. "If she wanted to get you she would have ripped out your throat by now."

Not exactly relaxing words. I hold my hand out and wait for the dog to take it off at the wrist but all she does is sniff at me. A soft tongue comes out and licks my hand. I guess we're friends now. She wags her tail when I scratch her head.

When I sit down the dog stretches and walks right up to me. Her nose is cold and wet on my face and she's so strong she nearly pushes me over in her desire to lick my face. "Whoa, whoa, whoa," I say, "it's okay, we're friends."

Chan has managed to calm Mrs. Chow down and the queen of crime is standing next to me watching the dog lick my face. "You can pet her, ma'am," Kevin says.

Mrs. Chow snorts but I can tell she's curious. She holds her hand out slowly and I have to suppress a laugh when I see it shaking. The dog sniffs her and sneezes. Mrs. Chow nearly jumps out of her shoes and backs away quickly. "It's okay," I say to the dog, "she's not half as dangerous as she thinks."

The dog shakes her head and walks slowly over to the cowering Mrs. Chow, nails clattering on the floor. Mrs. Chow holds her ground and puts her hand out again. This time the dog sniffs at her fingers and sits down, looking up at Mrs. Chow expectantly and wagging her tail.

"It's not going to bite me, is it?" Mrs. Chow asks.

"She just wants to be friends," Kevin says.

Mrs. Chow sits down and the dog wags faster. Soon Mrs. Chow is making cooing sounds and scratching one very happy dog's belly. It's a fascinating scene until Mrs. Chow shoots me a look that says, in no uncertain terms, that this is not happening and if I know what's good for me I won't tell a soul.

Chan touches my shoulder and says, "We should talk."

I nod and climb to my feet and suddenly feel the weight of the day on my muscles. The adrenaline must have worn off because I am damned tired. We sit at the bar and stare at each other in the mirror for a minute. "So," I finally ask, "what's up with the menagerie back there?"

"He's very magic sensitive," Chan tells me. "The Beast was after him but I managed to get him out in time. There was something else there, too, but I'm not completely certain what it was."

"Shouldn't his parents have taken care of him?" I ask.

"Captured," Chan says.

"The Beast has been busy," I say, rolling my eyes. "Attempted kidnapping and capturing parents."

"He's dangerous, Crow. Mark my words."

"Not to me, I'm done."

"The Beast is dangerous to everyone and everything. Unfortunately when you killed the Clock Man you released a lot of power. Don't worry, it had to be done or Chenming would have taken over everything, but there were some unforeseen consequences," Chan says.

"There are always consequences," I say and reach for a bottle. "So what now?"

"Now it's probably best that you lay low for a while. They'll figure out in time that you did what needed to be done, but in the short term you'll be in a heap of trouble. Mrs. Chow has offered to let you stay here."

"Oh, joy. I'm looking forward to seeing her smiling face every morning."

"Crow, you did something important…," Chan says.

"For once," I interject.

"But you've radically changed the power structure…"

"Because you didn't give me a choice," I say. "You and her and that blonde bitch dropped me into a pool of shit and now I stink to high heaven and things are worse than when I started."

Chan takes off his hat and sets it on the counter. He almost never takes off his hat. "We made a choice and decided this was the least bad option."

"What 'we'?" I ask, getting frustrated. "Who decided and why was I involved in the first place?"

"The Furious Fae and the dragon up North settled on this course of action. I got roped in last summer. Alyssa Zhang was already with them. I volunteered you because if someone was going to infiltrate The Clock Tower it would have to be someone who had a certain – how shall I put this? – moral flexibility," Chan says.

I feel my old buddy rage building up and clench my fist. Chan sees it and edges back slightly. "Never seen you back away pal," I tell him.

"You've changed, Crow," he says. His eyes are squinting, boring into me. "Something happened to you."

"I was locked in a tomb for what …"

"Two weeks," Chan says.

"No shit?" I ask.

He nods his head. "I was locked in a tomb for two weeks. Had a vision of some chick and a dragon. Woke up, found I could change things, killed some people, and killed a Clock Man. Yes. I'm different."

"You died in there. Died and came back and something came back with you."

I focus on the stool he's sitting on and see the little parts that make it what it is and give them a little push. Chan collapses onto the floor and looks up at me in amazement. "Yeah," I tell him. "Something came back with me. And I'm going to put it to good use. You're worried about The Beast? I'll take care of him and then give you something to really worry about."

The dragon bottle is full of rough *baiju*, but it feels so good going down. I drain the whole bottle and smash it down on the bar.

"Don't do this, Felix," Crow says. "You could help us."

"Help you do what? Waste time in the woods with your dragon? This city is ripe for the picking."

I grab my hat and jacket and head for the door. "Stay out of my way, Chan."

On the way out I stop to scratch the dog's ears and am rewarded with a happy wag. At least I've got one friend in the world.

I wonder if my little dragons are still hanging out.

Zona Peligrosa

The freeway outside the tiny convenience store has many names: Canam Highway, US Highway 85, Interstate 25. It's four lanes of asphalt laid down in the 50s that runs over a thousand miles from Las Cruces, New Mexico to Buffalo, Wyoming, running like a black ribbon through deserts and mountains. Though not as prestigious as the former Route 666 – now rechristened Route 491 after too many people worried about the Devil – Interstate 25 transmits goods, tourists, and copious amounts of drugs from the south to the desperate north.

Follow US Highway 380 west through San Antonio – the one in New Mexico, not the one in Texas – and that road runs smack dab into Interstate 25. Before continuing on, stop off at the Owl Bar & Café and have a beer and a green chile cheeseburger. After lunch, keep heading west, go under the Interstate and follow the dusty road off to the left. Down just a bit is the gas station that time forgot. Fortunately, the gas station has a sense of humor. Out front is a sign, probably painted in the last century, that proudly proclaims this is the last chance for gas for over a hundred miles. Go the other direction and there's a gas station less than a mile away. Heading west, though, the sign is actually a lie. The forgotten gas station is the absolute last chance for gas on that dusty little two-lane road. There was another gas station a little over a hundred miles away but it closed over fifty years ago.

The gas station is the last vestige of a once sprawling Whiting Brothers network, which is kind of interesting since the company is essentially dead and its corpses scatter the near-endless miles of Interstate 40. This last remnant is little more than a mechanical cash register, an old-fashioned credit card machine that may or may not work, and a variety of tchotchkes and stuffed things. But it does have gasoline; a truck drains and refills the tanks once a week even though the last time a car was filled here was years in the past. The lights are still on, the soda machine out front still works, and the ancient analog gas pump still dispenses fuel.

Inside the old gas station is a young man named Zapp Blander who has worked here full-time for the last two years. In that time he's helped three customers purchase ancient Zagnut bars (don't eat them) and filled one guy's Escalade with gas. He's gone months at a time without seeing a soul walk into his gas station. Still, the paychecks keep coming and Zapp keeps showing up for work every day. He spends his days reading books by Walter Gibson, Lester Dent, Warren Murphy, and Richard Sapir. Zapp figures if he can read one book a week Gibson and Dent alone should keep him in reading material until the end of his life. Add in the works of Murphy and Sapir and he'll have all the action and adventure he can have until the end of time.

Zapp considers his real job to be reading and drawing. He loves to read about the adventures of strong guys conquering evil and has a secret wish to be more like them. At five foot eight, though, he's hardly the action archetype. Zapp's also acutely aware of the irony of having the perfect name for an action hero when he can barely throw a football.

Today's adventure, a rollicking tale from the thirties, has the Man of Bronze himself facing down the evil John Sunlight. Like all tales from Doc's library it's an over-the-top adventure, filled with the baddest of the bad guys and the best of the good guys. Zapp is leaning back in his chair, feet on the counter when he hears a strange noise outside. In the normally silent world of the Whiting Brothers gas station, any noise is a strange noise. Zapp looks up from his book and sees a brief black blur as a car pulls up and passes just beyond the doors. A few moments later a man walks in flicking his keys around his finger. He's a big guy, dressed in leather like a biker but flashes Zapp a warm grin and disappears into the bathroom.

Zapp knows regulations require customers buy something before they use the bathroom but this is one of the first people to ever even walk into this place and the first one who just walked straight to the shitter like he owned the place. He manages to get a finger in the air, the universal sign of wait a moment, and says, "Wait," but Zapp's words fall into empty air as the bathroom door closes.

There's more noise outside and a beat up truck rolls across the gravel outside. Zapp jumps at the sight. Months of nothing and now he's got two customers at the same time. Two men, jumpy looking guys, walk up to the door. One of them looks around, like he's expecting to see something other than scrub brush and lizards. His buddy shoves him aside and kicks the open door. It flies open and slams back closed again, hitting the second guy in the nose.

"What the …, "Zapp asks no one in particular. He's known about the door's problems for a while, but never felt pressed to actually do anything about it.

The first guy pulls a shotgun from behind his back and points it at the door. Glass flies across the room when pellets hit it at close range, blowing a huge hole in the door. Zapp instinctively holds up his arm but none of the debris comes near him. He watches in a kind of horrid fascination as the guys outside examine the door. They were obviously expecting it to blow the glass clear out of the door but physics is a harsh mistress and thick glass doesn't always do as it's told.

The second guy shoves the first guy out of the way and pushes the door open. This time he's ready when it comes flying back at him and grabs it unsteadily before it can slam into his nose.

The two guys walk into the aging Whiting Brothers gas station like paranoid rabbits, jumping at everything in the small room. One of them sees a stuffed jackalope – a kind of hybrid antelope/jack rabbit statue that's common around the Southwestern United States. His eyes blink rapidly and a terrified squeal oozes from his throat. The guy points his shotgun at the stuffed rabbit and pulls the trigger, turning the fake critter into a mass of dusty fur and sawdust.

Zapp's been robbed enough times in other jobs to know these guys are just a pair of meth heads jonesing for a fix. The problem with meth heads, though, is they're completely irrational even at the best of times. A few years ago Zapp had to give a tweaker the whole cash drawer – even though the drawer was empty – before the guy would leave.

The first guy, a skeleton looking bastard in an old Iron Maiden t-shirt and a pair of jeans that should have been washed months ago, finally notices Zapp and stops dead in his tracks. These two were obviously hoping the place was abandoned and finding another person in the building has interrupted their fever dreams of getting in and out without being seen.

"Hi," Zapp says, waving his fingers nervously in the air. He assumed the standard hold-up position as soon as guys walked in, hands up and no sudden movements.

The second guy, a stringy Iggy Pop looking freak runs straight into the back of the first guy. They both jump and turn their guns on each other. It takes their drug-addled minds a long time to realize they're both on the same side but when they finally click the guys turn back to Zapp. The second guy smiles a toothless grin that should look menacing but only manages to look silly.

"Give us the … cash!" Iron Maiden yells.

"There's no money here, guys," Zapp says. "I haven't had a customer in years."

"Don't fuck with us!" the second guy yells. They're all about the yelling. "We're not retards. Open the fucking cash register and give us the cash."

Zapp works at the old analog cash register but it won't open. He smacks it and the old machine lets out a delighted ding. The cash drawer grinds partway open and Zapp has to tug it the rest of the way. He motions to the empty drawer but realizes the tweakers can't see it. With a huge amount of effort he turns the register toward the guys just in time to see their heads explode.

Behind them is the guy in leather who had walked in just before the tweakers. He watches calmly as the dead bodies drop to the floor, looking down the barrel of the biggest goddamned gun Zapp has ever seen. "Do you have any more of the jack rabbit things with horns?" the guy asks. "My gal would think that's the funniest shit she's ever seen."

Zapp stares at him in complete shock, struggling to comprehend what kind of man would blow away two guys and then ask about a jackalope. "You … you shot them," he stammers.

"Yeah," the guy says simply. "I woulda been here sooner but I couldn't find the toilet paper. I was at a Mexican/Greek joint up in Albuquerque earlier today. Don't know what you call it but it wasn't pretty if you know what I mean."

"You didn't have to shoot them," Zapp almost yells.

"Well, no, not technically," the guy says, "but I already had my gun out."

Zapp looks around the little store and wonders what to do. The guy has put his gun away, but there's still the matter of the blood, skull pieces, and brains scattered across the floor and walls. Unsure of what to do, Zapp brushes a piece of skull off the Man of Bronze.

He decides there's nothing else to do but move forward. "You didn't have to kill them," Zapp says.

The guy in leather shrugs and says, "They were wasting time and I needed a present for my gal." He snaps his fingers and adds, "Got any more of those rabbits? Maybe in the back."

Zapp motions around the small store and says, "There is no back. This is it; just a small store with old candy bars and fresh corpses."

The heady smell of copper hits Zapp's nostrils and he nearly chokes. Bile rises in his throat and his old familiar buddy nausea drops in for a visit. His stomach convulses, convinced the ageless Zagnut bars are at fault for the way he's feeling.

"You okay, bud?" the guy asks.

Zapp covers his mouth and shakes his head. "I'm fine," he mutters through clenched lips and tight fingers but he's not fine. He's about to add insult to injury and if he doesn't make it to the bathroom soon the insult is going to be added to the injury on the floor.

The guy stands stock still, waiting patiently for what everyone in the room knows is going to happen soon and violently and all over the place. Zapp tries desperately to keep his peanut brittle, cocoa, and coconut breakfast down in his gut where it belongs but his gut has plans to evict its current tenants.

Zapp's stomach seizes and acid rises in his throat. He's going to toss his cookies and there's nothing in the world that can prevent that but he still fights tooth and nail to stop it. Another seizure and he can feel little chunks making their way up.

"Just let it go, man," the guy says, "you can fight it all day but you're gonna lose."

Screw him, Zapp thinks and fights puking with everything he's got. His stomach spasms again and he squeezes his eyes shut and does his best to ignore the coppery scent of the blood and everything else that's spilled into the air since the tweakers died. Thinking about the smell heightens it and his guts erupt.

When the heaving ends and the dry heaves finally taper off to gags and the gagging edges back a general feeling of weakness, Zapp finds himself leaning on the counter and wishing he was dead. "Y'all done?" the guy asks him.

Zapp nods and pants.

"First time around a dead guy," the guy says, more a statement than a question, but Zapp nods anyway and wonders if this idiot will ever shut up.

"I usually kill 'em from a distance if I can," the guy says, either unaware that Zapp doesn't want to listen or simply doesn't care anymore. "These boots are pricey and hard to come by. My gal got 'em for me, personally, and she'd be a might bit pissed off if I got blood or brains or whatever all over 'em."

Zapp can't help himself and looks at the guy's boots. They seem unremarkable, a pair of decent looking engineer boots with rubber soles. The same kind of boots sold at a dozen stores in the area.

The guy must have caught Zapp's eye because he says, "I know, they don't look like much, but she had to skin a damned thing to get 'em. That's why I wanted one of them jackrabbits with the horns on 'em. They kind of look like some damned freaky pet and I think she'd get a kick out of that."

Zapp's voice is harsh, but he manages to say, "There might be one more over there by the drinks. Look on top of that shelf over there."

The guy turns and looks around while Zapp decides he needs to pilfer a Coke from the old fridge. He opens the top and finds a single warm bottle rolling around dejectedly. Good enough, he thinks, and reaches in. His grip is still weak, but Zapp manages to hold the bottle long enough to pop the top on the bottle opener on the front of the dead machine.

The Coke is probably thirty years old, but the fizzy drink goes down as smooth as it ever does and settles Zapp's grumbling stomach. He faces away from the mess on the floor and pretends nothing happened while he downs the old soda.

"Will you look at that," the guy says. "This one's even nicer than the other one. How much you want for it?"

Zapp waves a hand behind him, trying to tell the guy it's on the house but the stranger isn't having any of it. "Come on, I can't take this for nothing; wouldn't be proper."

"Saved … burp … my life," Zapp says.

"Yeah, but I enjoyed that. Hell, killin' bad guys is almost as much fun as a guy can get with his clothes on," the stranger says.

"I wouldn't know," Zapp says and finishes his Coke. He's got a god-awful mess to clean up and while he's not anxious to get it started, he is anxious to have it done.

"What?" the stranger asks, "Are you tellin' me you ain't never killed no one?"

Zapp shakes his head slowly. The stranger, stuffed jackalope under his arm, walks closer to the counter and looks at the book. The face of the Man of Bronze stares back at him. "Doc Savage, huh?" the stranger comments, "I used to read his stories, too, back in the day. Ol' Doc wouldn't have a problem lettin' the bad guys come to their untimely end. He never killed anyone, though, if memory serves. Didn't have no problem lettin' them fall to their doom or get crushed by stones, but he never pulled the trigger himself. After the war, of course. They never covered it in the books but I suspect ol' Doc killed plenty in the war. That why you ain't never killed anyone?"

"I'm not Doc," Zapp says quietly and for the first time in his life he realizes with absolute certainty that he is not one of the action heroes he so wants to be like.

"No," the stranger agrees, "you ain't. But hell, even Doc had to become Doc at some point in his life. Ain't nobody born Doc Savage. Guy like that has to be made."

"How do you make someone like Doc Savage?" Zapp asks quietly.

"Doc tested his mettle in World War I. Fought the Germans before they went completely off the rails and became Nazis. It was a brutal war and it changed him, arguably for the better. Everyone needs to break out of their comfort zone if they want to change."

Zapp looks around the room filled with a mess he'll wind up having to clean up and realizes he can stay here forever and have a safe life reading or he can walk out the door right now and try to be someone interesting. "What do you recommend?" he asks the stranger.

"You seriously never killed anyone?" the stranger asks with a cocked eyebrow like he's having trouble believing there are people in the world that haven't killed anyone.

"Never," Zapp says.

"You're sure. You've never killed anyone."

"Why is that so hard to believe?"

"Dunno," the stranger says with a shrug. "Just seems strange to me."

"I live in a quiet world," Zapp says. "I read. I do other things that are boring."

"You just had a shotgun pointed at your face."

Zapp pauses, remembering just how big those shotgun barrels looked. He gulps and visualizes the jackalope exploding into a mass of fake fur and sawdust.

"And you're still here," the stranger continues. "You wanna do something else interesting today?"

"I am not having sex with you in the bathroom," Zapp says.

The stranger bursts out laughing. His laugh is loud and boisterous and obviously not concerned with anything in the world. "No, buddy, you're not my type," he says, wiping tears of laughter from his face. "Besides, my gal would probably gut the both of us."

"You are the strangest person I've ever met," Zapp says.

"Much obliged," the stranger replies. "So, you up for a spot of fun or do you feel like staying here and cleaning up this mess?"

The shop is a total mess; it looks like the set of a Japanese horror movie involving tentacle monsters and ghosts. By his best estimates, Zapp figures he's looking at probably a full day of slogging through things that should have been left in bodies, a few mops, and at least the rest of the sponges.

He looks from the floor to Doc Savage's grimacing visage. What would Doc do?

"What's your name?" Zapp asks.

"Jack," the stranger says, "Yours?"

"Zapp."

"Zapp?" Jack asks.

"Zapp," Zapp replies. "With two ps."

"Far out, Zapp."

They stare at each other; Zapp pale and wan, Jack clutching a stuffed jackalope. "You ready, zapper?" Jack asks.

Zapp raises an eyebrow, wondering at the sudden familiarity but decides it's just how Jack is. "You know what, Jack, I think I am."

"Need to lock up or anything?"

"If someone's that desperate for Zagnut bars and thirty-year-old maps they can help themselves," Zapp says.

"That's the spirit buddy," Jack says with a huge grin. "Let's go shake the pillars of Heaven."

Zapp is unsure exactly what that means, but it sounds like something someone should say at a time like this. Shake the pillars of Heaven. Fight the good fight. If it bleeds we can kill it. Do the wrong thing for all the right reasons.

He steps over broken bodies and shattered glass, pulls the door open and holds it when it tries to snap shut, and finds a piece of history parked in front of his store.

Jack's car is a sleek auto from a bygone time and, unlike most people, Zapp immediately recognizes the brand. "Is that a Cord 810?"

"Nope," Jack says and keeps walking toward the driver's side door. "It's an 812."

The car is a sleek throwback to the time when car design reflected an organic aesthetic. It's a shapely and seductive ball of curves that draw the eye from the front to the back. The black paint has speckles of silver in it that glint in the late morning sun.

"This isn't a car," Zapp says.

Jack leans over the top of the car and peers at Zapp. "Oh yeah, son? What is it, then?"

"It's a dream on wheels," Zapp says.

Jack laughs that huge laugh of his, the one that says he doesn't have a care in the world. "Hop in, buddy. Dreams never stay still for very long and you don't want to be standing there when this one leaves."

Zapp takes a last long look at the Whiting Brothers store that's been a second home for years. This morning it all seemed perfectly normal: a place to go and someone would send him a check. Now the front door is shot out and the inside is covered with things that really weren't intended to cover stores. A part of him, a large part, wants to go back inside and keep the world he was used to. It was imperfect, it wouldn't lead anywhere, but it was safe and safety feels like a warm blanket.

He looks back at the car and his heart aches. He doesn't have a damned idea who the driver is, where the car is going, or what's down that road but it's not covered with brains and puke or filled with aging candy bars.

Zapp stares at the car but hesitates to get in. "What's wrong, buddy?" Jack asks.

"It's just ...," Zapp says and trails off.

"Just what?"

"Well, it's just ... I feel like I should be wearing a suit or a nice pair of sunglasses or something before I get in this car. My jeans and T-shirt just don't feel right," Zapp says.

Jack spreads his arms wide and stares at his reflection in the window. His beat-up leather jacket, Motörhead shirt, and faded jeans don't look much better but Jack seems completely at ease in his clothes and skin. He grins and looks up at Zapp. "You're right," he tells Zapp. "You do need something before you get in this car."

"What am I missing? It's the suit isn't it?" Zapp asks.

"Nope, wanna guess again?" Jack asks him.

"Glasses?"

"It is bright out here," Jack says, looking around at the world. He reaches into his jacket and pulls out a beat up pair of Ray-Bans and sighs with pleasure when he puts them on.

"We've got some glasses inside," Zapp says.

"Wouldn't hurt, but it ain't what you need." Jack tells him. "May as well grab those glasses, though, son. Mighty bright day today."

"Okay, then," Zapp says. "I'll bite. What do I need?"

"Attitude, son. You need attitude. You can't go through life thinking what you ain't good enough. All the suits and sunglasses in the world won't make you anything but you in a suit and sunglasses. Your buddy in there, Doc, you think he'd worry about glasses or a suit?"

"Probably not," Zapp replies. "But he was Doc."

"Yeah," Jack says. "He was Doc. One hundred percent of the time, Clark Savage Junior was Doc Savage."

Zapp stands up a bit straighter and nods, pondering the existential notion that Doc Savage could ever be anyone other than Doc Savage. "I see your point," he says.

"You're still gonna need them shades, though, son. Powerful sunny day today," Jack says. "It don't matter what pair you choose. It don't matter what color they are or what they got written on the side. If they keep the sun out of your eyes that's all you gotta worry about."

"I'll be right back," Zapp says.

He darts into the store, grabs the first pair of shades he finds – Wayfarer knockoffs with pink arms – and returns to find the engine running and the passenger door open. Zapp pulls his wits about him, sucks in a deep breath, and hopes to live up to the expectation.

The Cord 812 is smooth and sexy, so smooth Zapp barely feels it move. It's been so well maintained or restored or whatever that there's no way anyone would ever mistake this for a nearly hundred-year-old automobile. Zapp's car, an '89 Volkswagen Scirocco, can't even hit a bump with a part of it falling off but the Cord looks brand new. With a few after-market accessories, of course. Just like Doc, Jack doesn't seem the type to drive factory spec.

The inside of the car is appointed in buttery soft leather and enough polished wood to make a sizeable bar. That's where the tradition ends, though. It's unlikely the original Cord 812 came equipped with a heads-up display, a GPS unit, and a stereo that can blow women's clothes off. The stereo is currently blasting some kind of electronic swing, a thumping mixture of jazz horns and bass beats.

In the middle of the dashboard, right under a box that appears to do nothing more than hold a bunch of flashing lights, is a picture of a red woman with horns and a long tail. She's obviously naked but twisted around so nothing is showing. It's a skill apparently all women have developed.

"Who's the demon?" Zapp yells over the music.

Jack's head is bouncing in time with the beat, obviously lost in the music and the road. Zapp taps him on the shoulder and points at the picture. Jack presses a button on the steering wheel and the music stops. After the thumping jazz the silence feels almost oppressive. "What's up, buddy?" Jack asks.

Zapp points at the picture and asks, "Why do you have a picture of a demon woman on your dashboard?"

Jack nods sagely and says in an absolutely serious tone, "First, she's a devil not a demon. Never call a devil a demon lest you feel like seeing your innards."

"Why's that?" Zapp asks.

"Devils are smart, like us. Demons are automatons, critters the devils have made off in Purgatory or someplace like that. Calling a devil a demon is kind of like calling someone retarded. They don't take too kindly to that. Kind of a high strung group if you know what I mean," Jack says.

"Duly noted," Zapp replies. "If I'm ever in the company of a devil I'll make sure to not call it a demon."

"Him or her, not it," Jack says. "They're people. Well, mostly. They're really not that different from you and me. Sure their skin is different and the girls have those sexy tails, but devils are mostly just folk doing what they do."

"Okay, sorry. I didn't mean any offense," Zapp says. "Who's this girl?"

"That beautiful lady is my gal, Sally Anne," Jack says with a huge smile. "Pretty little thing, ain't she?"

"You're dating a devil?" Zapp asks, astonished. Like most people he'd always associated devils with evil and bad things and wonders what their relationship is like.

"Yup," Jack says. "Happiest I've ever been."

Zapp opens his mouth to ask more questions but decides it would be impolite to pry into the guy's personal life. He looks around the car and smiles. It's not often one gets to ride in car this old and well-restored. "Where'd you get the car?" Zapp finally asks.

"Won it in a poker game," Jack tells him. "The guy I beat wasn't too happy to lose it, either, but it was the car or his balls. He still took twelve hours to make up his mind and, personally, I think he made the wrong decision."

"Heck of a poker game," Zapp says.

"It's an honest trade," Jack replies.

They drive in silence for a few minutes down the road until Jack suddenly stops the car in front a dead end sign. He stares at the sign; brow furrowed and hands gripping the steering wheel. His knuckles turn white.

Without looking at Zapp, Jack points a finger and says, "Past this sign there's no going back. Sure you're still in?"

"What do you mean, no going back?" Zapp asks.

"I mean no going back. That sign isn't a lie," Jack says.

Zapp peers down the road but can only see one sign. "What, the one that says 'Dead End'?"

"That's the one," Jack says. "Most of the time those signs mean the road comes to an end unexpectedly. This is the eternal highway. At the end of it is a house."

"How can there be an end to an eternal highway?" Zapp asks.

"The house is the beginning and the end of the highway. Keep going and you'll always come back to that house." Jack is making strange gestures with his hands, kind of up and down waving patterns like he's imagining the car going over hills and around corners.

Zapp peers down the road and sees nothing more than an endless ribbon of cracked asphalt and shimmering mirages. "Okay, "he says, "If you go past the house and always come back to it, how do you get back off the eternal highway? Is there an exit ramp or something?"

"Something like that," Jack says, pointing at the sign in front of them. "There's only one way off this road and it's a heck of a first step."

"Okay, how about you be a little less obtuse and just tell me," Zapp says.

"That sign will tell you everything you need to know," Jack says, pointing forward.

Zapp looks around, wondering if he missed another sign out there somewhere but all he can see is the sign that reads "Dead End." He points at it and asks, "The one that says 'Dead End'?"

"That's the one."

"Okay," Zapp says, wondering where all this is going, "I'll bite. What is the sign trying to tell me?"

"You gotta die to get off this road," Jack says ominously.

"Die?"

"Die."

"I'm leaving," Zapp says and reaches for the door.

Jack's hand darts out, far faster than it should be able to move and lands on Zapp's shoulder. "Wait," Jack says, "hear me out."

"You're kidding right? I've got to die and you want me to hear you out? Are you insane?" Zapp asks.

"Yes. But not in the way you're thinking," Jack says seriously. "No, look, there are lots of different kinds of dying. Innocence can die. Your faith in humanity can die."

"My patience can die," Zapp adds.

"See, there you are," Jack says, gesturing wildly. "A part of you is already dying. Thirty minutes ago you were this quiet, shy guy and now you're throwing out zingers."

"So," Zapp says, "what is down that road that is worth dying for, even if it's just a metaphorical death?"

"You're in, buddy. You may not realize it, but you're in, balls to bone," Jack tells him.

"I'm not committing to anything," Zapp says. His fingers are still on the door but his mind is no longer paying attention. Curiosity has him in its grasp and he knows there's no way it will let go.

"You're committed, pal. You're ready to go the distance just to see what old Jack has up his sleeve. You just need to admit it to yourself. If I told you the most important thing in the universe was at the end of this road you wouldn't believe me so let's just say the most important thing in the universe at the end of this road," Jack says with a sly grin.

"I see what you did there," Zapp says with a sigh.

"Told you you wouldn't believe me," Jack says.

Zapp looks out the front window of the car. He's never been down the road in front of him but it promises action, adventure, and danger. Behind him is an empty stored filled with old candy bars and fresh blood.

Quality or quantity, which is better?

"What is it?" Zapp asks. "What's down there and why do you want my help? I'm just a guy who sits in an empty store and reads books."

"And dreams of action, right? Adventure? Who cares what the movies say, everyone craves action and adventure. Save the world, get the girl, live large, am I right? You can go forward and some part of you will have to die to get out or you can go back to your store. A quick death with a promise of a little fun is that way," Jack says, pointing through the windshield. He points his thumb backward and adds, "Or you can go back there, clean up blood and die by inches every day. You'll get a longer life if you go back to the store, but a better one if you go to the house."

Quantity of life or quality of life, Zapp thinks. Go out with a bang or with a whimper.

"Why do you need me?" Zapp asks again.

"At the end of this road, in that house I told you about earlier, is a thing I need to get before someone else grabs it. I can't touch it; I'm not innocent like you. It's worth a lot," Jack says.

"To who?" Zapp asks.

"What?"

"You said it was worth a lot. Who is it worth a lot to?"

"To me," Jack says quietly. "It's worth it to me to keep it away from the people looking for it."

"What makes you better than them?" Zapp asks.

"I don't want the damned thing. If I could throw it off the edge of the universe I'd do it but there ain't no edge of the universe and I can't touch it anyway. Only someone innocent can touch it," Jack says.

"That's why you want me to come, isn't it? Because I've never killed anyone. I'm innocent," Zapp says, feeling disheartened. He feels kind of pathetic hoping a guy like Jack might have been a friend.

"You're a good guy, Zapp. Not many people anymore I can say that about," Jack says, punching Zapp in the shoulder. "Besides, how many folk you know that get the Man of Bronze?"

Zapp's mood elevates slightly. What would Doc do in this situation? Would the man feel sorry for himself or would he tear off his shirt and go save the world? "This thing out there," he asks, "it's a big deal?"

"It can change the balance," Jack says. "Whoever gets it wins."

"What does that mean?" Zapp asks.

"Balance is important. Go too far in one direction and good things can go bad," Jack tells him. "Think of like this: there's this old joke I like. What's the difference between kinky and perverted?"

Zapp shrugs. To date he's only ever kissed one girl and it didn't exactly go well.

"Kinky tickles your ass with a feather," Jack says. "Perverted uses the whole chicken."

"Are you saying someone will tickle my ass with a chicken?" Zapp asks.

"Or something similar," Jack tells him.

"Kinky," Zapp says, thoughtfully.

"No," Jack says. "Perverted."

They sit in silence, each pondering their own problems. Zapp's mind keeps coming back to the idea of cleaning up blood and guts. He couldn't care less about balance or chickens or who wins, but he doesn't want to go back to slow death and he definitely doesn't want to clean up the mess back at the station.

"Can I drive?" Zapp asks.

Jack laughs. "Hell, no. Since I won it, I'm the only person that's ever driven this car and as long as I breathe I'm the only one that ever will drive this car. I will, however, make you a bargain."

Disappointment is clear on Zapp's face, but he didn't really think Jack would hand over the reins to the Cord. "What's the bargain?" he asks.

"One thing is information, the other is a gift," Jack says.

"Information? About what?" Zapp asks.

"After we're done, Hoss," Jack says. "You know that shed out back of your station?"

"Yeah, what about it? It's been locked ever since I started working there," Zapp says. He'd gone round to the shed from time to time over the years, wondering what was inside. No matter what he tried he could never get it open.

Jack reaches into his jacket and pulls out a shining key. "I think you'll like what's inside."

Zapp thinks over the deal. Information and a surprise. Knowing Jack, the information is some trivia about the pulp heroes of yore and the surprise is a shed full of stuffed jackalopes, but that's more information and more jackalopes than he has now. "Deal," Zapp says.

Jack's fist pounds of the steering wheel and he lets out whoop of joy. "Fuckin' A!" he yells. "Let's shake the pillars of Heaven."

A melancholy song, musings about the universe played on a Chinese pipe, starts quietly on the car's stereo. It sounds completely incongruous to Jack's exuberance. Jack is grinning ear-to-ear and the music sounds like a calm hit of magical mushrooms.

"You said that already," Zapp says.

"Gonna shake 'em again," Jack says and puts the old Cord into gear. His foot slams down on the accelerator and the giant engine roars. With a happy grin he pops the clutch and the car leaps forward.

They shoot past the Dead End sign and the road changes. New Mexico roads are notorious for having maintenance issues. The more remote the road, the longer it's been since anyone fixed it. A road this far off the freeway should be nothing more than potholes and cracked pavement but as soon as they pass the Dead End sign the road is smooth as silk.

A horn starts to play, layered over the mournful Chinese pipes. For about thirty seconds the horn and the pipes argue with each other over who should be in charge. Eventually the horn wins out and the song switches from meditative to the jazzy beats of a forgotten speakeasy. The horn finds its place in the world and soon the deep bass of modern electronic music adds its voice to the piece.

Scrub brush, small hills, and scraggly trees turn to blurs and then become crystal clear. The world outside the windows moves forward then backward then skips forward again. Time becomes unhinged and struggles to right itself.

"Happening what's?" Zapp asks. He shakes his head and tries again. "What's happening? Jumping trees around are the."

Jack holds up a finger and concentrates on the road.

Zapp looks around the cabin of the old Cord 812, desperately seeking anything to anchor his mind in time. The MP3 player on the dash is jumping around, endlessly repeating what should be the end of the song, the final farewell of the speakeasy horn, but the techno beat isn't yet ready to call it quits.

The horn calls quitting quits and the song moves on into a long drum solo. The solo is part cacophony, part planned, all energy.

Something lurches deep inside of Zapp's head and it feels like he tripped over an idea and sprawled face-first into the dust. "What just happened?" he asks breathlessly.

"Sorry, Hoss," Jack says, "Forgot to tell you there's a bump at the beginning."

"A bump," Zapp says.

"Well, you can't put an endless highway right in the middle of New Mexico," Jack says. "I mean, the place is pretty wide open but it's not endless."

The drum solo ends and the horn, the drum, the bass, and the pulsing techno beat continue on, working together to create a unified whole from such disparate styles.

Outside the Cord scenery flashes by. Things up close are blurry, the trees and scrub brush in the back are crystal clear. An occasional saguaro passes by, arms held out in a comical pose like it's surrendering to a bandito or dancing a jig in a shitty Juarez bar. "Those don't grow in New Mexico," Zapp says, pointing out the window.

"What doesn't?" Jack asks.

"Saguaro," Zapp says. Jack looks confused so Zapp adds, "The cactus with the arms."

"Those are cool," Jack says.

"Yeah, but they don't grow in New Mexico," Jack says.

"You missed the part where I said we're not in New Mexico anymore," Jack says. "You know what's interesting about this road?"

"Other than the saguaro?" Zapp asks.

"Yeah," Jack says. He raises his arms in the air and points them like up a cactus. "Saguaro,"

Zapp doesn't reply. A thousand snarky replies drift through his head but he chokes them down and coughs into his fist.

"This road is eternal, right?" Jack asks.

Zapp nods.

"Okay, the crazy thing about eternal is you can't think about it as having distance. It's eternal because it has no distance. No beginning. No end," Jack says.

Zapp nods slowly, completely confused.

"Think about it this way: eternal means unending but the only way to make something unending is to make sure it never starts in the first place. Hard to wrap your head around, I know, but that's how it is. This place goes on forever because it never actually starts," Jack says. He points a finger out the window at a house in the distance. "See that house," he adds.

The music is a pulsing, pounding beat, filled with joy and dancing and the sensational idea that there is no difference in time between the various styles; all are one.

Zapp peers out the window and sees a white house in the middle of nowhere. "Yeah," he says. "I see it."

"No you don't," Jack says.

"It's right there," Zapp says, pointing out the window at an empty expanse. He shakes his head like he's trying to clear it. "Where'd it go?"

"It was never there and it was always there," Jack says with a serious look on his face.

The song builds to a second, final crescendo. All the styles, all the times, all the instruments have worked together in unison to get to this point and they're all proud of themselves. The joy of a job well done is almost palpable in the music.

The car stops suddenly, slamming Zapp forward in his seat. The seatbelt bites into his waist but keeps him from flying through the window. He grabs his stomach and doubles over. "What are you doing?" he asks through gritted teeth.

With the sound of faint clapping, like the speakeasy was impressed, the song fades to an end.

Jack points through the window. "We're there. You gotta be careful or this place will get you every time."

Outside the window is a white house with green trim. The place has a neatly trimmed lawn and hedges. Everything about the place screams ideals; the ideal lawn, the ideal hedges, the ideal shutters that don't actually close but look ideal. It's the ideal house, so perfect it's kind of creepy.

"What now?" Zapp asks.

"Now, you go in and get the thing," Jack says.

Zapp stares in disbelief. "I go in? And get the thing?"

"Yep, you," Jack says. "Now, I appreciate it and I'll be in your debt. All you gotta do is go in that house and get the thing."

"You're not coming?" Zapp asks.

"I can't touch the thing while it's in the house," Jack says. "That's the thing about the house and the thing. While it's in there only someone innocent can touch it."

"Innocent?"

"Never killed anyone. Strange bit of rules about the universe: you ain't never killed anyone and you're considered innocent. No matter what else you done in this life, if you ain't killed anyone, you're innocent. And only innocent people can get the thing while it's in the house," Jack says.

"Whose bright idea was that?" Zapp asks.

"Mine," Jack says. "Light, dark, good, bad, whatever. They all killed someone at some point. It was the only way to keep the balance. Whoever gets it wins and I don't want it falling into anyone's hands I can't trust."

Zapp stares out the window at the house. Aside from the fact that it's in the middle of nowhere, its very … idealness … seems completely out of place. He remembers driving through Celebration with his folks when he was younger and the very perfection of the place made it seem strange and kind of frightening. This place has the same otherworldly feel.

"Why now?" Zapp asks.

"What do you mean?" Jack asks back.

"Why now?" Zapp asks again. "What's happening that you have to do this now?"

Jack leans back and for the first time since Zapp met him, the man looks nervous. All his effervescence and devil-may-care attitude slowly ebb away. "They found this place," he says, motioning at the house. "They're on their way right now."

"Who found it?" Zapp asks. "Who's on the way?"

"Everyone," Jack says. "They're all coming. Whoever gets in there first wins and then everyone loses."

"When?" Zapp asks.

"Any time now," Jack replies. "That's why I have to hurry. Why we have to hurry. If you like this world as it is, the balance must remain. All this will end the second the balance shifts."

"What if the good guys get it first?" Zapp asks.

"Well, we are here and we've got a lead, so the good guys can still win if you get in there and get it," Jack says.

"That's not what I meant," Zapp says.

"We are the only good guys in this game," Jack says calmly. "You need to understand that. You want to be free, you want to keep doing what you're doing? This is the only way. The light wins and everyone follows their game. The dark wins and everyone follows their game. Right now no one wins and that's the only way we – you and I – can win."

The sun is bright. Too bright even to be a New Mexico summer. Even through Zapp's cheap sunglasses the glare is almost debilitating. He looks around at the desolate landscape, just a two-lane road and scrub brush as far as the eye can see.

"What am I looking for?" Zapp asks.

"It can look like anything, you need to feel your way through it," Jack tells him. "It's powerful. You'll feel a tingle when you're near it."

"Walk in, grab something, walk out," Zapp says. "How hard can it be?"

"That's the spirit, son. That's moxie!" Jack says, pounding the steering wheel in excitement.

Now is the time, Zapp thinks, to become Doc. "I'll be right back," he says and opens the door.

"Go be the hero, big guy. Watch out for the guardian, though," Jack says.

"Guardian?" Zapp asks.

"Guardian," Jack confirms.

"What is the guardian?" Zapp asks.

"It's a guardian. You didn't think I'd leave it here unguarded, right? There's a guardian," Jack says.

"This guardian," Zapp says, "it's dangerous, isn't it?"

"Ferocious," Jack confirms.

"Can I kill it?"

"After you get the thing you can kill anything you feel like killing. Until then, no. You can't kill it," Jack says. "You don't have to save it, though."

Zapp straightens and looks at the house. That perfectly ideal house stuck in the middle of nothing. Inside the car Jack is grinning again. Fuck it, he thinks and closes the door. The white front door of the house is so bright he can barely look at it. Behind that door is a kind of destiny. It may not be easy or happy but it's a better destiny than selling maps and candy bars to lost sorority girls and drunken rednecks.

"Just remember, buddy," Jack says seriously, "you're in *la zona peligrosa* in there. Don't trust anything; that place was made to confuse you and kill you."

"*Zona peligrosa?*" Zapp asks. "Thanks for the tip, Sterling, but I already figured I was in the danger zone as soon as we hit that time warp."

"See," Jack says with that huge grin of his, "I knew you knew what was up!"

"I don't know a damned thing," Zapp says, "except I'm terrified beyond belief and want to get out of here."

He adjusts his glasses and they immediately slide back down his nose. Zapp snorts and walks straight at the door. The doorknob is warm to the touch but turns easily. "No reason to lock a door out here," Zapp says to no one in particular. The door swings open silently on well-oiled hinges.

Zapp steps through the door and into a kitchen straight out of the 1950s. "I wondered when you'd show up, sweetie," an old lady says.

"Do I know you?" Zapp asks.

The old woman ignores him and bustles around the kitchen. "Would you like a sandwich?" she asks.

She looks like his grandmother. Then again, she looks like everyone's grandmother. Gray hair pulled back into a bun, house dress with faded flowers, apron. Just like the house, the old woman is the ideal grandmother, too perfect to be real.

"Uh," Zapp starts.

The woman turns around and takes him in. Her old eyes sparkle as she sees him and Zapp feels like she's honestly happy he's there. "Oh, my," she says. "Look at you. So big. There's no way you want a sandwich, is there dearie?"

"I'm actually not really all that hungry, ma'am," Zapp says.

"No, of course not," she says. "But you really should eat more and get more exercise if you want to be the hero."

"Wait," Zapp says. "What? Hero?"

The woman leans back against the blue tile countertop and smiles at him, but doesn't answer immediately. The kitchen is a throwback to the fifties at least. An old percolator coffee pot stands in the corner, still plugged in. A clock on the wall, decorated with the face of a sun fading into a moon, ticks away contentedly, calmly measuring time in a timeless place.

Dominating the room is a faded lime green table with some repeated design drawn across it. The six chairs are chrome tubes with matching vinyl pads covered in clear plastic slip covers. In front of each chair is a place mat with some kind of repeating design.

"You wouldn't be here if you didn't want to be the hero," the grandmother says. "It's why they all came."

"I don't want to be a hero," Zapp says and realizes it's true. He'd much rather be in bed with a good book than in this strange place with this strange woman. His head is buzzing slightly like it's filled with bees.

"Good," the woman says.

A sense of unease fills Zapp's mind, a sensation that something isn't quite right and never will be again. He's reminded of all the times he walked into a store a week or so before it went out of business and the sense of malaise was palpable. This place is too perfect, too ideal to be real.

Or safe.

"I'm just looking for something a friend left," Zapp says lamely.

The old woman nods. "I know what you're here for."

"Can I have it?" Zapp asks. There's a desperation to leave, to escape building in his brain. Whatever the thing is, he needs to get it and get out of here.

"I don't know," the woman says with a shrug of her frail shoulders. "Can you have it?"

The question takes Zapp aback a step. Whatever the thing is, he needs to get it but he's having trouble focusing. The buzzing, the unease, the general edginess is making it difficult to think. Can he have it? "I hope so," Zapp says.

"Well then," the woman says. "All you have to do is find it and get it out of here."

She lights up a cigarette and inhales deeply. The smoke pours out her nose and for a moment she looks like a dragon. Gray and brown smoke swirls around her.

"Do you mind if I look around?" Zapp asks.

"Yes," she replies. "I do. You don't even know what you're looking for."

Zapp closes his eyes, wondering what he's gotten himself into. The whole scene is so bizarre, so otherworldly that it's putting the zap on his brain. He feels jittery, like he's been mainlining coffee. Deep breath. In. Out.

No good.

He opens his eyes and the purple countertop sparkles in the bright lights. Each tick of the clock seems louder, almost palpable in the silent kitchen. The old woman is still blowing smoke out of her nostrils and the tendrils twist and turn like a Chinese dragon.

Wait, Zapp thinks, purple countertop? It was blue a moment ago.

"You don't know what you're up against, Zapp," the woman says. She steps close to him and blows smoke rings in the air. "I was told to keep it here and I aim to do my job."

A ring of smoke floats quietly into Zapp's face. He closes his eyes and blinks against the sting. When he opens them the old woman is a young woman wearing nothing but lingerie and a smile. She turns on a heel and struts back to lean against the blue countertop.

Zapp reels, feeling like the world is falling out from under his feet. His vision blurs.

"You should sit down before your fall down, dearie," the old woman says. She fingers a lacy bra and grins a mouthful of yellow and brown teeth.

The door Zapp came in through is only a few steps away. Only a few measly steps to freedom but he can't make himself escape. Call it iron will, call it dedication, call it stupidity, but he refuses to leave and walk away with his tail between his legs.

Behind him is another door. His legs nearly collapse underneath him but he makes it through without falling. The new room is dark but Zapp can make out furniture against the wall. He pulls his phone out of his pocket and isn't surprised to see it's not getting a signal. No one to call, anyway, Zapp thinks and turns on the phone's flashlight.

The light reflects off gold-flecked wallpaper, a bridge table, and an olive green deco sofa that looks amazingly uncomfortable. It was probably a stylish room in the fifties but looks dated now.

Zapp continues playing the light around the room and finds carved wooden figurines and a thunderbird mosaic that looks handmade. The room is big, far bigger than it has any right to be. It's almost like someone took two or three rooms, smashed them together, and covered it all in wallpaper that's seen better days.

A hallway leads further into the house and Zapp hobbles down it, past the now the brown sofa and the mosaic of a midget with a whip. The clock in the kitchen shakes the walls with each tick. He passes a bedroom, empty save a pile of clothes and a cross with a cartoon mouse crucified on it.

Zapp hurries on, past a bathroom until he reaches the end of the hall. Doorways lead off to the left and right, both closed. On a whim, he opens the door on the left and finds a pair of twin beds with a pair of emaciated corpses. He chokes back a desire to run and creeps forward.

"Sure you want to go in there, big boy?" a voice asks from behind.

His head is full of bees, a relentless buzzing sound echoing between his ears. Zapp tries to spin around but winds up holding onto the wall to keep himself upright. She's right behind him, close enough that he should be able to smell her or feel the heat coming off her body, but the young woman in 1920s lingerie doesn't smell like anything and is exactly as warm as the air.

"You're not here are you?" Zapp asks. "You're the whole house, aren't you?"

She leans against the wall and licks her lips. Her eyes flick up and down his body, drinking him in and smiling salaciously. "Well, well, well," she purrs. "Look at the big brain on the zzzzzZappper. Come on big boy, take me to bed and we can be happy forever. I'm told I'm an excellent lay."

Zapp shakes his head, trying to clear it but the buzzing just gets worse. She's stroking her body now, down from her throat, across her breasts, down her stomach, and between her legs. Her eyes are alight. Zapp feels his heart pounding in his chest. Part of his mind swears he can smell her sex even though he knows she's not really in front of him.

"You're already inside of me," she says calmly. "Wouldn't you like to be inside of this body, too?"

He wants her more than anything he's ever wanted before. When he looks at her he sees the young, taut body in black lingerie. Her smile tells him to take her right there in the hallway; they could fuck on the floor like animals and she could be his forever. All he has to do is take her and make her his.

One foot moves forward, sliding across the shag floor without Zapp's consent. He wants out. He wants to find whatever it is he's looking for. He wants her.

"Come to me, baby," she whispers. "Let me take you all the way to the 86th floor."

86th floor. Doc's penthouse.

Zapp turns on his heel and sprints into the bedroom. He kicks the door shut just before the old lady in the slinky black lingerie can grab him. She pounds the door and he pushes backwards across the room on his ass.

Frying pan, fire, he thinks. The door is holding but it won't hold forever. Zapp frantically looks around the room, desperate for anything that can be used as weapon but all he finds are the two corpses and a nightstand between them.

Inside the room the noise in his head is gone. He knows he should be concerned that the whole house is trying to kill him but Zapp's more concerned with how he's going to get away. The room feels safe for now, like somehow it's not part of the rest of the house. It's safe, sure, but it's a cage. All she has to do is wait and eventually he'll die and she'll have won.

What would Doc do?

Zapp slowly gets up and looks around the room. The great detective would find information before he committed to a plan; he'd find what he was looking for while he still had the chance. Then, once that was secured, he'd find a way out.

The room is decorated like the rest of the house in faded 50s glory. Everything looks like it was top of the line at one point, but over the decades the gold thread has started to unwind and the once deep green tones faded to pastel. This room died when the occupants died.

Between the corpses Zapp spots a tiny thing, a thing almost perfectly hidden under an old paperback copy of "Houdini's Escapes and Magic". A tiny flicker of gold and ruby, still perfect and shiny after all the years in this dead place.

Zapp picks up the ring and stares at it. He's no expert on women's jewelry, but it looks like a wedding ring from sometime in the twenties or thirties, complete with a deco design.

"Sorry guys," Zapp whispers solemnly to the corpses, "but I need to take this."

He drops the ring in his pocket and stares at the dead couple for a moment. They were alive when Doc was alive. Well, as alive as a character can ever really get. He wonders if either of them listened to Doc's adventures or read his books. He wonders if they died together and hopes they at least met each other again somewhere and somewhen else.

Phase one finished, Zapp searches for a way out. He knows there's no way he can best the guardian in a fight. She may look frail or sexy or whatever she feels like, but Zapp understands that she was just choosing her forms to keep him off balance.

Speaking of which, his head feels fine in this room. As soon as he entered all the buzzing and nervousness went away, but he knows it'll come back as soon as he walks out the door.

There are two doors out of the room. One for sure leads right into her. Since the guardian is the house and the house is the guardian the other door probably leads straight to her, too. Zapp sighs and sits on the bed, jumping when his butt hits a bony leg.

"Sorry," he says to the dead woman, and shifts so he's not sitting on her.

He looks around the room again but doesn't see anything obvious. Two doors, a closet, a large window, two beds, an old TV, a pair of dressers, and a recliner. Not much of anything that looks like a weapon, but it's not like a gun would work against the whole house.

Zapp's mood plummets. He's got the thing, whatever the thing is. At least he thinks he's got the thing. Whatever. Now he's stuck in a room with a dead couple, a thing, and a guardian that will likely kill him as soon as he walks out the door.

Cleaning brains off the floor is looking more and more appealing.

He stands up and grabs the old T.V, straining under the weight of the ancient thing. With a huge amount of effort he hurls the T.V. at the window. It makes it less than halfway across the room before it falls to the ground and rolls.

"Damned thing probably still works," Zapp says with a sigh. He wonders if that asshole coach from High School Phys Ed is laughing somewhere. All those hours playing video games suddenly don't look like such a great use of time.

Zapp may not be able to toss T.V.s across the room but he can still run and he's still got a slight edge.

"Will you let me go if I toss it out?" he yells at the door.

Silence greets him and Zapp wonders if he's going to wind up like the couple in the bed. Maybe they were nice people. Spending eternity dead in a bedroom wouldn't be so bad if the other people were nice.

"Yes," the guardian answers finally. "I have no use for you."

He can smell the lie on her words. She lied about her shape, why wouldn't she lie about intentions?

Zapp scouts around the room, looking for anything that he can use. In the top drawer of a dresser he finds an old jewelry box. Most of the contents are degraded, faded like so much in this place, but a few things look promising. A couple rings, a necklace, a bracelet, and a watch look to be in reasonable shape. Pity about the watch, Zapp thinks, it's a nice Zenith and he'd love to keep it but he loves being alive more.

He quickly licks and polishes each piece on his shirt. The old jewelry tastes like time and lost causes but it polishes up okay. Zapp hurries to the door and pauses. "You promise?" he asks.

"I make no promises," the guardian replies.

Not surprising, Zapp thinks. He hurries across the room and makes sure the other door is unlocked and hustles back. "We had an agreement," he says. "I can die in here and you won't get what you want. We can help each other out here."

"If you are lying," the guardian hisses through the closed door, "I will rend your flesh from your bones and let you watch while I eat it."

Zapp gulps. He knows she's not kidding and there's a very good chance she'll do it anyway, but he decides to play it cool. "Careful," he says, "I eat a lot of Twinkies; my flesh may not be good for you."

"What are Twinkies?" the guardian asks.

"Heavenly eternity wrapped in plastic," Zapp replies.

"I wish to have these Twinkies you speak of," the guardian says. "Provide them and I'll let you go."

Zapp furrows his brow, wishing he actually had some Twinkies. Who carries Twinkies around? "I don't have any on me, but I can bring you some if you let me go."

"I do not trust you to bring me the Heavenly Twinkies."

"You'll just have to settle for the item then," Zapp says. "Step back from the door and I'll toss it out. Once you're satisfied you can let me go."

"Agreeable," the guardian says. Zapp hears her shuffling back from the door.

He breathes in deep and forces himself to be brave. He flings the door open and sees the guardian standing toward the end of the hall.

She's back to being the young woman in lingerie and is rubbing herself seductively. "Here," Zapp says, tossing the jewelry down the hall. "I got you some extras."

The jewelry hits the floor and shines feebly in the weak light. The guardian looks at the jewelry and back at Zapp. Her hands slide up and down her body. "Are you sure don't want me, too?" she asks.

"I'm good," Zapp says. "Have fun. They're sparkly."

He pushes the door shut and bolts for the other door, hoping it leads somewhere safe.

Beyond the other door is a bathroom with another door on the other side. Zapp sneaks through the bathroom and feels the familiar buzzing in his brain. His edginess returns full force and his heart starts pounding.

A pulsing sensation starts in his head, throbbing just behind his temples. He leans on the green tiled counter and stares at himself in the mirror. Zapp sees a stranger with hard eyes and a desperate expression. He lurches toward the other door just in time to feel the energy in the house change. Everything gets darker, heavier. It's the same feeling the air gets just before a huge storm breaks.

She's discovered his clever little ruse.

Zapp slams open the other door and tries to run through it. He hears the guardian bang on the bedroom door. Apparently she thinks he's still in the room. With a bit of luck it'll give him just enough time to get out.

The other door opens into a small room, probably a storage room that was converted to a bedroom. There are shelves all around the room filled with empty fish tanks. Zapp sneaks through the room and quietly opens the door to the hallway.

She's at the end of the hall, screaming and pounding on the bedroom door. He slips low to the floor and creeps down the hall, listening carefully for any break in her tirade. It's harder than he thought to sneak away. He has to fight with himself to not bolt and run for the door. Running is death, he repeats to himself, running is death.

At the end of the hallway he can go right go through the living area or left and go through the kitchen. He doesn't hesitate and breaks right.

Zapp knows he'll still have to go through the kitchen to get out, but he doesn't want the extra problem of having to run on the tile.

While he's sneaking he notices the world go quiet.

He bolts, dodging the bridge table and the chairs and focusing exclusively on the kitchen door. His hand is on the knob when she grabs him by the back of the head. He manages to turn the knob before she shoves his head through the window in the door.

It hurts more than he ever thought it could. He's seen people get their heads pushed through windows in movies over and over and the hero always gets up and finishes off the bad guy but there's blood all over Zapp's face and his neck hurts. A huge piece of glass pierced his cheek. He can feel it on his tongue. Even as the guardian pulls him back and rams his head into the wall, Zapp's hands are grasping at the glass in his cheek and tugging at in vain.

It hurts so much. Tears are streaming down his face, snot and blood are pouring out of his nose and oh God it hurts so much. Zapp wants to roll into a ball and die.

He finally pulls the piece of glass out of his cheek and holds it in front of his body. The guardian slaps it out of his hand and screams incoherently in rage. Zapp knows what she wants and desperately wants to give it to her, anything to stop the beating.

"Please, please, please," he repeats over and over.

In her rage at being deceived the guardian punches Zapp with all her might. One second he's standing, pleading for his life, the next he's flying through the kitchen door with at least a couple broken ribs. He hits the ground hard and the wind flies out of him.

The guardian screams in rage from the kitchen door but every time she tries to go through it something stops her. Zapp's barely functional brain recognizes she can't leave just before everything goes completely black.

Zapp wakes up to Jack's face hovering over him. The guy is grinning like a loon. He slaps Zapp on the shoulder and hoots. "Welcome back, Hoss," Jack says. "Thought I'd lost you, buddy."

"I hurt all over," Zapp says.

"Well, I gotta be honest with you bud, you're pretty messed up. She put you through the ringer but you made it out alive," Jack says.

"Why do I hurt so much?" Zapp asks.

Jack sits down in the grass next to Zapp and chuckles. "I didn't see the whole thing, just the part where you came flying out the door. Near as I can tell, though, she bashed you around pretty good before kicking your butt out."

"I don't think she meant to kick me out," Zapp says.

"Hold still," Jack says and reaches down. Zapp doesn't move, even when he feels a sting. Jack's hand comes back with a nasty looking piece of glass.

"Thanks," Zapp says.

"My pleasure," Jack replies. "Did you get it?"

Zapp digs in his shirt pocket and pulls out the ring. In the sunlight it glows. Golds, reds, even blacks light up and sparkle. He stares at the ring, fascinated. The ring is a reward, a memory of adventure, but the bruises and broken bones will probably be more than enough memory. He drops it into Jack's outstretched hand. "Where are you going to hide it now?"

"I'm not going to hide it; I'm going to put it on my girl's finger. No one will try it take then." Jack says.

"I'm having trouble remembering, who's your girl again?" Zapp asks.

"Hey! Look at you. Got a concussion your first time out. I didn't get one of those for years," Jack says and claps Zapp on the shoulder.

Zapp winces and holds his head. "I don't know if I'm proud of it."

"It'll pass, bro. It'll pass. You walked through the fire and you made it out the other side. The concussion, the bruises, you probably got a couple broken ribs, too. That's just skin and bones. You just faced down an Alunan guardian and walked away with all the power in the universe. That's the important part."

"What kind of guardian?" Zapp asks.

"Alunan. From Aluna. Look, I told you I'd give you two things in return for helping me out here. One was information the other was a gift. The gift is in the barn behind your store. Just break the lock off, no one will give a shit.

"The information, though, that's worth more than anything else. What's that old saying? 'Knowledge is power'? Something like that anyway. You, my son, just walked into a larger world. You've seen things that most folk haven't seen, and never will see. Here's your information: You don't have to follow the gods. Any of 'em. They're all full of shit, just a bunch of assholes with too much power. You're on my team, now, son. If you want to be, that is."

Zapp stares at the light blue cloudless sky. It seems so normal, so sane. Compared to the horrors inside the house and the lunatic babbling about gods, at least. "What does it mean to be on your team?" he asks.

"Ain't no good guys, ain't no bad guys. Forget what you've heard. We're the closest thing to good guys out there and we ain't all that good. We keep the balance and make sure no one gets ahead," Jack says. "Or you can go read books and clean up brains."

Zapp thinks about it for a moment. "Does it pay well?" he asks.

"I knew I had you," Jack says excitedly. "I knew it the minute you didn't freak out when I shot those guys."

Zapp tries to sit up but his head starts spinning and the world gets all blurry. He flops back down and holds his head in his hands. "You didn't answer me," he says.

"About the pay?" Jack asks. "Hell, yeah it pays well. Money, power, responsibility, the chance to make a difference."

His head is still spinning but Zapp's aware enough to make a coherent decision. "I'm in. I always wanted to part of a team. I want to hear you say it, though."

"Say what?" Jack asks.

"What we're gonna do to the pillars of Heaven," Zapp says.

Jack laughs out loud and shakes his fists at the sky. "Buddy," he says, "we are gonna shake the pillars of Heaven!"

With a little effort, and no small amount of wincing on Zapp's part, Jack gets Zapp loaded into the Cord. The music starts up again, loud drums banging on Zapp's battered skull, but he doesn't care anymore. The trip is quicker this time, maybe because going back always takes less time than getting there, and Jack drops Zapp in front of the old shed behind the dilapidated Whiting Brothers store.

"All yours now, bro," Jack says. "Get yourself rested up and I'll give you a holler. Enjoy the bike. Ah, shit. I gave away the surprise. Anyway, enjoy it."

Zapp leans against the wall of the shed and watches the black Cord speed off into the distance. It all seems so normal here and things he didn't realize he missed fill Zapp's senses: birds chirping, insects twittering, the slight breeze rustling through his clothes. The place in, well, wherever the heck it was, that place was perfectly silent outside. He shakes his head and wonders if maybe a hospital isn't in order.

After the shed, he'll go lay down somewhere. That will have to do for now.

The padlock looks solid but a single smash from a rock tears it from the rotting wood and it lands in the dust with a thump. Zapp tosses the rock over his shoulder and pulls open a door that creaks and whines at waking from its slumber. Sunlight shines inside revealing cobwebs and dust covering a huge wooden crate. "Hidalgo Trading Company" is stenciled on one side, but otherwise the crate is blank.

A crowbar is propped against the box. Zapp winces and wonders what to do with it. He's seen movies, so he just imitates the action he's seen on the screen. Find an opening toward the front, push the small part in and pull.

Give him a lever long enough and he can move the world.

The side of the box falls away revealing an old motorcycle. On the black gas tank is an Indian head and a note, yellowed and fading, reads "Clothes are in the closet behind you, always wear a helmet. -Jack."

Zapp forgets the pain, forgets the fuzziness in his head. The biker leathers fit perfectly. When he straddles the machine and puts on the helmet a heads-up display shows in front of him, telling him all sorts of things from the temperature outside (95F) to the status of the bike (Green). The motor comes to life easily.

A twist of the throttle and a new Zapp thunders down the road.

Eve

Three women stand on the edge of a cliff overlooking a battle raging down below. None of them move or blink even as the rivulets of water drip off their blond hair and down the front of their leather armor. The rain is more a drizzle than a downpour, just enough to be harassing but not enough to be oppressive.

The first woman wraps a cloak tighter around her over seven-foot-tall frame and watches the battle closely. Her breath fogs the air as she points and says, "Watch that one."

The other two women turn in unison and stare at a huge man covered in tattoos swinging a sword with one hand and smashing skulls with his shield in the other hand. He moves through the battle effortlessly, casually cutting limbs from bodies. His grinning face is covered with blood but his eyes are sparkling.

"Impressive," says the woman in the middle. Her gray eyes show no emotion, only a faint hint of interest. She grips the long bow tightly in her hand and adds, "but he might survive the fight."

"If he does, Kára, then it is because Odin wills it," the first woman says.

Kára nods, gray eyes not leaving the man on the battlefield. She raises an eyebrow as the man buries his shield in the face of a fallen warrior before running him through with a sword. "He would be quite useful, Radgridr," she says distantly.

"Indeed," Radgridr says.

"So far he is the only one who shows any skill," the third woman says. She's smaller than the others and clad in burgundy leather armor. At a paltry six foot eleven inches, Sanngrior is shorter than either Radgridr or Kára but she makes up for it with a fiery temper that masks her insecurity at being small.

Kára flicks a braided pigtail out of her face. She smiles as the man on the battlefield tosses a man to the ground, runs him through, and rolls out of the way before a flash of silver can remove his head from his shoulders. "His *Glima* is excellent," she says.

"Let us wait and hope he sees Valhalla," Radgridr replies.

The battle rages on and the man continues to evade death, much to the chagrin of the three women. His desire to live, even knowing what awaits him in the afterlife, continues to drive him forward. In his mind, the only way out of the battle is through winning it. Thoughts of his son and a desperate desire to hold his wife again fill his limbs with energetic precision. Swords arc at him but find nothing but air. Spears fly and miss.

All Vikings are special when it comes to fighting. They're good at it, they enjoy it; and for Vikings, the only way to get to Valhalla is to die in battle. A warrior who dies in battle and makes it to Valhalla get a shot at the fight that will come at the end of the world: Ragnarök. It will be a chance to fight side by side with Thor and Odin, taking the battle to the hated Jörmungandr and ensuring an eternity of peace.

So now, the battle rages. Large men, and some fairly tough women, hurl spears, smash each other with hammers, slash and cut with swords. Those who have lost their weapons are busy chucking each other around with a manic frenzy. The blood is thick on the ground, mingling with the frozen turf and making the ground treacherous.

If a warrior trips over a body here – and there are many dead or dying dotting the landscape – then someone will slide a blade between their ribs.

Water runs down Kára's brown leather armor. Her gray eyes search the battlefield for the man she wants to claim and is dismayed to find him still fighting. "The tide is turning against his army," she says quietly, hoping they hack him to pieces.

Sanngrior's blonde bobbed haircut is plastered to her forehead but her sharp black eyes are unperturbed by the increasing rain. She nods solemnly, waiting for the battle to end and the man to die. Only Radgridr hopes the man survives. Her blue eyes sparkle as she watches him deftly defy death time and again. Throughout the battle, she has taken a liking to this warrior and wants to see him go on.

A stray arrow pierces the man's back and he staggers to his knees, slipping in the bloody muck of the battlefield. Two warriors descend on him immediately but he falls to his side and slices the legs out from under one warrior and stabs the other in the groin with a dagger.

"He is amazing," Sanngrior whispers.

Radgridr clutches at her black armor and prays to Odin to let the man live. She knows her sisters want him dead. She's the nominal leader, if only because at seven and a half feet tall she's the largest of the women. Sanngrior will follow her lead, she knows this, but Kára has become more and more unpredictable lately. Radgridr sometimes worries that Kára has somehow become … corrupted; she seeks out warriors to bring to Valhalla with a single-minded intensity that frightens even the usually unflappable Radgridr

On the hill, the three women calmly watch the slaughter. Here, in this time, they're known as Valkyries. They're the choosers of the slain. They show up frequently at battles, seeking great warriors to come to Valhalla and, eventually, fight in the final battle of the world.

They're all blonde and all wearing varying themes on leather armor. The tallest, Radgridr, wears leathers dyed all black. Her hair is a mane of golden blonde hair that hangs down to the middle of her back and her icy blue eyes sparkle like a still mountain lake. Radgridr vacillates between consensus building and ordering the others, but always pushes for what she wants. Usually what she wants is for her sisters to act in a demeanor becoming their station. Unfortunately, she does not always get what she wants.

In the middle, holding a bow, and wearing brown leathers is Kára. Her hair, like the others, is blonde, but pulled into braided pigtails. The pigtails, coupled with stormy gray eyes, manage to make her look dangerous rather than cute. She's physically the strongest of the group, but is considered somewhat unpredictable by the others. Some have gone so far as to describe her as a stormy petrel, but never to her face and only from a safe distance. Her unpredictability makes her a fearsome foe.

The third is the smallest, but that's a relative term. Sanngrior is adorned in deep red leather armor, covered with a fine gray chain mail. Her hair, like the others, is golden blonde, but she wears it in a short bob that makes her look safe and charming. Her black eyes and severe face are a stark contrast to her hair. Sanngrior's black eyes have nothing that even approaches sympathy. Under the best of circumstances, she's not a pleasant person to be around. When she gets angry, she can make the gods run and hide. Her anger hides her insecurities; she feels small and weak around Radgridr and Kára and tends to lash out to prove her mettle.

These are not small women, the largest stands over seven feet tall, the shortest slightly under seven feet tall. The three of them could probably slaughter everyone on the battlefield without breaking a sweat.

There is a war coming, and these women were created to build an army that will win it. In the few years they've been around they've managed to raise an army nearly ten thousand strong, which is nothing compared to the army they'll need to build before the final battle comes. When the final battle against the Frost Giants is fought an army of hundreds of thousands will be needed.

The battle continues for hours, neither side willing to give an inch or cede to the other. Whatever kicked this fight off, some perceived slight or another, was too important to back down on. At the end, as the sun is setting, a single warrior is left standing. The man's drive to see his family again kept him alive where everyone else fell to the sword, the arrow, or the spear. He limps out of the battlefield, one leg badly cut, an arrow protruding from his back, and using the spear from a fallen foe as an improvised crutch.

"He was impressive," Radgridr says.

"Indeed," Kára replies quietly.

The man is almost out the field of battle when an arrow silently strikes him down. Even with a slashed leg and two arrows in his back piecing his lung, the man doesn't collapse immediately. He staggers several steps before falling to his knees and crawling forward.

The first two women look at Kára with something similar to shock in their eyes.

Kára lowers her bow and returns their gaze. "He would have died anyway," she says by way of explanation.

"Yes, but he did not die in battle. We cannot take him," Radgridr says.

"What you have done is against the orders," Sanngrior adds.

"My orders," Kára says, "were to find soldiers for the final battle. I just found one."

"He did not die in battle, though," Radgridr says again. "He cannot fight in the final battle."

"Kára," Sanngrior says, eyes riveted on the huge bow. "You know the rules. Why would you violate them?"

Kára glares at her sister and lowers the bow. "I have made my choice, Sanngrior. His wounds would have killed him; therefore he technically died in battle. I just hastened his demise."

"Kára, he is still alive. You did not kill him," Sanngrior says.

"Patience, sister. His heart and will are strong but his wounds are grievous. He will be dead shortly," Kára tells her.

Together, the three women watch as the man struggles to find his way home. The arrows sticking out of his back make him wheeze and every breath feels like breathing fire. The slash on his leg, already infected, no longer hurts, but he can tell the wound will cost him his leg. Thormod, the doctor in his village, is a miracle worker, but even his skills have limits and he has no doubt the leg will be removed.

The slash on the man's leg severed his femoral artery. He just wants to go home, to see his wife and newborn son, but the blood pumping out of his leg won't stop. His vision darkens, his limbs lose all sensation, but still he keeps crawling forward.

When the end finally comes, he sees a vision of his wife holding his son and knows that he lost. He promised Asta he would come home to her and Einar, but he has failed them. His final thought is a desire for vengeance. Revenge against the king that ordered him into this worthless battle, revenge against the bastard that slashed his leg, and revenge against whatever coward shot him in the back.

The man's name is Gosta, and through a technicality, he has bought himself a place in Valhalla.

*****

This wasn't the first time Kára stretched, bent, or outright broke the rules. As usual, Odin was less than appreciative of her efforts. "You have betrayed me again!" his voice thunders.

Odin is a large man with thunder in his eyes and ravens on his shoulders. His anger shakes the pillars of the heavens and earthquakes ravage the world below when he stomps his feet. He is unused to his orders being ignored. As the head of the gods, the All-Father, he is unused to not getting his way in all things and usually reacts violently to any transgressions against his authority.

"The man's wounds would have killed him. Wounds he received in battle. He died in battle," Kára replies, seemingly unaware or unconcerned with the man's rising ire.

"Then explain the arrow in his back! An arrow fired from your bow!"

The ravens, Huginn and Muninn, are agitated now, chittering to themselves nervously. Their tiny avian brains are incapable of any kind of advanced thought but they can know what happens when Odin's rage takes hold.

"I was putting him out of his misery. Consider it a mercy from the gods," Kára says.

"So you admit you killed him?"

"I admit no such thing. He was dead already, he just hadn't realized it," Kára replies

"You are incorrigible. You are ungrateful. You are reckless. You think the rules do not apply to you, do you?" Odin asks.

"The only rule I believe in is the one you imbued me with when you created me; I believe in creating an army to fight the final battle," Kára says with her back straight and her jaw squared.

"The rules exist for a reason! We only take those who fought valiantly and died bravely," Odin says quietly.

The words, and the quiet way he says them, fill Kára's heart with ice. Odin's rage is a common thing; he lets his anger take over whenever things don't go his way. For all his knowledge and wisdom, the All-Father is given to childish rages. Unlike regular childish rages, Odin's angry outbreaks are backed by all the power in the universe.

"He did fight valiantly, my lord," she says with her head hung. "He died bravely."

"He died with your arrow in his back, crawling back to his wife and son. He might have made it, too, had you not decided to intervene."

"He was the greatest warrior at the battle. He will be a great asset."

"He will be a great asset, but his son would have been better. Now, his son will grow up without a father to train him in the arts of war and we have potentially lost a hero."

"The child," Kára asks. "What will become of him?"

"We'll do the usual, send a hero to train him, hope the damage done hasn't been too extreme. His anger might cloud his judgment, though, and a warrior cannot afford outside anger," Odin replies, secretly happy that Kára is expressing an interest in things other than herself.

"Who are you sending?" Kára asks.

"Knut or Ivar, I haven't decided which yet." The All-Father replies.

"Either would be an excellent choice, my Lord, but..." Kára starts.

"But what?" Odin asks.

"Consider sending me instead." Kára says quietly.

"Why you?" Odin asks incredulously.

"Knut and Ivar are great warriors, but I'm better," she replies.

"Why should you wish to do this, Kára? It's not your place to train heroes; it's your place to choose the dead." Odin says, wondering if there's hope for her yet.

"Consider it an act of contrition," Kára says.

"You've never shown any sign of being sorry in the past; why start now?"

"Perhaps your wisdom is rubbing off on me."

The All-Father smiles at that. While his anger is an all-encompassing force, his ego truly knows no bounds. Kára knows this and has no compunction about using it against him. In her mind, he's a doddering old fool, focused on his power and his control and with no eye for the future.

In some ways, she's correct. He is an arrogant bastard who has become so focused on his power that he has forgotten the goal. The trappings of power have become more important to him than the reason he has his power.

His goal should be preparing for a fight at the end of time. In the past it was an all-consuming drive of Odin's, readying himself and his people for Ragnarök, but over the years his training has fallen off. He hasn't picked up his spear - save to run through those few that dared oppose him off - in years.

Kára knows the enemy trains relentlessly, and that's why she practices constantly. One woman, no matter how tough, might not change the tide of the war, but she's not going to be the one that loses the final battle.

Odin watches her with one good eye, seeking out the treachery he knows is there somewhere. He fails to find any deception, but is still wary. Still, if it will get her out of his hair for a while, sending her back across the Rainbow Bridge to Earth might be a good idea. "Fine then, Kára, you shall train young Einar in my arts. Make me proud."

*****

Einar and Asta live in a village on the shores of an ocean that's only slightly above freezing. The mountains and valleys are filled with trees that provide shelter and warmth and animals that provide food and clothes. The villagers are practiced fishermen and sailors.

It's a small village, under a thousand people, and unused to outsiders. Anyone caught skulking around the village is immediately suspect, but no one challenges a seven-foot-tall woman clad in the armor of the gods. In true Valkyrie fashion, Kára simply shows up on Asta's doorstep and promises to take Einar under her wing.

"The gods have sent me to train your son," Kára tells Asta.

Asta, who is less than five foot seven, stares up at the giantess on her doorstep. She takes in Kára's braided pigtails, red leather armor, spear, and shield and realizes that even though the gods have chosen to take her husband to Valhalla, they have seen fit to make sure her son was taken care of.

"He's by the shore," Asta says simply, "Dinner is in two hours."

Kára finds Einar by the shore, clumsily hacking away at a dead tree with an old rusted sword. He looks like his father, dark hair, dark eyes, but he lacks his father's grace and speed. Every move he makes is punctuated by his anger, forceful swings driven by rage and loss. He understands almost nothing of how to use the sword he grips tightly in both hands other than to swing with all his might and hope for the best.

"Pathetic," Kára thinks to herself and wonders if this is really the best course of action.

Where Gosta was elegant, Einar is an oaf. Where Gosta was fast, Einar has the moves of a drunkard. Where Gosta seemed to see the whole sword as a weapon, Einar understands only slashing and hacking.

Kára watches him for time, studies his movements and sees him wear himself down until he can barely stand. Amazingly, even though Einar is so tired he's staggering and can barely life the sword, he keeps going, keeps slashing away at the dead tree.

When she's seen enough she waits until he draws the sword back and hurls her spear with all her might. It hits the dead tree in the center and splits it in half.

Einar is so shocked he falls backwards, the sword falling from his young hands and landing quietly in the moist sand of the beach. He recovers quickly, though, grabs his sword and scrambles to his feet to challenge whoever had thrown the spear.

"I'm not here to fight you, Einar," Kára tells him. "I'm here to help you."

Einar stares down the giant woman. Fear flickers across his eyes and the sword shakes in his small hands, but he doesn't back down. "I don't need your help!" he yells.

"Yes," Kára said calmly, "you do. You're clumsy and one-dimensional, you let your anger guide your hand and you see only one way to use a sword."

"I'll show you how to use a sword," Einar hisses.

"Well, then, by the gods, strike me down if you can," Kára tells him.

Einar charges forward screaming, sword held over his head in both hands, ready to cleave this intruder in two. As he approaches, he sizes up his target and realizes she's much bigger than he is. No matter, his sword will cut her just like it will cut everyone else.

Kára doesn't move. She watches patiently as the child charges at her with his sword over his head. She knows the strike - if he can land it - will be a lethal blow to most any human. She's not human, of course, so the sword doesn't really matter to her, but it's important to make a good first impression on the boy. Her mind sizes up the attack and experience immediately presents her with various options for dealing with it: cut him across the stomach and watch his guts leak out, cut his legs out from under him, simply push her own sword forward and wait for him to impale himself on it.

None of these will get her back in the good graces of her boss, so she simply twists to the side as Einar strikes and trips him. He hits the sand hard and slides to a halt a few feet behind her. The only thing hurt is his pride, but those shots to the pride can sting.

Einar lands face down in the sand and wonders to himself what just happened. He had her, dammit! He had her dead to rights and now here he is with sand up his nose and in his mouth and his sword is somewhere, but he has no idea where that somewhere is.

"How old are you?" Kára asks, looking down at him.

"I'm eight," Einar says and kicks at Kára's leg. His foot hits her leg and stops dead without even moving her an inch.

"How long have you been training?" Kára asks.

"Since my father died," Einar replies, propping himself up on his elbows.

"Not long, then. I hope I'm not too late."

"Late for what?" Einar spits. His mind is already working, wondering who – or what – this strange woman is.

"To teach you. You've already developed too many bad habits."

Einar pushes himself up and sits in the sand staring at the strange woman in front of him. For the first time he takes her in and realizes he was a fool to have even thought of attacking her. The fact that she split a dead tree in half with a spear would have been warning enough for most people, but anger has a way of clouding judgment and Einar has spent a lot of time being really pissed off at the world.

He takes in her armor, her braided hair, her sheer stature, but it's her eyes that finally convinced him she's no ordinary woman. Those gray eyes that speak of stormy seas, rolling clouds, and the fog rolling in from the bay in the mornings that give him hope that perhaps the gods have not completely forsaken him.

"You will teach me?" he asks.

Kára squats down in the sand next to him and says, "Yes. I will teach you."

"Can you teach me how to kill the man that took my father?"

Kára pauses and lets the weight of that statement settle in. She was never one to run from her mistakes or to gloss them over with flowery language or flimsy justifications. She knows right then and there that he deserves the truth. Or at least a version of it. For now. When he's older, better able to handle the truth, she vows to tell him.

She closes her eyes and quietly says, "I can teach you to fight the one that took your father."

"Is that man still alive?" Einar asks, eyes sparkling with the hope that he'll be able to watch his father's killer take a final breath.

"No, your father cut his head off," Kára says. It's a partial truth; one of the arrows in Gosta's back did come from a man and Gosta did cut the man's head off. The wound that ultimately killed him – the cut on his leg – was delivered by a woman who died with Gosta's sword in her throat. Kára's arrow only hastened his death.

"How did my father die?" Einar asks.

"He died bravely," Kára said, her mind watching the man still trying to crawl home with her arrow in his back. "He died trying to make it back to you."

"If I die in battle, I can go to Valhalla and face my father's killer," Einar says.

"If you are chosen, yes you can," Kára says with a nod, knowing full well the boy will be chosen if she trains him well.

"What happens when I kill him?" Einar asks. "The man who killed my father, I mean."

"He'll be resurrected the next day," Kára tells him. "Once a warrior makes it to Valhalla he or she will live until Ragnarök."

"Is my father in Valhalla?"

"Yes he is," Kára says. She hasn't visited Gosta, but she knows he's there.

"Good," Einar seems relieved. Losing his father was bad enough, but it would have destroyed his heart to think his father didn't make it to Valhalla. "Who chooses who goes to Valhalla?"

"I do," Kára tells him. "Now, are you ready to learn how to fight?"

Einar stares at her in wonder. Everyone knows the Valkyries choose who is slain in battle and who gets to go to Valhalla. Some of them would even bring you mead in the Great Hall, but he has never heard of them training warriors.

A small part of his mind begins to ponder that. Why would she want to train him? Why is it so important to her? That small part will never go away and late at night it will eat away him, gnawing at him like a hungry rat. He pushes the thought aside for the time being and tells Kára, "I'm ready."

She spends the next hour teaching young Einar the basics of war and he shows he can learn quickly. He has a long way to go, but by the end of the first hour he's already showing marked improvement. His movements are still sloppy, but the anger is waning and he's concentrating on what he is doing rather than letting his rage drive him.

"Your mother said dinner was in two hours," Kára tells him as Einar takes a swing and collapses in an exhausted heap on the beach. "It is time to stop for now."

In many places if a seven-foot-tall woman shows up on the doorstep and promises to teach a child how to fight it's cause for concern, but in Einar's village it's considered a great honor and he and Asta treat Kára as an emissary of the gods. Young Einar learns how to fight by studying with a demigoddess and no one really thinks it's strange. Asta's esteem in the village grows by leaps and bounds and, as Einar grows up, he all but has to beat the girls off with his staff.

He turns out to be a natural fighter, aggressive, precise, and unemotional.

He doesn't fight without fear, though, and before his first battle he wets himself and prays to the gods that no one notices. No one does and he comes through the battle without a scratch. During the battle, Einar kills no less than twenty men personally.

On his eighteenth birthday, Einar is officially a man, and ready to take responsibility. He has grown up strong and smart and some small part of Kára feels he is her own son, too. At a party in his honor, she looks at him and sees his father again. Einar's no longer the angry boy she first met haphazardly hacking away at a dead tree on the beach. He's strong and smart and quite capable.

It makes Kára sad to watch him and she drowns her sorrows in mead and tells herself she's at least done some good. She might not be able to bring his father back or completely salve his deep internal wounds, but she helped make him strong. Strength is important in a world that will constantly test your mettle.

The village is used to her by now and recognizes when her spirits take a bad turn. She drinks alone and tells herself that this world is none of her concern, but she has grown to enjoy these people over the past ten years and will miss them when they're gone.

That's the damnable thing about immortality and even though Kára is a young immortal, she realizes these people will be dust long before she meets her final reward. She sighs sadly and drains a tankard of mead. Her usual anger, bitterness at the world that won't leave her alone, won't let her die, won't let her do what she was designed to do.

Einar watches her from his table but is too drunk to realize his teacher and friend is best left alone. He gathers his mead and plops down at her table with a huge grin. "Why are you drinking alone?" he shouts over the din.

Kára glares at him, wills him to leave, but he's too far gone to see that she wants to nurse her malaise in peace. Under the best of circumstances Kára is moody, but when the feelings of powerlessness wash over her like the freezing tide coming in, she gets dangerous.

"You should be happy!" Einar tells her. "It's a celebration!"

"I am celebrating," Kára replies, downing another tankard of mead.

"You are drinking your pain away, Kára, just like you always do," Einar says, face suddenly serious. "You once told me to face my pain, to gain strength from it, to ride it like the waves."

"It's too late for that," Kára tells him.

"It's never too late."

Kára changes the subject. "Why do you not change your hair color like all your friends do? They're all blonde and you keep yours black. Why?"

Einar leans forward and smiles at her. "I wondered when you would ask that. My father's hair was black, too. He told me he would never change it because it was his and it made him what he was. I guess I feel the same way. If it makes me stand out, so much the better!"

Kára smiles at that. So he has learned to believe in himself.

"See, you can smile!" Einar says, sliding another glass of mead at her. "Drink! Today we celebrate!"

"What are we celebrating?" Kára asks.

"The bastards that killed my father are dead! They met us in battle and we crushed them." Einar slams his fist on the table happily.

It's time. It's past time, Kára realizes, that Einar knows the truth.

"They didn't kill your father," she says quietly.

"Oh, really? They claimed to have put an arrow in his back as he ran in fear. At the very least that had to pay for that." Einar says, a glint of anger still burning in his eyes.

"I was there when your father died," Kára tells him. "I saw him die and escorted him to Valhalla personally."

"I know, you told me that," Einar says. "You told me some coward shot my father in the back."

"Some coward…," Kára whispers.

Those old gnawing fears of Einar's return in force, driven forward by drink. His fist clenches and he realizes he knows who killed his father. Deep down inside he's always known. He just needs confirmation. "Who killed him?" Einar asks. "Who put the arrow in his back?"

Kára downs the rest of her mead and slams the cup down on the wooden table.

"I did," she says.

*****

Einar stares and lets the truth sink in. The rats eating away at his mind all these years suddenly make sense. Their squeaky voices had been trying to tell him the truth but he drowned them out with anger and drink and an endless line of willing girls.

Of course Kára would help him, but not out of any desire to help the son of a fallen hero. She had trained him as a penance. He was nothing more to her than a way to pay for a crime. She has trained him and he has learned well. Pumped up by ego and a bellyful of mead, Einar decides to show her exactly the monster she's created. He lurches to his feet, sword drawn and pointed at her throat in an instant.

The celebration quiets down. Whispers can be heard among the revelers, "What is this? What is going on? Why is he threatening her?"

Bets are placed, mostly on Kára, but a few think Einar will have the upper hand.

Kára doesn't move a muscle. Just like the first time he attacked her she waits patiently. Patience is a skill Einar never quite mastered. If only there was more time, perhaps Kára could have taught him. Now she watches this young man who has grown to be her friend point a sword at her with murder in his eyes. She wishes it would work. She wishes he could slide the sword into her throat and end her right here and now, but she knows there is nothing he can do to kill her.

"Put it away, Einar," she tells him.

"I'll put it away after you're dead."

"You're strong," Kára says, "but not that strong. Put it away and let me explain."

Einar is crushed and the old rage that was buried but never destroyed comes boiling over him. "Fight me!" he cries. He can't quite bring himself to attack her until she attacks him first.

"No," Kára says. "I will not."

"Coward!" Einar shouts. "Fight me! Pick up your sword and fight me!"

"You wouldn't stand a chance; put it away. Go find your lovely girl and let her charms calm you down."

The dig at Inkeri is too much. She's more than just a girl to him, they'll be married soon. Einar spits at Kára and lunges forward, driving the tip of the sword toward his former teacher's throat.

The sword can't hurt her, Kára knows that, but ingrained instincts take over and she blocks his sword with the cup in her hand. She stands and flips the table up and over on its side, creating a barrier between her and her former student.

"Don't do this," Kára whispers.

Einar kicks the table at her. Kára kicks it back with enough force to break it in half.

The celebration that had quieted while everyone decided who to root for explodes back into a frenzy. Einar's sword flies in an arc, just Kára had taught him many years ago. The movement is a flash of silver and has taken the lives of many enemies over the years, but Kára fully expects the move and deftly blocks it.

Real fighting is dirty tricks; the finger in the eye, the foot in the crotch, the dagger in the ribs. Einar is a skilled fighter, trained by a demigoddess and prepared to be ruthless. He learned his lessons well and applies every trick he knows to beat her. Through Kára's training, Einar's sword has become a part of him. He wields it as easily as he points at the sea or hugs Inkeri.

Kára was never trained, per se. She sprang into the world already knowing how to fight like her creators. Over the years, she's added to her repertoire, a skill her creators didn't even know she had. Programmed things like her aren't supposed to be able to overwrite their programming, but Kára can change. Maybe not her body – that will last forever – but her mind is an ever-growing book. She's fought monsters, beasts, warriors, and gods and taken away something new from every encounter.

Like most fights, the battle between Kára and Einar is over quickly and leaves no small amount of blood for someone else to clean up. It's time for Kára to go home and Einar to meet his father.

*****

"Why do you do this, Kára? Why do you persist in twisting my orders?" Odin asks as Kára drops Einar's severed head in front of the throne.

"You wanted the son, you've got him," Kára replies calmly.

"He was supposed to die in battle," Odin says.

"He did. He fought bravely and died on his feet."

The ravens chitter madly to themselves as they watch the exchange. A godlike rage had grown in the man and the ravens know it. When Odin gets really mad, he doesn't yell, but his angry whispers make even the mountains seek shelter.

"I have had enough of this insolence," the man whispers. His voice sounds like the end of all things and Kára knows she might have overstepped herself this time.

"Is it insolence to follow your orders, my Lord?" Kára asks, desperately trying to salvage the situation.

"Of course it's not and you know it," Odin says. He's played this game with her countless times in the past. All those times he's sworn to himself that this time would be the last time, and each time he lets her do it again.

"Then how have I been insolent?" Kára asked innocently.

"You knew he had to die by human hand, yet you took it upon yourself to take his life," Odin says, trying to keep his anger in check. It's times like this he wishes could unmake his creations, but he designed the Valkyries too well. And she did manage to squeak by on a technicality. Again.

"He challenged me, my Lord, not the other way around. I was simply defending myself." She knows she started the fight, even if it wasn't her intention.

"You do not need to defend yourself. He could not have harmed you if he had a thousand swords and a thousand years. He could have hacked away at you day and night for an eternity and not harmed you at all."

Kára stares at the All-Father on his throne and wonders if perhaps she hasn't finally gone too far. *Oh, well*, she thinks to herself, *screw him.* If he had his one eye on the end game rather than the ass of that servant girl she wouldn't have to do this on her own.

The air chills with the man's anger as if the weather itself is throwing a cold shoulder at Kára for her defiance. She doesn't actually know the extent of Odin's powers, but he is the All-Father and it wouldn't surprise her if he could control the weather.

Enough of this, she thinks to herself, it's time to end this nonsense.

In a flash, Kára draws her sword and flings it elegantly at the old man on his throne. He, of course, had given an eye for knowledge of the future and was already moving before the sword had even left her fingers. It misses him completely and embeds itself in the back of his seat, tearing the old leather and pushing itself halfway through the oak.

Odin would say he knew it would happen, just like he knows everything that will happen. The truth is closer to him knowing every potential thing that can happen. There are countless possible outcomes of a simple event. Drop a ball and what can happen? It can bounce. It can fall flat on the floor. It can hover. Odin can see and understand all those possible outcomes and understand the subtle changes that will alter the outcomes.

He sees many possible outcomes of events related to Kára. In some, she calmly accepts his reprimand and goes back to being his favorite chooser of the slain. In others, they wind up in bed together, hoping against hope that Freya doesn't walk in. In still others, she throws the sword. Sometimes she waits until his back is turned and drives a dagger into him.

As soon as she took Einar's head, some of the possibilities collapsed in on themselves. As soon as Kára chose to drop the head in his throne room, more possibilities collapsed – including her winding up in his bed.

The terrifying and dangerous part of the future is it's never clear cut until just before it hits. Odin never tells anyone this. His people know he can see the future and wouldn't entirely understand that the future itself is not static. A future that changes from second to second is impossible to predict with any degree of accuracy. The universe isn't run like clockwork - people don't always follow rules - things that should never happen come to pass. It's easier to see the future as set in stone than to think reality is complex and hard to come to grips with even for the All-Father.

Still, Odin saw far enough forward to miss her strike and that's good enough. His unbreakable spear, Gungir, which has never missed a target, flies straight and true toward Kára's heart.

He created her, molded her out of his own power and a lust-filled night with a drunk human. He waited patiently while the woman's human body created the vessel for his power. As soon as the human was ready, he snatched the baby, kicked out the original soul and poured his own power into the void.

Kára is part of him, made from him, and though it pains him, Odin will destroy her without a second thought. She was designed to be immutable rather than eternal. Immortality is for the gods - they can live forever and truly live, grow, and change. Odin's creations were designed to be unchanging. No regular weapon can harm her; no mortal or beast can kill her.

Reality is complicated, even for a god. As possibilities collapse he picks the one that look best and decides it will become reality. In his mind, his spear will continue its perfect record, because that will be reality.

The spear flies like a bolt of lightning straight toward Kára's chest. It will hit, pierce her skin, punch a hole in her sternum, slide effortlessly through her heart, and exit out her back. Gungir is hardly a mortal weapon, it will slay her where she stands and no one will be able to stop it.

Odin chose the wrong reality, though. In his mind, he understands her, knows her strengths and weaknesses and can play her. She's grown though, changed in ways he cannot understand and did not foresee. Due to a small error in her development, one that slipped through Odin's wisdom and foresight, Kára has developed the ability to change herself.

As the spear flies at her, she deftly steps out of its way and darts forward, dagger drawn. Odin doesn't expect her to charge him and reacts on instinct alone, stepping out of the way of her charge and getting ready to spin around and end this nonsense.

She has multiple lifetimes of experience in fighting all manner of people and other things. She has learned to interpret and guess how someone will react. Kára expected Odin would simply get out of the way and slid to a stop before she passed him. When he spins and his back is to her, she slides the knife into his kidney and twists.

The All-Father falls to his knees, eyes wide, and hands desperately scrabbling for the knife she left in his back. His mouth opens and a scream that would scare the dead escapes his lips. The floor shakes and the walls tremble. The air freezes around them, turning to ice crystals that drift lazily through the chamber.

The attack has not gone unnoticed. Radgridr and Sanngrior are waiting behind Kára when she turns. The two have a knack for showing up at the worst possible times.

They sense that Kára is different. Her sisters have never trusted Kára; they see her as untrustworthy and unpredictable. Kára never trusted them, either, so the feeling was mutual. This fight was inevitable. Although all of them want the same thing – to see the end of the world – their methods vary drastically. Radgridr and Sanngrior are patient and content to let the world unfold as it should. Kára is less patient and sees it as her duty to hasten the end.

The battle is impressive, a swirl of swords and blonde hair, spears and leather armor. Two on one, especially when the two are demigoddesses, is hardly fair, but Kára had changed over the past years of training Einar. If you really want to learn something, as the saying goes, teach it.

Kára easily handles her sisters but has one minor problem: they're just as indestructible as she is. When Kára knocks one down the other Valkyrie immediately gets back up.

The fight would have continued until the end of time if the God of Thunder and Lightning didn't show up. He is a mass of muscle and hammer and, while he can't kill the women, he can easily break up the fight. Thor has no idea what's going on and he doesn't actually care; he lives for the fight and is happy to engage.

Once he shows up, the fight is over shortly and it is up to the old man to pass judgment.

*****

Odin has a problem. He created something, designed it to be indestructible, but now has to find a way to dispose of it. This is the problem with gods: they always think in terms of what will make them seem most impressive. Create something that can last forever and it looks impressive. Make damned sure it will last forever and you're really keeping up with the Joneses.

Things like this leave the old man in something of a quandary. He created Kára and her sisters to be eternal and now he is stuck with what to do with the one who had thrust a knife in his back. He knows he could kill her, his weapons – and his alone – could suck the life out her body. He could lock her up forever, but she'd find a way to escape and come after him again. Locking people up takes energy and effort, and he had other things on his plate to deal with.

Small matters like running a kingdom and plotting how to deal with the end of everything weigh heavily on his shoulders. These things have occupied his thoughts for as long as he can remember, keep him from relaxing, and keep him on the edge all the time. A roll around with his chamber maid – and whoever else he can find – is all that keeps him sane sometimes.

Of course, the knife didn't kill him. It takes more than even Asgardian weapons to kill him, but it hurt. A transgression had occurred and the perpetrator had to be made an example of. He won't kill her, not yet anyway, and he won't waste resources locking her up, but he will hurt her. And if he has his way, he will go on hurting her.

Kára was disarmed, chained, and presented to the old man. Radgridr and Sanngrior flank her, each looking for an excuse to rekindle the fight. The God of Thunder and Lightning stands at his father's side, calmly watching the proceedings.

"You have violated my laws for the final time," Odin says. His ravens chitter an angry agreement. He holds Gungir, thick as one of Kara's legs, in one massive hand. Storm clouds roil in his eyes. "For that you will be banished forever."

Kára rolls her eyes. She'd spent too much time among the humans to feel banishment will be much of a threat. "At least I won't have your clumsy attempts at nocturnal trysts to deal with," she spits back at him.

"You will never again be one of us. You will never again taste the mead of the Great Hall," Odin continues.

"I will never again taste your drunken lips on mine, either," Kára replies.

Odin smiles, an expression filled with cruelty and desperate revenge. "Don't be so certain, child," he says. "Immortality gives me a very long time to play with you."

Kára would hardly be the first woman Odin had travelled to Midgard to taste. His appetites are famous among the gods. "Freya," Kára asks Odin's wife, "are you going to allow this?"

Freya is suspiciously quiet, but there's an odd look about her. She is well aware of Odin's dalliances - everyone is - but is forbidden to speak of them. Kára hopes to press the issue and get Freya involved. Odin's power is without equal, but Freya has her ways of controlling him. Odin's wife lowers her eyes to the floor and says, "My king has spoken."

"You are weak," Kára says quietly. "I expected more from you."

The insult stings Freya but, like Kára, she has a role to play and it does not involve challenging her husband in the throne room. There will be plenty of time for that later. Just like the soft water eventually cuts through hard stone, Freya will eventually wear away at her husband. Eternity is a very long time and she aims to use it to her advantage.

"Kára, by my decree, you are forever banished from Asgard. You are to be stripped of your weapons, stripped of your clothes, and stripped of your power. You may keep your immortality that you can spend eternity regretting your transgressions. Perhaps some time I'll allow you to make supplications and consider allowing you to come back to Asgard. We can always use more chamber maids," Odin says.

The throne room erupts in laughter. Kára struggles against the chains that hold her tight. "We will meet again old man," she spits at him.

"Yes, my child, we will," Odin says. He points his mighty spear at her and smiles. Kára stands straight and tall, unwilling to yield even in the face of Gungir

Odin rises from his throne. Kára can feel his rage and his power even from the across the room and fights the desire to struggle and run. A massive arm hurls the spear at her chest. She watches Gungir soar through air and plunge straight into her chest. The pain is immense and she can't help herself, Kára screams in agony as the spear impales her. The power of the All-Father courses through her, shredding everything in its path. She feels the chains melt away as if even the metal is terrified. Her red leather tunic explodes away, shredded like so much paper.

The spear's power tears a hole in reality and shoves Kára through it. She falls from the sky, naked and screaming in agony. Through tear-stained eyes Kára sees the ground rushing up to meet her. She hits the dirt like one of the rocks that falls from the sky. The ground shakes and roars. The explosion is seen from a day's travel away.

At the bottom of a huge crater of sand and glass, an agonized Kára lies. She manages one last look of anger at the skies and the gods who had betrayed her before she gives up and darkness washes over her.

*****

Kára awakens to a new sensation. Pain courses through her body, an unwelcome visitor in her largely pain-free world. Pain is a body's way of reporting damage and one of the things about being essentially immutable is damage is a rarity. In her millennia of existence nothing has harmed her, but the All-Father's power is like nothing she's felt before.

With a groan she pulls herself together and brushes dirt from her body. Kára pulls herself to her feet and looks around the crater she made when she fell. Between her mass and Odin's anger she hit with enough force to put a twenty-foot-deep hole in the ground.

Kára is not one to feel sorry for herself and starts climbing. The soft dirt of the crater slips every time her hands dig in and it feels like she slides down two feet for every one foot she climbs. It takes hours, but at last Kára's hands finally reach the top of the hole. She glares at the sky, struggles to her feet and staggers across the empty plains.

At a quiet village she pilfers some tanned leather that was left out to dry and makes clothes and boots. She wants to leave money or something in return but all Kára has is the skin on her body. A thank you rune has to suffice.

Kára steals an axe from a metalworker and a sword from an armorer. After the third theft she realizes she no longer cares and doesn't bother to leave a note. She keeps her eyes to the stars, wondering what is happening at home. Has Freya finally fought back? What of her sisters? Radgridr in particular seemed angrier than usual, and that was saying something. Would Radgridr and Sanngrior come seeking her?

Like all tools without a purpose, Kára falls into a kind of depression. Valkyries are purpose-built creatures; their role is to find warriors and be warriors. Take that purpose away and the will ebbs. She builds a cabin, starts brewing mead, and proceeds to drink herself into oblivion.

Some people find solace in nature but Kára isn't one of those people. It could be argued, actually, that she really isn't people. The only solace Kára ever finds is in the bottom of a barrel of mead and that solace is fleeting. She drinks all night and wakes up with a demigoddess-sized headache the next morning.

This process of attempted self-destruction becomes a daily ritual. Day after day, year after year, Kára chases Jörmungandr, hoping the serpent will face her in a fair fight but day after day, year after year, the serpent ignores her and Ragnarök is postponed again and again.

She takes to drinking all the time in a desperate bid to escape reality. Drunkenness becomes the rule rather than the exception. It's during a particularly bad bender that Odin kicks in her door.

He doesn't say a word, doesn't have to. The All-Father has that evil glint in his eye that he used to get when he wanted her. Kára grabs her axe and flings it at him. Even in her drunken state her prowess is amazing. Odin barely dodges the spinning weapon and finds her sword at his throat before he can react.

"I said you would never have me," Kára hisses.

Odin grins and leers at her, completely unconcerned with the sword at his throat. He leans forward, pushing the razor tip of Kára's blade into his neck. "You think you can stop me with a mortal sword?"

Kára pulls the blade back and spins. The blade whips around in a huge arc and slams into the side of Odin's head. The All-Father staggers but remains standing. The strike would have severed the heads of a dozen mortals, but Odin isn't even scratched.

A fist that could crush a world wraps around Kára's throat and lifts her off the ground. With his other hand, Odin rips her leather clothes off and casually tosses them across the room. She struggles in his grip, desperate to escape, but he is simply too powerful for her.

He laughs at her struggles and takes her at his leisure. Every time she thinks he's done he comes back for more. And more. And more. He slams fists into her, kicks her while she is wrapped in a fetal position and violates her so many times she loses track of the world.

One morning, Kára awakes to an empty cabin. Her body is bruised and she aches all over. She claws her way across the floor to the remains of her clothes and finds he's urinated on them. The rough drapes provide enough cover for the time being.

He left a message for her, carved into the wall of her home with his spear. It simply says, "It will never be over."

Kára spits at the wall and then feels ridiculous for spitting on her own wall. Tears well up in her gray eyes but she chokes them back. An empty feeling of being beaten fills her gut, but she fights it down. Let him come again and again and again, she thinks. Let him get his kicks. He can't kill me. Someday, I'll get him.

But he can hurt her. Her aching body is testament to that.

Kára limps across the room and finds he'd only left her the dregs of her mead. She lifts the entire barrel and tries to drain what was left, but he's urinated in that, too. She spits it out and slams the barrel to the ground and watches it explode. The sudden, violent act reminds her of something she's lost. Anger wells up inside of her but she chokes it down. She needs to be focused and perfect if she is going to handle Odin.

A dagger lies on the table, forgotten by the All-Father when his lusts were satiated and Kára lay in a battered heap on the floor. It isn't much, a mere foot long, but it's Asgard workmanship. Kára can almost smell the blood Odin's dagger had spilled over the years.

It's powerful. Not enough to kill Odin, but enough to hurt him. Maybe hurt him enough to make him think twice.

She remembers a purpose long forgotten. In her years in the cabin she learned to work like the humans do and work became everything, obliterating her past and clouding her future. Kára was designed and built to help bring fighters to Ragnarök, an instinct that drove her to being flung from Asgard.

The only way Kára can beat the All-Father will be to keep moving. He likes to claim he knows everything but she knows that's a lie. It took time to find her here; it will take time to find her anywhere else. The only way to stop him will be to stop everything, bring on Ragnarök and end everything.

Odin knows a lot, albeit nowhere near as much as he claims, but he knows where to find her now. There is no reason to make things easy for him. Wrapped in a sheet, Kára grabs her axe and sword and walks out of the cabin.

"You have embarrassed us, sister," Radgridr says. She and Sanngrior are waiting right outside, swords in hand.

Sanngrior smiles an evil grin and flips her sword in the air and catches it. "We can't kill you," she says, "but we can certainly hurt you."

"You, too?" Kára asks. "Is there anyone left in Asgard that's not coming after me?"

"You embarrassed us," Radgridr says. "You embarrassed the whole order."

Anger rise up in Kára again, but this time she doesn't fight it. Bloodlust flows up like bile from her belly. Radgridr is closer but Sanngrior is the bigger threat. Kára throws her axe at the smaller woman and charges. Sanngrior ducks the axe but catches the sword in her gut. She screams as Kára twists her sword.

Radgridr charges forward, her broadsword high above her head, hoping for the single debilitating blow. Kára kicks Sanngrior forward and the woman flies off the sword, into a tree and collapses onto the ground. On a mortal, the wound would be lethal, but Valkyries can't be killed by mere moral weapons. Kára draws Odin's dagger and turns to face her other sister.

The taller woman was so certain she would claim victory that she doesn't notice the small weapon until Kára deftly dodges Radgridr's strike and rams the dagger into her stomach. The sword falls from Radgridr's hands and she staggers back in shock and pain. The All-Father's dagger slowly draws the life out of the tall woman and she drops to her knees in agony.

"You could have left it alone, Radgridr," Kára says. "If you had left me to my own devices I would have drunk myself into a stupor and you never would have heard from me again."

Radgridr gasps and screams and tries to pull the All-Father's dagger out of her stomach. "You betrayed us," she shrieks.

"He raped me and probably raped you and Sanngrior. Just because he made us doesn't mean he owns us," Kára replies.

Radgridr's eyes drop to the floor of the forest. Even though she doesn't say it, Kára knows her sisters have shared Odin's bed unwillingly, probably as penance for her actions. The bastard may be the All-Father, may have created them, but he doesn't have the right to take them against their will.

"Tonight you'll sleep in Valhalla, sister," Kára says. "When Ragnarök finally comes, we'll meet again. Sleep in peace, train hard. The end is coming."

Radgridr dies trying to say something, but all Kára hears is the whispering of the winds through the trees. The wind seemed to tell a tale of faraway places and people. Rustling behind her tells Kára Sanngrior is back up again.

"You killed her," Sanngrior says quietly. "You actually killed her."

"She would have tortured me for an eternity," Kára replies. "Just like you would have."

Kára yanks the dagger from Radgridr's stomach and watches as the woman's body turns to ashes that blow away in the breeze. She slowly turns and faces down her former sister. "Sanngrior," she says, "I need you to deliver a message for me. To Freya."

Sanngrior nods, still in pain and shock.

"Tell Freya what you saw here today. Tell her everything. That Odin was here that he took me. Tell her all the times Odin took you against your will. Tell her everything you've seen. Frey might not be able or willing to do anything, but she's the only hope we've got. The All-Father is far too powerful for us to take on by ourselves," Kára says

"What about us?" Sanngrior asks.

Kára steps further and puts her hands on Sanngrior's shoulders. Gray eyes search black eyes and hope there is still a spark of Sanngrior's anger in there, but find only sadness. Kára hugs her sister to her and holds her. "I must disappear now, sister. Odin will be searching for me now and he won't hold back his anger next time we meet."

"Where will you go?"

"Away. It's best you don't know. Just away. We'll meet again sometime, dear Sanngrior. Call Heimdall, travel the Bifrost home and tell Freya what you've seen," Kára says.

Sanngrior nods and fights back tears. One sister is dead and the other is vanishing. She feels empty inside, like her purpose and her being are blowing away like Radgridr's ashes in the breeze. She calls to Heimdall and the Bifrost appears; a rainbow to the heavens in the middle of the forest. Kára watches Sanngrior leave before gathering up her few remaining belongings and saying goodbye to the little cabin she'd built for herself.

There are new clothes to make, a world to see, and the end of it to plan. Apparently there are places to the south where it never gets cold and no one has heard of Odin. Kára turns and starts walking. If it turns out the desert isn't interesting, there are other parts of the world to see. It might take her centuries, millennia even, but she'll find a way to start

Ragnarök, if only because it will give her the perfect opportunity to kill Odin for all his sins.

Duérmete Niño

"Duérmete niño, duérmete ya," she sings.

Her voice sounds like quiet bells, shimmering sound echoing around the walls of the small room. All around her are pictures of *Luchadores* - the masked wrestlers of Mexico – and other superheroes. Above the boy's bed is a portrait of Mil Mascaras, flanked by pictures of Captain America and Wonder Woman.

The boy loves his heroes and hopes to someday grow up to be strong and proud and fall in love with Wonder Woman. His mother has explained to him over and over that Wonder Woman is not a real person, but the boy will have nothing to do with that. "She is real," he insists, tapping his chest. "She is real in here and that is all that matters to me."

"Que viene el Coco, y te llevará," his mother continues.

The boy giggles, but snuggles deeper into his heavy quilt.

"Duérmete niño, duérmete ya," his mother sings, her eyes filled with mischievous love for her sweet son.

She holds her hands out like claws and leans close to the boy's huddled form. Her fingers reach toward him and a glint of something glows in her eyes.

"Que viene el coco, y te comerá."

As she finishes the song she leans forward and tickles the little boy. He giggles and squirms under her tickling fingers, a huge grin on his face. They both laugh and the mother hugs her son tightly to her, smiling in wonder at how her little *niño* has grown so big so quickly.

"Mama," the boy says. "You know Coco isn't coming to eat me."

"I know, *mi hijo*," his mother says. "It's just a song my mother used to sing to me when I was a little girl."

"Was it when she wanted you to go to sleep?" the boy asks.

"Sometimes," she says. "She used to tell me Coco couldn't get me if I was asleep."

"That's silly," the boy replies. "Why couldn't he get you when you were asleep?"

"You know what? I never asked. I just assumed I was safe when I was asleep."

"You should have asked," he says. "It would be useful information."

The mother bites back a laugh at her precocious son. All kids grow up asking "why", but her son never grew out of it. Now that he's eight, he asks it even more than he did when he was four. He loves information and insists on having as much as possible about everything.

"I'll ask her next time I call her," she says. "I'm sure your *abuelita* had a very good reason."

"Grandma always says she has good reasons, but I think she's just making things up."

"She's telling you stories she was told when she was a little girl," she replies. "It's history."

The boy ponders this for a moment. "So they shouldn't be taken literally?" he asks.

"Of course not," she says with a smile. "They're just stories."

"Oh," he replies and yawns.

"You should get some sleep, *hijo*," she says. "You had a long day today."

"I don't like math," the boy says distantly as he snuggles deeper into the blanket.

She laughs quietly, not at all surprised by the *non sequitur*. "It's okay," she says as she tucks the covers under the boy's feet. "Math still likes you."

"Good night, mama," the boy tells her.

"Good night, baby bear," she replies, kissing the top of his mop of black hair. "I'll see you in the morning."

The mother flicks off the light and closes the door to her son's room. The faint glow of a star on the wall - a nightlight found on eBay – provides a bit of illumination. All around the boy, *Luchadores* and other superheroes keep silent watch.

In the corner of the room, deep in shadows where the star's light can't reach, a faint purple light glows. It flashes briefly, expanding and contracting in an instant. By the time the boy's eyes open the light is gone. He sits up in his bed, seeking whatever it was that woke him, but can't find anything.

He turns and looks up at Mil Mascaras. "You'll protect me, won't you?"

In his mind, he sees the mighty *Luchador* smile and nod. Satisfied, the boy snuggles back under the covers and closes his eyes. The room is his safe haven, a place away from the trivialities and mundanities of a mostly boring world. Here, in this place, the boy is the king of the world and his army of wrestlers and superheroes keep him safe.

As he drifts off to sleep a different pair of eyes opens in the dark shadows. The eyes see everything clearly, including the faint red outline of the boy. The owner of the eyes doesn't know who put the outline here. All he knows is he's programmed to always take the one outlined in red. It's a mission he's fulfilled for centuries.

If the boy were to open his eyes his scream would wake the neighborhood. All his life he's heard of Coco but never believed in the stories, but tonight the bogeyman has been sent for him. Someone, somewhere, sent a message to the creature to attack and devour the boy in this room.

The creature unfolds from the shadows, moving so smoothly it almost looks like he flowed straight of the shadow and into the real world. That's not actually too far from the truth. When Coco travels, he travels between worlds through the shadows that link parts of broken reality together.

As he moves, one of Coco's hands shifts smoothly into a single, giant claw. That claw has taken more lives over the centuries than even Coco himself can recollect. Somewhere in the universe someone is maintaining a toll of the creature's kills, the reason for the kills, and the general outcome.

Coco has never missed a target before. He's not much on the idea of skills, but he has a few up his tattered, black sleeve. He glides forward, silent as a mist.

The boy never sees Coco coming. It's better when the targets can be afraid and Coco can drink in their terror, but tonight the rules were plain: do it quietly.

Mil Mascaras, Captain America, and Wonder Woman watch impassively as the bogeyman performs his dirty work. The boy is not the real target, the parents are; repayment for some abstract failure or wrong action.

*****

Dark, scared eyes scan the countryside. Coco knows something is out there. For a being used to causing fear, feeling it is hateful. Fear is something others are supposed to feel. Not him. Not ever. He is the dispenser of terror, a creature designed to instill madness and horror.

And yet, Coco is afraid. He was pulled out of transit before he could make it to his lair and dropped in this rocky place. And that is something that has never happened before. Transit is always smooth, perfect. He performed his task, has a full belly, and wants to sleep. But something has interrupted his travels. An intruder is out there, something strong enough to interrupt him.

Something powerful enough to do that is scary.

His simple programming was designed to mimic the natural world, use the predefined rules that govern biological interactions. Buried among those multitudes of instructions was a simple one: invoke fear to protect the self. This would trigger a perfectly natural fight or flight response that would, in turn, ratchet up the creature's ability to survive.

In his hundreds of years stalking the forests and mountains Coco has never been afraid of anything. His mere presence is usually enough to reduce a target to a jabbering heap. But something is out there and Coco can't figure out what or where it is. Worse yet, the intruder isn't frightened. Coco's enhanced senses can detect traces of the intruder but the energy signature is strange: partly magical, partly mechanical. Whatever it is, it's not human and not an animal. It's … something else. Something his programming didn't account for.

Fear makes Coco angry. A simmering rage that something has deigned to stalk the great bogeyman fills his limited capacity mind. Fear has triggered the fight or flight response and he has chosen to fight.

In the distance he spots a faint glimmer of moonlight reflecting off a surface. In this dull and dusty place, moonlight doesn't reflect off anything natural. The target is out there, watching. Coco's gnarled fingers extend to claws, then to razor-sharp talons.

He has found its target and the hunt is on.

Coco's designers imbued him with a unique mode of travel; he can pass through shadows to travel. There are shadows aplenty in this place. Each tree, each shrub, each boulder casts a huge shadow that allows Coco to move about easily.

The decision to engage has been made and now begins the slow stalking. He moves quietly to the shadow of a tree and emerges through a different shadow fifty feet or so closer to the target. Talons tingle, anticipating the blood of the interloper.

The intruder stands just down range, partially hidden in the shadows. Perfect.

Coco dances through the shadows, each time emerging closer to his prey. After every hop he pauses and watches. Excellent. The intruder is completely unaware, still looking into the distance, seeking the place where Coco was instead of where he is.

A final hop and the bogeyman launches himself at the intruder. The hunt is coming to an end and the kill will taste so sweet. Coco's programming drives him to commit atrocities and while he was never designed to have emotions, the bogeyman of New Mexico has learned to feel over the years.

His feelings would be alien to almost anything else, but he feels a certain sense of contentment when he kills.

Sharp talons slice through air, seeking blood and warm flesh, the taste of a soul screaming into the aether. They find nothing. The intruder was right there! Where has it gone?

Something slams into to Coco from behind. The blow was immensely powerful, throwing him face forward into the dirt. The simmering rage explodes. Coco launches to his feet and seeks the target.

There. There it is; a human-shaped thing with bits of metal sticking out of its flesh. The intruder stares at Coco without moving. The intruder is standing with one leg forward, one back. Most of the intruder's weight is on the back leg and both hands are up, ready to intercept or attack.

Coco was never programmed with human fighting styles, and he's never faced a target that could fight back, let alone one capable of actually striking the bogeyman. He only understands speed and sharp talons. Muscle-like things tense and relax in Coco's body. He flashes forward, talons ready to rend the flesh from this strange creature's metal parts.

Again, the intruder reacts far faster than it should be able to, darting forward to catch the attack. The world spins around Coco and his brain struggles to figure out what happened and where he is. His vision alternates between bright stars and black ground before the hard packed earth slams into Coco's back.

His vision swirls briefly. For all his power, Coco was designed to be a quiet infiltrator, not a fighter. He doesn't quite know how to react to damage. Nothing has ever touched him before. He knows he should escape, run away but a kind of pride won't let him leave yet.

The intruder is standing directly over Coco, watching him impassively. One of the intruder's eyes is unlike anything Coco has ever seen before. The eye looks like a lens with lights slowly flashing inside. He stares into the eye, feeling a sense of a kindred spirit of sorts in the intruder; neither of them is exactly natural.

But Coco's feelings for others are weak and fleeting things. He rolls and rises to his feet, ready once more for his claws to sink into sink into skin. The talon is a blur, faster than any living thing has a right to move.

The intruder deftly blocks the incoming talon like it had all the time in the world. Coco slashes again and again, faster and faster but each time the intruder either dodges the razor sharp claws or calmly bats them out of the way.

A sense of dread grows in Coco. The pre-programmed – and frankly underdeveloped – fight response isn't working and he tries to disengage, to make his way to a shadow and run away, but the intruder switches from defense to offense and presses the attack. Each time Coco tries to run, the intruder kicks out a leg or grabs and trips the bogeyman.

The dreaded bogeyman feels blows rain down on his body; a shot to the jaw, a kick to the knee, a finger in the eye. Bit by bit, the intruder calmly wears Coco down until a final mighty punch sends the terror of New Mexico sliding across the dirt.

Alarm bells are going off in his head, warnings of damage sustained echo inside his body. Pain is a new sensation for Coco. The creature has never been touched, let alone hurt before. He's always relied on his speed and the terror his visits caused to stay out of harm's reach, but this new intruder is not scared and is so very fast.

For the first time in his long life, Coco feels outclassed and afraid.

Before Coco can get up and try to run again, the intruder launches itself into the air. A knee lands next to Coco's body and a shiny mechanical hand grips his throat. The strange eye glows bright green, burning into Coco's optic nerves.

Visions fill his head. A house. A man and a woman. A boy with a stuffed dinosaur. Yes. The boy. Kill the boy.

More visions waft inside of Coco's head. Like clouds in the sky, they twist and turn forming visions that disappear into vapor. Dragons and power. There are other things that need to be readied. The boy is a minor nuisance that could become a major problem. Nip it in the bud. The intruder's minions will take care of the parents – they might come in handy to create another boy, one that can be molded and taught. But the current boy must be destroyed. Due to his nature, the boy has to be destroyed by something not of this planet.

Something that can move without being seen. Something used to consuming children.

Something like Coco.

A new desire fills his mind, an inescapable desire to kill and consume the boy. Vague directions drop into his mind, a city not far from here full of lights and people. It won't be easy and the directions aren't exact, but Coco will comply. He will hunt and kill the boy because that's what he wants to do now. It's the only thing on Coco's mind.

The intruder pulls his hand from Coco's throat and delivers one last punch to his face. A five-fingered message: *do not fail*.

Then the intruder rises with a whine of motors and clacking metal. He gives Coco one final look before stepping over the prone bogeyman and walking off into the forest. Coco sees a flash of green and purple and feels the faint tingle of magic wash over his body.

And then he's alone and in pain, staring at the stars with a singular message pinging through his head: Kill the boy.

Kill the boy.

Kill the boy.

*****

Human cities are baffling things to Coco.

They're loud, brightly lit, chaotic places. Coco is a creature from the old times, back before there were lights and cars and blaring noises, and the general chaos of the place can easily overwhelm his senses if he isn't careful.

The houses, though… All human houses are the same as they've ever been. Little hidey holes so people can escape from the real world and surround themselves with lights and moving pictures and things that beep. Coco knows his way around houses. Infiltrating houses is, after all, one of his defined roles.

Infiltrate and consume.

That terrible sameness makes choosing the right house difficult. Normally when Coco is given a target there's a kind of light that draws the bogeyman to its intended victim. He then spends time learning the layout of the house and where the best shadows are. When the time is right, Coco strikes. His attacks are blindingly fast. Enter, slay, leave no trace.

Chaos and pain follow him; a river of missing children and shattered lives.

Coco himself is just doing what he was designed to do. All the heartache that he leaves in his path isn't personal and he doesn't choose his targets. He's really little more than tool employed by others, a thing that maintains balance. The balance is a nebulous thing, though. Balance is determined by others.

He appears through a shadow in the back yard and sniffs the air. Senses that transcend human understanding reach out and feel through the house. Something strange is going on inside. Coco can feel unknown things circling the house. He can't understand them, but they feel powerful – too powerful for him to fight.

The boy is inside, though. He must eat the boy.

Coco is far from rash. He was programmed for patience and his long existence has validated that underlying code. A scream pierces the night, and someone in the house is yelling. Coco retreats to a shadow and watches patiently, reaching out further with his senses.

Two adults – both keyed up – one frightened child, a dog, and the strange things are inside the house. The things feel alien. Coco relaxes and waits. Circles always break. Coco always wins.

At daybreak he hides in a convenient shed, surrounded by spiders and detritus. His senses tell him the house is awake. He rests and waits until night falls again.

Night falls and the house calms. The strange, powerful creatures are still there, but there's a sense of something happening in the house. A faint sense of primitive magic – human magic – leaks out. Coco perks up. Almost every time humans experiment with magic things go very wrong.

There's not much magic left on this planet, but what's out there is chaotic and less than predictable.

Power slowly builds in the house, focused approximately in the middle of the building. Coco's senses pick up the strange things floating in the endless circle. They approach the center of the magic and stop. Powers swirl and mix: alien and human magic combining together to make something different, something that smells very much like the intruder that planted the endlessly looping message in Coco's head.

Kill the boy.

Kill the boy.

Kill the boy.

He shakes his head and forces himself to wait, to see what's about to play out.

The strange things stop circling and the center of the magic moves rapidly toward the front of the house. His ears pick up humans arguing and then the magic flies through the air. It hits the ground with an explosion of power. Two of the humans – one of them the boy – exit the house.

The circle is broken. It's time to move.

He feels through the shadows in the house and is pleased to note the place is filled with them. Coco steps through a shadow in the shed and exits through a shadow in a room somewhere toward the back of the house. His dark eyes scan the room, looking for the best way to move forward.

A sense of magic builds in the front room of the house. Coco closes his eyes and reaches out, feeling the magic from the safety of his shadow. The magic is alien, not of this planet. It feels like the clicking man that planted the command to kill the boy, but not exactly the same.

The woman vanishes.

But the boy is still near. Coco waits.

The man enters the house and calls out, looking for the woman. Alien magic fills the house and the man vanishes just like the woman.

Perfect. Now there's just the boy.

Kill the boy.

Coco rises out the shadows. He stalks quietly through house, mind and senses focused on the boy.

"Mommy," the boy calls out. "Dad?"

The boy is sobbing now, terrified beyond belief. Coco soaks up the child's terror and feasts on it. He waits while he hears the child running toward another part of the house, toward the dog.

The dog is no matter. It's time to kill the boy.

Coco moves. A hand becomes a razor-sharp talon. He can already taste the blood and the delicious soul leaving the body. A grin – hideous and terrifying and full of teeth – forms on Coco's face. There are far too many teeth in that smile. His eyes glow red.

He's part way down the hall when magic fills the house again. The alien power feels like it's coming from behind him, so Coco dives into the first room he finds and hides in the shadows of the dark bathroom. The bathroom smells like humans and has the faint tang of alien and human magic mixing. Latent tendrils of magic swirl around him, probing and penetrating his essence.

Coco is a being born of a kind of constructive magic and dark code. His programming was designed to withstand the human world but magic was never given much thought because human magic is so limited. The chaotic mixture of magic in this room moves through him, flipping switches and changing things.

His brain shuts down briefly and when he awakens he catches glimpses of pure alien magic moving through the house, directly toward his target. He instinctively knows to avoid the thing moving and cowers further into the shadows.

He's waited this long, a little more won't hurt.

A burst of alien magic in another part of the house alarms him. His dark eyes grow huge and his senses probe the house. In another room, something is growing, changing, becoming. A thing that should not be here. A thing that smells like this planet but very old, much older even than himself.

Coco shakes in spite of himself. Danger is out there and he's no longer the most powerful thing in the house. The message keeps repeating incessantly, though: kill the boy.

Kill the boy.

Kill The Boy.

KILL THE BOY.

Coco bursts from his shadow and moves through the house like an angry fog. The boy must die and nothing will stand in his way.

He rounds a corner and comes face to face with a man in a large hat, holding the boy in one arm. The monster and the man exchange stares. An entire conversation passes between their gazes in a moment.

"He is mine."

"You'll never get him."

"He must be killed."

"Leave now."

"I must have him."

"Come take him."

Coco launches forward as the man calmly walks through a glass door. Before Coco can get there the man is gone and the door closes. He crouches and explodes through the door. Glass erupts and he lands with talons extended, ready to rend the man into pieces and take the boy.

But the room is empty.

Save for a couple rugs and some food in a bowl on the floor, the room is completely empty. He's in an outer room. Windows covers two of the walls and he can see the shed he hid in not too long ago. The man is gone, though, and the boy with him.

Coco howls. A scream filled with rage and pain and targets taken far away echoes through the night. He stalks around the room, peering into shadows, hoping to find the boy hiding. There is nothing. His senses tell him he's the only living thing in the room.

The boy escaped, but still the message plays through his mind: kill the boy.

But there is no boy. The boy is gone.

Coco slashes at the walls, tears the rugs to shreds, breaks the windows, kicks the food across the floor. Rage fills him and the message keeps playing in his head. Kill the boy. Kill the boy. Kill the boy. He shakes his head, trying to remove the insistent message but it's no use. The message keeps playing, over and over and over.

He finds the first shadow he can and dives into it, not caring where he winds up. He'll kill every child on this planet. It's against his programming, but the magic mixture from the bathroom and the message are overriding his programming and filling him with an urge to kill indiscriminately.

*****

Coco's rage and pain drive him. He exits the first shadow to find a small room with nine pairs of eyes gawking at him. For a moment nothing happens. A child screams. In a heartbeat, the fight is on. The first human male pulls a gun off the couch and fires wildly. Holes appear in the wall and the TV explodes, but Coco is already moving.

Fighting these pathetic humans is far easier than the thing in the wilds. They move so slowly he can almost see their thoughts. The man with the gun loses first one hand then the other to Coco's talons. Delicious blood spills and sprays the walls. It doesn't taste as good as child blood and is tainted with some chemical he doesn't recognize, but the blood is delightful nonetheless.

Coco takes his time, relishing the pain and the fear that coats the room. The blood dripping off his body is almost good enough to mute the message. Almost, but not quite. His head still throbs. Talons flash, shredding the human male, but still the message plays.

The light goes out in the man's eyes and Coco watches his soul escape before turning on the other adults in the room. His talons flash and blur. Pieces of people fly. His mind soars. Two people, a man and a woman fall to pieces in moments.

The last woman stands between Coco and four children. Four tasty, tasty children. One is a boy.

Maybe that boy will do.

Coco savages the woman, shredding the skin from her bones. He wants her to live, to feel everything. To his amazement she stays awake and conscious, screaming and weeping until he decides to release her.

The anarchic mix of human and alien magic has given him a new tool.

He turns on the children and gleefully shreds them. This is power, such wonderful power, and all he's ever felt after a kill is a deep sense of satisfaction that he has again fulfilled his purpose. But each time he kills now, he relishes it, loves it. Adores it.

Death will come to this town tonight.

All told it took less than three minutes to kill everyone in the room and paint the walls with their blood. Piles of shredded flesh and small limbs cover the room. His glowing red eyes take in the scene with a kind of joy and elation.

But the message is still playing, still endlessly looping in his head.

He must find a way to kill the boy.

But the boy is gone, taken far from his reach.

He must kill the boy.

Coco howls again, screaming his rage and pain at the world and the metal man who has destroyed his purpose. He shreds the couch, tears up the room, destroys everything he can find.

And the message still loops.

He picks up the little boy's arm and bites into it. The flesh tastes as sweet as it always does. He forces himself to believe this is *the* boy, but it doesn't work. The message keeps going.

Coco keeps going. He keeps eating, keeps destroying. His programming collapses under the weight of the constant message and the alien magic. He collapses into a chair and eats. Anger is a thing now. Hatred is a thing now. The mission, the programming, the desire to maintain the balance is gone. The balance is gone.

He eats and rages and paints his code on the walls with talons dipped in blood and guts. Coco is performing a kind of stack dump, digging through his own programming as he tries to find the interrupting message and purge it.

A faint voice interrupts his search. He stops and looks but the voice isn't in the room; it's in his mind.

"Run," the voice says quietly.

"Escape while you still can," it says.

"They are coming," it whispers.

Coco holds his head in his hands and wails at the pain.

He collapses into a chair and stares at the walls.

The door explodes open and three masked men burst into the room. Coco's anger drives him forward. He bats one of the men aside and severs pieces off the other two until they're two disembodied heads screaming soundlessly.

A talon poises to go to work on the other man when the voice repeats, "RUN!"

Coco looks toward the door again and senses something new. It's not the alien/human magical mix. This is raw and jagged and smells like pure, raw terror. Fear is coming.

"RUN."

Coco stares at the man on the floor. It would taste so sweet to spill his blood and eat his flesh. The message to run insinuates itself into his programming, fighting with the admonition to kill the boy.

"RUN!"

The message to run overrides the desire to kill. Coco bolts, diving into the nearest shadow.

*****

Fear and pain continue to drive him, forcing him far away from everything. For years, Coco wanders the rugged mountainous landscape of northern New Mexico. The incessant desire to kill the boy mutes slowly over time, but still pings around his head. The message to run never leaves him, though, so he constantly runs, constantly seeks the boy. No further messages come to hunt and kill children; he's all alone in the world with only the two competing commands.

He used to sleep between tasks, but even that simple ability has been stripped from him. The constant messages, the rage, and the pain eventually break him down. He is a being without a purpose; leastwise a purpose he can fulfill.

The boy is long gone and will likely never return.

So he runs. From what he doesn't know, but he runs.

Coco takes to randomly jumping through shadows. Desperation has driven him to constantly move, but after every jump he lands in the same miserable position he started in. As a final last ditch effort to end the misery, he runs and leaps into huge shadow, hoping it will take him someplace where the pain is gone and he can just sleep.

Something pulls him out of transit and Coco winds up in a park. There's a woman standing in front of him. He starts to charge, to tear her apart but she holds up a hand and he stops. She smells like power, one of the few true magic users left on the planet.

"You've been damaged," she says. "Let me help you."

It's the same voice that told him to run, to escape, but never told him where to go or what to do. She just planted a message to run. That message mixed with the message to kill the boy and effectively broke Coco's brain.

Coco growls, baring a mouth filled with teeth. His hands stretch into talons.

"*Calmate*," she whispers. "I can fix you if you will help me."

She tentatively reaches out to him and he pulls back, ready to strike. Gentle shushing sounds calm him, keep him from tearing her throat out. A hand strokes his face and Coco feels magic pouring through him.

"I can't completely fix you," she says, "but I can stop what's hurting you. I wish I could ask you who put the message in your head but I don't think you can talk."

Coco's eyes roll back in his head. His talons retract, shifting back into gnarled gray hands. Her magic plucks parts of his mind out and pushes others in. His connection with whoever created him is severed, probably forever, but a new connection to the little woman in front of him is established. Purpose flows back.

"I need you to do something for me," the woman says. "I have a problem that I need you to solve."

An image fills his head, a small statuette glowing red; a new kind of marker. Coco reaches out and senses the marker; it's far from here, in a small town.

"Kill them both and dispose of the bodies. I don't care how."

She touches his chest and he feels her power flowing through him. The messages are gone, the pain is gone. He finally relaxes.

"*Duérmete niño,*" she whispers. "Take care of me and I'll take care of you."

About the Author

Eric Lahti is just this guy, you know? He grew up searching for UFOs and hidden treasure in northern New Mexico before escaping to the weirdness of New Mexico's high plains for college. He currently resides in Albuquerque, New Mexico where he's a programmer, teaches Kenpo to kids and the occasional adult, and generally goofs off.

He wrote his first book – *Henchmen* – largely as a test to see if he could do it. It was either write a novel or play more video games and he found he enjoyed the writing enough to keep doing it.

Acknowledgements

No book is written in a vacuum. If you're harboring a desire to write just so you can avoid people this isn't the business to be in. But don't fret, people can be fun. Other authors even more so. The nice thing about other authors is they understand the desire to write and the general strangeness that can come along with that. Other authors, friends, acquaintances, that guy on the corner that keeps telling me to leave him alone, all people who deserve sincere thanks.

So, without further ado: extra special thanks Karin Allen for looking at one of the very first cuts of this book. Her comments and notes were invaluable. Other people include Tom Julian, Jan Riley, Max Power, Senan Gil Senan, Silas Payton, RobRoy McCandless, Val Tobin, and probably countless other people of IASD.

Also, more extra special thanks to my wife for putting up with me writing while we're watching TV and my son for letting me use Aluna. He created the place when he was a young 'un – and still has a map of the planet he drew hanging on his wall.

Finally, of course, thank you very much for reading this.

Chan, Crow, and Kevin will be back in "Greetings From Sunny Aluna". Wilford and Steven will be locking horns in Henchmen 3. I still haven't decided what to do with Jack and his devil girlfriend (look in the Holes anthology for a story about her), but they're too promising to ignore.

Thanks again!
Eric Lahti - 2015

www.ingramcontent.com/pod-product-compliance
Lightning Source LLC
Chambersburg PA
CBHW071241170626
46809CB00001B/40